CAPTAIN VORPATRIL'S ALLIANCE

BOOKS by LOIS McMASTER BUJOLD

The Vorkosigan Saga:

Shards of Honor • *Barrayar*
The Warrior's Apprentice • *The Vor Game*
Cetaganda • *Borders of Infinity*
Brothers in Arms • *Mirror Dance*
Memory • *Komarr*
A Civil Campaign • *Diplomatic Immunity*
Captain Vorpatril's Alliance • *Cryoburn*

Falling Free • *Ethan of Athos*

Omnibus Editions:

Cordelia's Honor • *Young Miles*
Miles, Mystery & Mayhem • *Miles Errant*
Miles, Mutants & Microbes • *Miles in Love*

The Chalion Series:

The Curse of Chalion • *Paladin of Souls*
The Hallowed Hunt

The Sharing Knife Tetrology:

Volume 1: Beguilement • *Volume 2: Legacy*
Volume 3: Passage • *Volume 4: Horizon*

The Spirit Ring

ALSO AVAILABLE FROM BAEN BOOKS

The Vorkosigan Companion, edited by
Lillian Stewart Carl and John Helfers

CAPTAIN VORPATRIL'S ALLIANCE

LOIS McMASTER BUJOLD

CAPTAIN VORPATRIL'S ALLIANCE

A Baen Books Original

Baen Publishing Enterprises
P.O. Box 1403
Riverdale, NY 10471
www.baen.com

ISBN: 978-1-4516-3845-5

Cover art by David Seeley

First printing, November 2012

Distributed by Simon & Schuster
1230 Avenue of the Americas
New York, NY 10020

Library of Congress Cataloging-in-Publication Data

Bujold, Lois McMaster.
  Captain Vorpatril's alliance / Lois McMaster Bujold.
      p. cm. — (Vorkosigan saga)
  ISBN 978-1-4516-3845-5 (hardback)
  1. Vorkosigan, Miles (Fictitious character)—Fiction. 2. Alliances—Fiction. I. Title.
PS3552.U397C37 2012
813'.54—dc23
                                                            2012023914

10 9 8 7 6 5 4 3 2 1

Pages by Joy Freeman (www.pagesbyjoy.com)
Printed in the United States of America

CAPTAIN VORPATRIL'S ALLIANCE

Chapter One

Ivan's door buzzer sounded at close to Komarran midnight, just when he was unwinding enough from lingering jump lag, his screwed-up diurnal rhythm, and the day's labors to consider sleep. He growled under his breath and trod unwillingly to answer it.

His instincts proved correct when he saw who waited in the aperture.

"Oh, God. Byerly Vorrutyer. Go away."

"Hi, Ivan," said Byerly smoothly, ignoring Ivan's anti-greeting. "May I come in?"

Ivan took about a second to consider the, at best, complicated possibilities Byerly usually trailed in his wake, and said simply, "No." But he'd hesitated too long. Byerly slipped inside. Ivan sighed, letting the door slide closed and seal. So far from home, it would be good to see a familiar face—just not By's. *Next time, use the security screen, and pretend not to be here, eh?*

Byerly padded swiftly across the small but choice living quarters of Ivan's downtown Solstice luxury flat, rentals by the week. Ivan had picked it out for its potential proximity to Solstice nightlife, which, alas, he had so far not had a chance to sample. Pausing at the broad glass doors to the balcony, Byerly dimmed the polarization on the seductive view of the glittering lights of the capital city. Dome, Ivan corrected his thought to Komarran nomenclature, as the arcology existed under a hodgepodge of seals to keep the toxic planetary atmosphere out and the breathable one in. Byerly pulled the drapes as well, and turned back to the room.

Yielding to a curiosity he knew he would regret, Ivan asked, "What the hell are you doing on Komarr, By? Isn't this off your usual beat?"

Byerly grimaced. "Working."

Indeed, an experienced observer, which Ivan unfortunately was, could detect a distinct strain around By's eyes, along with the redness from drink and perhaps recreational chemicals. Byerly cultivated the authentic look of a Barrayaran high Vor town clown given over to a life of dissolution and idle vice by actually living it, ninety percent of the time. The other ten percent, and most of his hidden income, came from his work as an informer for Imperial Security. And ninety percent of that was just more dissolution and vice, except for having to turn in reports at the end. The residue, Ivan had to concede, could get dicey.

Ratting out your friends to ImpSec for money, Ivan had once heckled By, to which By had shrugged and replied, *And the greater glory of the Imperium. Don't forget that.*

Ivan wondered which it was tonight.

In reflexive response to the manners drilled into him in his youth, Ivan offered, "Something to drink? Beer, wine? Something stronger?" He contemplated By's boneless flop onto his living room couch. "Coffee?"

"Just water. Please. I need to clear my head, and then I need to sleep."

Ivan went to his tidy kitchenette and filled a tumbler. As he handed it to his unwelcome guest, By said, "And what are you doing in Solstice, Ivan?"

"Working."

By's open hand invited him to expand.

Ivan sat across from him and said, "Trailing my boss, who is here for an Ops conference with his assorted counterparts and underlings. Efficiently combined with the annual Komarr Fleet inspections. All the excitement of a tax inventory, except in dress uniform." Belatedly, Ivan realized By had to already know all this. He'd found Ivan, hadn't he? Because By's random social calls, weren't.

"Still working for Admiral Desplains?"

"Yep. Aide-de-camp, secretary, personal assistant, general dogs-body, whatever he needs. I aim to make myself indispensable."

"And still ducking promotion, are you, Captain Vorpatril?"

"Yes. And succeeding, no thanks to you."

By smirked. "They say that at Imperial Service Headquarters, the captains bring the coffee."

"That's right. And I like it that way." Ivan only wished it were true. It seemed barely months ago, though it was over a year, that the latest flare-up of tensions with Barrayar's most traditional enemy, the Cetagandan Empire, had pinned Ivan to military head-quarters 26.7 hours a Barrayaran day for weeks on end, sweating out all the most horrific possibilities. Designing death in detail. War had been averted through nontraditional diplomacy, mostly on the part of Barrayaran emperor Gregor's weaseliest Imperial Auditor and, to give credit where it was due, his wife.

That time. There was always a next time.

Ivan studied Byerly, who was only a few years older than himself. They shared the same brown eyes, dark hair, and olive skin common to Barrayar's somewhat inbred military caste, or aristocracy, whatever one wanted to call it, and, indeed, common to most Barrayarans. By was shorter and slighter than Ivan's six-foot-one, broad-shouldered fitness, but then, he didn't have a Desplains riding him to keep up the recruiting-poster appearance expected of an officer serving at Imperial Headquarters. Granted, when they weren't squinting from the dissolution, By's eyes had the startling beauty that distinguished his famous, or infamous, clan, to which Ivan was connected by a few twigs in his own family tree. That was the problem with being Vor. You ended up related to all sorts of people you'd rather not be. And they all felt free to call on you for favors.

"What do you want, Byerly?"

"So direct! You'll never become a diplomat that way, Ivan."

"I once spent a year as assistant military attaché to the Barrayaran Embassy on Earth. It was as much diplomacy as I cared for. Get to the point, By. I want to go to bed. And by the looks of you, so do you."

By let his eyes widen. "Why Ivan! Was that an invitation? I'm so thrilled!"

"Someday," Ivan growled, "I might say yes to that old line, just to watch you have a coronary."

By spread his hand over his heart, and intoned wistfully, "And so I might." He drained his water and gave over the vamping, the face so often arranged in a vague smarminess firming intently in a way Ivan always found a touch disturbing. "Actually, I have a little task to ask of you."

"Figured."

"It's quite in your line. I may even be said to be doing you a good turn, who knows. I'd like you to pick up a girl."

"No," said Ivan, only in part to see what By would say next.

"Come, come. You pick up girls all the time."

"Not on your recommendations. What's the catch?"

Byerly made a face. "So suspicious, Ivan!"

"Yeah."

By shrugged, conceding the point. "Unfortunately, I'm not entirely sure. And my duties with, if I may say it, the unusually unpleasant people I am presently accompanying—"

Spying on, Ivan translated this without difficulty. And the company By kept was usually unpleasant, in Ivan's opinion. *Unusually* unpleasant implied...what?

"—leave me little opportunity to check her out. But they have an inexplicable interest in her. Which I suspect is not friendly. It worries me, Ivan, I must say." He added after a moment, "She's quite well-looking, I assure you. You need have no fear on that score."

Ivan frowned, stung. "Are you implying I'd refuse to supply assistance to a homely girl?"

Byerly sat back, eyebrows flicking up. "To your credit, I actually don't believe that's the case. But it will add a certain convincing verisimilitude for the outside observer." He pulled a small plastic flimsy from his jacket and handed it across.

The background was too fuzzed to make out, but the picture showed a striking young woman striding down a sidewalk. Apparent age could be anything between twenty and thirty standard-years, though that was no certain clue as to real age. Tumbling black hair, bright eyes, skin glowing an interesting cinnamon brown against a cream tank top. Decided nose, determined chin; either the natural face she was born with, or the work of a real artist, because it certainly didn't bear the stamped-from-the-same-mold blandness of the usual body sculpture, a biological ideal that lost its appeal with repetition. Long legs in tan trousers that hugged in all the right places. A nicely full figure. *Nicely* full. If the face was natural, might the other prominent features be, too? With weakening reluctance, Ivan said, "Who is she?"

"Supposedly, a Komarran citizen named Nanja Brindis, lately moved to Solstice from Olbia Dome."

"Supposedly?"

"I have reason to suspect that might be a recent cover identity. She did move here about two months ago, it does seem."

"So who is she really?"

"It would be a fine thing if you could find that out."

"If she's hiding her identity for a good reason, she's hardly going to tell me." Ivan hesitated. "Is it a good reason?"

"I suspect it's a very good reason. And I also suspect she is not a professional at the game."

"This is all pretty vague, Byerly. May I remind you, my security clearance is higher than yours."

"Probably." Byerly blinked in doubt. "But then there is that pesky need-to-know rule."

"I'm not sticking my head into one of your dodgy meat grinders— *again*—unless I know as much as you know. At *least*."

Byerly flung up his well-manicured hands in faux-surrender. "The people I'm with seem to have got themselves involved in a complex smuggling operation. Rather over their heads."

"Komarr local space is a major trade nexus. The place is lousy with smugglers. As long as the transients don't try to offload their goods within the Imperium, in which case Imperial Customs deals sharply with 'em, they get ignored. And the Komarran trade fleets police their own."

"That's two out of three."

Ivan's head came up. "The only thing left is the Imperial Fleet."

"Just so."

"Crap, Byerly, if there was even a hint of that sort of thing going on, Service Security would swoop in. Damned hard."

"But even Service Security needs to know where and when to swoop. I am doing, as it were, a preliminary pre-swoop survey. Not only because mistakes are embarrassing, especially if they involve accusations of Vor scions with arrogant and powerful relatives, but because they tip off the real crims, who then promptly escape one's tediously set net. And you've no idea how tedious that can get."

"Mm," said Ivan. "And once military personnel get involved with, they think, simple civilian crime, they become vulnerable to more treasonous blackmail."

By bared his teeth. "I'm so pleased you keep up. One of your saving graces."

"I've had practice." Ivan hissed alarm. "Desplains should know about this."

"Desplains will know about it, in due course. In the meanwhile, try to remember you *don't* know." Byerly paused. "That caution is canceled, of course, should my dead body turn up in a lewd and compromising position in some ditch outside the dome in the next few days."

"Think it might?"

"The stakes are very high. And not just the money."

"So how's this girl connected, again?"

Byerly sighed. "She's not with my crew. She's definitely not with the non-Barrayarans they're dealing with, though it's not outside the realm of reason that she could be a defector. And she's not what she pretends to be. What's left, I am forced to leave to you to find out, because I can't risk coming here again, and I'm not going to have time in the next few days for side issues."

Ivan said slowly, "You think she's in danger of her life?" Because why else would By bother to set even a side-friend on this side issue? By didn't make his living through charity.

But he did make his living through a weird sort of loyalty. And, somewhere underneath the persiflage, camouflage, and just plain flage, he was high Vor of the highest...

"Let's just say, you would gratify me by staying alert. I should not care to explain any accidents that might befall you to your lady mother."

Ivan allowed the concern with a rueful nod. "So where am I to find this so-called girl?"

"I am fairly certain she's a real girl, Ivan."

"You think? With you, one never knows." He eyed By dryly, and By had the grace to squirm just a bit, in acknowledgement of his cousin Dono née Donna of lamented memory. Donna, that is. Count Dono Vorrutyer was all too vivid a presence on the Vorbarr Sultana political scene.

By dodged the diversion and, so to speak, soldiered on, though the idea of By in any branch of the Service made Ivan wince in imagination. "She works as a packing clerk at a place called Swift Shipping. Here's her home address, too—which was unlisted, by the way, so unless you can devise a convincing reason for turning up there, probably better to run into her coming into or out of work. I don't gather she does much partying. Make friends, Ivan. Before tomorrow night, by preference." He rubbed his face, pressing his hands to his eyes. "Actually—by tomorrow night without fail."

Ivan accepted the contact data with misgivings. By stretched, rose a bit creakily to his feet, and made his way to the door. "Adieu, dear friend, adieu. Sweet dreams, and may angels guard your repose. Possibly angels with clouds of dark curls, sun-kissed skin, and bosoms like heavenly pillows."

"Dry up."

By grinned over his shoulder, waved without turning around, and blew out.

Ivan returned to his couch, sat with a thump, and picked up the flimsy, studying it cautiously. At least By was right about the heavenly pillows. What else was he right about? Ivan had an unsettling premonition that he was going to find out.

Tej was conscious of the customer from the moment he walked in the door, ten minutes before closing. When she'd started this job a month ago, in the hopes of stretching her and Rish's dwindling resources, she'd been hyperaware of all customers who entered the shop. A job that exposed her directly and continuously to the public was not a good choice, she'd realized almost at once, but it had been the entry-level position she could get with the limited fake references she commanded. A promotion to the back office was mentioned, so she'd hung grimly on. It was being slow in opening up, though, and she'd wondered if her boss was stringing her along. In the meanwhile, her jagged nerves had slowly grown habituated. Till now.

He was tall for a local. Quite good-looking, too, but in a way that fell short of sculpted or gengineered perfections. His skin was Komarran-pale, set off by a long-sleeved, dark blue knit shirt. Gray multipocketed sleeveless jacket worn open over it, indeterminate blue trousers. Shoes very shiny yet not new, in a conservative, masculine style that seemed familiar but, annoyingly, eluded recognition. He carried a large bag, and despite the time noodled around looking at the displays. Her co-clerk Dotte took the next customer, she finished with her own, and the fellow glanced up and stepped to the counter, smiling.

"Hi, there"—with difficulty, he dragged his gaze from her chest to her face—"Nanja."

It didn't take that long to scan her nametag. *Slow reader, are you? Why, yes, I get a lot of those.* Tej returned the smile with the minimum professional courtesy due a customer who hadn't, actually, done anything really obnoxious yet.

He hoisted his bag to the counter and withdrew a large, asymmetrical, and astonishingly ugly ceramic vase. She guessed the design was supposed to be abstract, but it was more as if a party of eye-searing polka dots had all got falling-down drunk.

"I would like this packed and shipped to Miles Vorkosigan, Vorkosigan House, Vorbarr Sultana."

She almost asked, *What dome?* but the unfamiliar accent clicked in before she could make that mistake. The man was not Komarran at all, but a Barrayaran. They didn't get many Barrayarans in this quiet, low-rent neighborhood. Even a generation after the conquest, the conquerors tended to cluster in their own enclaves, or in the central areas devoted to the planetary government and off-world businesses, or out near the civilian or military shuttleports.

"Is there a street address? Scanner code?"

"No, just use the scanner code for the planet and city. Once it gets that far, it'll find him."

Surely it would cost this man far more to ship this…object to a planet five wormhole jumps away than it was worth. She wondered if she was obliged to point this out. "Regular or premium service? There's a stiff price difference, but I have to tell you, express won't really get there much faster." It all went on the same jumpship, after all.

"Is it more likely to arrive intact with premium?"

"No, sir, it will be packed just the same. There are regulations for anything that goes by jumpship."

"Right-oh, regular it is."

"Extra insurance?" she said doubtfully. "There's a base coverage that comes with the service." She named the amount, and he allowed as it would do. It was in truth considerably less than the shipping charges.

"You pack it yourself? Can I watch?"

She glanced at the digital hour display over the door. The task would run her past closing time, but customers were fussy about breakables. She sighed and turned to the foamer. He stood on tiptoe and watched over the counter as she carefully positioned the vase—a glimpse of its underside revealed a sale tag with four markdowns—closed the door, and turned on the machine. A brief hiss, a moment of watching the indicator lights wink hypnotically, and the door popped back open, releasing a pungent whiff that stunned her sense of smell and masked every other scent in the shop. She bent and removed the neat block of flexifoam. It was an aesthetic improvement.

Ivan Vorpatril, read the name on his credit chit. Also with a Vorbarr Sultana home address. Not just a Barrayaran, then, but one of those Vor-people, the conquerors' arrogant privileged class. Even her father had been wary of—she cut the thought short.

"Do you wish to include a note?"

"Naw, I think it'll be self-explanatory. His wife's a gardener, see. She's always looking for something to stuff her poisonous plants into." He watched her slide the foam block into its outer container and affix the label, adding after a moment, "I'm new in town. Yourself?"

"I've been here a while," she said neutrally.

"Really? I could do with a native guide."

Dotte closed out the scanners and turned off the lights as a broad hint to the laggard customer. And, bless her, lingered by the door to see Tej safely free of the shop and him. Tej gestured him out ahead of her, and the door locked behind them all.

The oldest human habitation on the surface of Komarr, Solstice Dome had a peculiar layout, to Tej's eye. The aging initial installations resembled the space stations she'd grown up in, with their labyrinths of corridors. The very latest sections were laid out with separate, street-linked buildings, but under vast, soaring, transparent domes that mimicked the open sky the residents hoped to have someday, when the atmospheric terraforming was complete. Middling areas, like this one, fell between, with much less technologically ambitious domes that still gave glimpses of an outside where no one ventured without a breath mask. The passage that Swift Shipping fronted was more street than corridor, anyway, too broad for the persistent customer to easily obstruct her.

"Off work now, huh?" he inquired ingenuously, with a boyish smile. He was a bit old for boyish smiles.

"Yes, I'm going home." Tej wished she could go home, really home. Yet how much of what she'd known as home still existed, even if she could be magically transported there in a blink? *No, don't think those thoughts.* The tension headache, and heartache, were too exhausting to bear.

"I wish I could go home," said the man, Vorpatril, in unconscious echo of her thought. "But I'm stuck here for a while. Say, can I buy you a drink?"

"No, thank you."

"Dinner?"

"No."

He waggled his eyebrows, cheerfully. "Ice cream? All women like ice cream, in my experience."

"No!"

"Walk you home? Or in the park. Or somewhere. I think they have rowboats to rent in that lake park I passed. That'd make a nice place to talk."

"Certainly not!" Ought she to invent a waiting spouse or lover? She linked arms with Dotte, pinching her in silent warning. "Let's go to the bubble car stop now, Dotte."

Dotte gave her a surprised look, knowing perfectly well that Tej—Nanja, as she knew her—always walked home to her nearby flat. But she obediently turned away and led off. Vorpatril followed, not giving up. He slipped around in front, grinned some more, and tried, "What about a puppy?"

Dotte snorted a laugh, which didn't help.

"A kitten?"

They were far enough from Swift Shipping now that customer politeness rules no longer applied, Tej decided. She snarled at him, "Go away. Or I'll find a street patroller."

He opened his hands in apparent surrender, watching with a doleful expression as they marched past. "A pony...?" he called after them, as if in one last spasm of hope.

Dotte looked back over her shoulder as they approached the bubble-car station. Tej looked straight ahead.

"I think you're crazy, Nanja," said Dotte, trudging with her up the pedestrian ramp. "I'd have taken him up on that drink in a heartbeat. Or any of the rest of the menu, though I suppose I'd have to draw the line at the pony. It wouldn't fit in my flat."

"I thought you were married."

"Yes, but I'm not *blind.*"

"Dotte, customers try to pick me up at least twice a week."

"But they aren't usually that incredibly cute. Or taller than you."

"What's that have to do with anything?" said Tej, irritated. "My mother was a head taller than my father, and they did fine." She clamped her jaw shut. *Not so fine now.*

She parted company with Dotte at the platform, but did board a bubble car. She rode to a random destination about ten minutes away, then disembarked and took another car back to a different stop on the other side of her neighborhood, just in case the man was still lingering out there, stalkerlike, at the first one. She strode off briskly.

Almost home, she started to relax, until she looked up and spotted Vorpatril lounging on the steps to her building entrance.

She slowed her steps to a dawdle, pretending not to have noticed him yet, raised her wristcom to her lips, and spoke a keyword. Rish's voice answered at once.

"Tej? You're late. I was getting worried."

"I'm fine, I'm right outside, but I'm being followed."

The voice went sharp. "Can you go roundabout and shake him off?"

"Already tried that. He got ahead of me somehow."

"Oh. Not good."

"Especially as I never gave him my address."

A brief silence. "Very not good. Can you stall him a minute, then get him to follow you into the foyer?"

"Probably."

"I'll take care of him there. Don't panic, sweetling."

"I'm not." She left the channel open on send-only, so that Rish could follow the play. She took her time closing the last few dozen meters, and came to a wary halt at the bottom of her steps.

"Hi, Nanja!" Vorpatril waved amiably, without getting up, looming, or lunging for her.

"How did you find this place?" she asked, not amiably.

"Would you believe dumb luck?"

"No."

"Ah. Pity." He scratched his chin in apparent thought. "We could go somewhere and talk about it. You can pick where, if you like."

She simulated a long hesitation, while calculating the time

needed for Rish to get downstairs. Just about...now. "All right. Let's go inside."

His brows shot up, but then his smile widened. "Sounds great. Sure!"

He rose and politely waited while she fished her remote out of her pocket and coded open the front entrance. As the seal-door hissed aside, he followed her into the small lift-tube foyer. A female figure sat on the bench opposite the tubes, hands hidden in her vest as if chilly, voluminous patterned shawl hiding her bent head.

A slender gloved hand flashed out, aiming a very businesslike stunner.

"Look out!" Vorpatril cried, and, to Tej's bewilderment, lurched to try to shove her behind him. Uselessly, as it only cleared the target for Rish. The stun beam kneecapped him neatly, and he fell, Tej supposed, the way a tree was said to, not that she'd ever witnessed a tree do such a thing. Most of the trees she'd seen before she'd fetched up on Komarr had lived in tubs, and did not engage in such vigorous behavior. In any case, he crashed to the tiles with a vague thrashing of upper branches and a loud *plonk* as his head hit. "Owww..." he moaned piteously.

The quiet buzz of the stunner had not carried far; no one popped out of their first floor flat door to investigate either that or the thump, alarming as the latter had seemed to Tej.

"Search him," Rish instructed tersely. "I'll cover you." She stood just out of reach of his long but no doubt tingling arms, aiming the stunner at his head. He eyed it woozily.

Tej knelt and began going through his pockets. His athletic appearance was not a façade; his body felt quite fit, beneath her probing fingers.

"Oh," he mumbled after a moment. "You two are *t'gether.* Thass all right, then..."

The first thing Tej's patting hand found was a small flimsy, tucked into his breast pocket. Featuring a still scan of her. A chill washed through her.

She seized his well-shaved jaw, stared into his eyes, demanded tightly: "Are you a hired killer?"

Still weirdly dilated from the stun nimbus, his eyes were not tracking quite in unison. He appeared to have to think this question over. "Well...in a *sense*..."

Abandoning interrogation in favor of physical evidence, Tej

extracted the wallet he'd flashed earlier, a door remote much like her own, and a slender stunner hidden in an inner pocket. No more lethal weaponry surfaced.

"Let me see that," said Rish, and Tej obediently handed up the stunner. "Who is this meat really?"

"Hey, I c'n answer that," their victim mumbled, but fell prudently silent again as she jerked her aim back at him.

The top item in the wallet was the credit chit. Beneath it was a disquietingly official-looking security card with a heavy coding strip identifying the man further as one *Captain Ivan X. Vorpatril, Barrayaran Imperial Service, Operations, Vorbarr Sultana*. Another mentioned such titles as *Aide-de-Camp to Admiral Desplains, Chief of Operations*, with a complicated building address featuring lots of alphanumeric strings. There was also a strange little stack of tiny rectangles of heavy paper, reading only *Lord Ivan Xav Vorpatril*, nothing else. The fine, black, raised lettering bumped under her curious fingertips. She passed them all up for Rish's inspection.

On sudden impulse, she drew off one of his polished shoes, which made him twitch in a scrambled reflex, and looked inside. *Military* issue shoes, aha, that explained their unusual style. 12 Ds, though she couldn't think of a reason for that to be important, except that they fit the rest of his proportions.

"Barrayaran military stunner, personally coded grip," Rish reported. She frowned at the handful of IDs. "These all look quite authentic."

"Assure you, they are," their prisoner put in earnestly from the floor. "Damn. By never mentioned any lethal blue-faced ladies, t' ratfink. Izzat...makeup?"

Tej murmured in uncertainty, "I suppose the best cappers would look authentic. Nice to know they're taking me seriously enough not to send cut-rate rental meat."

"Capper," wheezed Vorpatril—was that his real name? "Thass Jacksonian slang, innit? For a contract killer. You expectin' one? That 'splains a lot..."

"Rish," Tej said, a sinking feeling beginning in her stomach, "do you think he could really be a Barrayaran officer? Oh, no, what do we do with him if he *is*?"

Rish glanced uneasily at the outside door. "We can't stay here. Someone else could come in or out at any moment. Better get him upstairs."

Their prisoner did not cry out or try to struggle as they womanhandled his limp, heavy body into the lift tube, up three flights, and down the corridor to the corner flat. As they dragged him inside, he remarked to the air, "Hey, made it inside her door on t' first date! Are things lookin' up for Ma Vorpatril's boy, or what?"

"This is not a date, you idiot," Tej snapped at him.

To her annoyance, his smile inexplicably broadened.

Unnerved by the warm glance, she dumped him down hard in the middle of the living room floor.

"But it could be," he went on. "...To a fellow of certain special tastes, that is. Bit of a waste that I'm not one of 'em, but hey, I can be flexible. Was never quite sure about m'cousin Miles, though. Amazons all the way for him. Compensating, I always thought..."

"Do you ever give up?" Tej demanded.

"Not until you laugh," he answered gravely. "First rule of picking up girls, y'know; she laughs, you live." He added after a moment, "Sorry I triggered your, um, triggers back there. I'm not attacking you."

"Dead right you're not," said Rish, scowling. She tossed shawl, vest, and gloves onto the couch, and dug out her stunner again.

Vorpatril's mouth gaped as he stared up at her.

A black tank top and loose trousers did not hide lapis lazuli-blue skin shot with metallic gold veins, platinum blond pelt of hair, pointed blue ears framing the fine skull and jaw—to Tej, who had known her companion and odd-sister for her whole life, she was just *Rish*, but there were good reasons she'd kept to the flat, out of sight, ever since they'd come to Komarr.

"Thass no makeup! Izzat...body mod, or genetic construct?" their prisoner asked, still wide-eyed.

Tej stiffened. Barrayarans were reputed to be unpleasantly prejudiced against genetic variance, whether accidental or designed. Perhaps dangerously so.

"'Cause if you did it to yourself, thass one thing, but if somebody did it *to* you, thass...thass just *wrong*."

"I am grateful for my existence and pleased with my appearance," Rish told him, her sharp tone underscored by a jab of her stunner. "*Your* ignorant opinion is entirely irrelevant."

"Very boorish, too," Tej put in, offended on Rish's behalf. Was she not one of the Baronne's own Jewels?

He managed a little apologetic flip of his hands—stun wearing off already? "No, no, 's gorgeous, ma'am, really. Took me by surprise, is all."

He seemed sincere. He hadn't been expecting Rish. Wouldn't a capper or even hired meat have been better briefed? That, and his bizarre attempt to protect her in the foyer, and all the rest, were adding to her queasy fear that she'd just made a serious mistake, one with consequences as lethal, if more roundabout, as if he'd been a real capper.

Tej knelt to strip off his wristcom, which was clunky and unfashionable.

"Right, but please don't fool with that," he sighed. He sounded more resigned than resistant. "Tends to melt down if other people try to access it. And they make issuing a replacement the most unbelievable pain in the ass. On purpose, I think."

Rish examined it. "Also military." She set it gingerly aside on the nearby lamp table with the rest of his possessions.

How many details had to point in the same direction before one decided they pointed true? *Depends on how costly it is to be mistaken, maybe?* "Do we have any fast-penta left?" Tej asked Rish.

The blue woman shook her head, her gold ear-bangles flashing. "Not since that stop on Pol Station."

"I could go out and try to get some..." Here, the truth drug was illegal in private hands, being reserved to the authorities. Tej was fairly sure that worked about as well as it did anywhere.

"Not by yourself, at this hour," said Rish, in her *and no backtalk* voice. Her gaze down at the man grew more thoughtful. "There's always good old-fashioned torture..."

"Hey!" Vorpatril objected, still working his jaw against the stun numbness. "There's always good old-fashioned *asking politely*, didja ever think of that?"

"It would be bound," said Tej to Rish, primly overriding his interjection, "to make too much noise. Especially at this time of night. You know how we can hear Ser and Sera Palmi carrying on, next door."

"Houseless grubbers," muttered Rish. Which was rude, but then, she'd also had her sleep impeded by the amorous neighbors. Anyway, Tej wasn't sure but that she and Rish qualified as Houseless, too, now. And grubbers as well.

And that was another weird thing. The man wasn't yelling for help, either. She tried to decide if a capper, even one who'd had the tables so turned upon him, would have the nerve to bluff his way out past an influx of local police. Vorpatril did not seem to be lacking in nerve. Or else, against all the evidence, he didn't think he had reason to fear them. Mystifying.

"We'd better tie him up before the stun wears off," said Tej, watching his tremors ease. "Or else stun him again."

He did not even try to resist this process. Tej, a little concerned for that pale skin, vetoed the harsh plastic rope from the kitchen stores that Rish unearthed, and pulled out her soft scarves, at least for his wrists. She still let Rish tug them plenty tight.

"This is all very well for tonight," said Vorpatril, observing closely, "especially if you break out t' feathers—do you have any feathers? because I don't like that ice cube thing—but I have to tell you, there's going to be a problem come morning. See, back home, if I didn't show up for work on time after a night on the town, nobody would panic right off. But this is Komarr. After forty years, assimilation into the Imperium's going pretty well, they say, but there's no denying it got off to a bad start. Still folks out there with grudges. Any Barrayaran soldier disappears in the domes, Service Security takes it up seriously, and quick, too. Which, um . . . I'm thinking might not be too welcome to you, if they track me to your door."

His comment was uncomfortably shrewd. "Does anyone know where you are?"

Rish answered for him: "Whoever gave him your picture and address does."

"Oh. Yes." Tej winced. "Who *did* give you my picture?"

"Mm, mutual acquaintance? Well, maybe not too mutual—he didn't seem to know much about you. But he did seem to think you were in some kind of danger." Vorpatril looked down rather ironically at the bindings now securing him to a kitchen chair, dragged out to the living room for the purpose. "It seems you think so, too."

Tej stared at him in disbelief. "Are you saying someone sent *you* to *me* as a *bodyguard*?"

He appeared affronted by her rising tones. "Why not?"

"Aside from the fact that the two of us took you down without even getting winded?" said Rish.

"You did too get winded. Dragging me up here. Anyway, I

don't hit girls. Generally. Well, there was that time with Delia Koudelka when I was twelve, but she hit me first, and it really hurt, too. Her mama and mine were inclined to be merciful, but Uncle Aral wasn't—gave me a permanent twitch on the subject, let me tell you."

"Shut. *Up*," said Rish, driven to twitch a bit herself. "Nothing about him makes sense!"

"Unless he's telling the truth," said Tej slowly.

"Even if he's telling the truth, he's blithering," said Rish. "Our dinner is getting cold. Come on, eat, then we'll figure out what to do with him."

With reluctance, Tej allowed herself to be drawn into the kitchen. A glance over her shoulder elicited a look of hope from the man, which faded disconsolately as she didn't turn back. She heard his trailing mutter: "Hell, maybe I should've *started* with ponies...."

Chapter Two

Ivan sat in the dark and contemplated his progress. It was not heartening.

Not that his reputation for success with women was undeserved, but it was due to brains, not luck, and steady allegiance to a few simple rules. The first rule was to go to places where lots of women already in the mood for company had congregated—parties, dances, bars. Although not weddings, because those tended to put the wrong sorts of thoughts into their heads. Next, try likely prospects till you hit one who smiled back. Next, be amusing, perhaps in a slightly risqué but tasteful way, until she laughed. Extra points if the laughter was genuine. Continue ad lib from there. A 10:1 ratio of trials to hits was not a problem as long as the original pool contained ten or more prospects to start with. It was simple statistics, as he'd tried to explain to his cousin Miles on more than one occasion.

He'd entered that shop knowing the odds were not in his favor; a pool with only one fish required a fellow to get it right the first time. Well, he *might* have got lucky; it wasn't unprecedented. He wriggled his wrists against his scarf bonds, which were unexpectedly unyielding for such soft, feminine cloth. Some sort of metaphor, there. *This is not my fault.*

It was By's fault, he decided. Ivan was a victim of poor intel from his own side, like many a forlorn hope before him. Ivan had encountered overprotective duennas before, but never one who'd shot him from ambush the first time he walked through the door. The unfriendly blue woman...was a puzzle. He disliked puzzles. He'd never been good at them, not even as a child. His impatient playmates had generally plucked them out of his hands and finished them for him.

Rish was incredibly beautiful—sculpted bones, flowing muscles, stained-glass skin shimmering as she moved—but not in the least attractive, at least in the sense of someone he'd want to cuddle up to. Sort of a cross between a pixie and a python. She was shorter and slimmer than Nanja, and very bendy, but, he had noticed when the two women were dragging him up here, much the stronger. He also suspected genetically augmented reflexes, and the devil knew what else. Best appreciated from several meters' distance, like a work of art, which he suspected she was.

Whose work? That degree of genetic manipulation on humans was wildly illegal on all three planets of the Barrayaran Imperium. Unless one had it done to oneself, offworld, in which case it might still be better to go live somewhere else, after. Nanja was certainly neither Komarran nor Barrayaran, or she'd have had a more visible reaction to that famous name and address where he'd shipped the ghastly vase. Not only Not From Around Here, but also Not Been Here Long.

Her companion's elegant gengineering was almost Cetagandan in its subtlety—but the Cetagandans didn't make human novelties as such. Their aesthetic boundaries in that material were very strict, not to mention restricted, reserved for more serious and long-range goals. Now, animals—when Cetagandans were working with animal or plant genomes, or worse, both at once, all bets were off. He shuddered in memory. He would be *glad* to cross Cetagandans off his list, renegade or otherwise. He would be *ecstatic*.

Ivan peered around the dim living room. He was not, he assured himself, tied up in a small, dark place. It was a spacious, dark place, and not pitch-dark in any case, given the ambient urban glow from the window. And on the third floor, well aboveground. He sighed, and remembered to keep wriggling his weary feet. The nasty plastic ropes securing his ankles to the chair legs did seem to be slowly stretching. Perhaps he should have tried harder to escape, earlier. But the two women had been taking him right where he'd wanted to go, inside, for just the purpose he'd come, to talk. True, he'd been envisioning *friendly chat*, not *hostile interrogation*, but what was that quote Miles was so fond of? *Never interrupt your enemy while he is making a mistake.* Not that they were enemies, necessarily. He hoped. By could have stood to be clearer on that point, in retrospect.

The next most likely suspect on the body modification front was, of course, the planet and system of Jackson's Whole, an almost equally unsavory hypothesis supported, alas, by any number of small hints the two women had let fall.

Jackson's Whole did not have a unified planetary government—in fact, it claimed to have no government at all. Instead, it was ruled by a patchwork of Great Houses—116 of 'em the last Ivan had heard, but the number shifted in their internecine competitions—and countless Houses Minor. They tended not to hold large, unified territories on the planet's surface, but rather, interpenetrated more like competing companies. Granted, the system, or lack of it, did make it less likely for the Jacksonians to pull together for, say, a major military invasion of their neighbors. But a person who had no House allegiance or employment there was a very unprotected person indeed.

Ivan had no trouble imagining all sorts of colorful reasons for the two young women to be on the run from the Whole. Any sensible persons not aligned with the power structure—structures—would be better off emigrating, if they could manage it. The real mystery was why anyone from there would be *chasing* them. Assassination wasn't that casual a business expense, not with interstellar distances in play. If the two had made it all the way to Komarr but were still this afraid, someone with resources must really care, and not in a good way.

The room was not growing smaller. Nor darker. Nor damper. Nor changing in any way. But dear *God* this chair was getting hard. He hitched his shoulders and wriggled his butt, recalling all those dire warnings about deep-vein thrombosis and long rides in shuttle seats. As if he didn't have enough paranoia running through his aching head right now. Though his legs had stopped with the post-stun pins-and-needles, and were down to just pins.

So how had the two women fallen in together, and what was

their relationship, really? Was the blue woman friend, business partner, servant, lover, or bodyguard to the other? Some combination, or something even more arcane? When, inevitably, he'd had to pee, Rish had taken the con in the argument over whether it was safe to let him up. Ivan's plaintive, *How long do I have to spend not attacking you to prove I'm not attacking you?* had moved the warmer Nanja, but not the gold-eyed other. In the end, Nanja had left the room, and Rish had held a plastic jug.

Decanting his bladder was too much of a relief by then for Ivan to be embarrassed, much. Rish's strange beauty did not diminish close up; it just grew ever more detailed, almost fractal, but he'd stayed shriveled in her hand nonetheless, too alarmed to be aroused by her cool touch. She'd been as impersonal and efficient as a trained medtech. Which was *undoubtedly* just as well. Ivan couldn't vouch for how things would have gone had the task fallen to her partner.

So had undertaking the chore indicated anything except the price of winning the argument, or that Rish was protectively older, or what? Maybe the two women were escaped slaves. They could ask for asylum—slavery was entirely illegal in the Imperium, even more disapproved than gaudy gengineering upon humans, despite the inevitable legal brangling about where mere unfavorable indentures left off and the real thing began. If Rish was a created slave, she might be valuable enough to pursue. Hell, maybe Nanja had *stolen* her, now there was a thought. That'd tick someone off...

For a planet with a mere nineteen-and-something-hour sidereal day, this was turning into a damned long night. Ivan eyed his out-of-reach wristcom and tried to estimate the time left till dawn, and his nonarrival at work. His credit chit, used at the shipping shop, would surely give ImpSec a Last Known Location. Nanja's co-clerk would come under questioning about as soon as the investigating officer could scramble there, and probably wouldn't even need fast-penta to identify Ivan. ImpSec—not Service Security, for reasons Ivan had not yet confided to his quarry—would probably be knocking on the door before the two women had finished arguing over whether to feed their famished prisoner any breakfast. Pleasant, well-upholstered Nanja, Ivan imagined, would take his side...

His breath stopped at a faint scratching noise from the living room window. The flat was three floors up; there was no wind within a dome to move, say, tree branches against the polarizing glass, even assuming there were any trees on that side of the building. He hadn't had a chance to look. He opened his mouth again, exhaling as quietly as possible. Well—he scraped for optimism—maybe ImpSec hadn't waited for morning...? *And if you believe that, I have a cousin who will sell you the Star Bridge in Vorbarr Sultana...*

A hiss, a faint glow, as a narrow plasma beam cut a large hole in the window. Ivan thought he could see two dark shapes briefly limned in the dark beyond. Three floors up? They had to be riding some kind of float pallet, out there above the alley. The panel of normally unbreakable glass was eased back soundlessly out of the way.

Ivan had quite expected ImpSec to come collect him, yet another reason not to exert himself unduly in pointless escape attempts. But not at this hour, and not by that route. It seemed Nanja's paranoia was more urgently justified than he'd thought.

Ivan became uncomfortably aware that he was still tied to the bloody chair. Even if he could, by some heroic effort, rip his feet out of their restraints (shedding his shoes in the process), his wrists would remain bound to the chair arms. The most he'd be able to manage would be a sort of barefoot, crouching waddle toward his probably-armed foes. Maybe he could swing around and hit them in the shins with the chair legs...? Ivan had no desire to be stunned twice in one day, even optimistically assuming they bore stunners and not some more lethal weapons.

Ivan sank back and waited till both dark shapes had oozed through the gap and stood up, before calling out in a carrying voice: "If you're after those two women, I gotta tell you, you're hours too late. They packed their bags and flew ages ago."

A low-voiced huff from the dark that might have been, *What the hell...?* A faint double gleam from night goggles as two startled heads turned toward him.

"You may as well turn on the lights," Ivan continued, loudly. "You could stand to untie me, too." He bounced in place and thumped his chair legs, as if for emphasis.

The shapes trod forward. One reached to shove up his goggles and hit the light pad on the wall; the other yelped, "Ow!", clapped his hands over his eyes, and hastily dragged down his own light-amplifying eyewear. Cheap civilian models, Ivan observed, wincing against the sudden glare, not that anything more exotic would be required for this sort of sortie.

The first intruder strode toward him. Waving a stunner, Ivan noted wearily. "Who the hell are you?" the man demanded.

Two males. Komarran accents. And heights and general builds, though Komarran phenotypes were not nearly so uniformly blended as Barrayaran. It was all their centuries of trade, and passing traders, when Barrayar had been cut off from the Nexus at large. Dark clothing that might pass as street wear.

"A few minutes ago, I'd have said I was a completely innocent bystander, but now I'm starting to think I might be someone who was mistaken for you," said Ivan amiably. "I don't suppose you could untie me?"

"And why are you strapped to that chair?" added the other, staring.

"Tortured, too," Ivan supplied inventively. *Nanja, Rish, wake up!* "Horribly. For *hours*."

The second man peered in suspicion. "I don't see any marks."

"It was psychological torture."

"What kind?"

"Well," Ivan said, beginning with the first thought that rose to his mind, "they took off all their clothes, and then—"

The first man said, "Don't talk to him, you fool! The job's gone wrong. Toss the place and let's split."

"Hey, it gets better—don't you want to know about the ice cubes...?"

"Should we grab him, instead?"

The stunner wavered in doubt, steadied, pointing all-too-directly into Ivan's face. "Decide on the way out. Stun him first."

And ask questions later? In some nastier locale, much harder for ImpSec to find...? Dammit, *Miles* could have talked two such goons into untying him. Yeah, and probably suborned them to his cause before the ropes hit the floor, to boot. The trigger finger tightened...

The staccato buzz of a stunner beam came not from the Komarran, but from the shadows of the darkened hallway. Two pulses, two direct head-hits, the most effective if you could make the aim. The range was short. The invaders dropped like sacks of cement.

Ivan controlled his involuntary flinch. "About time you two woke up," he said cheerily, swiveling his head.

Rish padded into the light, followed at a more cautious tiptoe by Nanja. Neither woman wore filmy nightwear, Ivan saw to his disappointment. And apparently neither slept bare, more's the pity. Instead, both wore body-hugging knits suitable for the gym. Or for snapping awake in the middle of the night and dealing with unpleasant surprises.

"You know, if anything I said maybe led you to think I didn't quite believe you, I mean, about being a touch twitchy about uninvited visitors, I take it back," Ivan began. He nodded to the two lumps on the floor. "Anybody you know?"

Rish knelt and turned them over. Nanja followed to stare down into their faces.

"No," said Rish.

"Local rental meat," said Nanja, in a more disgusted tone. Her face grew suddenly tenser. "They've tracked us. Not only to Komarr, but all the way to *here*. Rish, now what do we do?"

"Follow the plan." The blue woman rose and stared down at the unconscious pair. "Kill them first, I suppose."

"Wait, wait!" said Ivan, a twinge of panic running through him. She *meant* that, even if she didn't sound very enthusiastic about it. "I mean, I agree with your diagnosis, local hirelings. Suggests they probably don't know much. And I don't think they were assassins—cappers. They were kidnappers, I bet." He added after a moment, "And don't I get any reward for saving you from them, just now? I mean, a kiss would be nice, but untying me would be more practical."

Nanja, after a long look at him, nodded. Under her blue companion's disapproving glare, she knelt and undid Ivan's bonds. He vented a *whoosh* of relief, rubbing his wrists and ankles before carefully standing up. The room only spun a little.

He really shouldn't push it, but faint heart never won, and all that. He bent his head and presented his cheek to her, just to see what would happen.

A hesitation. A widening of her eyes, which, close up, were a clear sherry color, lighter than her skin, very striking framed with her long black lashes. To his unconcealed delight, she stretched her neck and bestowed a neat peck on his cheekbone.

"See?" he said, in an encouraging tone. "That wasn't so hard." The spot tingled pleasantly.

He poked an invader with his toe in passing, as Rish knelt

to go through their pockets, then stuck his head out the big rectangular hole in the window through which a faint draft now coursed. A float pallet of much the sort used by techs to effect repairs on tall building faces hovered just below the frame. It bore a large plastic bin, typical of receptacles used to haul away soiled linens in hotels or hospitals. Empty. You could just about fit two stunned women into it, Ivan judged, if you folded them up snugly. Ah, the classics. But a cheap, common object; no one would look at it twice, so long as it wasn't trundled through some very inappropriate location.

He drew back inside and turned to the two women. "Yep, kidnapping. Not murder. Unless they meant to kill you and then cart away the bodies, tidily. Any guesses which?"

Nanja stood hugging herself, looking cold. "It could be either, I suppose. Depending."

"Any idea who would be sending you budget ninjas in the dark before dawn? No, silly question, belay that. Would you care to *share* with me who would, and so on?"

She shook her head. The clouds of curls bounced in a forlorn fashion.

"No IDs, no money, no nothing," reported Rish, rising. "Just stunners, gloves, and pocket lint."

The invaders, Ivan noticed for the first time, did indeed wear thin transparent gloves. Cheap, commercial, millions used to protect hands from dirty jobs all over the planet. Nothing unique, nothing traceable, which pretty much went for all of their equipment. Low rent, or cleverer than they seemed?

"You know, those goons could well have some sort of backup waiting outside," Ivan opined.

"We have an escape route. Over the roofs," said Nanja.

"Have you ever practiced it?"

"Yes," said Rish, scowling at him, which was no clue, as she pretty much scowled at him all the time. "Start packing, Tej."

Tej? Well, Ivan had known that *Nanja* was an alias. The blue woman hadn't made that slip of the tongue in front of him before. Starting to trust him, or just rattled?

"Do you know where you're going? That is, do you have a place to go?" Ivan asked.

To which Rish replied, "No business of yours," and Nanja-Tej said, "Why do you ask?"

Ivan promptly addressed himself to the latter. "I was thinking you might like to hole up at my place for a few days. Take stock, make your plans when not in a panic. I can almost guarantee I have no prior connection with you for your enemies to trace. It's likely as good a safe house as you could get on short notice. And it's free."

Nanja hesitated. Nodded. Rish sighed.

"What do we do with these, then?" said Rish, nodding at the lumps. "Safest to kill them..."

Ivan was still having trouble figuring out which woman was in charge. But the lumps did indeed pose a puzzle. The most obvious thing was to call ImpSec Komarr and have them send a professional cleaning crew to take the whole mess in hand. Reminded, Ivan retrieved his wallet, stunner, and wristcom. No one objected. The thing was...

Very belatedly, it occurred to Ivan to wonder what kind of fix Byerly was in, to send an HQ desk pilot to cover these women instead of, say, a trained ImpSec bodyguard or even squad, with all the high-tech trimmings. *By's idea of a joke* was not out of the running as a hypothesis, but... just how delicate was By's investigation? Was he simply out of range of his usual handlers, contacts, and blind drops, or was there some more sinister reason in play? By's hints had suggested that his current bag of creepy playmates had high connections in the Service—how high? And which branches? Could By be on the track of some corruption within ImpSec Komarr itself?

Dammit, the purpose of a briefing was to tell you everything you needed to know to do your job right. It shouldn't be a frigging *IQ test*. Or worse, *word puzzle*. Ivan hissed in growing frustration. Next time he saw By, he was going to strangle the smarmy Vorrutyer whelp.

The smarmy Vorrutyer whelp who, Ivan had reason to know, did sometimes, if very rarely, report directly to, and receive orders directly from, Emperor Gregor...

"Don't kill them," said Ivan abruptly. "Pack up as quick as you can, we'll take your escape route, and then go to my digs. But on the way out I'll call Solstice Dome Security, report that I witnessed a break-in from down in the street. Leave the door open for them, everything in place. Plenty enough funny business here that I guarantee they'll take these goons in charge, maybe put them on ice for a good long time. When the local patrollers arrive, any backup out there will scatter, if they haven't already. Does that work for you?"

Slowly, Rish nodded. Nanja-Tej was already on her way to their bedroom.

Ivan did yield to the temptation—temptation should have the right-of-way at all times, in his view—to peek after her into the room. The flat only had the one sleeping chamber, windowless, curiously enough. Twin beds, both rumpled, hm. What did that mean...?

The two women were ready in less time than Ivan would have believed possible, having fit everything they wanted into a mere three bags. They had to have drilled this. Ivan coiled up the ropes and scarves and stuffed them into various of his jacket pockets, and returned his chair to its demure place under the kitchen table. As a practical matter, he abandoned any of his fingerprints, loose hairs, or shed skin cells to their fates. Maybe they would pose an interesting test of Solstice Security's crime scene procedures.

Tej, dry-mouthed with worry, jittered along the edge of her building's roof as the Barrayaran spoke into his wristcom. He did an extremely convincing drunken drawl.

"...Yeah, you should see, I'm down in the street watching this right now. No horseshit, these two guys with, like, a window-washer's float pallet, goin' right through this third-story window. I don't see how they're washing windows in the dark, d'you know? Oh, my God. I just heard a woman scream...!" With a faint smile, Vorpatril shut down his link to the Solstice emergency number.

Solstice Dome never really slept. Enough general illumination from the city lights gave adequate vision for the next task, even if the colors were washed out to a mix of sepia and gray, checkered with darker shadows.

"You first, Tej," said Rish. "Careful, now. I'll toss you the bags."

Tej backed up a few steps for her running start and made the exhilarating broad jump to the next building. Three floors up. She cleared the ledge with ease and turned to catch the bags, one, two, three. Rish followed, loose garments fluttering as she somersaulted in air, landing on balance half a meter beyond Tej, motionless and upright like a gymnast dismounting.

Vorpatril stared gloomily at the gap, backed up quite a way, and made a mighty running jump. Tej caught his shoulders as he stumbled past her on landing.

"Ah," he wheezed. "Not as bad as it looked. A little gravitational advantage, thank you, Planet Komarr. Almost makes up for your miserly day-length. You wouldn't want to try that on Barrayar."

Really? Tej wanted to ask more, but didn't dare. And there was no time. Rish led off. As they made the second leap, the flashing lights of a dome patrol airsled were visible in the distance, closing rapidly.

Vorpatril balked at the next alley, half a dozen meters across. "We're not jumping *that*, are we?"

"No," said Tej. "There's an outside stair. From the bottom, it's only a block to the nearest bubble-car station."

By the time they'd distributed the bags and walked the block, carefully not hurrying, everyone had caught their breaths again. The few sleepy-looking early, or late, fellow passengers crossing the platform scarcely spared them a glance. Rish twitched her shawl around to hide her head better while Vorpatril selected a four-person car, paying a premium for its exclusive use and express routing. He politely took the rear-facing seat, punched in their destination, and lowered the transparent canopy to its locking position. The car entered its assigned tube and began to hiss along smoothly.

The night was fading into dawn, Tej saw, as the car rose on a long arc between two major dome sections. A shimmering red line edged the horizon beyond the limits of the sprawling arcology. As she watched, the tops of the tallest towers seemed to catch fire, eastern windows burning sudden orange in the reflected glow, while their feet remained in shadow. From a few lower sections, higher domes rose in a strange random spatter-pattern, catching gilded arcs.

Her fingers spread on the inside of the canopy as she stared. She'd never seen practically the whole of Solstice laid out like this, before. Since they'd arrived downside, she had only left their refuge to scurry out for work or food, and Rish hadn't ventured out at all. Perhaps they should have. Their immobility had given only an illusion of safety, in the end. "What *are* those domes?"

Vorpatril swallowed a jaw-cracking yawn and followed her glance. "Huh. Interplanetary war as urban renewal, I suppose. Those are sections destroyed during the fighting in the Barrayaran annexation, or later in the Komarr Revolt. Making way for fresh new building, after." He eyed her with tolerant amusement. "Real Komarrans would have known that, of course. Even if they weren't from Solstice."

She clamped her teeth and sat back, flushing. "Is it so obvious?"

"Not at first," he assured her. "Until one meets Rish, of course."

Rish's gloved hand pulled her shawl down lower over her face.

Several minutes and kilometers brought them to the business and governmental heart of the dome, an area where Tej had never ventured. The platform on which they disembarked was growing busier, and Rish kept her face down. They crossed the street and marched a mere half block till they came to a tall, new building. Vorpatril's door remote coded them within. The lobby was larger than Tej's whole flat, lined with marble and real, live potted greenery. The lift tube seemed to rise forever.

They debouched into a hushed, deeply carpeted corridor, walked to the end, and entered, through another coded door, another foyer or hallway and then a living room, with a broad view of the cityscape opening beyond a wide balcony. The décor was serene and technologically austere, except for a few personal possessions dropped at random here and there.

"Ah, no, look at the time!" Vorpatril yelped as they entered. "First dibs on the bathroom, sorry." He broke into a jog, leaving a trail of clothing in his wake: jacket, shirt, shoes kicked aside. He was unbuckling his trousers as he called over his shoulder, "Make yourselves comfy, I'll be out in a tick. God, I'd better be..." The bedroom door slid closed behind him.

She and Rish were left staring at each other. This sudden stop seemed even more disorienting than their prior panicked rush.

Tej circled the living area, inspecting a swank kitchenette that seemed all black marble and stainless steel. Despite its culinary promise, the refrigerator contained only four bottles of beer, three bottles of wine (one opened) and a half-dozen packets which the undecorative wrappings betrayed as military ration bars. An open box of something labeled *instant groats* graced the cupboards in lonely isolation. She was still reading the instructions on the back when the bedroom door slid open and Vorpatril thumped out again: fully dressed, moist from his shower, freshly depilated, hair neatly combed. He paused to hop around and shove his feet into his discarded shoes.

Both she and—*hee, I saw that!*—Rish blinked. The forest-green Barrayaran officer's uniform was quite flattering, wasn't it? Somehow, his shoulders seemed broader, his legs longer, his face...harder to read.

"Gotta run, or I'll be late for work, under pain of sarcasm," Vorpatril informed her, reaching past her to grab a ration bar and hold the package between his teeth as he finished fastening his tunic. He shoved the bar temporarily into a trouser pocket and seized her hands. "Help yourselves to whatever you can find. I'll bring back more tonight, I promise. Don't go out. Don't make any outgoing calls, or answer any incoming ones. Lock the doors, don't let anyone in. If a slithering rat named Byerly Vorrutyer shows up, tell him to come back later, I want to talk to him." He stared at her in urgent entreaty. "You aren't a prisoner. But be here when I come back—please?"

Tej gulped.

His grip tightened; laughter flashed in his eyes. He pressed his lips formally to the backs of her hands, one after the other, in some Barrayaran ethnic gesture of unguessable significance, grinned, and ran. The outer door sighed closed on sudden silence, as if all the air had blown out of the room with him.

After a frozen moment, she gathered her nerve, went to the balcony door, and eased it aside. Judging from the angle of the light, she would get an excellent view of Komarr's huge and famous soletta array, key to the ongoing terraforming, as it followed the sun across the sky, later. She'd never been able to see it from her own flat.

She'd been cowering in the shadows for a long, sick time, it seemed in retrospect. Every plan she'd ever been given had come apart in chaos, her old life left in a blood-soaked shambles far behind her. Unrecoverable. Lost.

No going back.

Maybe it was time to take a deep breath and make some new plans. All her own.

She ventured to the railing and peeked down, a dizzying twenty flights. Far below her, a hurrying figure in a green uniform exited the building, wheeled, and strode off.

Chapter Three

Tej and Rish spent their first few minutes alone scouting the exits. The luxurious flat had only the one door, but the corridor had lift tubes at either end, and emergency stairs as well. There was also the balcony, Tej supposed, but to be survivable, escape by that route would require either antigrav or rappelling gear, which they did not currently possess. They next explored the interior space for any hidden surveillance equipment or other surprises; there either was none, or it was very subtle. The lock on the outer door was much better than average, and Rish set it with satisfaction; but of course no ordinary door would stop a truly determined and well-equipped invader.

Rish did find a compact launderizer concealed in the kitchenette, and applied herself to laundering all the dirty clothes they'd hastily packed, perhaps in the hope that their next escape, whatever it turned out to be, could be more orderly. Tej discovered the captain's sybaritic bathroom, and decided to treat her chill weariness with a long soak.

The scent of *him* still lingered in the moist air, strangely pleasant and complex, as if his immune system was calling out to hers: *let's get together and make wonderful new antibodies.* She

33

smiled at the silly image, lay back in the spacious tub of hot
water, and frankly enjoyed his dash of inadvertently displaced
flirtation in the old evolutionary dance, all the better because he
couldn't know how he was observed. It was, she realized after a
bit, the first spontaneously sensual moment she'd had since the
disastrous fall of her House, all those harried months back. The
realization, and the memories it trailed, were enough to destroy
the moment again, but it had been nice while it lasted.

She stirred the water with her toes. Since they'd gone to ground
on Komarr, fear and grief had slowly been replaced with the less
stomach-churning memory of them, till last night had kicked it
all up again. It was not in the least logical that she should feel—
relatively—safe in this new refuge. Who was this Ivan Vorpatril,
and how had he discovered her, and *why*? She floated, her hair
waving around her head like a sea-net, and breathed his fading
scent again, as if it could supply some hint.

The water didn't cool—the tub had a heater—but at length her
hands and feet grew rather wrinkly, and she surged up out of the
cradling bath and dried off. Dressed again, she found that Rish had
discovered that the flat's comconsole was not code-locked, and was
searching for any Solstice Dome Security reports on their intruders.

"Find anything?"

Rish shrugged her slim shoulders. "Not much. Just a time
stamp, and our address. 'In response to a witness report of a
possible break-in, officers arrived and apprehended two men in
possession of burglary equipment. Suspects are being held pending investigation.' It doesn't sound like anyone's stepped up to
outbid the arrest order yet."

"I don't think they do it that way here," said Tej, doubtfully.

Rish scanned down the file. "'Officers called to domestic alter-
cation...vandalism reported at bubble-car platform...attempted
credit chit fraud by a group of minors...' Oh, here's one. 'Beating interrupted of man spotted by bar patrons stealing public
emergency breath masks. Suspect arrested, patrons thanked.' I
suppose I can see why no one would have to pay for *that* arrest
order... The Solstice patrollers were busy enough last night, but
really, the crime here seems very dull."

"I think it's restful. Anyway, bath's yours, if you want it. It's
really nice, compared to that dreadful sonic shower we've been
living with lately. I can recommend it."

"I believe I will," Rish allowed. She stood and stretched, looking around. "Posh place. You have to wonder how he can afford it on a Barrayaran military officer's salary. I never had the impression those fellows were overpaid. And their command doesn't let them hustle on the side." She sniffed at this waste of human resources.

"I don't think it's his real home, that's back on Barrayar. He's just here for some work thing." Recently arrived, judging from the contents of his kitchenette, or maybe he didn't cook? Tej nodded at the comconsole. "I wonder how much we could find out just by looking him up?"

Rish's golden eyebrows rose. "Surely this benighted Imperium doesn't allow its military secrets out on the commercial planetary net of its conquest."

Throughout the Jackson's Whole system, information was tightly controlled, for the money, power, and security it could bestow, and for that narrow edge that could mean the difference between a deal succeeding or failing. At the other extreme, Tej's favorite tutors from her youth, a trio of Betans her parents had imported at great trouble and expense, had described a planetary information network on their homeworld that seemed open to the point of madness—suicide, perhaps. Yet somehow Beta Colony remained, famously, one of the most scientifically advanced and innovative planets in the Nexus, which was *why* the tutors had been imported. Of all the instructors she'd been plagued with, the Betans were the only ones whose departure she'd mourned when, homesick, they had declined to renew their contracts for another year. Most other planetary or system polities fell somewhere between the two extremes of attempted information control.

"I think we may be thinking too hard," said Tej. "We don't need to start with his secrets, just with what everybody else knows." *Everybody but us.*

Rish pursed her lips, nodded, and stepped aside. "Have at it. Shout out if you find anything useful."

Tej took her seat. Stuck hiding in their flat, Rish had been allowed far more time to learn the arcana of making this net disgorge data than Tej, but how common could that odd name be? She leaned over and entered it.

A Komarran database was the first to pop up above the vid plate, bearing the promising title of *The Vor of Barrayar.* All in alphabetical order, starting with V and ending with V. *Oh.* There were, it seemed, hundreds and hundreds of Vorpatrils scattered across the three planets of the Barrayaran Empire. She tried reordering the names by significance.

At the top of that list was one Count Falco Vorpatril. The Counts of Barrayar were the chiefs of their clans, each commanding a major territorial District on the north continent of their planet. In their way, Tej supposed they were the equivalents of Jacksonian Great House barons, except that they came by their positions by mere inheritance, instead of having to work and scheme for them. It seemed a poor system to her, one that did nothing to assure that only the strongest and smartest rose to the top. *Or the most treacherous*, she was uncomfortably reminded. Count Falco, a bluff, hearty-looking, white-haired man, had no son named Ivan. Pass on.

Several high-ranking military officers followed, and some Imperial and provincial government men with assorted opaque and archaic-sounding titles. There was an Admiral Eugin Vorpatril, but he had no son named Ivan either.

Belatedly, she remembered the little paper cards from Vorpatril's pocket. There were several Ivan Vorpatrils, including a school administrator on Sergyar and a wine merchant on the South Continent, but only one Ivan Xav.

His entry was short, half a screen, but it did have a confirming vid scan. It seemed to be of him as a much younger officer, though, suggesting that he had improved with age. Tej wasn't sure how such a stiff, formal portrait could still look feckless. His birth date put him at 34 standard-years old, now. The entry listed his father, Lord Padma Xav Vorpatril, as deceased, and his mother, Lady Alys Vorpatril, as still living.

Her eye paused, arrested. His father's death date was the same as his birth date. *That's odd.* So, her Ivan Xav was half an orphan, and had been so for a long time. That seemed...painless. You could not miss, fiercely and daily, a man you'd never met.

She was reminded of his horrible vase. Who had he sent it to, again? She bit her lip, bent, and spelled the awkward name out very carefully. All those Vor names tended to come out as a blurred *Voralphabet* in her mind, unless she paid strict attention. *Double oh.*

A very uncommon name, Vorkosigan; barely a dozen or so living adult males. But she should have recognized it nonetheless.

The clan Count of that surname appeared, when she reordered the entire database by significance, second on the whole list, right after Emperor Gregor Vorbarra. Count, Admiral, Regent, Prime Minister, Viceroy... Aral Vorkosigan's entry scrolled on for what seemed several meters of closely written text. Unofficial titles included such nicknames as *Butcher of Komarr*, or *Gregor's Wolf*. He did have a son named Miles, of just about her Ivan Xav's age. VorMiles also had an entry much longer than Captain Vorpatril's, if much shorter than his sire's.

Tej was not as vague as most Jacksonians about the history of this patch of the wormhole nexus. But she'd never expected even to visit here, let alone be trapped for months, so she hadn't exactly studied up. Her original evacuation route had called for a direct transit across the Barrayaran Imperium, not even touching down on the surfaces of Komarr or Sergyar, just making what orbital or jump-station transfers were needed to reach her final destination of Escobar. Or even, when that goal had begun to seem unsafe as well, to Beta Colony of imagined-happy memory. No one would blink at Rish there. Well, all right, they probably would blink, she was *made* to be riveting, but no one would harass her. Anyway, the point was, this stop had never been on any sensible planner's itinerary.

Barrayar had one of the most bizarre colonization histories in the whole of the Nexus, which was full of the relics and results of audacious human ventures. The story extended far back to the twenty-third century CE, when wormhole travel had first been developed, launching a human diaspora from Old Earth. A prize because of its breathable atmosphere, the planet drew an early settlement attempt of some fifty thousand would-be colonists. Who promptly disappeared from all contact when their sole wormhole link proved unstable, collapsing with catastrophic results. Missing, presumed dead, and over the next six centuries, all but forgotten.

Till, little more than a hundred years ago, a new jump route was prospected from—to its ultimate regret—Komarr. The explorers discovered a thriving but backward world. Subsequently, twenty years of Komarran-supported Cetagandan occupation had failed to civilize the savage planet, but did succeed in militarizing it.

A generation after the expensive withdrawal of the Occupation, the Barrayarans had come boiling out of their cul-de-sac to seize Komarr in turn, presumably to block any further galactic attempts to civilize them. The momentum of their Komarran success had led in turn to an ill-advised overreaching, as the Barrayarans of the day then went on to try to conquer more distant Escobar the same way. That expedition had failed, disastrously, in the face of strong Escobaran resistance aided by every neighbor the victim possessed, including clever Beta Colony; high-ranking casualties had included the Barrayaran crown prince himself.

It was still a matter of profound respect and awe, to Jacksonian students of the great Deals of history, how evil Emperor Ezar had managed to hang on to the newly discovered planet of Sergyar during the treaty settlements, adding it firmly to his empire before dying and leaving his throne to a five-year-old grandson. After that, the Imperium had settled down a lot, more concerned with consolidating the boundaries they'd gained than expanding them beyond their power to defend. But in all, the Barrayarans remained uncomfortable neighbors. Jacksonians generally were just as glad they weren't right next door, but rather, buffered by a complex multi-jump route through the open system of the Hegen Hub and the free planetary polity of Pol.

All of which, plus two out of three systems of the Imperium, a person had to cross to reach the safety of Escobar, or Beta Colony beyond, sigh.

Tej returned to Ivan Xav's entry. Really, there was little more here than what had been revealed by the contents of his pockets, though she supposed this confirmed their validity. He was what he seemed, a middling Vor officer of middling responsibilities and middling rank. Just middling along.

So why was he looking for me? But before she could explore further, Rish emerged refreshed from her bath to offer a shared brunch, which perforce consisted of half a military ration bar, nasty but nutritious, and half a bottle of wine each. It was surprisingly good wine, though Tej suspected the beer would have complemented the entrée more stoutly. And after *that*, she fell into an exhausted doze on the sofa. Even after her months downside, Komarr's short day length remained physiologically awkward. She hadn't slept soundly since they'd arrived.

Nor since before . . .

Ivan was only a few minutes late, which he was honestly able to blame on the morning bubble-car clump-up on the tube from

Dome Center out to the military shuttleport—happily, the slow-down had been in a high section with a nice view, not in the disturbing underground stretch. Barrayar's Komarr command HQ was somewhat awkwardly split between the downside installation next to the 'port and the orbital and jump-point stations, but no pop-ups to orbit were scheduled today for the visiting admiral and his loyal assistant.

Desplains, a spare and quietly competent officer in his late fifties, took in Ivan's neat but squinty appearance with an ironic eye. "Heavy drinking last night, Vorpatril?"

"No, sir, not a drop. I was kidnapped by two beautiful women and held prisoner in their flat all night. They didn't let me get a wink of sleep."

Desplains snorted amusement and shook his head. "Save your sex fantasies for your friends, Ivan. Time to saddle up."

Ivan gathered the notes and agendas and followed him out.

The three-hour-long morning meeting with the downside local staff was more torture than last night's ordeal had been, in all, and Ivan only kept awake by surreptitiously pinching his earlobe with his fingernail. The afternoon's schedule promised to be more entertaining, a private planning session with Desplains's own inspection team, a cadre of keen and occasionally evil officers known to the inspected as the Vor Horsemen of the Apocalypse, though only two of the group had surnames burdened with that prefix.

This left Ivan his lunch hour to pursue his own affairs. He grabbed a rat bar *again*, poured a cup of tarry coffee, popped two painkillers in an attempt to clear the sleep-deprivation cotton batting from his head, unwillingly contemplated his secured comconsole, and instead of starting a tedious and possibly frustrating search, called the building next door. Admiral Desplains's name cleared his route at once.

ImpSec Galactic Affairs shared its downside offices with ImpSec Komarr, although how much the two sets of spook-handlers talked to each other was anyone's guess. Once past the lobby security, the hushed, windowless corridors reminded Ivan all too much of ImpSec's parent headquarters back in Vorbarr Sultana: utilitarian, secretive, and faintly depressing. *They must've imported the same interior designer, just before he hanged himself.*

The top Galactic Affairs analyst for Jackson's Whole here was one Captain Morozov; Ivan had been interviewed by him twice

before, over his cousin Mark's affairs. The personal touch always
sped things up, in Ivan's experience. Morozov also met, adequately,
Ivan's current *who-do-you-trust* calibrations. Ivan found him
presiding over a similar cubicle and comconsole to that of a few
years back, even more packed with books, cartons of flimsies,
and odder memorabilia. Morozov was a pale scholar-soldier with
a square, bony face, and an unusually cheerful outlook on life
and his work—ImpSec regulars could be morbid.

Morozov greeted Ivan with either a wave or an ImpSec-style
salute, it was hard to tell which, and drew up the spare swivel
chair with an extended foot. "Captain Vorpatril. We meet again.
What can Galactic Affairs do for Admiral Desplains today?"

Ivan settled himself, finding a place for his feet amongst the
cartons. "I"—he conscientiously did not say *we*—"have a query
on an unusual person with a suspected Jacksonian connection."
Carefully, if vividly, Ivan described Rish, withholding her name
for now—it could be just another alias, after all. There seemed
no point in describing Tej. There might be whole planets full of
cinnamon-skinned beauties out there somewhere, for all Ivan
knew. Rish, he suspected, was unique. *Keep it simple.*

Morozov listened intently, his eyebrows climbing, fingertips
pressed together in a gesture copied, Ivan was fairly sure, from
his infamous former boss. As Ivan wound up, he vented a *Huh!*
Before Ivan could inquire just what kind of *Huh!* it was, Morozov spun to his comconsole and zipped through its file listings
too fast for Ivan to follow. He sat back with a triumphant little
Tah-dah! gesture as a still vid formed over the plate.

Ivan leaned forward, staring. "Good grief! There's a whole set!"
With a conscious effort, he closed his mouth.

The vid showed a group portrait, posed and formal. Rish, it
was clearly Rish, knelt on one knee, second from the left. She was
wearing very little: a gold thong and a winding pattern of gold
foil that appeared to be glued on, barely covering other strategic
points and twining up to her neck as if to present her face as an
exotic blossom. Surrounding her were four other women and a
man. They had slightly varying heights and builds, but all looked
equally lithe and shimmering. One woman was white and silver,
one yellow and metallic gold, one green and gold, one red and
garnet, and the man was jet black and silver. Six faces differently
but equally exquisite, smiling faintly, serene.

"Who *are* they?"

Morozov smiled like a particularly satisfied stage magician. Ivan had to admit, that was one hell of a rabbit.

"Their names are Pearl, Ruby, Emerald, Topaz, Onyx, and the blue one is Lapis Lazuli. Baronne Cordonah's famous living Jewels. That scan was taken several years ago."

"Jacksonian genetic constructs?"

"Of course."

"What, um, do they do? Besides stand around and look stunning."

"Well, the Baronne was known to use them as décor from time to time—from all reports, she was a woman who knew how to make an entrance. Also as a dance troupe, for very favored visitors. Servants, and I suspect much more. They are certainly jeeveses."

"Uh...what?"

"A *jeeves* is a Jacksonian slang term for an obligate-loyal servant or slave. Made variously, either by psychological conditioning or genetic bias or both, and unswervingly devoted to their object of attachment. They're said to pine if they are separated from their master or mistress, and sometimes even die if he or she dies."

They actually sounded a bit like his cousin Miles's loyal armsmen, but that select cadre of stern men wasn't nearly so photogenic. Ivan kept this reflection to himself. "Baronne Cordonah? Any relation to Cordonah Station?" One of five vital jump-point stations guarding the wormholes into and out of Jacksonian local space. Fell Station, which served the jump point out to the Hegen Hub, was usually of the most interest to Barrayar, but the others were important, too.

"Until recently, Shiv and Udine ghem Estif Arqua, Baron and Baronne Cordonah, were the joint masters of House Cordonah and all its works."

"Until how—wait, what? Ghem Estif?" A pure Cetagandan name. "How the hell did that happen?"

"Oh, now that's a tale and a half." A glint of enthusiasm lit Morozov's eye. "How far back should I start?"

"How far back does it go?"

"Quite a way—you'd be amazed."

"All right, begin there. But keep in mind that I get mixed up easily." Ivan cast an eye on the time, but quelled an urge to tell Morozov to fast-forward it. An ImpSec analyst in a *forthcoming* mood was a wonder not to be wasted.

"The name of General ghem Estif may be dimly familiar to you from your history lessons...?" Morozov paused in hope. More dim than familiar, but Ivan nodded to encourage him. "One of the lesser Cetagandan generals who oversaw the last days of the Occupation, and its assorted debacles," Morozov generously glossed. "At about that time in his career, he actually was awarded a haut wife."

The highest honor, and burden, a Cetagandan ghem lord could acquire; such a spouse was a genetic gift bestowed by the upper tier of Cetagandan aristocracy, the haut, a super-race-in-progress, or so they imagined themselves. Having met a few daunting haut ladies, Ivan could imagine that the reward had been a very mixed blessing for the old general.

"When most of his brother ghem officers returned to Eta Ceta to lay their somewhat terminal apologies before their emperor, ghem Estif and his wife understandably lingered on Komarr. It must have been a strange and wrenching life for them, expatriate Cetagandans in the domes. But ghem Estif had his connections, and eventually his daughter Udine, who was actually born here in Solstice, married an extremely wealthy Komarran shipping magnate."

"Uh, how many generations of Udines are we talking about...?"

Morozov held up a hand. "Wait for it... Ghem Estif's schemes were unfortunately knocked asunder by us once more, when Barrayar annexed Komarr. The family fled in various directions. The daughter and her husband got out at the last possible moment, under fire, with the protection and aid of a mercenary captain from the Selby Fleet, which Komarr had hired to augment their defense. A somewhat eccentric Jacksonian sometime-smuggler and hijacker by the name of Shiv Arqua."

"Was the Komarran husband killed, then?"

"Nope. But by the end of the voyage, young Udine had definitely switched allegiances. It is unclear just who hijacked whom, but Shiv Arqua's rise to prominence in House Cordonah began at about that time."

"I see." *I think.* Ivan wondered just what accumulated frustrations on the part of the defeated ghem general's expat daughter had triggered such an elopement. Or had it been a more positive choice? "Er, was Shiv an especially glamorous...space pirate, then?"

Morozov rubbed his chin. "I'm afraid even ImpSec has no

explanation for women's tastes in men." He bent forward again and called up another scan. "The official portrait, when Arqua took the Baron's seat, twenty years back. He'd be grayer and stouter now, if that helps."

A man and a woman appeared standing side by side, staring into the pickup with grave, closed expressions. Both were dressed in red, her gown deep carmine, his jacket and trousers almost black. The woman drew Ivan's eye first. Oh, yeah, she had the height, the luminous eyes and skin, the superb sculpted bone structure, the marrow-deep confidence that marked a liberal serving of haut genes. A thick, black hank of shining hair bound with jeweled ribbons was drawn over her shoulder, to hang, visibly, past her knees, very much harking to the haut style.

The top of her husband's head was barely level with her chin, though Arqua was by no means unusually short. Middle height, stocky build, the remains of a muscular youth softening in middle age; black hair of unknown length, but drawn back, probably, into some knot at his nape. Maybe some faint streaks of silver in there? Rich, deep mahogany skin. A heavy, rather squashed face that looked as if it would be more at home running a gang of enforcers, but featuring liquid black eyes that would, Ivan suspected, be dangerously penetrating if turned on you in person.

Ivan wasn't sure, but by the angle of their arms, he thought the two might be holding hands behind that velvety fold of skirt.

"Impressive," said Ivan, sincerely.

"Yes," Morozov agreed. "I was actually rather sorry to lose them. Arqua and his wife were pretty even-handed in their dealings. Arqua got out of the hijacking trade and into the middleman, ah, recovery business quite a while back. House Cordonah had the best record for getting hostages back alive of any of the Houses that dabble in that commerce. Reliable, in their own special way. They were just as happy to sell Barrayaran information to Cetaganda as Cetagandan information to ImpSec, but if the data the Cetas received was as solid as what we got, they should have been satisfied customers. And the Cordonahs were willing to return favors, both above and below the table."

"You keep using the past tense. So what's Barrayar's current relationship with House Cordonah, then?"

"It's in disarray, I'm afraid. About seven months ago, House Cordonah suffered an especially hostile takeover by one of their rival jump-point control cartels, House Prestene. With this much time gone by without an attempt at a countercoup, it's almost certain that both the Baron and the Baronne are dead. A real loss. They had such *style*." He sighed.

"Are, uh, the House's new masters less helpful to us, then?"

"Say rather, untested. And uncommunicative. Several data lines were lost during the shifts, which have not yet been replaced."

Ivan squinted, trying to imagine what that last sentence would translate to if it weren't in ImpSec Passive Voice. *Trail of bodies* was a phrase that rose to mind.

"It was not known if the late Baronne's Jewels were captured, killed, or scattered in the takeover," Morozov went on. "So I have a keen interest in any sightings, if perhaps academic at this late date. Just where did you see Lapis Lazuli?"

"We need to talk about that," Ivan evaded, "but I'm out of time." He glanced at his wristcom; it wasn't a lie, oops. He scrambled up. "Thank you, Captain Morozov, you've been very helpful."

"When can we continue?" said Morozov.

"Not this afternoon, I'm afraid; I'm bespoke." Ivan picked his way over cartons to the cubicle door. "I'll see what I can fit in."

"Stop by any time," Morozov invited. "Oh, and please convey my personal best wishes to your, er, stepfather, which I trust will find him much recovered."

"Virtual stepfather, at most," Ivan corrected hastily. "M'mother and Illyan haven't bothered to get married yet, y'know." He managed a somewhat wooden smile.

As he fled in disorder down the dingy corridor, it occurred to him that there could be *another* reason he was getting such an unusual degree of cooperation from the ImpSec old guard these days, and it had nothing to do with his association with Admiral Desplains. He shuddered and ran on.

Ivan headed for the door at day's end with his brain jammed with everything from personnel promotion debates to surprise inspection schemes to the lurid history of House Cordonah, but mostly with urgent mulling of just where to stop for a takeaway dinner that would most please Tej. *If she's still there.* He was anxious to get home and find out. It was, therefore, no joy to see, out of the corner of his eye, a lieutenant from the front security desk waving frantically and hurrying to catch him. "Sirs! Wait!"

Too late to speed up and pretend not to have seen the fellow. Ivan and Admiral Desplains both paused to allow him to come up, slightly out of breath.

"What is it, Lieutenant?" inquired Desplains. He did a better job than Ivan of concealing his dismay at their impeded escape, only a faint ironic edge leaking into his resigned tone.

"Sir. Two Solstice Security people just turned up at the front desk, saying they want to interview Captain Vorpatril."

Interview, not *arrest,* Ivan's suddenly focused mind noted. Although he imagined any attempt by civilian dome authorities to arrest a Barrayaran officer from the midst of Barrayaran HQ could be a tricky proposition, jurisdiction-wise.

Desplains's brows rose. "What's this all about, Vorpatril? It can't be the Imperial Service's largest collection of parking violations, again—you don't have a vehicle here. And we've only been downside four days."

"I don't know, sir," said Ivan, truthfully. *Suspect* was not the same thing as *know,* right?

"I suppose the fastest way to find out is to just talk to them. Well, go along, try to make them happy." Unfeelingly, his boss waved Ivan away. "Tell me all about it in the morning." Desplains made a swift strategic retreat, leaving Ivan as the sacrificial rear guard.

It could have been worse. Desplains could have wanted to sit in. . . . Ivan sighed and trudged unwillingly after the too-efficient lieutenant, who told him: "I put them in Conference Room Three, sir."

There were a handful of such reception rooms off the HQ building lobby, holding-pens for people HQ didn't care to admit to its inner sanctums. Ivan expected that every one of them was monitored. Conference Room Three, the smallest, had approximately the ambiance and intimacy of a tax office waiting area, Ivan discovered as the lieutenant ushered him inside. He wondered if it was made that dismal on purpose, to encourage visitors not to linger.

"Captain Vorpatril, this is Detective Fano and Detective-patroller Sulmona, Solstice Dome Security. I'll just leave you to it, then, shall I? Detectives, please return to the front desk and sign out again when you're finished." The lieutenant, too, beat a retreat.

Fano was a stocky man, Sulmona a slim but fit-looking woman.

He was in civvies, she in uniform complete with such street gear as would be expected on a patroller's belt, including a stunner holster and shock-stick. Both were youngish but not young. Not grizzled veterans, but not rookies; born post-Conquest, then, though perhaps with older relatives possessing unhappy memories. Sulmona's left hand bore a wedding ring, Ivan noted automatically.

"Thank you for agreeing to see us, Captain," said Fano formally, standing up. He gestured to a chair across the table from the pair. "Please, sit down."

Taking psychological possession of the space, Fano was, in proper interrogation-room style. Ivan let it pass and sat, granting them each a neutral nod. He had suffered through a course in counterinterrogation techniques once, long ago. *I suppose it will come back to me.* "Sir, ma'am. What can I do for Dome Security?"

They exchanged a look; Fano began. "We're following up on a peculiar B&E arrest—that's breaking and entering—early this morning in the Crater Lake neighborhood."

Dammit, how had this pair nailed him so fast? *Don't panic. You didn't do anything wrong.* Well, all right, he'd done several things wrong, starting with listening to Byerly Vorrutyer. But he didn't think he'd done anything *illegal. Yeah, I'm the victim, here.* What he said out loud was, "Ah?"

"Oh," put in Sulmona, pulling a vid pickup from her pocket and setting it in front of them, "do you mind if we record? It's standard procedure in these investigations."

Why not? I'm pretty sure my people are. Yes, and the transcript would be copied to Admiral Desplains first thing tomorrow morning, no doubt. *Ouch.* "Sure, go ahead," said Ivan, trying for a tone of easy innocence. He offered a friendly smile to the detective-patroller. She seemed to be immune to his charm.

Fano went on, "The flat that was broken into is listed as rented by a young woman named Nanja Brindis, lately moved to Solstice from Olbia Dome. Unfortunately, Sera Brindis is not to be found, either last night or today—she didn't report to her work this morning. We understand you had contact with the young woman earlier last evening. Would you care to describe it? In your own words."

The better to hang myself. How much of the story did this pair already possess? They had obviously seen some scan of the credit chit he'd used at the shipping shop, and maybe talked to the coworker, and who knew what else. So he'd likely better stick as closely to the truth as possible, without betraying Byerly or Nanja-Tej. Or the Imperium. Or himself, but it was pretty easy to see where he sat in that hierarchy, should a goat be required. He sighed, because he didn't think the Komarrans would understand it if he bleated.

"Yes, well, I'd stopped in at the shop where she worked to ship a package home. It was closing time, so I offered to take her out for a drink or dinner."

Sulmona frowned at him. "Why?"

"Er...haven't you seen a picture of her yet?"

"There was a scan for her work ID," said Fano.

"Then it didn't do her justice. She was a very eye-catching young woman, believe me."

"And?" said Sulmona.

"And I'm a soldier a long way from home, all right? She was pretty, I was lonely, it seemed worth a try. I know you Komarrans don't always think us Barrayarans are human, but we are." He matched her frown. She didn't drop her eyes, but she did rock back a bit; point taken.

"And then what happened?"

"She said no, and I went my way."

"Just like that?" said Sulmona.

"I can take no for an answer if I have to. Someone else will say yes eventually."

The pair exchanged another unreadable look. Fano prompted, "And then what? Did you follow Sera Brindis to her flat?"

"No, I thought I'd stroll back to look at that lake, where they rent the boats, you know. Since it seemed I was to have time on my hands." Wait, was that in the right direction? Well, he could feign to have been turned around. "And I ran into Sera Brindis again, coming the other way. A happy chance, I thought."

"I thought you took no for an answer," murmured Sulmona.

"Sure, but sometimes women change their minds. It never hurts to ask again."

"And if they change their minds in the other direction?"

"Her prerogative. I'm not into that rough stuff, if that's what you're thinking." And Ivan could see it was—well, they were cops, they had to have seen some ugly scenarios. "I prefer my bed-friends friendly, thanks."

"And?" said Fano. Weariness was beginning to color the patience in his voice.

"So she invited me inside. I thought I'd got lucky, was all." Ivan cleared his throat. "This is where it gets a trifle embarrassing, I'm afraid." *Did* they know about the blue roommate? Well, they might, but Ivan decided that he wouldn't. "I thought we were going to sit down for a drink, some get-to-know-you conversation, maybe dinner after all, all the civilized stuff, when suddenly she pulled out a stunner and shot me."

"Were you trying to attack her?" said Fano, abruptly cold.

"No, dammit. Look. I know I've been a desk pilot for a while, but I did have basic training, once." And the ImpSec refresher course on personal defense once a year, but that was a nonroutine and dubious benefit of his *other* rank. No need to mention it here. "If I'd been trying to attack her, I'd have succeeded. She was only able to zap me because it came as a complete surprise. I'd thought things were going *well*."

"And then what did you think?" said Sulmona dryly.

"Nothing. I was frigging *unconscious*. For a long time, I guess, because when I woke up, I was tied to a chair and the flat was dark. Seemed empty. I wasn't sure if it was safe to yell out or not, so I just started working on trying to get loose."

"Safe?" said Sulmona, in a disbelieving tone.

He didn't have to play a total fool, Ivan decided. He fixed her with a frown. "If you two have worked at your jobs for any length of time, you have to have cleaned up a couple of cases of Barrayarans, especially in uniform, out in the domes who ran into Komarrans with old grudges. I didn't know if I'd fallen into the hands of crazy people, or terrorists, or spies, or what. Or if I was about to be tortured or drugged or kidnapped or worse. So getting myself loose seemed a better bet than drawing attention."

The pair's return stares were tinged with enough embarrassment that Ivan was pretty sure he'd scored a hit. Develop this theme, then.

"I was just starting to make progress when these two guys showed up at the window—third-story window, mind you—and started cutting through it with a plasma arc. I didn't figure this was exactly how Komarrans went visiting their friends, y'know? Especially at that hour. For all I knew, they'd come to collect me."

"The perpetrators," said Fano, "in their first testimony, stated that they were in process of returning the float pallet to the person they'd borrowed it from, and saw you by chance in passing. That you cried out frantically for help, and that's why they broke in."

"Ha," said Ivan darkly. "Good story, but not true. They cut their way in before they ever saw me." He hesitated. "First testimony? I hope you fast-penta'd those suckers."

He'd actually neither hoped nor expected anything of the kind. Surely any kind of serious agent had to have undergone resistance treatment to the truth drug?

"Later," said Fano. "As soon as we'd collated enough evidence and inconsistencies to legally permit us to conduct a nonvoluntary penta-assisted interrogation."

"What, they weren't allergic? I mean, they seemed like pros to me. What little I saw of 'em."

"Professional petty criminals in the domes don't normally adopt such extreme military techniques," said Fano. "Instead, they rely on a cell system. They never know who hired them, or why they were set to their task. Low tech, but effective enough, and very annoying. To us, that is."

"I'll bet," Ivan commiserated. "So—*were* they after me?" And thank *God* he'd stuck as tightly to the truth as he could, so far.

Fano frowned, and admitted, "No. It seems they were hired to pick up Sera Brindis and her maidservant, and deliver them to a location where they would be handed off to yet another cell for transport. We haven't been able to find out anything about this maidservant. Sera Brindis was the only resident listed in the flat. Did you see a second woman?"

Ivan shook his head. "Not before I got stunned." He gave it a beat. "Nor after, for obvious reasons."

"Did you stun the two men?" asked Fano.

"I was still tied to the damned chair, unfortunately. And blinded by the lights. I tried to con them into untying me. The shots seemed to come out of nowhere. I did hear footsteps behind me, running out the front door, but by the time I finally got free and was able to look around, nobody was there."

"How many pairs of footsteps?"

"One, I thought, but I couldn't swear to it. The whole night was like a damned farce, except I was the only one without a script. By then I was mainly interested in getting out of there before someone else came back and started in on any fun let's-torture-the-Barrayaran games."

Sulmona leaned forward and fiddled with her recorder. "We received an anonymous tip about the break-in, which led back to a data wall that none of our programs could penetrate. Happily, it seems we now have a positive voice match." Ivan's own slurred voice began to sound: "...yeah, you should see, I'm down on the street watchin' this right now..." Remorselessly, she let the call play all the way to its abrupt end. She added, "We also found a charge to your credit chit for a bubble-car ride from Crater Lake Platform to downtown Solstice, just a few minutes after the time-stamp on this call." Because it never hurt a case to add a little redundancy, Ivan glumly supposed.

"*Did* you hear a woman scream?" asked Fano.

"Uh, well, no, not really. I just figured it would hurry up the response. I wasn't sure how fast those two goons were going to wake up. And I didn't think they should be let to go wandering off on their ownsome. Better the whole mess should be turned over to the proper authorities. That would be you. Which I did."

"You know, Captain Vorpatril, both leaving the scene of a crime and making falsified emergency calls are against the law," said Fano.

"Maybe I should've hung around, but I was going to be late for work. And I was still pretty shaken up."

Fano gestured to the recorder. "Were you drunk?"

"I won't deny I might have had a drink or two earlier." He could, but he wasn't going to—better if they thought he'd been a trifle alcohol-impaired, which they might well buy. He could see it played to their prejudices. "But have you ever had a heavy-stun hangover?"

Fano shook his head; Sulmona's brows drew down, possibly in unwilling sympathy, about the first he'd got from her.

"Let me tell you, they're downright *ugly*. Your head buzzes for hours, and your vision is messed up. Balance, too. It's no wonder I sounded drunk." And that for Admiral Desplains, and whoever else on Ivan's own side that was going to be listening to this. Because there were limits to self-sacrifice, and this was all bad enough, *damn* Byerly.

Fano's lips twisted. "And what at your work was more important than leaving a crime scene in which, to hear you tell it, you were a victim?"

Ivan drew himself up, letting the admiral's high Vor aide-de-camp out for the first time. He, too, could deliver unpleasantness in a chilly tone. "A great deal of my work is highly classified, Ser Fano. I won't be discussing it with you."

Both Komarrans blinked.

Sulmona riposted, "Would you be willing to repeat your testimony under fast-penta, Captain?"

Ivan leaned back, folding his hands, sure of his ground on this one. "It's not up to me," he replied easily. "You would have to apply to my commanding officer, Admiral Desplains, Chief of Operations, and then after that the request would have to be approved by ImpSec HQ in Vorbarr Sultana. By General Allegre personally, I believe." Damned well knew, actually. "An ImpSec operative would have to sit in, administer the drug and the antagonist, and record everything. You would both have to be personally investigated and cleared by ImpSec first." Ivan added kindly, "You're welcome to apply, of course. I expect you could get an answer in about two weeks." And he would be on his way back to Barrayar before then.

The detectives shot him twin looks of dislike. That was all right. Ivan didn't exactly like them, either.

"Yes, but didn't you even report this incident to your own security, Captain?" asked Fano.

Really disliked them. "I reported it in brief to my commanding officer." True in a *sense*, but oh God, wasn't Desplains ever going to fry him in the morning over that. "As I didn't end up in the hospital or the morgue, and I wasn't questioned, tortured, bugged, or even robbed, I have to classify it as a misadventure encountered on my own time. Bit of a mystery, true, but mysteries get turned over to ImpSec"—*or originate from ImpSec*—"which is, thank God, not my department. I'm Ops, and happy to be so. Every ImpSec officer I ever had to do with was twisty as hell, y'know?" *Especially my relatives.* "But when ImpSec decides what I'm supposed to think, I'm sure they'll tell me."

Fano said, unhopefully, "And would ImpSec be willing to share any findings with Solstice Dome Security?"

"You can apply," said Ivan. He bit his lower lip to stop himself from baring his teeth.

Sulmona drummed her fingers on the tabletop. "We still have a missing woman on our hands. Or not on our hands. I don't like it. If whoever was trying to kidnap her missed her, where is she?"

"At a guess, she probably pulled up stakes and went to hide somewhere else," said Ivan. "It would seem the sensible thing, if someone was after you."

"The *sensible* thing would be to go to Dome Security for help," said Sulmona, mouth pinching in frustration. "Why didn't she?"

Ivan scratched his head. "Dunno. She didn't exactly confide in me, y'know? But if she's only lately moved here, it would make sense that her mysteries probably have their roots back where she came from. Where was that, again?"

"Olbia Dome," said Fano, automatically.

"Then shouldn't you folks be directing your attention to Olbia Dome?" *Instead of to, say, my flat, argh?*

"That will be our next task," sighed Fano. He pressed his palms to the table and levered himself upright, and Ivan wondered how much of his night's sleep he'd missed over this. *Not as much as me.* Reluctantly, he opened his hand in dismissal of Ivan. "Captain Vorpatril, thank you for your cooperation." He didn't add *such as it was* out loud, but Ivan thought it was implied.

"My personal embarrassment doesn't seem the most important issue, here. Doesn't mean I enjoy it. But you're welcome. I really do hope no harm has come to Sera Brindis."

Ivan rather pointedly escorted his visitors to the security desk to sign out. The harrowing interview over, he fled the building.

Chapter Four

Captain Vorpatril returned nerve-wrackingly late after dark, when both sun and soletta had set. Tej forgave him almost immediately for the sake of the several large, heavy, handled bags he bore, from which delectable odors issued.

"We have to talk," he wheezed, but the two famished women overbore him without much resistance on his part.

"We have to *eat*. Do you realize you left us nothing but those awful ration bars?" Tej demanded. "That was all we had for lunch. Well, and the wine," she added fairly. "That was pretty good."

"*I* had rat bars for breakfast *and* lunch, and no wine at all," he one-upped this.

Rish, whose metabolism was permanently set on high, sped to lay out plates and eating tools on the round glass table across from the kitchenette. The bags disgorged three kinds of pasta, grilled vegetables, a sauté of spinach, garlic, and pine nuts, sliced vat beef, roasted vat chicken with rosemary, salads both leafy and fruit, cheeses, cheesecake, three flavors of ice cream and two of sorbets, and more wine. Tej could only think *I do like a man who keeps his promises.*

"I wasn't sure if you had any special dietary things, customs, needs," Vorpatril explained. "So I tried to get a range. All Komarran-style; there's a good place just up the street."

"I'll eat anything that wasn't ever a live animal," Rish avowed, setting-to in demonstration.

"I was beginning to think about compromising on that live animal part," Tej added.

Vorpatril, she was pleased to see, was a man who appreciated his food. Given the rat bars, she'd begun to picture him concealing a level of Barrayaran barbarism that even the holovids hadn't hinted at. But the selection demonstrated an unexpected level of discernment and balance. The attunement of his senses couldn't match her or Rish's innate aptitude and formal training, of course, but it was far from hopeless. And he seemed unwilling to damage the dining ambiance with upsetting discourse, which suited Tej just fine.

He was still working up to whatever he'd wanted to disclose when he went off to the lav and to shed his jacket and shoes, returned via the couch, sat, and more or less fell over. "Just need to close my eyes f'r a minute..."

The eyes stayed closed; after a while, the mouth opened. He didn't snore, exactly; it was more of a soothing purring sound, muffled by the cushion he clutched.

Rish crossed her arms and regarded him. "I'll concede, these Barrayarans are cute when they're asleep. They stop talking." Her head tilted. "He even drools fetchingly."

"He does not drool!" Tej smiled despite herself.

"Don't get attached, sweetling," Rish advised. "This one is dangerous."

Tej stared down at the sleeping officer. He didn't look all that dangerous, not with that curl of dark hair straying over his forehead, just begging for a soft hand to put it to rights... "Really?"

"You know what I mean."

"Should we wake him up?" asked Tej doubtfully. "I don't think he slept at all last night. I thought he would doze in the chair."

"Eh, let sleeping creatures lie." Rish glanced at her wristcom. "Besides, my favorite 'vid comes on right now..."

Rish, immured in their flat for weeks on end, had developed an addiction to an array of Komarran holovid serial dramas, a fondness Tej did not especially share. After a day of grubbing, the short Komarran evening left her little time for relaxation.

Rish went off now to the bedroom, which had the best holovid remote link, and closed the door. First turning off the lights to make sure she was not visible from a distance, Tej slipped onto the balcony and stared out for a time at the strange, sealed city. Was her long journey doomed to end here—one way or another? It could be worse. But it was not her choice, just an accumulation of chances.

She returned at length, carefully locking the balcony door and drawing the drapes, then set herself to quietly cleaning up after their meal. There was plenty left over to sustain them through tomorrow, at least. The captain appeared to be planning on keeping her and Rish, not that the decision was his. She returned to the couch and tentatively tried to poke him awake, pulling away the cushion. He clutched it back with surprising strength and determination for an unconscious man, mumbling and turning over to protect it, so Tej gave up and just sat down across from him to contemplate the view. She had to admit, it was a good view, genetically speaking. For a wild-caught.

After another few minutes, Rish came out to join her, smiling in a pleased way. "I was right about Hendro Fon," she informed Tej. "He *was* faking the amnesia. And the DNA sample had been substituted. Sera Jenna was a real clone! I'll bet the trade fleet merger is off now." She sat beside Tej and nodded at Vorpatril. "Still out, is he?"

"Yes. He must have been exhausted. I wonder what it is they make an aide-de-camp do all day, anyway?"

"I have no idea," said Rish.

Quiet held sway for a time.

Tej finally murmured, "Rish, what do we do next? We're good here for tonight, probably tomorrow, but then what? I can't go back to my job."

"Small loss. I know you worked hard, sweetling, but your grubber job was far too slow in filling the bag. I said so at the time."

"You did. I thought Nanja would get something better soon." And the commonplace shop had seemed to be ideal for lying very low indeed. Tej had learned how to do every task required of her in less than two days. Which was good, because she doubted she'd have been up to mastering anything more challenging, just then. *I'm so sick of this struggle.* "Nanja Brindis used up my last identity package, and she was barely deep enough to pass even a cursory inspection." Maybe that was a good thing. Her next identity would surely be less predictable to their pursuers if even she couldn't predict it.

Nor afford it.

If they could get to Escobar, better identities might be made available to them there, but if they couldn't get off Komarr without better IDs . . .

"I really realize, now, what it is to be Houseless."

Rish gripped her hand in brief consolation. "I suppose we could try going to ground in a different dome. Maybe Equinox, or Serifosa. If we can't afford a jumpship, we could at least afford the monorail. Get out of Solstice, where we know we've been smoked." Her voice was unpressing.

"A smaller dome would make it even harder to hide, though."

Rish stood, stretched, and wandered over to prod their host. When he did not stir, she leaned over and neatly forked his wallet from his pocket. She brought it back to Tej, and they went through it together, again.

"Not much cash," said Rish, "and we can't use his credit chit. Though I suppose his IDs would fetch a good price, if we could find the right buyer."

"This"—Tej fingered the thin stack of local currency, then tucked it into the wallet again—"would only sustain us for a few days. We've a couple of days for free right here. This much wouldn't get us ahead. Just put it back."

Rish shrugged and did so, as deftly as she had extracted it.

Tej leaned her head back, her own eyes closed for a time.

"I saw this vid show," Rish offered after a while, "all about Sergyar, and the colonization effort. It looked like a nice world, breathable atmosphere and all."

"Did they show anything about that horrid worm plague?" Tej shuddered.

"Not a word. I think they were trying to persuade people to move there. Gruesome pictures of colonists all bloated up like lumpy sausages wouldn't much aid that. But I gathered you could go as some sort of indentured laborer, and pay for your passage after."

It sounded like the first step on the slippery slope into contract slavery, to Tej. What she said aloud was, "But Sergyar has an even smaller population than Komarr. And it's all stocked with Barrayarans. How would you hide there?"

"It's a very mixed population, I heard. The current Vicereine is making an effort to draw immigrants from all over. Even Beta Colony. It won't be like Barrayar, or even Komarr, if that keeps on."

They were both silent for a while, contemplating this option. It depended on their being able to make it to orbital embarkation alive and uncollected, which didn't seem a good bet right now.

"There's Captain Mystery, here." Rish nodded to the sleeping figure across from them. "Captain Vormystery, I suppose he would correct that."

"Ivan Xav, the one and only. I think he likes me."

"Oh, I can *smell* that." Rish smirked. "He also has a slight breast fetish."

"Don't they all." Tej sighed. The corners of her mouth drew up. "Though not, in his case, for *slight* breasts."

"If he were a random Komarran stranger off the street, I'd advise—though only as a second-to-last resort—that you attach yourself to him and ride as far as you could. But he's not Komarran, he's definitely not random, and that's far too strange."

"Mm."

Another long silence.

Rish finally said, in a very low voice: "I would die before I allowed myself to be taken back and used against the Baron and Baronne."

In an equally quiet tone, Tej returned, "There's no Baron and Baronne left to be used against. We'd just be used." She blinked eyes gone abruptly blurry. *No. I won't cry any more. If weeping were going to help, it would have done so by now.*

Both stared straight ahead. Rish's voice went darker, bleaker. "Once they grab us, the chances for the last escape will grow very constrained. *Too soon* could become *too late* too fast to target."

No need to say out loud what the last escape was; they'd discussed it twice before, though they'd twice evaded it, once by bare minutes. "How, here?"

"Too dangerous for either of us to go out looking for a painless termination drug, though I did notice a sign for a veterinary hospital on the way, could be raided, but... I read about this method, once, that they used on Old Earth. Lie back in a hot bath and just open your veins. It only hurts for a moment, a little sting, less than a hypospray jab, they say. There's that great big tub in the bathroom. We could just ease back and...go to sleep, sweetling. Just go to sleep."

"It would be a bit tough on Ivan Xav when he came home, though, wouldn't it? Not to mention tricky for him to explain to the dome cops."

"Not our problem by then."

Barely turning her head, Tej glanced aside at her companion. "You're tired, too. Aren't you."

"Very," Rish sighed.

"You should have taken a nap this afternoon, as well." Tej scrunched her eyes in thought. "I don't know. I think I'd rather seize some last chance for...something. Go to the highest tower in Solstice, maybe, and step off the roof. The fall would be great, while it lasted. We could dance all the way down. Your last dance."

"Bitch of an *arrêt* at the end, though," said Rish.

"And no encore. The Baronne always loved your encores..."

"I vote for the tub."

"The balcony out there might do, if we were cornered."

"No, too public. They might scrape us up and put us back together. And then where would we be?"

"That's...really hard to guess."

"Ah."

More silence. The sleeping captain snorted and rolled over again.

"You'd have a better chance of hiding out minus me," began Rish.

Tej sniffed. This, too, was an old argument. "My loyalties may not be bred in my bones, odd-sister, but I'll back nurture against nature any day you care to name."

"Nature," breathed Rish, starting to smile.

"Nurture," said Tej.

"Nature."

"Nurture."

"Tub."

"Tower." Tej paused. "You know, we need a third vote, here. We always end up in a tie. It's a gridlock."

"Deadlock."

"Whatever." Tej tilted her head in consideration. "Actually, the *best* method would be something that made it look like our pursuers had murdered us. The local authorities would think they were killers, and their bosses would think they botched the snatch. Get them coming and going."

"That's pretty," Rish conceded. "But it would only cook the meat. The best revenge would fry the *brains*."

"Oh, yes," Tej sighed. *Oh, yes.* But she didn't see how to reach all the way home to effect such a deed from the Unbeing, given that she couldn't even do so while still breathing.

Vorpatril rolled back and made a strange wheezing noise, like a distant balloon deflating, then went quiescent again.

"Eyeable show, that, I grant you," said Rish, nodding to him, "but there's not much of a plot."

"Think of it as experimental dance. Very abstract."

More quiet.

Rish yawned. "I vote we take over the bed. Leave him out here."

"You know, I think you might get a unanimous—" Tej froze as the door buzzer sounded, loud in the stillness. Rish jerked as if electrocuted and leaped to her feet, golden eyes wide.

Tej lurched across to the other sofa and shook its occupant by the shoulder, saying in an urgent undervoice, "Captain Vorpatril! Wake up! There's someone at your door!"

He mumbled and hunched in on himself, like an animal trying to hide in a hole too small for it. The buzzer blatted again.

Tej shook him again. "Ivan Xav!"

Rish stepped across, grabbed his sock feet, and ruthlessly yanked them to the floor. The rest of him followed with a thud. "Hey, *ah*, wazzit?" he mumbled indignantly, rolling over and sitting up at last, then clapping a hand over his eyes. "Ah, too bright!"

The door buzzer sounded and did not stop, now, as if someone held it down with a thumb and leaned in.

"Who the hell'd be out there at this time of night?" Vorpatril blinked in a blurry attempt to focus on his wristcom. "What *is* this time of night?"

"You've been asleep almost three hours," said Rish.

"Not 'nough." He tried to lie back down on the floor. "God, what's that noise in my head? Swear I didn't drink that much..."

"Answer your *door*," Tej hissed, hauling on his arm. To the buzzing was now added a thumping, as if someone was hitting the door with a bunched hand. *Surely* kidnappers wouldn't be this noisy...?

He lumbered up at last, visibly pulling himself into focus. "Right. Right. 'L go find out." He waved them off as he started for the short hallway leading to the door onto the corridor. "You two go hide."

Tej stared wildly around. The place had only the living room, kitchenette, bedroom, and bath, spacious as they were, plus two closets and the balcony; any search for cowering women would be short and foregone. Should she allow herself to be cut off from access to that balcony? Rish darted into the open bedroom doorway and frantically motioned her to follow; instead, Tej nipped to the other corner and peeked around into the entry hall.

The door slid aside. From a shadowy shape occluded by Vorpatril's broad shoulders came a terse voice, male, Barrayaran accent: "Ivan, you idiot! What the hell happened with you last night?"

"You—!"

To Tej's considerable surprise, the captain reached out, grabbed his visitor by the jacket, and swung him inside and up against the hall wall. The outer door hissed closed. She caught a bare glimpse of the man before shrinking back out of sight: neither old nor young, shorter than Ivan Xav, not in any recognizable uniform.

"Ivan, Ivan!" the voice protested, shifting its register from irate to placating. "Easy on the jacket! The last time anyone greeted me with that much passion, I at least won a big, sloppy kiss out of it." A slight pause. "Granted, that was my cousin Dono's dog. Thing's the size of a pony, and no manners—it *will* jump all over—"

"Byerly, you, you—ImpWeasel! What the hell did you set me up for?"

"Just what I wanted to ask you, Ivan, my love. What went wrong? I thought you would bring the woman back here!"

"Not on a first date, you twit! You always end up at her place, first time. Or some neutral third location, but only if you're both insanely hot."

What...?

"I stand enlightened," said the other voice, dryly. "Or would, if you would let me down. Thank you. That's better." Tej fancied she could almost hear him shooting his cuffs and adjusting his garb.

Ivan Xav's voice, surly: "You may as well come on in."

"That was what I'd had in mind, yes. I'd have thought the five minutes I spent leaning on your door buzzer would have been a clue, but oh well."

Tej retreated on hasty tiptoes across the living room and around the bedroom doorframe. Rish stood plastered against the wall on the far side, listening intently. She raised a warning finger to her lips. Tej nodded and breathed through her open mouth.

The light, exasperated voice continued, "The latest updates from Solstice Dome Security on the break-in remain very unenlightening, but—tied to a *chair*, Ivan? However did you manage that?"

"I haven't seen the latest—oh, God, they didn't give my name, did they?"

"Do they know your name?"

"They do now."

"Ivan! You should know better!" A hesitation. "The next begged question being, of course, how did you get untied?"

The captain heaved a sigh. "Before you say anything more, Byerly—ladies, you'd better come out, now."

Whoever this man was, he seemed to know Ivan Xav, and far too much about Tej's affairs. Should she trust in her host's cavalier disclosure of them? *Do we have a choice?* Tej let out her breath, nodded across to Rish, and stepped out of the bedroom doorway. The new man swung around to take her in, his eyebrows climbing.

"The hell! Do you mean to tell me I've been running mad since midmorning trying to trace the woman, and she was here all the—"

Rish stepped out from behind Tej and regarded the newcomer coolly.

He was abruptly expressionless—now *there* was a curious first response—his face unreadable. But not the rest of him. His eyelids did not widen, but his pupils flared. Rish could actually pick up heart rates, a degree of discernment beyond Tej's capacity, though she fancied his heart did not speed, but actually slowed, seeming to take bigger gulps in its shock. Of the surprise, fear, and arousal all present in the first faint scent of him, wafting to her, she suspected he was only conscious of the first two.

He blinked, once. Closed his lips with a visible effort. "My word," he said faintly.

"Yeah, that's what I said. More or less," said Vorpatril. "Or would have, if she hadn't just grassed me with a stunner."

"Mademoiselle." The man named Byerly favored Rish with a flowing half-bow, only partly a parody of the gesture. "May I just say, a stunner seems redundant? So, introduce us, mon coz." He was back in control of himself, now. Rish's eyes were very narrow, watching him intently. Taking him in, far more literally than he could guess.

"He's not my cousin," said Vorpatril, with a jerk of his thumb at his visitor. "The relationship's more removed, although, alas, not removed nearly far enough. Tej, Rish, meet Byerly Vorrutyer, commonly known as By. Just plain By. Not Lord Vorrutyer or Lord Byerly—those titles are reserved for the sons of the count."

In coloration, the two might have been siblings, though the underlying bones denied that first impression. Yet clearly, the two men shared a generous measure of Vor genes. *Caste* might be the precise term. The visitor wore a vaguely military-looking jacket and trousers, decorated with braid and piping that she suspected were more artistic than indicative of rank. The jacket swung open, revealing a fine shirt and colorful braces. And a brief glimpse of a discreet stunner holster.

Ivan Xav was dangerously engaging. This man was dangerously... tense? Tired? Wired? Yet despite his manhandling in the hallway, there was no flinching in his posture, no effort to distance himself from his host. No fear of Vorpatril, nor of Tej for that matter. Rish—by the flicker of his eyes, the angle that he held his body, he was keenly conscious of Rish. Trying to account for her?

Vorpatril went on, "By, meet Tej, also known as Nanja Brindis— but you knew about her, didn't you? And her...friend, Rish. Who was a surprise to us all, but I believe the dome cops have her down on their playlist as *the maidservant, missing.*"

Tej swallowed. "How do you do, Byerly Vorrutyer," she said formally. "That tells us who you are, but not, I'm afraid, what you are." She let her eyebrows rise in an inquiry divided equally between the two Barrayarans.

Vorpatril folded his arms and stared off into space. "That would be for By to say."

The other Barrayaran drew a long breath—buying time to think?—and cast an inviting wave toward the angled pair of couches. "Indeed. May I suggest we all sit down more comfortably?" Another moment or two purchased, while she and Rish alighted where they'd been before, and the two men took Vorpatril's late sleeping slot. But after settling himself next to his removed relative, who removed himself yet farther to the couch's end, Byerly still looked rather blank. "Um. So. How...did you all end up here?"

Tej said, in chill tones, "Captain Vorpatril invited us."

"They wanted a safe place to lie low," Vorpatril put in. "Which must be working, if you couldn't find 'em." He added after another moment, "On purpose, anyway."

Tej frowned at Byerly. The mismatch between his foppish mannerisms and his body's testimony was as grating to her senses as clashing colors or a musical discord. "Who *are* you?"

"Good question. Who are you?"

"I can tell you one thing," said Vorpatril. "Got it from Morozov, the Jackson's Whole guru in Galactic Affairs out at HQ—Rish, here, is also known as Lapis Lazuli. She used to be part of a whole gengineered dance troupe belonging to the, evidently, late Baronne Cordonah of Cordonah Station. Seems that about seven months ago, House Cordonah was swallowed up by some pretty nasty competitors."

Tej trembled.

Rish looked up, eyes hot with rage, swiftly banked. "Not competitors. Predators. Scavengers. Hyenas, jackals, and vultures."

"A veritable zoo," said Byerly, his brows lifting above widened eyes. "Were you, ah, there at feeding time?"

Tej held up her hand. "We won't tell you anything." She waited while his face tightened in frustration, and then offered her only card, or the illusion of it. Pure bluff, exhilarating and sickening. "But we might deal you for it. Answer for answer, value for value."

Would he go for it? The deal was utterly hollow. The man could pull out his stunner, drop Rish where she sat, and take Tej before she was half launched at him—though perhaps less easily the other way around. She could wake up tied to a chair like poor Ivan Xav, except with the cool kiss of a hypospray of fast-penta held to her arm. In minutes, she'd be spilling everything she knew, along with fits of giggles. Why should he buy what he could so easily steal?

Instead, he sat back. There ensued a long, thoughtful, silence.

"All right," said Byerly at last. "I'll deal."

Rish's brows rose in surprise. So did Vorpatril's.

"What's your real name, Sera Brindis?" By began at once.

Tej's mouth drew down, concealing both elation and terror. His supple adaptation was almost Jacksonian, and yet he was as purely Barrayaran as Vorpatril. Did he understand what he was doing—what she was doing? *Only one way to find out.* "That's a question worth my life. What have you to offer of equal weight?"

His head tilted. "Eh, perhaps we won't start with that one, then.

As for what happened last night, I can get that free from Ivan, so I shan't waste a trade on it. What *did* happen last night, Ivan?"

Vorpatril started. "Eh? You want the short version? No thanks to you, these ladies mistook me for a hired goon sent to stalk them, a misunderstanding we didn't get straightened around till the real goons showed up. You owe me for a lost night's sleep, a stunner hangover, having to jump *tall buildings* with a stunner hangover, and, let me add, a major personal disappointment. We bailed, left the goons out cold on the floor, called in the break-in to the dome cops, and came here with barely time left for me to get to work."

Byerly ran his hands through his dark hair, disarranging it. "Dear *God* Ivan, *why* did you call Dome Security?"

"They were bound to turn up eventually. I didn't want the goons to get away, sure as hell didn't want to take 'em with me, and I wasn't sure if I could trust"—he hesitated—"other authorities, given some things you'd said." He went on, sounding more aggrieved, "And to cap it, the two most unsympathetic dome cops *ever* tracked me to work just at quitting time and cornered me for forty-five minutes of grilling. They were just itching to arrest me for stalking, rape, kidnapping, murder, who knows what else—being Barrayaran, I expect."

"Ah, shi—did you mention me?"

"Kept your existence entirely out of it. Had to tap-dance around their physical evidence like a loon to do it, too, so you can say *Thank you, Ivan*."

"That may be premature."

Vorpatril's scowl deepened. "Yeah, and to make things worse, this all took place in an Ops conference room, where you just know it was monitored. It'll all be in *my boss's* inbox by tomorrow morning, and I might lie to the dome cops for you, By, but I'm damned well not going to lie to Desplains."

Byerly pounded his forehead with his fist. "*Ivan.* If you knew that, why didn't you take them out somewhere else for that interview—coffee shop, park bench, *anywhere*? You haven't the instinct for self-preservation that God gave a canary. How *ever* have you survived so far?"

"Hey! I do fine, on my own. It's only when you Im—you damned weasels show up in my life—uninvited, generally—that it gets this complicated."

"All right, I have a question," said Tej, interrupting all this—how long would they keep it up? "Who sent Captain Vorpatril to me, who gave him my picture? Was it you?" She frowned at the other Voralphabet.

He spread a hand over his chest and offered her a sitting bow. "None other. I trust you found him satisfactory?"

"Why?"

"That's two questions."

"So keep score." Her eyes narrowed. "Did you know Rish and I were going to be attacked last night? How?"

Vorpatril bit his knuckle.

Byerly's face set in a faint, empty smile for a moment—processing?—then relaxed into its ironic default expression once more. "I hired them."

Tej's heart plummeted. Were they deceived—again...?

"What!" cried Vorpatril indignantly. "You might have said!"

"I was not certain to what degree I could rely on your acting abilities."

Vorpatril crossed his arms and sat back with a snort.

Uh, what...? thought Tej. Rish's empty hand slipped quietly back out of her trouser pocket, even her guarded face bewildered.

Byerly continued to Tej, "I am presently engaged in studying some people. Frequently, the best way to gain a close view is to make myself useful, which I do—selectively. While it is not always true that the enemy of my enemy is my friend, in this case I thought it well to give the appearance of cooperation while diverting its result, at least until I could find out more about you."

So he'd betrayed her with one hand, and his acquaintances with the other? "That's...pretty ambidextrous."

He shrugged, unoffended. "Hence Ivan—a third hand, if you like, whom I admit was a last-minute stopgap, but this all came up rather suddenly. *My* plan—as there was no indication whatsoever that your strangely elusive maidservant lived in—was that he should take you out frolicking, leaving the cupboard bare for your midnight visitors. Pleasant for you both, frustrating for them, entirely unconnected with me. I still don't know why they wanted you kidnapped, mind you." He looked up and batted his eyes invitingly.

"You're an agent." Commercial, governmental? Surely not military. "What kind?"

"Now, that *is* a piece of information worth your name."

Ivan put in, "Er, Tej, if your enemies know who you really are already, why should your friends be kept in the dark? Does this make sense to you? Because it doesn't to me."

"You've not proved yourselves our friends."

"What, I have too!" said Vorpatril. He jerked his thumb at the other man, and conceded, "Him, maybe not so much."

Tej rubbed her mouth. Ivan Xav had a point. "Is he trustworthy?" she asked him straight out.

"No, he's a damned weasel." Vorpatril hesitated. "But he won't betray Barrayar. If what you are poses no threat to the Imperium, you have nothing to fear from him. Probably."

Byerly cast Vorpatril a look of exasperated disbelief. "Whose side are you on?"

"You've been known to make mistakes. I distinctly recall pulling your, and your Countly cousin's, feet out of the fire on one of 'em, spectacularly. But do I get respect? Do I get gratitude? Do I get—"

Byerly, hunching, said, "You got another job."

For some reason, this settled him. "Huh."

Byerly massaged his neck, looked up, and met Tej's gaze with a mild smile belied by his intent eyes. "Very well. I will now deal for your name." He inhaled. "I am an Imperial Security surveillance operative. My specialty is normally the high Vor social milieu centering around Vorbarr Sultana. I am out of my usual venue because the people I am following left there and came here in pursuit of their affairs, which are certainly criminal and potentially treasonous."

Tej shook her head. "The ones who are after us are not Barrayarans."

"I know. Yours are the people my people are dealing with. Locating you for them was to be a favor, to sweeten a pot presently in process of going sour."

Vorpatril's face scrunched. "Hey. Was finding Tej and Rish one of the little ways you made yourself useful, too?"

Byerly shrugged.

"For God's sake, By! What if those goons *had* snatched 'em?"

"I thought the experiment might yield much useful information, whatever way it fell out," said Byerly, sounding pressed. "In no case would their captors have been allowed to carry them out of the Imperium. But if Tej and Rish can tell me even more about their, ah, foes, then this affair has fallen out better than I might have expected. Although there are other consequences... well." Very reluctantly, he added, "Thank you, Ivan."

"It's not just my life at risk," said Tej slowly. "Rish's is, too."

Byerly said, "I am working with two associates. If I—what is that Jacksonian phrase?—*get smoked*, it is probable that they will be, too. So you see, I am not without my further responsibilities, either."

It occurred to Tej that this exchange had just given the Barrayaran agent a very good professional reason to keep her and Rish as far away as possible from kidnappers and hostile interrogators, regardless of his other agendas. Her bluff had won them a very real prize. Or else he'd want them safely dead, but she did not sense the excited tang of such a hidden lethal intent upon him. Tej glanced at Rish, who had been following this with all her attention—and superior senses. *Is he telling the truth?* Rish returned a cautious nod. *Yes, go ahead.* With maybe a *So far* implied.

Yes. This man's coin is information. Not... coin. Rish would appreciate the aesthetic clarity, to be sure.

Tej swallowed. "Very well." Her throat felt very tight and thick, as if it were closing off in some deathly allergic reaction. "My full name is Akuti Tejaswini Jyoti ghem Estif Arqua. My parents are—were—Shiv and Udine ghem Estif Arqua. Baron and Baronne Cordonah."

She looked up to gauge the effect of this news. Byerly had gone expressionless again, as if not merely processing, but locked up. Vorpatril's face had fallen into a fixed smile. She had once owned a favorite fur and fabric bear, very huggable, with eyes that glassy, but she felt no urge to hug the Barrayaran now.

Chapter Five

Ivan's mind had gone so blank, the first thought that arose in it sped out of his mouth wholly without impediment. "How did all that name get stuck on one girl?" And how the devil did she *spell* it?

Tej—Ivan could see why the nickname, now—tossed her clouds of curls in impatience. She made a truncated gesture, as if to deny—what? "When we kids started to come along, my father found this book—I don't know from where—*Ten Thousand Authentic Ethnic Baby Names From Old Earth, Their Meanings and Geographical Origins*. He had trouble choosing. I have a sister named Stella Antonia Dolce Ginevra Lucia, but by the time I arrived, he'd reined back a little." She added after a moment, "We called her Star."

"You're . . . not an only child, then?" asked By. "Not the heiress of your House?"

Oh, *there* was a good question. And an appalling thought.

Tej gave By a cold stare. Waiting for a trade?

"I'm an only child, myself," Ivan offered.

"I know that."

"How?"

"I looked you up on the comconsole. You're really you, too." She frowned at Byerly. "I wonder what I'd find if I looked you up?"

"Not much. I am a scion of an undistinguished cadet branch of my family." By's glance flickered to Rish, listening with those pointed turquoise elf-ears. "Disinherited, technically, but since my branch possesses nothing to inherit, that was something of an empty gesture on my father's part."

"He has a younger sister, I think," said Ivan. "Haven't ever met her. Married and living on South Continent, isn't she, By?"

By's smile, already thin, flattened further. "That's right."

"There's no point in withholding anything Captain Morozov could tell us," Ivan pointed out helpfully to Tej. This whole deal thing was alarming, really, all too Jacksonian and adversarial. "That'll include anything that's public knowledge, or that's hit the Nexus news feeds." And likely a good bit more than that, and Ivan was now sorry that he hadn't lingered to learn more. But it would have been bound to lead in turn to questions he hadn't wanted to answer just then, such as, *How many mysterious women are you hiding in your rental flat, Ivan?*

Tej rubbed her eyes with one slim brown hand. "I'm the second-youngest. My oldest brother was the heir, but he was reported killed in the takeover, too. I'm pretty sure my two older sisters made it out of Jacksonian local space through other jump points, but I don't know what happened to them after that. My other brother...got out a long time ago."

"How did that work? Your escape?" asked By.

Tej shrugged. "It's been set up for ages, for all us kids in case of a House emergency. There was a drill. When we were given the code word, we weren't supposed to ask questions or argue or delay, we were just supposed to follow our assigned handlers. I'd been through it once before, a few years back—we made it to Fell Station before the turnaround order caught up with us. I thought that's what would happen again."

"So you weren't an eyewitness to the Cordonah Station's, er, forcible change of management?"

"I think Star got out just as the station was being boarded, but the rest of us were hours gone by then. The evacuation drill was never something my parents took chances with." She swallowed, her throat obviously tight with some upsetting memory.

"Everything we learned, we learned later through the news feeds, though of course you can't trust *them*."

"Twice," said Rish, unexpectedly. "Surely you weren't too young to remember?"

"Was that the trip we took when I was six? Oh! No one ever told me what that was all about. Just that we were going on a ride, and a visit."

"We wanted to keep you calm."

"What, *you* couldn't have been older than fifteen." Tej turned to Ivan, though not to Byerly, and said, "Rish used to baby-sit me a lot when I was younger, in between dance practice and other chores the Baronne assigned."

You call your mother the Baronne? Well, the tall woman in Morozov's scan had looked formidable, more beautiful than warm. The man...had been harder to gauge.

"Is Rish your assigned handler?" asked By.

Tej shook her head. "We had a real bodyguard, a courier. I'm afraid he may be dead, now. That happened on Fell Station. We almost didn't get away."

Had the man bought their escape with his life? Seemed like it, from the quiver in her voice, and the chilled look in Rish's eyes. But if Rish wasn't the official bodyguard, what was she? Ivan looked at her and asked, "So are you really a jeeves?"

Those spun-gold eyebrows rose. "What would you trade for that information?"

"I..." Ivan glanced aside. "I think it's Byerly's turn, now."

By shot him a look of annoyance, which left Ivan unmoved.

"Actually," Ivan went on to him, "I think you owe *me* a bucket of information, By. Before I put my foot in it by accident, again, and I'm not taking any more *Ivan, you idiots* off of you when you can't be troubled to give me a decent briefing!" This ringing declaration left him a little winded, and By edging slightly away, good. If Ivan had to shout to be heard, maybe it was time to bellow a bit. "Name names, Byerly!"

Byerly looked as if he'd rather knock out several teeth and hand them across. Nevertheless, after a narrow frown at the two women, he rubbed his forehead and began, "All right, then. Ivan, d'you know Theo Vormercier?"

"Barely. Not my crowd."

"Quite. Lately, he was cut out of a long-expected inheritance when his aging uncle, Count Vormercier, remarried and began springing offspring."

"Really? I mean, I'd heard about the marriage, from m'mother y'know, but I didn't think the new wife was that much younger than him."

"Technology, of course. They used genetic assembly and a uterine replicator. I understand they now have a brand-new gene-cleaned bouncing baby boy and another on the way." Byerly smirked. "Say, any chance that your mother and old Illyan would—"

"No," said Ivan firmly. Not that a certain formidable auntly person hadn't actually *suggested* it, Betan that she was. He glanced at Tej, listening intently if with a somewhat baffled expression. "You were saying about Vormercier."

By's eyes glinted with fleeting amusement; he nodded and went on, "Theo had been living on his expectations for quite a long time, and not frugally. To say that this development took him aback would be understating the case. In the meanwhile, he had a younger brother in the Service—a quartermaster officer in the Sergyar Fleet's orbital depot. Brother Roger's expectations, while considerably more modest, were equally thwarted. About a year ago, Theo went out to visit him. And, evidently, they talked."

"Sergyar Fleet is Commodore Jole's patch," said Ivan. "Not to mention...huh. Not a good place to play games."

"Doubtless that had something to do with the extreme caution and cleverness with which they went about it. Roger's embezzlements began small, with theft of a load of outdated military equipment and supplies that had been slated to be destroyed. Perfectly understandable temptation, almost an admirable frugality when you think about it. The receiver contacts they'd made with that scam led to bigger and better contacts, and the next effort was much more ambitious."

"How'd you get all this from Vormercier? You fast-penta him when he wasn't looking?"

"Alcohol and braggadocio, Ivan. And stretched patience and a strong stomach on my part, if I do say so." By sighed. "The conspirators divided the task. Roger takes care of the heavy lifting. Theo launders the money. There is no money trail back to the actual military thieves. The loads go as opportunity permits from Sergyar orbit to Pol Station, where they are slipped to their non-Barrayaran receivers and into a void. Money comes out of a void into the hands of a contact on Komarr, who finds various apparently legal ways to hand it on to Theo, who takes it back to Barrayar and invests it. At a much later date, the military minions stop by and collect, under an inventive variety of pretexts. But like many another gambler before them, the brothers Vormercier appear never to have heard of the dictum *Quit while you're ahead.*"

"My Dada used to say that," said Tej. Rish nodded.

Byerly, after a bemused pause, cast them a small salute and continued. "The old phrase *No honor among thieves* also seems apropos. I have reason to think Theo has been embezzling from the funds entrusted to him. In any case, he was quite on-edge when it became time to take his yacht, his entourage, and his trusted hanger-on—that would be me—to Komarr for a soletta-viewing party. And gather in his next payout for goods delivered from his Komarran contact. Unfortunately for Theo, the goods have not been delivered. The ship was unexpectedly delayed in Komarr orbit, and has missed its Pol Station rendezvous. I believe your people had something to do with that, Ivan?"

Ivan pursed his lips and whistled. "So it's gotta be the *Kanzian*. Only Sergyar Fleet vessel in-system right now. The Vor Horsemen snagged it for the fleet inspection. Desplains likes springing little surprises like that, though I bet it wasn't a surprise to Jole. He'll likely reciprocate, next chance."

Byerly nodded, as if satisfied to have another stray piece of his puzzle slot into place. "While Theo's contacts appear to be relatively unruffled by the development, Theo is in a lather. The contacts have declined to advance him moneys on a cargo as yet in limbo, but offered as a sop a surprisingly substantial bounty on your two guests." Byerly nodded across at the women. "Beggars not being choosy, Theo promptly seized the sop and set me on the task, and here we are."

By paused as if for a round of applause, and appeared disappointed to only receive three long stares. "Collecting the identity of Theo's Komarr contact was a bit of a coup for me, but hardly enough to justify my expense reports. But, as Ivan could no doubt explain in his exemplary military manner, the best way to capture a wormhole is from both ends at once." He spread his arms wide, then brought his hands slowly together, caging air, or something only he could see. "If one could get a handle

on those people in the void beyond Pol Station, one might well
work backward to trap everything that lies between them and
Komarr." He looked up with undisguised interest at Tej and
Rish. "Do you figure the people who bid for you are from the
syndicate that seized your House?"

Tej's fists clenched, opened. "Prestene? I . . . don't know. Maybe.
Or they might be anybody, looking to collect the arrest order fee."

"Said fee posted ultimately by the syndicate? Why do they
want you? The size of the prize suggests quite a special interest."

Tej's lips tightened; then she shrugged. "Rish, as one of the
Jewels, would be an outward sign of Prestene's triumph over
House Cordonah, if they could capture and display her. Even
more brag if they can collect the set. I suppose they think I'm
a loose end, wild to come back and destroy them if I could,
and take back my parents' House. Maybe they watch too many
holovids, I don't know."

"And are you? Wild for revenge?"

"I never wanted to be a baronne. The only thing I want is my
parents back, and my brother." She bit her lip. "Won't happen
in this life."

Byerly turned to Rish. "So—*are* you a jeeves?"

She eyed him, then gave a short nod as if to say, *fair trade*. "I
was one of the Baronne's created children, and will always remain
so. All further loyalty treatments were discontinued after that
scare years back. The Baronne said she didn't want her Jewels
to be damaged or suffer if she died unexpectedly."

"I didn't know that," said Tej, sounding surprised.

Rish made a graceful turn of one blue hand, though what she
meant by it, Ivan could not guess. "You were six."

"So what kept you from running off?" asked By.

She raised her chin and looked down her nose at him, a neat
trick given that she was shorter. "Didn't you claim you were
disinherited? What keeps you from betraying your Imperium?"

By opened his hands as if to surrender the point. "So what
other tasks did you perform for Baronne Cordonah? Besides
baby-sitting."

Rish touched her lips and gave him a peculiar smile. "Living
sculptures."

"Ah?"

"At receptions, the Baronne would position us Jewels around

the chamber, and we would maintain various poses, as still as marble for minutes at a time, then shift to new poses. After a while, the guests invariably began to behave as if we were real statues. None of them seemed to realize how very keen our hearing was. Or how good our memories. We would compete with each other, to see who could get the best tidbits to report to her at the end of an evening." Her gaze at By grew speculative. "But I think you know exactly how that works. How freely people will talk, when they take you for a block. Not so?"

He returned her a reluctantly appreciative nod.

"So what does it all mean?" asked Ivan plaintively.

By cocked an eyebrow at him. "That seems a rather philosophical question, to be coming from you."

"No, the name thing." Ivan gestured somewhat inarticulately at Tej. "Aj-Tejas-whatever. From your da's book." He added conscientiously, "Ivan in old Russian means John in English. Dunno what John means, come to think."

Tej got a strange look on her face, but answered—was the deal still on?—"*Akuti*, princess, *Tejaswini*, radiant—or maybe intelligent, I'm not sure which—*Jyoti*, flame. Or light."

"Princess Radiant Flame," Ivan tested this on his tongue. He'd attempt the other pronunciation later. Or Princess Bright Light, whichever. *Princess*, in either case. "Sounds like your da thought the world of you, huh?"

Tej swallowed and looked away, as if the far end of the room had suddenly grown riveting. She answered in a would-be-pedantic quaver, "The geographical origin was supposed to be South Asian. Star's was South European, or South American, or south something, anyway. Or maybe it was the other way around. We never spent much time on Old Earth history."

"So what kind of a name is *Vorrutyer*?" Rish asked Byerly, possibly to give Tej a moment to regain her composure.

He sat back looking surprised at the question, or maybe just at its coming from her, but answered readily: "The origin of the prefix *Vor* is much debated, except that it arose during the Time of Isolation and came to refer exclusively to members of the then-warrior caste. We are fairly certain that the *Rutyer* was a mishearing or misspelling of the Old Earth German *Rutger*."

Tej, back in control of her voice, asked, "So what about Vorpatril?"

Ivan cleared his throat. "Not sure. Some say it's British, some claim it came from the Greek or French, maybe as a corruption of *patros* or some word like it. A lot of Barrayaran names got twisted around during the centuries after the Firsters were cut off. Or shortened—Serg from Sergei, Padma from Padmakar, and Xav's a contraction of Xavier."

"Mutated over time, makes sense," said Tej, then paused to take in matching glares from both By and Ivan. "Why do you look like you just swallowed a bug? The usage is precise. A mutation is a copying error. Everyone knows that."

"Do *not*," said Ivan firmly, "use that term to a Barrayaran. It's a pretty deadly insult to imply that someone's a mutant. Even if you're just spelling their names."

"Oh." Tej looked baffled, but said amiably, "All right. If you say so."

By glanced at the time on his wristcom and muttered a curse. "I have to be somewhere else. Several minutes ago." He dragged his hands through his hair and stood up. His gaze swept Ivan, Tej, and Rish, all three. "I guess this is as good a bolt-hole for you as any other, for now."

"For how much longer?" asked Ivan.

"I don't know. A day, two days, three? I meant to play this out as long as I could, in hopes of getting in beyond Theo's contact. I'm making progress, but we're close to pulling the plug. At which point I'll need to vanish, if I want to maintain my cover and my liveli-hood. And my skin. So until we meet again, dear friends, adieu."

With a wave that did not quite mimic an ImpSec salute, By made for the door; Ivan accompanied him out.

In the corridor, By lowered his voice. "If things go sideways, Ivan, you should probably take those women to Morozov."

"They won't want to go. They don't trust ImpSec."

By shrugged. "Morozov could cut them a deal, I'll bet. ImpSec Galactic Affairs would be happy to lap up whatever they wanted to spill about this syndicate of theirs."

"Or maybe more than they wanted."

"We can discuss that. Later." By strode off, a tired man hurrying.

Ivan sealed the door, made sure it was locked, and returned to his living room to find Tej and Rish deciding who was to have the first turn in the bathroom before bed. Ivan glanced at his wristcom and cringed to count the scant hours till Komarran dawn. *I hate this strangled day length.*

"That is a strange man," commented Rish, looking toward the door after Byerly.

"You're not the first to note that," said Ivan ruefully.

"How did he get into his line of work?"

Ivan squinted, wondering why that question had never before occurred to him. "I have no idea. It's not the sort of thing you ask these ImpSec fellows. I think he was around twenty-standard when he moved to Vorbarr Sultana—his parents lived out on the west coast, t'other side of the continent, see. He hung around on the edges of things for years before I ever found out about his ImpSec moonlighting. The fact that he was estranged from his family never seemed to need an explanation—that is, if you knew many Vorrutyers. The whole clan is, um... either on the vivid side, or downright antisocial."

"Ah," said Rish elliptically, and went off to claim the bath.

Ivan sat back down, watching Tej watch her friend pad silently away. This couch would do for his bed, if only people would let him lie here in peace for enough hours... "Baby-sitter?"

Tej's laugh was no more than a puff of air through her nose. "I don't know that she exactly volunteered for the job. I used to follow her around like a kitten chasing a string. I was just fascinated by all the Jewels, when I was younger. I would watch them at their dance practice, and make them try to teach me, too."

"What kind of dance?"

"Oh, every kind. They collected skills and styles from all over, and were always trying to put them together in new combinations. I wanted to be one of them, to be allowed to *really* dance—you know, in their performances. But puberty was cruel to me."

On the contrary, Ivan thought puberty had been very generous to her. He just managed to stop himself from saying so out loud, converting it to, "How so?"

"The best dancers are all thin and small and strong, very whippy. Like Rish. By age fourteen, it was plain I was going to be built more like my Dada—my other sisters all took after my mother, willowy. I just grew too tall, too big, too heavy. Too top-heavy." She sniffed as if in some weird—in Ivan's view, anyway—female self-disapproval. "By age fifteen it was obvious that no matter how hard I worked, I could never be as good as the Jewels. So I stopped."

"Gave it up?" said Ivan. "That's no good. Just because someone else is some sort of natural flaming genius, doesn't mean that you're an idi...um." *Um.* "Doesn't mean that you should..." He tried rushing the notion. "Should hide your light under the covers."

Her smile grew wan. "My sister Star said the only reason I wanted to perform with the Jewels was to make myself the center of attention. I expect she was right." She hoisted herself wearily to her feet and went off to change places with Rish.

She'd forgotten to demand a trade. Watching her vanish into the shadows of the next room, all Ivan could think was: *Actually, y'know...I expect you wanted to dance because you wanted to dance.*

Tej dreamed.

She was running through writhing space station corridors, pursued by a nameless menace. Ahead of her, the Jewels scattered right and left, leaping in grands jetés down cross-corridors, flashes of red and green, blue and obsidian, gold and pearl-white somersaulting in fantastical triple turns in the air, but by the time she caught up, the corridors were silent and echoing, empty. She ran on.

A side door slid open; a voice hissed, "Quick! Hide in here!"

It was Captain Vorpatril. He was wearing his green military officer's uniform over a bear suit. His chest was crisscrossed with bandoliers of power charge packs, and he held a very large weapon, perhaps a plasma rifle. Or was that a water gun? He grinned at her from the round, furry frame of the bear hood. The gun went away, and then they were kissing, and for a moment or two, the dream went good. His kisses were expert: neither too shy, tickling annoyingly, nor too invasive, like someone trying to shove a slug down her throat, but just right, firm and exploratory. Tej noted this, thinking, *I'll have to try very hard to remember this part when I wake up...*

"I want to touch your skin," she told him, when they broke for breath. "It's very pale, isn't it? Is it smooth, or hairy? Are you that pale all over? Do you have silver veins like Pearl?" Where *was* Pearl...?

"Here, let me show you." He grinned again and zipped the bear suit down from neck to crotch. Both fur and skin peeled away, revealing glistening red muscle, white fascia, and the thin blue lines of veins.

"No, no, just the fur!" Tej cried in horror, backing up. "Not the skin too!"

"Oh, what?" said Vorpatril, in a tone of some bewilderment. He stared down, the bewilderment changing to dismay as the blackening crackle of a plasma arc burn spread out in a widening circle on his chest. Smoke and the smell of burning meat filled the air, and then it wasn't Vorpatril anymore, but their ill-fated courier, Seppe, back on Fell Station....

Tej gasped and awoke. She was in bed in the dark of Vorpatril's flat; Rish lay in silence beside her, unmoving, unaware, yet elegant even in sleep. Tej wanted to ask her where the Jewels had been flying to, but of course, people didn't share each other's dreams reciprocally. Tej wouldn't wish hers on anyone else, certainly.

I'm glad to be out of that *dream . . .* Most of it. The beginning and the end were just like most of her dreams lately, altogether too much like her real life. The kiss, though, had warmed her right down to her loins. *Hi there, loins. Haven't heard from you for a while . . .*

The strange rushing noise at the edge of her hearing resolved itself at last as the shower. It turned off, and then she could hear rustlings from the bathroom and its attendant dressing room/closet. In a while, a faint hiss sounded as the door slid aside, but the captain had evidently turned off the lights before he'd opened it. So as not to disturb his sleeping guests? Or, she wondered as his unshod footsteps wandered nearer to the bed, something more sinister?

She opened her eyes, turned, and stared up at his shadowed shape. He seemed to be fully dressed in his uniform again. No bear suit. His skin was firmly in place, good. Masked by fresh soap and depilatory cream, his scent was mildly aroused; as was her own, she supposed, but fortunately Rish was not awake to razz her on it.

"What?" she breathed.

"Oh," he whispered back, "sorry to wake you. I'm just on my way out to HQ."

"But it's still dark."

"Yeah, I know. Damn nineteen-hour days. Anything special you'd like me to bring back tonight?"

"Whatever you pick will be fine," she said, with some confidence.

"All right. I'll try not to be so late this time, but I never know what'll come up, so don't panic if I'm delayed. I'll lock up behind me." He made to tiptoe away.

"Captain Vorpatril!" She hardly knew what she wanted to say to him, but the dream-scent of burning flesh still unnerved her. She settled on a vague, "Be careful."

He returned a nonplussed, "Uh...sure."

The bedroom door closed behind him; she heard him rattling in the kitchenette, and then the sigh of the outer door, and then... then the flat sounded very empty.

Tej rolled back over, hoping for a sleep without dreams.

Despite everything, Ivan managed to arrive at Komarr down-side HQ right on time that morning, half an hour before his boss was due—though more often than not Desplains managed to bollix that schedule by arriving early. Ivan started the coffee, sat at his secured comconsole, grimaced, and fired it up to find out what all had arrived in the admiral's inbox since last shift.

Ivan had developed a personal metaphor for this first task (after the coffee) of the day. It was like opening one's door to find that an overnight delivery service had left a large pile of boxes on one's porch, all marked "miscellaneous." In reality, they were all marked "Urgent!" but if *everything* was urgent, in Ivan's view they might as well all be labeled miscellaneous.

Each box contained one of the following: live, venomous, agitated snakes on the verge of escape; quiescent venomous snakes; nonvenomous garden snakes; dead snakes; or things that looked like snakes but weren't, such as large, sluggish worms. It was Ivan's morning duty to open each box, identify the species, vigor, mood, and fang-count of the writhing things inside, and sort them by genuine urgency.

The venomous, agitated snakes went straight to Desplains. The garden snakes were arranged in an orderly manner for his later attention. The dead snakes and the sluggish worms were returned to their senders with a variety of canned notes attached, with the heading *From The Office of Admiral Desplains*, ranging from patiently explanatory to brief and bitter, depending on how long it seemed to be taking the sender in question to learn to deal with his own damned wildlife. Ivan had a menu of Desplains's notes, and it was his responsibility—and occasionally pleasure, because every job should have a few perks—to match the note to the recipient.

As he had both expected and feared, an urgent—*of course*—note from ImpSec Komarr with his full police interview of yesterday attached was nestled among this morning's boxes. And the supply of venomous, agitated snakes in today's delivery was disappointingly low.

After a brief struggle with his conscience, Ivan set the note in the garden-snakes file, although he did put it at the very bottom of the list. Desplains was possibly the sanest boss Ivan had ever worked for, and the least given to dramatics, and Ivan wished to preserve those qualities for as long as he could. Forever, by preference. So every once in a while, Ivan let something trivial but amusing filter through to the admiral, just to keep up his morale, and today seemed a good day to stick in a couple of those, as well. Ivan was still looking for a few more things he could legitimately enter when Desplains blew in, collected his coffee, and murmured, "Ophidian census today, Ivan?"

"All garden variety, sir."

"Wonderful." Desplains took a revivifying sip of fresh-brewed. Ivan wished he could remember which famous officer had once said, *The Imperial Service* could *win a war without coffee, but would prefer not to have to.* "What ever came of your interview with the dome cops yesterday?"

"I put the ImpSec note in File Three, sir." File Three was the official designation of the garden-snakes crate, because, after all, sometimes Desplains did suffer a substitute aide, if Ivan was on leave or out ill or requisitioned for other, less routine duties, and some shorthands took too long to explain. "I expect you will want to look at it eventually." Ivan made his tone very unpressing.

"Right-oh."

"Meeting with Commodore Blanc and staff in thirty minutes," Ivan reminded him. "I have the agenda ready."

"Very well. Snakes aweigh."

Ivan hit the send pad. "On your desk now."

Desplains raised his coffee cup in salute and passed into his inner office.

He would never, Ivan reflected, ever want to be promoted to admiral, to be greeted the first thing every working day by a desk populated entirely by live, hissing snakes. Perhaps he could resign his commission if such a threat ever became imminent. Assuming he made it to that stately age without being court-martialed, a consummation depending closely in turn on his doubtful ability to avoid relatives associated with ImpSec bearing... gift pythons. Gift pythons with snazzy reticulated blue-and-gold skins this time, it seemed.

He bent to his comconsole and returned a crisp note to Imp-Sec Komarr: *From the Office of Admiral Desplains: Urgent memo received* and the date stamp. *Hold pending review.*

Chapter Six

"Tej, get away from that edge," said Rish, irritably. "You're making me nervous."

"I'm only watching for Ivan Xav." Tej gripped the balcony railing and craned her neck, studying the scurrying evening throng in the street far below. She'd had several false alarms already, of foreshortened dark-haired men in green uniforms exiting the bubble-car station and turning in her direction, but none of them had been the captain. Too old, too young, too stout, too slight, none with that particular rolling rhythm to his stride. None bearing bags. "Besides, he's bringing dinner. I hope."

Rish crossed her arms tighter. "If only the Baron and Baronne had known, they could have had all your parade of suitors offer you provisions, instead of those high House connections."

Tej's shoulders hunched. "I didn't want high House connections. That was Star's and Pidge's passion, and Erik's. And the Baronne's. I thought there were enough Arquas trying to build economic empires. Family dinners got to be like board meetings, once they were all into it." Tej had long since given up trying to get in a word at meals without a crowbar, certainly not about her own piddling interests, which, since they did not include schemes for House aggrandizement, interested no one else there.

Pidge, officially named Mercedes Sofia Esperanza Juana Paloma, was Tej's other older even-sister, born in the era before the Baronne had finally made her spouse ease back on his inspirations, or maybe she'd hidden the book by the time the last few Arqua offspring were decanted from their uterine replicators, who knew? The Baronne always called her Mercedes; Dada, from the time she'd started precociously talking—and never again shut up, as far as Tej could tell—had dubbed her *Little Wisdom* as a play on *Sofia*, but as soon as her other siblings discovered that another meaning of *Paloma* was *pigeon*, her family nickname had stuck. Well, except when Erik transmuted it to *Pudge*, to get a rise out of her, which it reliably did.

Did you get out safely, Pidge? Have you made it to your assigned refuge yet? Or did your flight go as sour for you as mine did for me? Her elder sisters had supplied Tej with what she suspected was no more than the normal amount of adolescent hell, but she worried for them now with all that was left of her shredded heart. Erik...knowing that Erik had not got out, but not knowing how, had supplied the stuff of nightmares, both asleep and awake. Had he died fighting? Been captured and coldly executed? Tortured first? *However it happened, he's beyond all grief and pain and struggle and regret now.* After all these months, Tej was beginning to be reconciled to that cold consolation, if only for want of any other. Amiri...her middle brother Amiri was still safe as far as Tej knew. *And your hard-bought new life will not be betrayed through me, that's an ironclad contract.* Even if she made the deal only with her own overwrought imagination.

She rose on her toes and leaned out, causing Rish, who stood well back with her shoulders snug to the wall, to make a strained noise in her throat. "Oh, there he is! And he's got lots of big bags!" Tej watched that long stride close Ivan Xav's distance to the building's entry till he turned in out of sight, then gave up her spy-vantage. When they went inside, Rish locked the glass door firmly behind them.

Vorpatril bustled in with the dinner and what proved to be sacks of groceries, and cheerfully emptied them out onto the counter while Rish rescued the restaurant containers and set the table.

"It's Barrayaran Greekie, tonight," he told the women. "Wasn't easy to find. Got a tip about this place from one of the fellows out at HQ. A Barrayaran Greekie sergeant whose family'd been in the restaurant business back in his home District married a Komarran woman and retired here, set up shop. It comes highly recommended—we'll see."

"Barrayaran Greekie?" asked Rish, brows rising in puzzlement.

"The smallest of our main languages," he told her. "The First-ers actually arrived in four disparate settlement groups—Russian, British, French and Greek, as their home regions on Old Earth were back then. Over the centuries of the Time of Isolation, everyone pretty much blended together genetically—founder effect, you know—but they kept up those languages, which still gave folks plenty to fight about. I think there were some more minor tongues as well, to start, but those got rubbed out in what you galactics call the Lost Centuries. Except we weren't lost, we were all right there. It was just the Nexus that got misplaced."

Tej considered this novel view as he continued unpacking sacks, including, she was glad to see, fresh fruit and teas and coffees and vat-dairy cream and milk. How many days was he planning for?

He added, "Fortunately, we kept a lot of the food styles. Modified."

"But not mutated," murmured Tej.

"*Indeed* not." But his lips twitched, so her tiny joke hadn't really offended him, good. He drew out another large carton and folded the bag. "More instant groats. They're a traditional Barrayaran breakfast food, among other things."

"I saw that little box in your cupboard. I wasn't sure what a person was supposed to do with them."

"Oh, is that why you weren't eating them? Here, let me show you . . ." He drew boiling water from the heater tap and mixed up a small bowl of the stuff, and passed it around the table to sample as they sat to the new largess. Tej thought the little brown grains tasted like toasted cardboard, but perhaps they were some childhood comfort food of his, and she oughtn't to criticize them.

Rish made a face, though. "A bit bland, don't you think?"

"You usually add butter, maple syrup, cheese, all sorts of things. There's also a cold salad with mint and chopped tomatoes and what-not. And they use them at weddings."

The Greekie food, as he dished it out, looked more promising;

her first bites delivered some quite wonderful aromas, flavors and textures. "How do they prepare your groats for weddings?"

"They don't serve them. The grains get dyed different colors, and sprinkled on the ground for the wedding circle and what-not. Some sort of old fertility or abundance symbol, I suppose."

It also seemed the food least likely to be regretted in that sacrifice, a suspicion Tej kept to herself.

Ivan Xav seemed much more relaxed tonight, and she couldn't figure out quite why, except for the lack of his strange friend Byerly to stir him up. She would have thought that the revelation of her true identity would have alarmed him more, but maybe he disliked mysteries more than bad news?

"This is all right," he said, leaning back replete when they'd demolished the Greekie dinner. "When I rented this place to sample the Solstice nightlife, I'd forgotten just how short the nights were. There's time to either party *or* recover before work, but not both. So staying in actually suits, though not on your ownsome. That would be dull."

He rose to go rummage at the comconsole. "My cousin told me about this dance thing you and Rish might like to see, if I can find an example..."

"Do you have a lot of cousins?" Tej asked, leaning over his shoulder. "Or just a lot of one cousin?"

He laughed at that last. "Both, actually. On my father's side, there's only my cousin Miles—not exactly a cousin, our grand-mothers were sisters. That part of the family got pretty thinned out during Mad Yuri's War, which came down soon after the end of the Occupation. I've half-a-dozen first cousins on my mother's side, but they don't live near the capital and I don't see much of 'em. Ah, here we go!"

His search had turned up a recorded performance of the Minchenko Memorial Ballet Company, from a place called the Union of Free Habitats, or Quaddiespace. Tej had never heard of it, but as the vid started up Rish drifted in and said, "Oh! The gengineered four-armed people. Baron Fell had a quaddie musician, once. I saw a vid of one of her gigs. Played a ham-mer dulcimer with all four hands at once. But she jumped her contract and left, and no one's heard of her since. I didn't know they could *dance*..." Her face screwed up. "*How* do they dance, with no feet?"

"Free fall," said Ivan Xav. "They live in it, work in it, dance in it . . . my cousin and his wife saw a live performance when they were out that way on, er, business last year—told me all about it, later. Very impressive, they said."

Dance the quaddies did, it seemed, in zero-gee: hand to hand to hand to hand, singly, in pairs, but most amazingly, in groups, glittering colored costumes flashing through air. The Jewels gave the illusion of flying, at times—these dancers *really* flew, wheeling like flocks of bright birds. Both Rish and Tej watched in rapt fascination, Rish putting in mutters of excited critique now and then, and bouncing on the edge of her chair at especially complex maneuvers, her arms waving in unconscious mimicry.

Tej shared the sofa with Ivan Xav. His arm, laid out along the back, crept nearer, easing down over her shoulders till she was quite snugged in by it. After a few moments of silent consideration, she declined to shrug it off. It threw her back into a memory of watching shows with Dada, in her childhood—how patient he must have been with her choices, in retrospect—snuggled into his warm side, a stouter one than Ivan Xav's, but smelling equally, if rather differently, masculine. She wasn't sure if the recollection helped or hurt, but there it was. For a little hour, some simulacrum of peace.

It ended soon enough, when Ivan Xav turned off the holovid at the close of the performance and Rish said, "So how long were you planning to stay on Komarr, Captain Vorpatril?"

"Mm? Oh." He sat up, and Tej edged regretfully away. "This whole duty—the annual inspections and conferences—usually runs about ten days or so. I've been here, um, let me see . . ." His lips moved as he counted on his fingers. "Seven nights, so far, including this one. So not much longer. I trust that By will be done with his business sooner, though. Seemed like his pace was picking up."

"So this safe house"—a graceful blue hand spiraled—"will go away when you do."

"Uh . . ." he said. "I'm afraid so. Though I could book it an extra week for you, but . . . I figured to wait and see what By comes up with."

Rish glanced significantly at Tej.

Ivan Xav cleared his throat. "Would you two consider making a deal with ImpSec? I mean, more than just with Byerly.

I bet you know lots of things they'd like to share, for suitable considerations."

Tej grimaced. "If there was one lesson both my parents took care to pound into me, it's that it's impossible to deal safely if the power differential between the two sides is too great. The high side just skins, and the low side gets stripped. Your ImpSec has no *need* to be nice to us."

"Well, they've no need to be gratuitously nasty, either," said Ivan Xav uneasily. "That I can see."

"What if they decide they *need* to establish a fresh working relationship with the new House Cordonah, and that Rish and I would make dandy bargaining chips? I have nothing to stop them with—*nothing*." She choked down her rising tone, refusing to turn her head toward the balcony. That *nothing* would stop them, too literally true.

"Look, I know they're all weasels over there at ImpSec, but they're pretty honorable weasels."

"I thought they were a security organization," said Rish. "Their honor has to consist of putting Barrayar's interests first."

Ivan shrugged somewhat helplessly, but did not deny this.

"We'll think about it," said Tej. "Meanwhile . . . do you want first claim on the bath, Captain? You have to get up before us."

He glanced at the time and made a face. "I guess I'd better." He looked as if he'd like to stay and argue more, but swallowed whatever he'd been going to say, and went off.

When the bedroom door had closed after him, Rish said, "Was that a *Maybe yes* we'll think about it, or was that a *No, but we won't confirm it till we make it safely to the exit* we'll think about it?"

"Have you spotted a safe exit? I haven't."

Rish set her fine jaw. "Tomorrow. I think we should run tomorrow, as soon as he goes off to that HQ of his. The cash in his wallet would get us to another dome, at least."

It would have to be one of the domes with its own commercial shuttleport. That cut it down to a couple of dozen choices planet-wide, all larger arcologies, which was a good feature, but none were close. Tej's heart sank at the thought of another scurrying, fearful journey among strangers, from nowhere to nowhere, in the vague hope that their lost House's enemies would look for them . . . nowhere.

"And are you sure we're not being watched out for?" said Tej. "Are you sure *he* isn't watched, for that matter?"

Rish shook her head. "I think we ran out of good choices a while back. We're now down to the least-bad."

Tej rubbed her aching forehead. "I'll think about it."

Rish flounced in her seat, a maneuver only she could imbue with such stylish censure. "And you have to stop cuddling that Barrayaran. It's not as if you can keep him, or take him along with us, or whatever."

"Oh, so it's just me?" said Tej. "*You* liked his weasel friend well enough. Even I could smell it."

"Did not!" Rish denied. "I just thought he was...interesting. A walking human puzzle who...works on human puzzles, I suppose."

"Ferreting them out?" Tej snickered.

"Apparently." Rish frowned. "He sure found us. Twice."

A disturbing observation. Tej was still thinking about the implications when her turn came for the bath.

The door buzzer sounded in the half light of dawn, just as Ivan was finishing dressing for work, all but his shoes. And kept on sounding, continuously.

Byerly in a toot? Strange hour for it. It was too late for him to have been up since yesterday, and *far* too early for him to be up for today. Ivan padded to the door, and this time prudently checked the security vid. Yes, By, leaning on the buzzer and shifting from foot to foot. Maybe he really, really had to go to the lav. *You wish.* Ivan released the lock, the door slid aside, and Byerly tumbled within and hit the pad to close it with his bunched fist. "Ivan. Thank *God* I caught you," he said. "We have a problem."

"What, a new one? Or just more of the same one we have already?" said Ivan, refusing to be stirred by By's histrionics at this hour. He gave way as By surged down his short hallway, beginning to rethink that stance already. By never surged; he sauntered. Or strolled. Or sometimes swayed, or even evaporated. But right now, he looked downright condensed, altogether too much here.

The two women, awakened by this entry, appeared through the door of the bedroom as Ivan followed By in from the hall. Tej looked deliciously bed-rumpled, warm and soft but for her frown. This was a woman who ought to greet each day with a sleepy, seductive smile, which Ivan wished he knew how to supply. *Hell, I do know; I just haven't had a chance to.* Rish was her usual sleek self, concerned and fully alert mere seconds after being jerked from a sound sleep. Both women wore the tank tops they slept in and loose Komarran trousers, pulled on hastily; Rish spotted By and tucked her stunner back in her pants pocket. Tej wore no support garment under her top, and the effect as she moved forward was wonderfully distracting. *Not now*, Ivan told himself. Part of himself, the part with a single mind of its own.

"What's going on?" asked Rish.

"Theo Vormercier has blindsided me," said By bitterly. "When my hired goons didn't produce you, instead of turning to me for my next solution, he implemented his very own brilliant idea, or so he thinks. He turned your identities and descriptions over to Komarran Immigration Services as illegal entries. He figured to let them do the legwork of locating you, and then snatch you somehow from incarceration after your arrests."

Tej's eyes grew big. Rish just went very, very still.

"So?" said Ivan. "They're hidden for now. No way for Immigration to know they're here . . . is there?"

"Unfortunately, Immigration shares databases with the dome cops, and your name, which you so thoughtfully supplied them, came up. The Immigration people will be on their way to check you first thing today."

"They'll have to catch me at work again. Nobody home here, right?"

"What if they break in to search?" asked Tej uneasily. "There's no place to hide." Her gaze shifted to the balcony door, where the first faint color in the sky was beginning to mute the city lights, and she swallowed.

"They have to have some sort of warrant," said Ivan, beginning to share her unease. "I would think."

"Ivan, those people *issue* warrants," said By impatiently. "They don't have the broad powers ImpSec does, but they've plenty enough for this. Probably more than they used to have back when Komarr was an independent polity. They don't even have to break anything—they can make the building manager open the door."

"We have to get out," said Tej. "We can't let ourselves be trapped in here."

Ivan had some sympathy for that sentiment. Even though the

flat wasn't dark, or constricted, or wet. Also, they weren't alone....
Maybe they were overreacting, really.

"That's what I came to tell you," said By.

"Wait, no," said Ivan. Once they got away, and lost themselves,
how would he ever find Tej again? The women had to be pretty
good at hiding, or they wouldn't have evaded their determined
pursuers across four systems for what, seven months? Or maybe
By had a plan—he wouldn't have come boiling in here without
one, would he? Some way to keep a string on them—

"You'll have to get your things together—" By began, but was
interrupted by the door buzzer. Two stern blats. Tej jumped and
Rish tensed. By wheeled. "What the hell? They can't be here
already."

Ivan nipped out to the short hallway and checked the security
viewer. Unfortunately, he recognized his visitors. Detective Fano
and Detective-patroller Sulmona, up bright and early, or dark and
late, whichever. Fano leaned on the buzzer again, and Sulmona,
after another moment, pounded on the door. "Vorpatril?" she
shouted through it. "Answer your door."

No polite *please* with that, Ivan noted as By and the women
came up to peer anxiously around his shoulders.

"That's not Immigration," said By.

"No, it's the dome cops. Same pair I talked to t'other day.
Would Immigration have sent them?"

"No, they have their own uniformed squads for this sort of
thing. There are procedures. This must be something else."

Another buzz, longer. Sulmona pounded again. "Vorpatril? We
know you're in there. Open up."

Ivan hit the com and called, "Why?"

By winced.

Fano drew a long breath. "We have a felony warrant for your
arrest. That gives us the right to break down this door if you
don't open it."

"Arrest! What the hell for? I haven't done anything!"

"Kidnapping."

"*What?*" said Ivan, outraged.

Fano's jaw jutted. "We know you lied. The security vids from
the Crater Lake bubble-car platform finally surfaced. They clearly
show you and an unknown person escorting the missing Nanja
Brindis into a bubble car. She hasn't been heard from since. The

abduction charge is enough to get us in your door, but the one I'm really after is murder. But you know that, don't you, Captain?"

Ivan was struck nearly speechless, except for the wheeze of his hyperventilation.

"Don't open it!" whispered Tej. Truly, Ivan didn't want to. By and Rish dragged him back to the living room for a hissed conference.

"But I have to let them in," said Ivan, harried. "In the first place, it's *another* felony not to, and in the second place, Tej, you can make the kidnapping charge go away by telling them I didn't abduct you, I just invited you. Not to mention murder, good God!"

Tej said, "We can't let them in, they'll *take* us."

"Tell them through the intercom," Ivan suggested. Would that work?

"How would they know you weren't holding a weapon to her back?" asked By, unhelpfully.

"And don't you believe for a minute that Prestene's agents can't whip us out of their custody before you can get back with help, and anyway, your help is *worse*," said Tej. "ImpSec! I'd almost rather take my chances with Prestene!"

"Hey!" Byerly protested.

Rish turned in a complete circle, gold eyes dilated, reaching as if for some rope that wasn't there. "We can't get out. There's no way out!"

Tej grabbed her hands, stopping her rotation. "It'll have to be the balcony after all. Oh, Rish, I'm so sorry I led you into this!"

"What's on the balcony," Ivan began, but was interrupted by a chime from his wristcom. That particular tone wasn't one he could ignore. He held up a hand, "Wait!" and opened his link. "Sir?" he said brightly.

"Vorpatril!"

Ivan rocked back. Desplains *never* bellowed. "Uh, yes?"

"What the hell is all this?"

"Are you at work already, sir?"

"No, I'm in my quarters. Just received an emergency heads-up from ImpSec Komarr that Dome Security has filed a felony charge on my aide-de-camp, so I finally opened their memo. That was no garden snake!"

"I can explain, sir." The door buzzer sounded again, and more pounding. Muffled shouts. "Later. I have a bit of a situation on my hands right now." Ivan gulped and cut the com. He'd never cut off any admiral, *ever*, let alone Desplains.

The pounding stopped. More muffled voices.

"We've got to block the door. Buy time," said Ivan.

"Time for what?" said By.

"Time for me to think of something."

"*That* could take all *day*."

Ivan shot him an irate look, teeth clenching hard.

"The couches," said Tej. "They'll be through the door codes soon enough—we have to make a physical barrier." The two women leapt to begin dragging furniture into the hall and propping it up against the door. By looked as if he didn't think this would work, but, carried along by the fog of cold panic that seemed to be permeating the place, fell into helping them nonetheless. *Damn* but Rish was strong for her size...

Ivan peered into the security vid. The two detectives had been joined by four more people, three men and a woman. One man was the building manager. The other three were in unfamiliar uniforms. They appeared to be debating with each other, comparing official-looking forms displayed by their wrist holos. Unless it was some really arcane style of video arm wrestling? *Dueling jurisdictions?*

Ivan shoved By up to look in the vid. "That wouldn't be Immigration, would it?"

"Uh, yes?"

The building manager fumbled with a code key. By opened his jacket and jerked out his stunner.

"Can you take down all six of them before they get you?" asked Tej uneasily. Picturing her and Rish escaping over a wall of bodies? Possibly including By's and Ivan's?

Still peering, By swore, set his stunner on high, and jammed it up against the electronic lock. It buzzed angrily, and after a long moment, sparks shot out of the mechanism. "At least that'll hold the building manager," said By, a glint of strained satisfaction in his eye.

"You've locked us in!" Ivan protested. "And now I can't open the door."

"Good!" said Rish, heaving another heavy armchair atop the pile and wedging it in tight.

They all retreated temporarily to Ivan's emptied living room.

Tej swung around, stared deeply into Ivan's eyes, gasped, "I'm so sorry it has to end this way, Ivan Xav. I know you tried," and flung her arms around him. Ivan found himself holding what would, under other circumstances, be an absolutely delightful bundle of warm, soft woman. He opened his mouth to her frantic kiss nonetheless, and his arms wrapped her in turn, snugly and securely. He wasn't sure what was happening here, *but O God don't let it stop...*

She stopped. Pushed him away. He managed not to whimper. "That's it," she said simply, and turned to take her blue companion's hand, with a nod toward the balcony. "It's time, Rish."

Rish nodded back, face very grim. They started for the door. By, uneasy, moved to block the glass.

"Where do you think you're going?" By asked.

"Over the balcony."

"But you don't have grav belts! Or anything!" said Ivan.

Tej wheeled back and raised her chin at him. "That's right."

"But we're twenty stories up!"

"Yes, that ought to be enough."

"You'll be killed!"

Rish stared at him in disbelief. "Are you *slow*, Captain?"

"But the dome cops will think I flung you off, or worse!"

Tej was plainly moved by this, but steeled herself and said sternly, "If you haven't got a better plan, *right now*, we're going. Because later will be too late."

"No, yes, what—" Ivan's wristcom chimed, insistently. He opened the link, yelled, "*Not now, sir!*" into it, and closed it again. After a moment, it chimed once more. Louder. No override for this code.

"By, don't let them get out!" said Ivan, ran to the kitchenette, ripped off his wristcom, opened the refrigerator door, tossed it in, and slammed the door shut again. The wristcom still whimpered, but very faint and plaintive.

He turned back to the women, and By, who stood with his back tight against the glass. Both he and Rish had their stunners out, pointed at each other. Rish's was shaking in her death-grip. The new pounding from the hall was growing louder, more disturbingly mechanical. Not just fists anymore. The flat's doors were designed to keep air from getting out, in a dome-pressurization emergency. Not determined policemen, backed up by building maintenance personnel, from getting in.

What else had he just seen sitting out on that kitchen counter...
"Don't shoot!" Ivan cried. "And don't jump! I have an idea!"

This held the tableau, if only in morbid curiosity, long enough
for him to run back into the kitchenette and grab the instant
groats from the countertop, the large economy-size box that he'd
purchased yesterday evening. He ran back into his living room
and brandished it. "This'll do the job!"

"You're going to throw cereal at them?" asked Rish, perplexed.

"Or shall we all sit down and have a hearty Barrayaran breakfast together while the police break in?" asked By, in an all-too-
similar tone. But both stunners drooped.

Shrugging off the sarcasms, and dear God hadn't he had enough
practice at that in his life, Ivan drew a long breath. "Tej. Will
you marry me?"

"*What?*" she said. It wasn't a thrilled sort of *what?* either, that
ought to greet such a proposal, more of a *have-you-lost-your-mind?*
what. Ivan cringed.

"No, this'll work! A woman who marries a Barrayaran subject
automatically becomes a Barrayaran subject. It's one of those fundamental oaths that underlie all other oaths, biology before politics,
so to speak. From the moment we finish speaking, Immigration
won't be able to arrest you. And the dome cops won't be able
to arrest me, either." What he was going to do about Desplains,
Ivan was less sure. His wristcom was still thinly chiming in its
exile, cold and lonely and far off. Ivan ripped open the box and
began dancing sock-foot through the living room, dribbling out
a circle of cereal on the carpet.

"Don't we have to go somewhere and register it, even for a
simple civil match?" asked Tej. "We'd never make it to wherever!
They'll seize us as soon as we go out the door!"

"But not," said Rish blackly, "the other door." By braced his back
harder against the latch, though he still stared, confounded, at the
growing circle. His eyes were as wide as Ivan had ever seen them.

"No, that's the beauty of it!" Ivan explained. "In Barrayaran
law, the couple marry themselves. It's a Time-of-Isolation thing,
you wouldn't understand. Your breath is your bond. You each
prop up your Second—your witness—on the edge, you step into
the circle, you speak your oaths, you step out, it's done. The
core oaths are really simple, though people gussy them up with
all kinds of additions to stretch the ceremony out, God knows

why, it's usually racking enough." He appealed for support. "Tell them I'm right, Byerly!"

"Actually"—By coughed, swallowed, found his voice—"he is. About the legalities, anyway."

"I can use my military dependent travel chits to get you back to Barrayar," Ivan went on. "Five jumps farther away from your pursuers, and besides, once you're married to me, you'll have ImpSec totally on your side because, um, because. This'll buy time. And as soon as you've figured out what you really want to do, we can go get a divorce in the Count's Court. Not quite as easy as getting married—my Betan aunt thinks it should be t'other way around—but Count Falco's an old friend of Mamere's. Ten minutes, in and out, I swear! And you'll both be on your way."

"On our way where?" asked Rish, sounding confused.

"I don't know, somewhere! I can't think of everything all at once, you know!"

"Oh, so not a *permanent*—but I don't know your oaths," said Tej faintly, staring at him in a kind of hypnotized fascination as he stood before her waving the emptied box in time with his urgent persuasion.

"That's all right, I have them memorized. I must have been dragged to about a thousand high Vor weddings in the past decade. I could probably recite them in my sleep. Or my nightmares. We won't tell the dome cops about the divorce, of course. None of their business."

Tej glanced toward the balcony. Toward him. Toward the balcony. Toward him. *Why is this a hard choice?*

From the hallway, a teeth-gritting mechanical whine began, as of someone cutting through an airseal door.

"You can't tell me you'd rather jump off a twenty-story building and smash in your skull than marry me," Ivan went on desperately. "I am *not* a fate worse than death, dammit! Or at least not worse than *that* death, good God!"

"But what about Rish?" asked Tej. Her chin came up. "You can't marry us *both* . . . can you?"

"Uh," said Ivan. He cast a beseeching look at By, who held up his hand as if to fend off an attacking mini-drone.

"No," said Rish, coolly.

"*Thank* you," said By. His expression grew inward for a moment. "I think . . ."

"I'll, I'll, I'll...hire you for something, after," said Ivan. "Lady's maid? Lots of Vor women have them. M'mother does, I know. At that point, you'll be properly employed by a Barrayaran subject, a *Vor* subject, and we can fudge it with Immigration later. From a safe distance."

"Then who will protect us from ImpSec?" said Rish.

"I will," Ivan promised recklessly. "I can call in some favors. And if not, I know people who can. Starting with m'mother's gentleman friend, if I have to. Or maybe as a last resort." *Definitely as a last resort.* "Can't I, By?"

This last proposal left By standing like a mesmerized waxwork effigy. But he did manage to make his mouth move—it was By, of course he managed to make his mouth move. "I don't know if I want to watch when you tell your mother about this, or flee the Empire. Given that you're making me complicit as your Second, maybe Old Earth would be far enough...no, farther than that..." He shook himself out of his paralysis and turned to the women. "Much as I hate to admit it, this notion of Ivan's would work. Temporarily. It's the long-term consequences that terrify me."

"And after what you just did," Ivan went on to Tej, disregarding By's last comment, "you can't convince me that you'd rather kiss the pavement than kiss me." *My mouth is still tingling.* "Not that you'll have to kiss me, if you don't want to. Totally up to you, what happens after, I hope that goes without saying."

More alarming thumps and crashes from the hallway. Rish wet her lips and said, "Do it, Tej. And we'll find out if it works soon enough. We're out of time to debate. Or for the tub." She reset the safety and slipped her stunner back into her pocket in wordless acquiescence.

Ivan held out his hand to Tej. "Tej, will you please try this?"

She rubbed her forehead, and said doubtfully, "I guess so..." As the first acceptance to a marriage proposal that Ivan had ever received in his life, this lacked a certain something, but she took his hand and stepped over the line of groats into the circle.

Ivan pointed. "By, Rish, you stand on either side, facing each other. You're the witnesses, so watch."

"I doubt I'll be able to look away," murmured Byerly, holstering his stunner as well and stepping up to his assigned spot. "It'll be just like watching a monorail wreck." Rish rolled her eyes—in agreement?—and took her place opposite.

"All right, I'll go first," said Ivan to his bride-to-be, "and then I'll coach you through your part. Wording's about the same. 'I, Ivan Xav Vorpatril, being of sound mind and body—'"

"That's for *wills*, Ivan," muttered By. "I thought you said you knew this stuff?"

Ivan ignored him and plowed on. "Do take thee, uh...what did you say your name was, again?"

By buried his face in his hands.

Tej repeated it. All of it.

"Do take thee, Akuti Tejaswini Jyoti ghem Estif Arqua"—and he'd got the pronunciation right the *first time*, and didn't even choke on the *ghem* part, hah!—"to be my spouse and helpmeet, forsaking all others..." The core of the oath was only three sentences. He got them out somehow, and coached Tej through her half. "...*do take thee, Ivan Xav Vorpatril, to be my spouse...*" Her hands were shaking, held in his. So were his.

"And that's it!" said Ivan. "We now pronounce each other spouse and spouse, before these witnesses, and I get to kiss you. Again. For the first time. Because before, you kissed me, right?" He locked himself to her lips, rolling his eyes as By stepped forward and swept a break through the groat barrier with his shoe. They swung out of the circle together, Byerly stretched his neck and pecked her on the cheek in passing, and six irate, swearing Komarrans stumbled over each other out of Ivan's hallway and advanced upon them, stunners at the ready.

Ivan drew a wad of cash from his wallet, thrust it into the startled Rish's hand, and added, "You're hired. Officially."

And, as a uniformed woman reached out to seize Tej, who shrank away, Ivan continued in a forceful bellow modeled directly on Count Falco: "Unhand Lady Vorpatril!"

Chapter Seven

Tej had spent days steeling herself for death. This wrenching turn in her affairs left her stomach floating as if she *had* just jumped over that beckoning balcony, except that this fall didn't come to an end. She felt weightless, like a drowning woman. The mad captain seemed to have clamped a rescuing arm around her neck and be towing her along, but was it toward some unseen shore, or farther out into deeper waters?

She should have spotted that Ivan Xav was insane before this. Surely there had been *clues*. But he had, despite it all, seemed so easy-going, so affable, so *comfortable*—or at least unwilling to be thrust out of his comforts—a welcome rarity, among the people in her life. And then, with no warning, this.

Maddest of all was that his ploy seemed to be *working*. The Komarran Dome cops neither arrested him, nor seized him to be carried off for some psychiatric observation. Byerly Vorrutyer, introduced as an acquaintance from Vorbarr Sultana and present-ing valid identification, blandly testified to the ceremony he had just witnessed, pointing out the circle of groats ground into the carpet as supporting physical evidence. Rish backed him up, if in a slightly choked voice. There followed much frantic consultation of wristcom hololinks on the parts of both the dome cops and the Immigration officers, which apparently returned some very unwelcome answers. Ivan Xav retrieved his now-silent wristcom from the refrigerator and, anxious to get to his military HQ, cut the attendant explanations quite short.

The dome cops were plainly not happy that the discovery of Tej, transmuted from kidnap victim to runaway bride, had spoiled their hoped-for case against the Barrayaran. They retired thwarted and surly, with mutters about subpoenas for material witnesses to be promptly forthcoming, as they were still left with the puzzle of the budget ninjas on their hands. But they couldn't arrest Tej for being a crime *victim*. The Immigration people, too, retreated like a force planning a rematch, but the important thing was that it cleared the doorway *now*, except for a brief argument with the building manager about the damages. Vorpatril, affronted, pointed out *he* hadn't created the mess, but impatiently short-circuited the sting by telling the manager to put the repair costs on his rental charges. The two tense Barrayarans then gave Tej and Rish barely time to throw on street clothes and grab their most important possessions—not many left of those by now—before hustling them out the wrecked doorway, down the lift tubes, and through the lobby.

Outside, Vorpatril swung Byerly aside and backed him up into a wall niche behind a tall, potted evergreen. Tej could hear very little of their rapid, low-voiced exchange over the street noise, but it seemed to involve a lot of jaw-clenching and teeth-baring. Under a flowing headscarf, Rish all but pricked her ears. Tej leaned toward the pair, but only caught Ivan's Xav's forceful *You* owe *me, and I'm collecting . . .* and, as he finally eased back and released his unwilling auditor, *Go do what you have to do.* Byerly was more successful at pitching his voice not to carry, so all Tej had to go on was his body language. She'd never before seen someone swear quite so emphatically in body language. But when they started again toward the bubble-car platform, Byerly hastened off in the opposite direction.

They were about to cross the street when Vorpatril herded her and Rish abruptly into the doorway of a shop not yet open, spinning Tej around to face him—and, she realized, to shield him from view. "What is it?" she whispered, acquiescing to the tactic as soon as she recognized it.

"Service Security," he muttered into her hair. "A whole patrol. Just came charging out of the bubble-car station—yep, heading for my building, all right. Two enlisteds, a sergeant, and a colonel, *hoo* boy. Desplains must have dispatched them for me. I wonder if they mean to rescue me, or arrest me? . . . I think we don't want to stick around to find out. They can have a nice, long chat with the building manager. He deserves it, and it'll hold 'em for just long enough, I think. Come on, hurry."

Vorpatril's wooden smile and this-is-all-normal posture didn't slip till he'd bundled them into a bubble car and it was bowling along the route out to the military shuttleport. He slumped in his seat and addressed himself to his wristcom with the caution of a man defusing a bomb. At some return code, he muttered in relief, "Oh, good, he's got it on voice delay," and continued more brightly, "Admiral Desplains, Vorpatril here, sir. Sorry about the holdup this morning, but I have the misunderstanding with the Komarrans all straightened out. Nobody's trying to arrest me anymore"—his lips silently mouthed, *I hope*—"but I have one more short stop to make at ImpSec Galactic Affairs to settle a few details. I'll meet you and the Horsemen out at Dock Six. I'll explain everything else when I get there." He made to cut the com, but then raised it to his lips and added, "Please don't leave without me. It's important."

He blew out his breath, then entered another code, and made an appointment with someone named Captain Morozov to meet them in a few minutes at some lobby security desk. Tej and Rish looked uneasily at each other.

"That's your ImpSec person you mentioned who studies Jackson's Whole?" asked Rish.

"Morozov, yes. Good scout, bit of a boffin, but he's really *interested*, you know. I mean, above and beyond what he has to be for his duties as an analyst, which I suppose is what makes him a top boffin. I thought I'd leave you two with him for the day. You can't go back to my flat—after all that uproar this morning, it's gotta be smoked."

"True," said Rish, reluctantly.

"But however you feel about ImpSec, I can pretty much guarantee that nobody's rent-a-goons can get at you inside their HQ."

"But surely this Captain Morozov will want to know things," said Tej. "What should we tell him?"

Ivan Xav shrugged. "Everything. He's even cleared to know about By, though I doubt he does—not his department."

"Even about the—the wedding thing?"

He sighed. "I'll tell him about that."

When they exited into the busy bubble-car station out by the shuttleport, Rish said, "I have to pee," grabbed Tej, and towed her into the ladies' lavatory. Vorpatril made frustrated gestures of protest, but stopped short of following them inside. They left him standing in the corridor alongside a couple of other males with glazed, waiting expressions.

It didn't matter; there was only the one door, and no windows, Tej automatically noted as they entered. A woman dealing with a wailing infant, and another attempting to shepherd two hyperactive and not-well-trained toddlers through their ablutions, gave plenty of sound cover and guaranteed that no one was paying them the least attention.

Rish retreated to a corner and turned Tej around, strong blue hands gripping her shoulders. "Talk to me, Tej. You look like someone hit you on the head with a mallet, and you're just waiting to fall down. You're scaring me, sweetling."

"Am I?" Tej blinked. "I sure didn't see that blow coming. I wonder if he really thinks he married me?"

Rish shifted her head and eyed Tej narrowly, as if checking to see that her pupils were still the same size. "Do you think you really married him?"

"I have no idea. I guess the important thing is that everyone else seems to." Tej took a deep breath. "And till we find out what all else this *Lady Vorpatril* business is good for, we'd likely better go along with it."

Rish pursed her lips, nodded, and stood back, releasing her worried grip. "Point taken." Her mouth tightened. "So what are we going to tell this Morozov fellow? Think, sweetling, think."

Tej rubbed her forehead. "I'd be perfectly happy to feed everything we know about those House Prestene bastards to Barrayar, if only I could be sure they weren't about to become new best friends afterward. Though if the Prestene syndicate is really on the other end of this smuggling scheme, I think the Barrayarans aren't going to be too well-disposed toward House Cordonah's new management. I know even Dada and the Baronne took care how they crossed these Imperium crazies. It's rumored that all of House Ryoval was taken down by a single ImpSec agent, after the old baron pissed Barrayar off somehow."

Rish whistled. "Really?"

"That's the tale Star told me, anyway. She got it from someone in House Fell. So I think..." Tej wished she could think. Her brain seemed to have turned to mush. "I think we should tell this Morozov almost everything. Bury him in details, so's he won't have either the time or the motivation to move on to the fast-penta."

"Ah."

"Our story will be that the syndicate is after you as a flashy prize, and me as a baby enemy they want to strangle in the cradle." Yes, that had seemed to work for the Byerly person. And besides, it was true. "Hold back only anything about where Amiri is. Anything about Amiri, come to think. And don't volunteer anything about Star and Pidge. Or Grandmama."

Rish nodded understanding.

They both made quick dashes for the stalls, returning to the station corridor before Vorpatril overcame his social conditioning and came in looking for them, although, by the glare he cast them, it had been a near thing.

"Crowded?" he inquired.

"Lots of little kids," Tej said truthfully. "I think they must have eaten straight sugar for breakfast." That was the best deal, yes. Truth.

Just not *all* of it.

To Ivan's relief, Morozov was already waiting at the ImpSec Galactic Affairs reception desk when he guided the two women inside the lobby. Morozov's eyes widened as Rish turned to face him, but then he managed a boffin-y bow.

"Lapis Lazuli. A visit to ImpSec's humble quarters by an artist of your caliber is quite an honor." His lips parted in equal surprise as he took in Tej. "And, if I am not mistaken, one of the Misses Arqua as well! This is excellent, Vorpatril."

"You're mistaken," said Ivan. "Or anyway, behind the times. Captain Morozov, may I present the new Lady Vorpatril."

Morozov blinked. Three times. And rose to the challenge: "Congratulations to you both. Er... a recent happy event, was this?"

"About"—Ivan glanced at the time on his wristcom, *ouch*—"an hour ago." He drew breath. "But it's all right and tight and legal, we had the groats and the oaths and the witnesses and everything. Which means she is now officially an Imperial Service officer's dependent. And Rish is her, um, personal assistant. In my employ. Officially."

"I see. I think...?" Morozov laced his hands together; Ivan wasn't sure if that lip-biting expression concealed dismay, or unholy glee.

"An officer's dependent who some very unpleasant people have been trying to kidnap and maybe murder," Ivan forged on.

That got the analyst's full attention. "Ah. I *see*. We can't have that, can we?"

"Right. So I'm leaving them with you for the day till I can get back downside and deal with, uh, everything. They probably ought to stay in the building. I thought you all could talk."

"It would be my very great pleasure," said Morozov, brightening right up. Tej and Rish did not look nearly as thrilled as he did.

"And no damned fast-penta," Ivan continued. "I think you'd have to ask my husbandly permission anyway, but just in case there's a question, you don't have it. My permission, that is."

Morozov's brows twitched. "Noted. Er...if I may ask a personal question...does your mother know about this marriage yet?"

"Nobody knows about this marriage yet, but that'll change soon enough. One thing at a time. I'm due to accompany Desplains upside in, oh God, twenty minutes ago. I hope they're holding the shuttle."

Morozov waved an ImpSec salute at him. "Then I shall consider myself detailed to guard the new Lady Vorpatril from all harm until your return, shall I?"

"Please." Ivan turned away, turned back. "And feed them. They'll like that. Nobody's had breakfast yet." He started off and stopped again. "But not rat bars."

"I'll send my clerk to bring up something from the cafeteria. Ladies, will you come with me? I can offer you coffee or tea in my office." Morozov gestured the uneasy women away down the corridor, and continued in the tone of a town Vor dame, or possibly Byerly Vorrutyer, at the most gossipy: "And I'm dying to hear all about your wedding, Lady Vorpatril! I'm sure this will come as a delightful surprise to all of Captain Vorpatril's friends..."

Ivan pushed through the doors and ran. He made sure to make it that special bland run that said, *I'm late and in a hurry*, and not the wild bolt that said, *This building I am fleeing is about to explode*, because he didn't want to spread panic. He had enough panic tamped into his head right now to blow up a battalion. *This'll work this'll work, this had better work...*

He found, thanks be, the admiral's shuttle still waiting in Dock Six. Desplains and all four of the Horsemen were aboard, fuming with impatience. The shuttle was already moving as Ivan flung himself into the seat where the scowling Desplains pointed and snapped his belts closed.

"We're off to inspect the flagship *New Athens*, right?" Ivan wheezed.

"So glad you remembered," said Desplains, drawing a long breath for what promised to be a classic bolt of scouring sarcasm, but Ivan shook his head.

"Change it to the *Kanzian*."

Desplains stopped dead in mid-rant-launch. "What?"

"The *Kanzian*. Tell the shuttle pilot to dock at the *Kanzian*."

Desplains sat back, eyes narrowing. "Why?"

"Because hidden somewhere aboard it—or possibly clamped outside of it—are several cargo pods full of equipment, weapons, and supplies stolen from the Sergyar Fleet Orbital Depot. Which their conveyors are no doubt trying frantically to camouflage right now, in anticipation of our scheduled inspection tomorrow." Ivan nodded to the inspection team chief, leaning over the aisle to hear this. "Forget the rest, that's what the Horsemen should look for."

"How do you know this, Vorpatril?" asked Desplains.

"I had a tip-off from an ImpSec agent."

"ImpSec didn't tell *me*."

"This was one of their left-hand men, the sort the right hands don't talk to. Frigging weasels. But he's known to me. The reasons I've been late for work the past few days weren't just personal ones, sir."

"Are you sure of this?"

"Very." *IhopeIhopeIhope...*

"ImpSec." Desplains sat back, his scowl transmuting to his thinking-frown, scarcely less alarming. "I suppose you would know."

"I do in this case, sir." Adding *I'd stake my career on it* seemed redundant, since he just had. "But you can't even hint where you got the tip, sir. There are ImpSec agents still on the ground in the matter who are at high risk till they get clear."

"Hmm..."

There ensued rumbling and grumbling, but the Horsemen were good; they had the new inspection plan roughed out before the shuttle slid into its docking clamps at the Komarr Fleet orbital station. Next to the *Kanzian*.

Captain Morozov proved a disappointment to Tej, considering ImpSec's reputation. He wasn't in the *least* scary.

By the time he'd ordered in a gratifyingly substantial lunch, the tale of her and Rish's escape and subsequent odyssey across three systems was almost told. The first not-too-alarmed flight to Fell Station, and then all their false sense of security blown to shocked bits when their bodyguard was shot; the escape to the Hegen Hub, the weeks turned to months of slipping from station to station around the Hub like some sort of lethal shell game—brief, stressed, frightening periods of motion alternated with long, boring, frightening periods of hiding; the bad news catching up with them in agonizingly slow hammer blows; the gradual relaxation of their months downside on the free planet Pol, almost sure they'd shaken pursuit, till it turned up again. The final flight to Komarr, with their every resource of money, identity, and resolution nearly tapped out. She tried to hold back how their identity shifts had worked, but since the fellow promptly guessed nearly every detail, Tej ended up being frank about all that, as well.

Morozov might not be properly intimidating, but he was something better; he *understood*. Tej discovered, when he volunteered a few inviting anecdotes of his own during the lulls and hesitations, that some years back he had actually been a junior ImpSec field agent in the Whole. They were all out-of-date tales of amusing misadventures, but Tej began to sense that in the gaps lay some adventures that hadn't been so amusing, nor misses.

"No one is allowed to become an analyst without field experience," he explained. "They are not at all the same skill-set, but when one is given the task of interpreting field reports, it's a source of considerable illumination to have once been the fellow writing them." He seemed quite content with his headquarters job now, though, and perhaps the holovid of the middle-aged woman with children, tucked almost out of sight on his cluttered desk, suggested why.

As they portioned out sandwiches, teas, and assorted deep-fried vegetables and cheeses around the cubicle, Tej, with editorial interjections from Rish, brought the tale up to the moment with a description of her bewildering wedding at dawn.

"I wish I could have been a witness, too," said Morozov, his eyes crinkling. "That was quite a quixotic impulse on your, er, bridegroom's part. Well, faint heart ne'er won fair lady, I suppose."

"I think it was his admiral calling on his wristcom that finally pushed him..." she swallowed the words, *over the edge*, and substituted, "into his inspiration. When it wouldn't stop chiming, he finally took it off and threw it into the refrigerator."

Morozov choked on a bite of sandwich. But, "Really," was all he said when he got his breath back.

"Is this Admiral Desplains of Ivan Xav's a, um, very important admiral?"

"Chief of Operations for the entire Imperial Service? You could say so, but it would be a charming understatement."

"Oh," said Tej. "So... Ivan Xav's not just some sort of military clerk?"

"You could say so." Morozov's lips twitched. "But it would be a charming understatement." Morozov finished his last bite, leaned back in his station chair, and tented his fingertips together. "I should likely explain, I served several years of my apprenticeship in Analysis at ImpSec headquarters in Vorbarr Sultana, back when the legendary Chief Illyan was still running the place."

Illyan's, at least, was a name Tej dimly remembered hearing on her father's lips, more than once. Usually accompanied by swearing. She nodded uncertainly.

"Domestic Affairs was never my department, but one cannot serve long in the capital without acquiring some familiarity with the high Vor scene."

"Did you know Ivan Xav there?"

"No, we never met in person till the affair of his cousin's clone brought him into my orbit, some time later."

And why did that have anything to do with Jackson's Whole? And which cousin? "Am I—are we—likely to meet his cousin? Or his clone?" She hesitated. "Is this the Cousin Miles he keeps talking about? Is he anyone important?"

Morozov squeezed his eyes shut, briefly. Opened them to give her a rather pained look. "Just how much *has* your new husband told you about himself?"

"Not much. I looked him up."

"Where?"

"Maybe I'd better show you..."

A few minutes at his comconsole found Tej's database. "Why ever did you look in a Komarran database for Barrayaran affairs?" Morozov inquired mildly.

"It seemed...as if it would be more reliable...?" Would he take that as an insult?

Morozov looked over Ivan Xav's entry and sniffed. "Correct but incomplete, and sadly out of date. You shouldn't have stopped there, m'dear."

"I ran out of time."

"Well." Morozov swung around again. "High Vor family relations tend to be complex, interlaced, and mined. Before you set foot in them, I strongly advise you to study up."

"Is Ivan Xav high Vor, then? I thought he was just...middling. He *acts* middling." Tej was beginning to be peeved about that. Just what kind of a tricky deal had she landed herself in, anyway?

"Oh, yes," said Morozov, as if that explained anything.

Tej glared at him.

He held up a warding palm and suppressed a smile. "To understand Captain Vorpatril's peculiar position in the capital, one must travel a bit farther up his family tree. His mother is of good Vor stock, and certainly not to be underrated, but it's on his father's side that things become interesting."

"He said he was an only child. So was his father—or anyway, he didn't have any siblings listed."

"Up farther than that. Captain Vorpatril's father's *mother* was Princess Sonia Vorbarra, who, along with her elder sister Olivia, were the daughters of Prince Xav Vorbarra. Who was the younger son in turn of Emperor Dorca Vorbarra, later called Dorca the Just. And the younger half-brother of Emperor Yuri, later called Mad Yuri, but that's another tale."

Perhaps more than names out of history texts for the Baronne or Grandmama, but mere distant tales to Tej. Yuri had led the brutal and bloody rebellion against the Occupation on the ground, while his brother Xav had run all over the Nexus gathering off-world support for his forces, not so much for Barrayar, as against Cetaganda. And—um, yes—that was the whole sum of Tej's knowledge of them. "So...Ivan Xav's great-grandfather was this really important prince. And his great-great-grandfather was this really important emperor?" She looked suspiciously at Morozov, who had his hand pressed to his mouth, his eyes alight with annoying amusement. "Or is that another charming understatement?"

"It will do for now. To bring it back to the present, Ivan Xav Vorpatril from the hour of his birth has been high on the list of potential heirs-presumptive to the throne of Barrayar should anything untoward, God forbid, happen to Emperor Gregor. Or he was, till Gregor married Laisa Toscane and the boys came along, to many people's relief."

"A list? Is it a long list?"

"Not especially, though it still contains several latent opportunities for civil conflict. First on the list has always been—ah, you see, Sonia's elder sister Olivia married Count Piotr Vorkosigan. Who thus became the sire in turn of Count Aral Vorkosigan, who is the father of Miles Vorkosigan, Ivan's notable cousin. Lord Auditor Miles Vorkosigan, now. If you linger in Vorbarr Sultana for longer than ten minutes, I can almost guarantee you will meet him. But it's always been realized by anyone with even half a wit that none of the Vorkosigans would have touched the throne, seeing as how Lord Miles was born so damaged, should it have fallen vacant before Gregor had sired his own heirs. Instead, they would doubtless have swung their considerable weight behind Ivan Vorpatril. And pushed."

Rish was listening to all this like a blue marble statue. Tej hoped she was tracking the complications better than Tej was. Tej had a hot date with a comconsole soon, there could be no doubt. *Homework.* Tej hated homework. *No choice now.*

"The upshot of it all is that Vorpatril has been a potential plot magnet for disaffected political parties all his life, partially shielded by his cousin's clan, partially protected by his own . . . I suppose I could describe it as *notoriously nonferrous* lifestyle. Pressures have eased off for him lately, to a degree."

"Wouldn't Ivan Xav's mother have been anxious to promote him?" asked Rish, clearly puzzled by this maternal lapse. "Or see him promoted, anyway?"

"I gather that Lady Alys has always been much more anxious to protect him from risk. Her only child, you see. Though she is a formidable woman. *Had* anything untoward ever happened to Gregor, I am sure that—after first seeing those responsible properly hanged with all due ceremony—she would undoubtedly have been drawn into guiding her son in his new duties."

"I thought she was a secretary," said Tej faintly. "The database called her some kind of secretary." She looked at Morozov, looking back at her in wonder. "Charming understatement...?"

"Social Secretary to the Imperial Residence. Official hostess for Emperor Gregor for decades, now first assistant to Empress Laisa. One of the most powerful women in the capital, in her own quiet way. I know Chief Illyan never underestimated her."

Would Ivan Xav take her to meet his mother, when they arrived in Vorbarr Sultana? And if so, should they perhaps tell her about the divorce before they mentioned the wedding?

While Tej digested the implications, Morozov gathered up the lunch debris and set the tray in the corridor. When he returned, his thoughts had plainly shifted back to his own more immediate duties, for he opened with a chatty, "And how ever did the Baronne come to create you Jewels, Rish? It must have been a fascinating project for her..."

And then it was time to gather what was left of her wits and evade, again, and push Ivan Xav to the back of her mind. Where he loomed like a very indigestible lump indeed.

Just as Ivan had hoped, his arresting lure drew Desplains's attention entirely off of the erratic personal affairs of his high Vor aide-de-camp for the next several hours, especially after the first cargo pod was found in the process of being stashed under a fake antenna. There followed a fire drill of the most chaotic: Service Security everywhere, surprised perpetrators playing hide and seek all over the ship, the *Kanzian*'s captain out for blood, livid with outrage and chagrin to discover that he'd missed the criminal scheme taking place under his nose. Ivan faded into the background, documenting and taking notes on the whole circus like the excellent admiral's assistant he was. At the end of the long day, Admiral Desplains and the Horsemen were being regarded by the *Kanzian*'s entire crew and most of the orbital station's personnel as possessing supernatural powers granted by some dark god, and they wouldn't have been human if they hadn't enjoyed the effect, at least a little bit.

Desplains was almost mellow as he settled into his shuttle seat for the trip back to downside HQ. His gesture this time for Ivan to take the seat across from him was more of a wave of friendly invitation. The admiral leaned his head back against the seat in a moment of well-earned weariness, but opened his eyes again and regarded his subordinate in some bemusement.

"Good work today, Ivan. You do have your uses."

"Thank you, sir."

"And here I thought—never mind. I owe you one."

Ivan was good. Ivan was *Ivan* when the admiral was pleased with him, *Vorpatril* when the mood was neutral, and *Captain* when Desplains was irritated. This was probably the best opportunity Ivan would get to broach the next subject. Also, given the short duration of the flight, the only opportunity, so. *Go.* He took a deep breath. "I'm glad you think so, sir. As it happens, I am in need of a somewhat personal favor just at the moment. Not unrelated to this." His wave around reminded his listener of the *Kanzian* coup, just bagged.

"Oh?" Desplains knew better than to offer a free pass in advance, but his benign tone and nod invited Ivan to go on.

"I need a permission to get married, and approval for two passages from Komarr to Barrayar for Service dependents."

Desplains's eyes flew wide. "Ivan! This is sudden. You never breathed a word—is it some Komarran girl? Nothing wrong with that, of course, quite the fashion these days, but—does your mother know about this?"

"Backdated to yesterday," Ivan forged on, before the admiral could build up any more elaborate fantasies of secret interplanetary romances in his mind.

Desplains went still. Sat back. Continued in a much cooler tone, "I see. When did these nuptials actually take place, Vorpatril?"

Not *Captain* yet; Ivan still had turning room. "At dawn this morning, sir. So I suppose a permission dated to today would also do, but there will hardly be time before we land downside."

"I think you had better begin at the beginning."

"I intend to, sir." Ivan marshaled his thoughts, trying to figure out how to put as much of the culpability on Byerly as possible. Traditionally, Ops had no objection to criticizing ImpSec for any screwup, from minor to monumental. *Yes, blame the absent, always a good plan.* "The beginning would be three nights ago, when the ImpSec deep cover agent came to my flat and asked for my help—"

⊂℞⊃ ⊂℞⊃ ⊂℞⊃

It was almost Komarran midnight when Ivan at last made it back to the ImpSec Galactic Affairs building where, the night clerk assured him, Morozov was still in his office, very late, isn't it, sir? Ivan declined to respond to this invitation to drop tidbits, which disappointed the clerk but did not surprise him.

The door to Morozov's cubicle was open, spilling light into the corridor and, Ivan was heartened to hear, rather cheerful-sounding voices. He arrived to discover Morozov and his two guests perched variously in the debris, disemboweled food cartons spread all over and deflated soda bulbs piled up, deeply engaged in some sort of game—a brightly colored, if rather tattered, box lay open on the floor, and each player manned a vid board, balanced on their laps. As Ivan walked, or rather, picked his way inside, something beeped and twinkled, Tej hooted, Morozov groaned, and Rish grinned like an evil blue elf.

Tej was the first to look up. She cast him an oddly penetrating glance. "Ivan Xav! You're back!"

"Sorry it took me so long. I have some guest quarters arranged for us tonight here in the HQ compound, so it's only a step over to bed. Nothing fancy, but safe. Looks like you got dinner. Uh..." *Have you been all right here?* seemed to be a question already answered. "What's the game?"

"*Great House,*" said Tej. "It's an old Jacksonian children's game. I used to play it when I was girl, with my sibs and the Jewels, but they always beat the pants off me, unless I cheated. Though you're allowed to cheat."

"Each player starts with a small stake," Morozov explained, "and the object is to deal with and against each other, till the winner ends up owning the virtual world. It can be played with only two people, barely, but it's far more interesting with three or more. It's not often that I get a chance to play it with actual Jacksonians." He added after a moment, "I've lost five rounds straight. I suspect collusion."

Rish smirked.

"Thank you for staying so late," Ivan began, but Morozov waved this away.

"It's been a very enjoyable day, quite a nice break in my routine." The ImpSec analyst rose with a groan, and stretched. "I concede. You two can wrestle it out for second and first."

The two women eyed each other, bared teeth, and bent to a

flurry of beeps and twinkles. Morozov jerked his head at the doorway, and followed Ivan out. They moved a few steps down the corridor beyond earshot of the cubicle.

"I like your new wife, Captain Vorpatril," said Morozov.

"Uh, thanks. Only temporary though, you know."

"So she explained." Morozov smiled at his shoes.

"Did you get anything useful out of the day? From ImpSec's viewpoint, that is. From your interrogation."

"Interrogation? Oh, nothing so crude among friends. Or cultural relatives-in-law. We just had one delightful, riveting conversation after another. You must get her to tell you the full tale of her flight from the Whole—it sounds to have been a ghastly adventure, in all. I quite hope it may have a happier ending than beginning."

"Er," said Ivan. "We really haven't had much chance to talk yet."

"So I gathered." Morozov rubbed his neck; his voice took on a more serious tone. "Everything the pair of them told me that I already knew about, checked out well, allowing for point of view and so on. So I have a high degree of confidence in the new information they purveyed. As far as it went."

Ivan waited for it. Then grew impatient—he was exhausted— and prodded, "But . . . ?"

"Tej began by withholding details about her family, reasonably enough, but just about everything I could want to know and more about the Arqua clan has come out in the last three hours of *Great House*—*very* valuable game. Lively, too."

Who won? Ivan suddenly realized, could be a question with more than one answer.

Morozov slipped from serious to grim. "My considered professional analysis is that the syndicate that seized House Cordonah is going to keep on coming. It's plain they still fear a countercoup. They want these women—alive, probably; dead, in a pinch. Each Arqua they can obtain gives them a stronger handle on the out-of-reach remainder. You'd best be prepared."

"Ah." Ivan swallowed. He tried to figure out what that meant, then realized he had a top figurer-outer standing right in front of him. *Use your resources.* "For what, exactly?"

"Small-scale kidnapping teams, most likely. Deploying all sorts of tactics, including deception. Import teams have greater logistical challenges, but are known quantities to their handlers. Local hirelings blend better, and know the ground. Any successful abduction must fall into two halves: seizing the victims—which actually may be the easier part—and their removal beyond the Imperium's boundaries."

Somebody kidnaps my *wife, and they'll find the Imperium's boundaries can stretch a hell of a long way,* Ivan found himself thinking with unexpected fierceness. Wait, no. This thing with Tej was only a temporary ploy, not a real marriage. Well, no, it *was* a real marriage, that is, a legal marriage, that was the whole reason why it had worked. But not permanent. Nothing to be alarmed about there.

Anyway, it was surely allowable to shoot kidnappers regardless of who they were trying to carry off, right?

"I'll be escorting them both on to Barrayar in little more than a day's time," said Ivan. "They should be safe out here at Komarr HQ till then—don't you think?"

"Commercial or military ship?"

"Admiral Desplains's jump-pinnace, actually. He was kind enough to assign me some spare berths. Wedding present, he said."

"That should be exceptionally safe. I imagine it will take their pursuers some time to regroup after the, ah, curve ball you threw this morning. I don't think that could have been anticipated in anyone's schemes."

Including mine.

"Meanwhile," said Morozov, "I'd think you, as the lady's new husband, would be as closely placed as humanly possible to find out more, eh?"

Puzzles. *I hate puzzles.* Ivan liked flowcharts—nice and clear and you could always tell just where you were and what you should do next, everything laid out neatly. No ambiguities. No traps. Why couldn't life be more like flowcharts?

Morozov went on jovially, "After all, a man who can't persuade his own wife to trust him is a man in trouble in many ways."

So many ways. Ivan could only nod.

Chapter Eight

The military compound's guest quarters proved to resemble a small, faintly shabby hotel, designed to temporarily house officers, dependents, or civilian contract employees either in transit to elsewhere, or downside on Komarr for duties too brief to billet them in permanent housing. Its security, Tej judged, was only fair, but still vastly better than anything she'd had to rely upon lately, and it didn't feel like a prison. Ivan Xav escorted Tej and Rish to a clean if narrow chamber with two beds, and, yawning, himself went to ground in a room directly across the hall. As Tej's very first wedding night ever, this would have left something to be desired, if she hadn't been so exhausted by the disruptions of the past days as to fall asleep nearly as fast as she could pull up her covers.

When they awoke the next morning Ivan Xav had already gone off to aide-de-camp his admiral some more, though he left a note of reassurance, scrawled on the back of a flimsy and shoved under their door. Captain Morozov turned up to escort them to a long, chatty brunch in a private room off the ImpSec building cafeteria, where he asked yet more uncomfortably shrewd questions, seeming as satisfied with the evasions as the answers, which was a bit disquieting, on reflection. In the afternoon, a uniformed enlisted man arrived with all of their and Ivan Xav's remaining possessions from his rental flat, and dumped them on Rish's bed to be sorted out. Minus the groceries, evidently abandoned; Tej would rather have liked to have kept the emptied groats box for a souvenir.

Tej sat herself down at the room's little comconsole and began to try to study up on Barrayaran history. Which the Barrayarans appeared, from a first glance, to have made *far* too much of. Rish, trammeled by the confined space as usual—these past months had been especially hard on her—started her dance exercises, or as least as many of the thousand-moves-kata as she could fit into the constricted area. She had wandered into their tiny bathroom to practice the neck, face, ear, eye, and eyebrow movements in front of the mirror—ten reps each—when a hearty knock on the door shot Tej from her chair and almost out of the window. Only one floor up, now, so unlikely to be lethal—had Ivan Xav arranged that?

In any case, it was his voice that called, "Hi, Tej, you in there?" Trying to calm her pounding heart, she went to unlock the door.

He stuck his head in and said, "Saddle up, ladies. Our shuttle awaits."

"So soon?" said Tej, as Rish came out of the lav.

"Hey, you two may have slept in, but it's been a long day for me."

"No, I mean, I thought—I thought this thing with the smugglers might have thrown you off schedule."

"It's Service Security's problem now. That's what delegation is for. They're scrambling like mad to cover their lapse—this is the sort of rattlesnake they're supposed to hand *to* Desplains, neatly pithed, pinned on a card, and labeled, not the other way around. Very disorienting for 'em. Though all of their further reports will doubtless catch up with us en route. Travel time with the boss is not break time, alas." He gathered up his delivered gear and went off to pack his duffle.

The ride up to orbit on the military shuttle felt like escape from a deeper pit than just a gravity well. Tej stared out her tiny window. Scabrous patches of green terraforming clung like lichen around the barren, poisonous planet, and the lights of the dome arcologies, strung like bright beads along the faint monorail lines, made promises for the future, but not for the now. For someone who'd spent as much time growing up on space installations as

Tej, Solstice Dome ought to have felt spacious, but it hadn't. If a place wasn't going to be a proper station, it ought to be a proper planet, but Komarr had seemed to be something caught between.

I don't know where I'm going. But this wasn't it. Was she going to have to sort through the entire Nexus by process of elimination to find her final destination? *I hope not.*

The shuttle docked, and Ivan Xav led them on a very short walk through the military orbital station to another portal. A zero-gee float through a personnel flex tube gave Tej a bare glimpse of a ship about the size of a rich man's yacht, but not nearly as cheery-looking—an effect of the warty weapons housings studding the armored skin, perhaps. The tube spat them out into a small hatch bay, neat but decidedly utilitarian. Three men awaited them: an armed soldier in ship gear, an unarmed enlisted man in a plain green uniform, and a spare, gray-haired man in a less-plain green uniform like Ivan Xav's. He did not particularly exude arrogance, but Tej recognized how people stood or moved when they owned the place, and this man did; it hardly needed Ivan Xav's salute and, "Admiral Desplains, sir," to identify him. "May I present to you my wife, Lady Tej Vorpatril, and her personal assistant, Lapis Lazuli, also known as Rish."

The admiral returned the salute in a more perfunctory manner. His polite smile broadened into something more genuinely welcoming, or maybe that was just genuinely amused, as he looked over his guests. Somebody must have warned him about Rish, for he didn't gawk. "Lady Vorpatril. Miss, ah, Lazuli. Welcome aboard the *JP-9*. My ship has no more memorable name, I'm afraid."

Tej gathered her wits enough to return, "Thank you for inviting us, sir," and didn't correct Rish's address. A Chief of Operations wasn't exactly a House baron, more like a senior House security officer, but it might be well to treat him just as circumspectly.

"I understand you were of material aid in helping us trap our home-grown smugglers, yesterday," Desplains went on.

Not at all sure what Ivan Xav had told him, Tej tried smiling mysteriously, and murmured, "They were no friends to me or mine."

"So Captain Morozov gave me to believe," said Desplains.

Oh. Of course Morozov had to be reporting to someone. Their chats hadn't been just for his entertainment, or his back-files, however much he managed to make one feel so. "Has Morozov much special training in interrogation?" Tej asked, belatedly curious.

"Actually, he trains interrogators," said Desplains. "One of our top men, you know." He dragged his gaze back up to her face—so, old but not dead, though Tej had trouble estimating Barrayarans' ages. "I begin to see why Captain Vorpatril's chivalrous inspiration took the form it did, Lady Vorpatril. I suddenly realize his duties with me have not left you much time together since your wedding yesterday, ah, morning was it?"

"Not any," she confirmed. She tried a doleful look on him, curious to see what would happen.

It won a quirky smile, anyway. "We shall have to find some way to make it up to you. In the meanwhile, Ivan, show our guests around the ship and give them the safety drill."

He made a motion to the enlisted man, who collected their bags. Tej and Rish parted reluctantly with theirs, till Ivan Xav whispered, opaquely but reassuringly, "Admiral's batman, it's all right." As they left the hatch bay, Desplains and the other bent their heads together in some conference.

The ship was small and the tour brief, as the engineering and Nav-and-Com areas were evidently off-limits. While they were about this, Tej more felt than heard the faint thumps and clanks that told her they had detached from the station and were on their way already. The amenities were few: a kind of dining room-gathering place that Ivan Xav dubbed the wardroom, a small observation lounge, a compact but well-equipped exercise room that Rish eyed with interest. Tej guessed a crew of less than twenty, split among shifts, and a capacity of perhaps a dozen passengers, maybe twice that in an emergency. The jump-pinnace was bigger and slower than a fast courier, but not by much.

Getting lost on board was not going to be a problem, or even an option. Ivan Xav focused on escape routes and emergency pods and equipment how-to's, and conscientiously made them both go through the entire pressurization-or-other-emergency safety routine, till he seemed satisfied that they understood it.

"Do you do this for passengers a lot?" asked Rish, freeing herself from a breath mask and handing it back.

"We carry high-ranking non-Service supercargo from time to time, depending on the mission. Or the admiral sometimes includes his family on these more routine jaunts, but they had other things going on at home this week."

"Have you worked for Desplains long?" asked Tej.

"About three years. He brought me along with him when he was promoted from Admiral of the Home Fleet to Chief of Operations, two years back."

The batman-person appeared. "If you will come this way, Captain, Lady Vorpatril, Miss Lazuli." He led them down to the end of a short corridor; an airseal door labeled *Admiral Desplains* slid open at his touch on the pad. Inside was a tiny suite—a sitting room and two bedrooms with a connecting bath. One bedroom had four neat bunks. The other boasted a double bed. Their three bags and Ivan Xav's duffle waited, placed ambiguously on the floor of the sitting room.

"Admiral's compliments, Lady Vorpatril, ma'am, but he begs you and the captain will accept the use of his quarters for the duration of the journey. He says the space is underutilized, without Madame Desplains or the children along. Which, indeed, it is." The batman pointed out a few basic features and bowed himself out with a murmured, "There is a call button on the wall if you require anything more, but I trust I have provided most of the necessities."

Ivan Xav stared around, seeming vaguely stunned. "Huh! Guess I'm forgiven, then..." He pulled himself together, peeked into both bedrooms in turn, wheeled to the women, and said, "Er... take your pick?"

Tej and Rish looked at each other. Rish said, "Excuse us a moment," grabbed Tej by the arm, and dragged her into the bunk room, letting the airseal door slide closed behind them.

"Quit *smirking*," said Rish.

Tej chirped, "Oh, but how *nice*. Ivan Xav's boss has given us the honeymoon suite. It would seem a shame to waste such a grateful gesture, don't you think?"

Rish ran a hand over her platinum pelt in a harried swipe, blue ears twitching. "All right, I can see how it might be a good deal if he pair-bonds to you. Maybe not so good if you pair-bond to him. Don't lose your head, sweetling."

Tej tossed her curls. "It's only a *practice* marriage. So I ought to get in some practice, don't you think?"

"And quit prancing, too. It's not like he's an allowed suitor. That call button won't bring in a brace of the Baron's bodyguards to eject him from your bedroom if he displeases you. There's only me. And while there are places where I'd back myself to take him on, this isn't one of them. This ship is Barrayaran, bow to bulkhead. With no place to run."

"He's allowed if I allow him." Tej's voice went bleak. "Who else is left to make that call, Rish?"

Rish took a breath, but let it out slowly, unused.

"I know this isn't a deal from strength, but here we are," said Tej. "For the next six days. And afterward, too, for some unknown amount of time. There's no harm in setting up a basic biological reward-loop as a minor safety net. You know I won't mistake it for anything more." Tej hesitated. "Although how you can look at what Dada and the Baronne had, and dismiss it as minor, I don't know."

"Exception that proves the rule, sweetling." Rish paced the floor, two steps each way. "Oh, hell, go on and have your treat. Maybe it'll be the fastest cure for this madness."

Tej's smile tucked up, irresistibly. "Not for him—I'll wager my training on that. Anyway, his admiral practically handed him to me gift-wrapped. And you know how I like opening presents."

This pulled a reluctant chuckle from Rish. She thumped a fist gently into Tej's shoulder. "In that case, break a leg. Preferably one of his, not one of yours."

"Nothing so violent."

They went back out to the sitting room, where Ivan Xav was standing with the glazed look of those men who'd waited outside the women's lav, except that the fingers of his right hand were drumming rapidly on his trouser seam. He jerked to attention with a weird, twisted smile. "So what's the verdict?"

"Rish will take the bunk room," said Tej, "and you and I will take the other room."

His mouth opened. Closed. Opened again. "That . . . sounds great, but you know, you don't have to do this if you don't want to. Of course, if you *do* want to, that's . . . that's just great!"

Rish rolled her eyes, picked up her bag, and withdrew to the bunk room, calling, "Good night, good night, to all a good night. I claim first dibs on the bath, though."

Barely seeming to hear this, Ivan Xav blinked at Tej, and said, "And the *other* good thing is that on board here, we're back on Fleet time, which is Vorbarr Sultana time. Twenty-six-point-seven hour sidereal day, you know, with the night proportional. Makes for a *much* more leisurely evening."

Unexpectedly, he stepped forward, wrapped an arm around Tej's waist, and swung her around like a dancer and down onto the room's little sofa, bolted to the floor in case of artificial gravity mishaps. "How do you do, Lady Vorpatril? I'm so pleased to meet you."

Yes, I can tell already, Tej did not say out loud. "Hi there, Lord Vorpatril." What was he a lord *of,* anyway? She would have to find out. Later. "Say my whole name. Bet you can't."

His chin jerked up at the challenge. "Lady Akuti Tejaswini Jyoti ghem Estif Arqua Vorpatril."

Tej, impressed, raised her brows. "You're a fast study, Ivan Xav."

"When I have to be." One finger went out to tease a curl from her forehead, then hesitated. "Er...how old would you happen to be, Tej? I mean, you look maybe twenty-something standard, but Jacksonians, all that body modification...Cetagandans, all that genetic manipulation...could be anything from ten to sixty, I suppose."

"As it happens, I am just turned twenty-five."

"Oh. Whew."

"What would you have done if I'd said ten?" she asked curiously.

"Cried. And turned you back over to your baby-sitter."

"Or sixty?"

"Now, that I could have dealt with. Older women—it's a fantasy, y'know. Or can be."

"Have you ever fulfilled that fantasy?"

"I...don't think this is the time to go into my past, y'know? Tonight should be all about you." His voice was growing smoother, more confident. But then he hesitated again. "Ah...Great House baron's treasured daughter and all, I expect you led a very sheltered life, huh? Very protected. Lots of armed guards and all that."

"Yes, till the House fell."

He tilted his head back and forth, as if thinking. Or puzzling. "Uh...I need to ask this, don't mean to embarrass you or anything, and any answer is fine, as long as it's true. Because I kind of need to know. Are you still a virgin?"

"Good heavens, no. Not since age fifteen."

"Oh, was it fifteen for you, too? I mean, oh good. That's not a problem for me, I don't have any of that Time-of-Isolation baggage about marrying a virgin, that would be hypocritical, after all. Especially for a temporary-though-legal marriage. Easier the other way around anyway, really." He paused again. "Contraceptive implant?"

"Also since age fifteen," she assured him.

"Ah." He smiled beatifically, and closed in for a kiss.

It was a good kiss, quite as good as her dream or better. She snaked her fingers up between them to deal with his first button. The flattering uniform seemed to have rather a lot of them. For the first time, his hand strayed below her shoulders, in a tentative, reverent touch; good, he wasn't going to be grabby.

"So what happened when you were fifteen?" she asked, during their next break for air. "Was it a positive experience?"

This surprised a laugh from him, and a look of fond reminiscence. "I was a desperately randy adolescent—almost any experience would have seemed positive, but yes, I guess it was. She was one of the girl grooms at my great-uncle's stables down at the long lake, a summer fling at a summer place, pretty damned idyllic, really. I thought I seduced her, but in retrospect, I realize she seduced me. Older woman, y'know—she was nineteen. Dear God, but I was a clumsy young lout. But fortunately, or maybe it was mercifully, she didn't trample on my young ego. Though she would probably have had to gallop one of the dressage horses across it to make a dent, I was so chuffed with myself."

Tej laughed at his laughter, pleased for his covertly tender former self.

A finger ran lightly over her cheekbone, tracing its curves. He started to speak, shook his head, but then, as if he could not help himself, asked, "And you? I hope you weren't afflicted with a clumsy and self-absorbed young lout."

"By no means. The Baronne wanted to make sure we knew what we were about—me and my siblings and the Jewels. So she imported an eminent team of licensed practical sexuality therapists from the Betan Orb for us, for erotic arts training. A man, a woman, and a hermaphrodite. They stayed two years—I was so sorry when they went back home. It was the only thing I was ever better at than my sisters."

The hand stopped. He made a weird little noise down in his throat that she was completely unable to interpret. "I've never been to the Orb," he said at last, in a faraway voice. "My cousin Miles has been there, though he won't talk about it. Mark and

Kareen have been there. Hell, even Commodore Kou and Madame Drou have been there..."

"Well, I've never been there, either," she said. "Except by proxy, I suppose. But I did like the arts. They meshed well with my perception drills. It was like dance, in a way. For a little while, you live in your body, in the now, not all up in your head, all torn between the past and the future and missing the moment."

That gentle hint brought him back to the now; the hand began to move again.

"I had two allowed suitors after that," she went on. "But they didn't work out. There's another fortunately-in-retrospect for you."

"Allowed suitors? I don't know what—is that a Jacksonian term?"

"You don't have allowed suitors on Barrayar?" she asked. He shook his head. She couldn't say she was surprised, merely surprised at his ignorance. "It's for when one is considering some sort of House alliance by marriage. Try before you buy, and I'm glad I did. The first was plainly far more interested in House politics than in me. When I told him that in that case maybe he should go to bed with my father, instead, he wasn't too pleased. And nor was I. The other...I don't know. There was nothing *wrong* with him, I just didn't like the way he smelled."

"Did he...not bathe?" Ivan Xav's arm made an abortive jerk, as if he thought, but then thought better, of trying to sniff his own armpit.

"No, he was perfectly hygienic. Just not, I don't know...compatible. The Baronne suggested later that maybe our immune systems were too similar, but that didn't seem quite right to me. I thought he was just boring."

"Oh," said Ivan Xav.

She took the opportunity of his distraction to unwrap his shirt a few more buttons. Ah, nice chest hair. Not too much, not too little, a fine masculine dusting. The dark color made a pleasing aesthetic contrast with his pale skin, and she made sure to savor it. One should *notice* one's partner's gifts, and let them know one was pleased, or so her erotic arts training had emphasized. She curled a bit of hair over her finger, in signal of appreciation, and danced her fingertips down his torso.

The bunk room door slid open partway, and he flinched at the slight noise. Rish's voice floated out. "Shower's yours. I'm going to *sleep* now, so close *both* doors between when you're done, eh?" The door slid shut, firmly.

"Rish has very sensitive hearing," said Tej, "but she sleeps like a brick."

"Ah," said Ivan Xav, faintly. "Well. It's been a long day, perhaps I'd better hit the lav—uh, unless you'd like first crack?"

"Or we could share the shower..." Her fingers twirled some more.

He shook his head in regret. "Not this one. It's only a sonic, and two people wouldn't fit." He brightened. "But when we get back to my place in Vorbarr Sultana, I know that, um...another time?"

They should have taken advantage of the amenities back in his Solstice flat, but how were they to have known? Timing. The best chances of life all ran afoul of timing.

He kissed her again, then peeled himself away, lips last.

When they rendezvoused again in the bed, most of the unwrapping was already done, to Tej's mild regret, but perhaps there would be other occasions. She slid between the sheets he had warmed. Clean sheets, she noticed in appreciation, a thoughtful touch from the busy batman, at a guess. Ivan Xav rolled over, and up on one elbow, his hand hovering uncertainly over her, as if he didn't know where to begin.

She smiled up at him. "Are you *shy*, Ivan Xav?"

"No!" he denied indignantly. "It's just...I've never made love to a wife, before. I mean, to my wife. A wife of my own. Not having had one. I don't know how a few words in a groat circle can make what should be familiar feel very strange all of a sudden. Power of suggestion or something."

She rolled up on her own elbow, to free a hand to reach his face, trace the bones beneath the skin. Good bones. Her body shifted with the motion, and then he wasn't looking deep into her eyes anymore, but he was looking, pupils wide and black. Noticing gifts with due reverence needn't always take the form of speech, she was reminded.

"I always kept it light, y'know?" he gasped.

"I can do light," she said, leaning in. "My name *means* light."

He leaned to meet her. "So...so illuminate me," he breathed, and then there was much less talking.

The admiral's batman brought breakfast on a trolley—not intending it to be indolently consumed in bed, Ivan suspected, but rather to make sure Ivan was out of his in a timely fashion. The military servant knocked politely on both bedroom doors and set up the meal in the sitting room, effacing himself promptly as soon, Ivan also suspected, as he'd ascertained who had slept with whom last night, the better to report that intelligence back to their mutual boss. Desplains had very obviously left it up to Ivan and his guests to sort themselves out, but he had to be curious as to the results.

Ivan felt... chipper, he decided, was a good word. Remarkably chipper. He put himself together in immaculate military order, waved to Rish, who was blearily sucking tea, kissed *his wife* goodbye—make that, *his beautiful bed-rumpled exquisitely edible wife*, who, to cap his enchantment, did not appear to be chatty in the mornings—and chippered off to work, approximately twelve steps down the corridor to Desplains's onboard office, adjoining the ship's compact tactics room.

Desplains was there before him, not unexpectedly—the admiral found the constraints of jump travel minus combat boring, and, unless Madame Desplains was along, worked longer shifts to fill the time. Since this often resulted in his generating yet more things for his subordinates to do, it was one of Ivan's duties not mentioned in the manual to make sure he didn't extend those hours indefinitely. But this shift, Ivan felt ready to wrestle a *thousand* snakes. He greeted the admiral with a snappy salute and a "Good morning, sir!" and fell to.

Desplains merely raised a brow; they slid at once into the practiced routine, Ivan triaging the messages coming in semi-continuously over secured tightbeam, shooting notes back and forth, the occasional spoken query or order, returning memos, messages, and orders in a steady stream back to Komarr Operations or ahead to Ops HQ in Vorbarr Sultana, still five flight-days away. As Ivan had anticipated, the uncovering of the theft and smuggling ring had generated a load of new traffic, though not yet the interesting explosions that would no doubt ensue when word had finally made it all the way to Commodore Jole's Sergyar Command and back.

"Ivan?" said Desplains, about an hour into this.

"Sir?"

"Stop whistling. You sound like an air leak."

"Sorry, sir. Didn't realize I was doing that."

"So I eventually concluded."

When the first wormhole jump came up, Ivan took a break to warn the ladies, which was when he discovered that both were susceptible to jump-sickness, Rish far more than Tej. He then pulled off the world's easiest heroics by popping to the infirmary and collecting jump medication—the admiral's ship carried the *good* stuff—and hand-delivering it, though Tej had to forcibly excavate the whimpering Rish from her bedding to administer her dose. "Five jumps in five days, why did I agree to this?" she moaned. But within twenty minutes she was sitting up blinking in agreeable surprise, reconciled once more with her inner ears, her stomach, her vision, and, apparently, her hearing—unpleasant auditory hallucinations from jump sickness were a new one to Ivan. All he ever experienced was a brief twinge of nausea and having everything appear to turn green, requiring him to remember to use caution in interpreting indicator lights for about a minute.

He returned to work, intensely aware that mere meters away, a pocket paradise awaited.

At the end of the shift, Desplains cordially invited Ivan and his female entourage to join him for dinner, which was laid on privately, just the four of them, in the little observation lounge. While ship food was not elaborate—Desplains was an indifferent gourmet—Ivan detected the hand of his loyal crew in fresh produce picked up before they'd left Komarr, and Ivan himself had long ago made sure that the admiral's all-Barrayaran wines were something to be proud of. And the batman's service was impeccable.

Observation lounge proved an apt description, as Ivan quickly became aware that Desplains was using the opportunity to study Ivan's new bride and her companion. Well, evaluating personnel was one of the man's jobs, after all. Tej did quite well, Ivan thought. It occurred to him that a Jacksonian Great House might be not-dissimilar to a District count's household, with its demands for the regular entertainment of assorted business associates and odder guests, and a lot of potentially hazardous politics going on under the table. She certainly had the how-to-make-small-talk and which-fork-to-use down smoothly.

Desplains drew her out on her recent flight, avoiding the most distressing parts because this was, after all, dinner. A few of her stories were unconsciously hair-raising, but mostly they were neutral-to-opaque. Morozov might have done some groundwork, there, unconsciously supplying her with clues of what to say to Barrayarans, and she hadn't missed the turns. Rish, more wary, spoke less.

In any case, Desplains seemed to have enjoyed the diversion and the company, for the invitation was repeated on succeeding evenings, with various of the ship's crew gradually added in as shifts permitted—the captain, the off-duty pilots, the chief engineer, and Desplains's physician, because the admiral traveled with his own as per Service regs. But by whatever mercy, Desplains did not let the meals stretch too far into the night, for which Ivan was intensely grateful.

During the dayshift hours when Ivan was closeted with Desplains, Tej seemed to be reasonably content reading and watching vids, or primping, or playing games with Rish. The crew of *JP-9* were among the more sophisticated fellows the Service could supply, and any comments they had to make on Rish's boggling physical appearance they at least kept out of her keen hearing. Rish made heavy use of the exercise room, first alarming and then impressing some of the crewmen who shared it. She somehow discovered three more addicts of Komarran holovid dramas, and ganged up with them during their off-duty time to obtain fresh episodes snuck in during slack periods in the tightbeaming.

At one of Admiral Desplains's suggestions, Tej also discovered the onboard language tutoring programs, and dipped into the Barrayaran dialects of Russian, French, and Greek, none of which she claimed to have been taught before. Or plunged into, Ivan thought, when he ducked his head in to check her progress. So far from a trudge, she seemed to find the task tolerably amusing.

"Oh, *languages* aren't work," she explained cheerily. "They're a game. Now, economics, *that's* boring." She made a face at some pedagogical memory Ivan couldn't guess at.

For almost the first time, Ivan saw a glimpse in her of her haut genetic heritage, not only in the scary speed of her acquisition, but the purity of her accent, as she wandered around the ship to find bemused bilingual crewmen to practice upon. Her Komarran accent had certainly fooled him, and presumably the Komarrans as well. No question, she had a keen ear, and he wondered if she possessed perfect pitch, too, like a certain part-ghem Barrayaran he knew.

The off-shifts arranged themselves, though Ivan was beginning to think that even 26.7 hours was too short for a day, or rather, for a night.

The first snake in Ivan's garden raised its head briefly on the fourth day out. He'd forwarded a memo to Desplains's comconsole from General Allegre, Chief of ImpSec, marked *Personal, Eyes Only*. A few minutes later, Desplains looked up and remarked mildly, "Ivan—you *have* messaged home with an account of your adventures, have you not?"

"No reason to, sir. I mean, you know all about it. And my mother stopped asking about my girlfriends after I turned thirty."

"Vorpatril, I decline to get between you and your mother on any of your personal matters."

"As well you shouldn't have to, sir."

And that was, Ivan hoped, the end of that, but a number of hours later—they were, after all, getting closer to Barrayar—he fielded another *Eyes Only* message, from an all-too-familiar address. Though the temptation to make it vanish between his comconsole and Desplains's was *very strong*, Ivan nobly resisted it, a spasm of virtue that he suspected no one was going to appreciate.

About fifteen minutes later, Desplains remarked, "May I ask why, if Lady Alys Vorpatril wishes to know what is going on in her only son's life, she applies to me and not to you?"

Ivan blinked. "Experience?"

The silence from across the room took on a curious frigid quality, and Ivan looked up. "Oh. That was one of those, what d'you call it, rhetorical questions, was it, sir?"

"Yes."

Ivan cleared his throat. "You don't suppose ImpSec's been feeding her their reports, do you? That's bound to be confusing. I mean, look at the stuff they send *us*."

That last line almost worked. But, alas, not quite. Desplains's lips tightened. "As she works directly, every day, with General Allegre and his key staff on matters of the emperor's personal security, and lives with the man who ran ImpSec out of his head for decades before that, and you are her closest living relative, I would think you were in a better position to guess the answer to that question than I am, *Captain*."

"I'll, ah"—Ivan swallowed—"I'll just fire her off a little reassuring note right now, shall I, sir?"

"You do that."

Ivan hated that dead-level tone. Ugly unnerving thing, it was. Reminded him of his Uncle Aral in a mood.

But a written note, that was the ticket. A vid recording was nothing but an invitation to blather, with no living person in real-time opposite you to give a visual or verbal cue how you were getting on, or when to stop.

Ivan bent to his comconsole, setting the header and the security codes. Medium security would likely do. Enough to shield the message from the eyes of people who didn't need to know, not enough to make it sound like some sort of emergency.

Dear Mother.

He sat a moment, while lights blinked at him.

I don't know what ImpSec's been telling you, but actually, everything's all right. I seem to have accidentally got married, but it's only temporary. Don't change the headings on your cards. I will explain it all to you when we get there.

Love, Ivan.

He contemplated that for a moment, then went back and cut the middle lines as redundant. If he was going to explain it all when he got there, surely he needn't explain anything now.

I don't know what ImpSec's been telling you, but actually, everything's all right. I will explain it all to you when we get there.

That looked much better. Now a little short, though. A slow smile turned his lips. He bent and added: *P.S.—Byerly Vorrutyer has the whole story, if you can catch up with him.*

Actually, he didn't expect By to be back in Vorbarr Sultana till some days after he and Tej and Rish arrived, at the earliest. But what was that tale from Old Earth, about throwing one's fellow traveler out of the troika to distract the pursuing wolves? Yeah, like that, only more virtual, since Mamere wouldn't be able to lay her hands on By, either. But it *sounded* good.

He sent the message on its way, racing ahead of them at the speed of light.

Chapter Nine

For a capital that had hosted so many wars, both civil and interplanetary, Vorbarr Sultana seemed in remarkably good shape to Tej's eye. From her readings of Barrayaran history aboard the *JP-9*, she'd half expected to see gutted buildings with blackened timbers still smoking, bomb craters in the streets, and haunted, emaciated people scurrying like rats among the barricades. Instead, it was fully modernized, if not always fully modern, chock-a-block with galactic-standard transportation and architecture, with citizens—no, subjects, she corrected the term—out everywhere, looking busy and well-fed and alarmingly assertive. Terms like *lively* or even *vibrant* rose to Tej's mind. It was extremely disorienting.

All right, the traffic congestion was appalling. The auto-cab that they'd taken from the military shuttleport took twenty minutes to crawl across what Ivan Xav assured her was a very famous bridge, but it did give her and Rish time to stare up and down the river valley, from the high bluffs crowned with strange archaic castles lit, their guide promised, with pretty colored floodlights at night, to the hillsides crowded with fine houses hogging the views, to the level areas sprouting high-rises, universities, and medical complexes. They pulled up in front of a tall residential building quite close to the center of things, or at least to the military headquarters. The government complexes were closer to the Old Town, nearly lost in the center of the sprawl, but Ivan Xav explained that the historical area was all cleaned up these days, with some quite fine restaurants to be found if one knew how to avoid the backcountry tourists.

The building harboring Ivan Xav's flat reminded Tej very much of his place in Solstice, but the security was rather better; a human guard manned a reception desk, and Ivan Xav paused to have them scanned and entered as bona fide residents in the electronic database. The vidcams were unobtrusive but maintained a redundant overlap. He then whisked them up a lift tube and down a hallway, pulling out a remote to unlock a sliding, but not airsealed, door. "Home at last," he announced cheerfully, "and boy, am I glad of it."

His flat, too, reminded her of the place on Komarr—it lacked the separate entry hall, and the kitchen was bigger, but it boasted a balcony overlooking the street and a bit of the city. Not as high up. The rooms were larger, but they were much more cluttered, seeming closer and warmer somehow despite the stuffy smell of a place not occupied for the better part of a month.

"Ah, good," Ivan Xav went on, striding to the bedroom and tossing his duffle down on a broad bed. "The cleaning service has been in. We're all set."

Having worked for nearly three weeks straight, Ivan Xav was due several days of leave, Admiral Desplains had told Tej upon parting for his own leave and Madame Desplains, who'd been waiting at the shuttleport to pick him up. He trusted Captain Vorpatril would use the time well to organize his affairs, right, Ivan? Ivan Xav had nodded earnestly. Just what that meant, Tej had no idea.

They were here. *Now what?* In her exhaustion and stress on Komarr, she'd scarcely thought past *escape from. Escape to* hadn't even been on her mental horizon.

"Where do I sleep?" Rish inquired, wandering around and looking things over, her expression dubious.

"The sofa folds flat. It's not too bad." Ivan Xav stretched mightily and came back into his living room. "There are three people I'd most like to avoid in Vorbarr Sultana—m'mother, Miles, and

Gregor, in that order. Well, and Falco, but he's not so hard to dodge. He may well be up in the District. Though I suppose we'll have to chase him down in due course. But other than that, what would you two like to do here in the great metropolis?"

Tej looked down at her travel-rumpled garments. *Do?* That implied *Go out*, surely. "We only have these Komarran clothes. Are they all right to wear on Barrayar, or should we find something to help us blend in better?"

Rish extended a slim blue hand and snorted. She then raised her arms and did a slow backbend, kicking over to a handstand and then up to her feet again.

"You know what I mean," said Tej.

"Yeah, sure," said Ivan Xav. "M'mother gets her clothes custom designed, but my other gir—I've been dragged around to enough other places, I'll bet I could find you something nice. But Komarran styles are trendy, too—Empress Laisa, you know. Maybe you want to look around and see what you like, first, and then go picking."

A pleasant chime sounded.

"T' hell?" said Ivan Xav. "Nobody knows I'm back yet. Not expecting company..." He wandered to his door and carefully checked his security vid. It was far too early, Tej reminded herself, for her pursuers to have regrouped and caught up with her.

"Ah," muttered Ivan Xav. "Christos. Maybe... maybe we're not home just yet. Still caught in traffic, yeah."

"Come on, Lord Ivan, open up," came a man's voice, balanced on some cusp between amused and irritated. "I know you're in there. Or at least check the messages on your wristcom."

"M'mother's driver and errand boy," Ivan Xav told Tej and Rish over his shoulder. "And bodyguard—the man's a retired commando sergeant. Like my cousin's armsmen in all but title and oath. I swear he aspires to the role. Came in about four years ago—he didn't actually dandle me on his knee as a small boy, he just acts like it." He added reluctantly after a moment, "Good at his job, though."

Which one? Tej wondered.

Ivan Xav hit the pad to open the door.

The man looked big, gray-haired, and affable; for a change, his clothing did not resemble a uniform, just a neat shirt with wide sleeves, trousers with baggy cuffs tucked into short boots, and a sleeveless jacket with strange but attractive embroidery. But mostly, he looked big.

He eased around Ivan Xav, spotted Tej and Rish, and said, "Ah," in a satisfied tone. He came to a species of attention before her. "Good afternoon, Lady Vorpatril, Mademoiselle Lapis Lazuli. I'm Christos, Dowager Lady Vorpatril's driver. M'lady has charged me to convey you to a private dinner at her flat. And also to convey her earnest invitation for said dinner, should it unaccountably"— he cast a knife-flick of a glance at Ivan Xav—"have become lost somewhere on Lord Ivan's wristcom."

"Oh," said Tej, glaring a plea at Ivan Xav. What was she supposed to do?

"We just got off the shuttle," Ivan Xav began.

"Yeah, I know." Christos held up a viewer. "I brought a book for while you clean up. I'm to wait while you get ready. Because she didn't want me to miss you, if you took yourselves out or whatever." He smiled thinly, trod into the living room, and helped himself to a chair, settling back for a comfortable read. He added as he keyed it on and found his place, "Dress is casual, she said. Which only means, not formal."

"Trapped," Ivan Xav muttered. "Like rats..."

"What now?" Tej whispered to him.

He scratched his head and sighed, as if in defeat. "Well, we've all got to eat sometime. And at least the food'll be first-rate."

"If we get this over with *now*," murmured Rish, "we won't have to sit around anticipating it, you know. It does seem an inevitable meeting."

Ivan Xav grimaced, but Tej nodded. Even if Ivan Xav's mother was a horrible harridan in hysterics, as his actions seemed to imply, the news of the impending divorce ought to calm her down. It seemed unlikely that she would pull out a weapon and shoot her son's new bride over dinner, and besides, that would be redundant. She had only to stake Tej and Rish out where the enemy syndicate could find them, and the problem would be carried out of her ken without her having to lift, or tighten, a finger. Still...poisons? Rish could detect an astonishing number of these, if presented in food or drink. But—redundancy, again. Tej decided she was letting travel weariness and her nerves turn her thoughts just too strange. It would all be made plain soon enough.

A flurry of turns in the bath and dithering over their tiny

selection of garb resulted in Rish in black Komarran trousers and top, with a long-sleeved jacket and her head-shawl, Tej similarly attired in shades of cream, a little shabby but easy on her acute color sensitivity, and Ivan Xav in civilian clothes similar to what he'd been wearing the first time they'd met, but pulled clean from his capacious closet and not crumpled and smelly from his duffle. The driver shepherded them out with bland courtesy.

A large groundcar with a separate driver's compartment awaited them in the basement garage. As Christos handed them into the spacious back passenger compartment and started to close the silvered canopy, Ivan Xav held up a hand and said, "Uh, Christos—will Simon be there, do you know?"

"Of course, Lord Ivan." The canopy snapped closed, sealing them in.

Ivan Xav sat back with a wince, but for a few minutes Tej and Rish were too busy craning their necks and trying to see the city for Tej to pursue this new mystery. Nearing sunset of what seemed to be a late fall or early winter day, traffic was heavy, but the car was bearing generally upriver and uphill.

Ivan Xav cleared his throat. "I should probably explain Simon," he began, then stalled out, muttering, "No, there's no explaining Simon..."

"All right, who is Simon?" said Tej. If they were being flung into this headfirst... "Aren't you the one who was complaining to Byerly Vorrutyer about inadequate briefings?"

"How do I put this?" Ivan Xav rubbed his forehead. "Simon Illyan was Chief of Imperial Security for upwards of thirty years, from the War of Vordarian's Pretendership till about four or so years back, when he suffered, um, a sort of stroke. Neurological damage to his memory functions. Retired out on a medical, y'know."

Wait, *that* Simon Illyan? The same ImpSec boss whom Morozov, without a trace of irony, had dubbed the *legendary*?

"—and took up with m'mother. Why *then*, and not any time in the preceding three decades that they worked together, I have no idea, but there you are. So he's like *there*, all the time now. With her. Unless she's at the Residence working. They stick to each other like glue. It's pretty damned unnerving, I can tell you."

"Oh," said Rish, finally unraveling this. "They're *lovers*. Why didn't you say so?"

Ivan Xav tilted his head back and forth and made little flailing motions with his hands. "Haven't got used to it yet, I guess."

"After four years?" Tej blinked in new dismay. In other words, *the* Simon Illyan was almost-sort-of Ivan's stepfather and *he hadn't mentioned it till now*? "Does he really have a cyborg brain?"

"What?"

"That was the rumor in the Whole. Illyan, the Barrayaran Imperial Security chief with the cyborg brain." The whispers had suggested a sinister super-humanity. Or super-inhumanity.

"I wouldn't call it *that*. When he was a young ImpSec lieutenant—twenty-seven, I think he said, good grief, that's almost eight years younger than I am now..." Ivan Xav trailed off, then took up his thread again. "Anyway, then-Emperor Ezar sent him all the way to Illyrica, a trip that took months, to be fitted with an experimental eidetic-memory chip. Which was kind of a bust—nine out of ten of the subjects came down with some sort of chip-induced schizophrenia, and the project was canned. Illyan was a tenth man. So ever after that he had to cope with two memories, the perfect one off his chip, and his original organic one. Ezar, of course, died, and Illyan had to find his own way—he became one of the Regent's key men around the time of the Pretendership."

"So, so he had a stroke, and..." Tej puzzled through all this spate of belated information. "It did something to this chip?"

Ivan Xav cleared his throat. "Actually, it was the other way around. The chip broke down. Had to be surgically removed. But Illyan's brain had sort of, it's hard to describe—even harder to live through, I guess—rerouted itself around the chip in the, what, almost thirty-five years that he had it. When it was so abruptly yanked out, it was really hard for him to readjust.

"So the thing about Simon is," Ivan Xav forged on, "the thing about Simon is, he used to have this terrifying total recall, but now he sometimes doesn't track. He's pretty quiet, so you're not always sure what's going on in his head, not that you ever were. So, um...make allowances, huh?"

He was—Tej tried to sort it out—he was anxious for his mother's lover's dignity, then? And not just for how it reflected on his mother, it seemed. He seemed anxious for Simon Illyan in his own right. That was...unexpected.

And Illyan was now her...stepfather-in-law? Or would he see her that way? It was unclear whether he and Ivan Xav were close. But it seemed that the legend was in some sort of medical eclipse. Well, old people. It was said Barrayarans aged faster than galactics.

It was all very curious. If the looming Christos were to offer them escape from their date with fate right now, she wasn't sure that she would take him up on it.

They arrived at length at another tallish residential tower, this one high on the river ridge and so commanding an even better view. "Is this where you grew up?" Tej inquired, as they entered yet another underground garage.

"No, m'mother moved here recently. She has the top two floors. She used to live in an older building much closer to the Imperial Residence. That was where I grew up as much as anywhere, I guess."

"Nice digs," murmured Rish as they rose in a transparent lift tube through level after level of elegantly appointed foyers. "Are higher floors more expensive?"

"Dunno. She owns the building, so it's not like she pays the rent." He added after a moment, "She still owns t'old one, too." And, after another, "And mine. Has a business manager to look after 'em all."

Tej was beginning to wonder if Lady Alys Vorpatril qualified as a House Minor in her own right. And then they were crossing out of the tube into another foyer, and escorted by Christos through a pair of sleek doors clad in fine wood marquetry to a hushed hallway graced with mirrors and fresh flowers. And then into a broad living room backed by wide glass walls taking in a sweeping panorama of the capital, with the sun going down and the dusk rising to turn the city lights to jewels on velvet for as far as the eye could see, under a cloud-banded sky.

In two comfortable-looking armchairs angled close together at the room's far corner sat a man and a woman; both rose and advanced as Christos announced, "Milady, sir; Lord Ivan Vorpatril, Lady Tej Vorpatril, Mademoiselle Lapis Lazuli," and bowed himself out, delivering his captives and escaping in the same smooth movement.

Tej scrambled to recognize the couple from assorted vid scans she'd recently seen, although, as always, people in person were subtly different from their graphic representations—in scent, in sound, in sheer palpability. And these people were *palpable.*

Lady Alys was a woman past youth and into an indeterminate age one might dub *dignified*, but certainly not old; she moved with ease, and the streak of silver in her bound-back hair seemed to rest there as mere tasteful decoration. Dark brown eyes like Ivan Xav's, large in her pale, oval face; fine skin well-cared-for. A long-sleeved, dark red dress with a hem at her mid-calf was topped by a darker loose sleeveless vest of equal length, the colors appropriate to her skin tones, her surroundings, and the season.

Simon Illyan was dressed not unlike the driver, except in shades of sober cream and charcoal. He was barely taller than Lady Alys, who was surely of no more than average height for a Barrayaran woman. Thinning brown hair was succumbing to a tide of gray rising around the sides. Scans she'd seen of him from earlier in his career, always in the background of some Imperial event—and if she'd *known*, she'd have paid him more attention—had seemed to convey a sharp tension in his posture and grim expression. He smiled at her now with an amiable vagueness that went well with the slight pudge around his middle, but sat oddly with his reputation.

Lady Alys cast a look at her son that seemed to say, *I'll deal with you later*, and turned to take the startled Tej's hands in cool, slim fingers.

"Lady Tej," she said, looking her guest in the eye as if...searching? "Welcome to my home. Congratulations on your marriage. And, I am so very sorry for your late losses."

The last words floored Tej. *No one* had offered her condolences for the slaughter of her family, not one person in all the long months of their erratic flight from the Whole to here. Granted, the only people who'd known who she was were the ones trying to add her to the tally. *But still, but still, but still.* She gulped, breathless and trembling. Managed a constricted, "Thank you," blinking back the blur in her eyes. Ivan Xav looked at her in concern.

With a peculiar little nod, Lady Alys squeezed her hands and released them. Ivan Xav moved in to slip an arm around her shoulders and give her an uncertain hug.

"And you too, Lapis Lazuli," Lady Alys continued, turning to Rish, but offering more of a handshake. "Or do you prefer Rish?"

"I prefer Rish," said Rish. "Lapis Lazuli has always been more of a stage name."

"May I make you both known to my long-time friend, Simon Illyan."

Illyan, too, shook their hands in turn, his clasp firm and dry. He lingered to look Tej up and down; his smile broadened slightly. But he made no remark.

"Please, won't you come sit down." Lady Alys made a graceful wave toward the seats in a close conversational grouping at the room's far end. Ivan Xav grabbed Tej's hand and kept her by him, aiming them onto the two-person sofa; Lady Alys and Illyan took their former chairs, and Rish perched on a rather antique-looking carved chair with new silk upholstery. The whole room, Tej noted, was put together with a quiet, firm taste, a mixture of the old and new that complemented rather than clashed, and, oh blessings, with an impeccable eye for color. Well, Rish stood out a little.

Lady Alys touched a jeweled pin on her vest, and in a moment a staidly dressed, middle-aged woman servant appeared trundling a sort of drinks trolley. "May we offer you an apéritif? Or there are teas."

Tej, mind still swimming, rather blindly selected a Barrayaran wine she recognized from Admiral Desplains's table, and Rish chose some native cordial, apparently for the strange name; the others were handed what were apparently their usual tipples without query by the servant. The glasses were small and finely wrought, inviting appreciation, not inebriation. The servant trundled away as discreetly as she'd entered.

Lady Alys took a sip and turned to Rish—to give Tej time to recover herself? "Someone was kind enough to forward me a short vid of one of your performances with your fellow Jewels. Very impressive. I understand your emigration was forced upon you, but do you have plans or hopes for continuing your art in a new venue?"

Rish grimaced. "No plans, certainly. Performance arts do not mesh well with hiding for one's life. Success requires—and generates—fame, not obscurity."

Lady Alys nodded understanding. "Teaching or choreography... no, I suppose the same difficulty would arise."

Illyan rubbed his chin, and offered, "Could you change your appearance? Cosmetic alterations to blend with the target population?"

A blue hand tightened on a black-clad knee. "That would be repugnant to me. And...when I started to dance, people would know who I was anyway."

He gave a conceding nod, falling back into his listening quiet.

Tej decided she'd calmed enough that her voice wouldn't crack. She set down her glass, gripped Ivan Xav's hand for courage, and said, "Lady Alys, you should know right away that you needn't worry about the marriage. Ivan Xav and I will be getting a divorce."

Ivan Xav freed his arm only to put it around her shoulders, hugging her in tight. He endorsed this: "That's right, Mamere. Just as soon as I can catch up with Count Falco, that is."

Lady Alys tilted her head and stared at them. "Has my son proved such an unsatisfactory husband in a mere week? Surely you should give him a longer chance."

"Oh, no, no!" said Tej, hurrying to correct this strange misconception. "I think Ivan Xav would make a wonderful husband!"

"So I had always hoped," murmured Lady Alys, "and yet, somehow, it seemed never to be..."

Ivan Xav squirmed slightly, inching closer to Tej, or trying to. There weren't any inches left.

Tej said sturdily, "He has so very many good qualities. He's brave, he's kind, he's smart, he has excellent manners, and he thinks quickly in emergencies." When pressed hard enough, anyway. "Very good-looking, too, of course." She probably ought not to add *good in bed* here; Barrayarans seemed to have funny notions about sex, which she didn't quite understand yet. "And, um..." What was that unusual word Desplains had used? "Chivalrous, too, which is why he rescued us and brought us here, but really, he owes me nothing."

Lady Alys pressed a finger to her lips. "That is not what those words in the groat circle say, however. Assuming Ivan managed to remember the right ones."

"I did," asserted Ivan Xav indignantly. "And anyway, I shouldn't think you would be in such a tearing hurry to become the *Dowager* Lady Vorpatril."

"My dear and only child, how did you come by that misapprehension? I've longed for it any time these past ten years. And anyway, if the title comes to seem too dreadfully aging, I now have other resources to correct the problem." She glanced at Simon Illyan, who raised his brows and smiled back. Very private smiles that made Tej feel an intruder, though she wasn't sure on what.

"So," Lady Alys went on, "it is to be a marriage of convenience, then?"

Illyan put in, "Or inconvenience," and pressed a concealing hand across his jaw. His eyes were alight, betraying his upward lip-twitch nonetheless.

"The inconvenience," said Lady Alys, "would seem to reside not in the marriage, but in this Jacksonian syndicate that pursues the girls. About which, I confess, I understand very little as yet. But I feel constrained to point out to you, Ivan—just in case you have overlooked it—that there is no point in your catching up with Falco for a divorce until you have figured out what happens to Tej and her companion after the protection of your name and position is removed. You dragged them here to Barrayar, after all."

"I, uh...hadn't got that far yet," Ivan Xav admitted.

Lady Alys turned to Tej, and asked seriously, "Do you know what you would want?"

It came to Tej then, belatedly, that Lady Alys had just spent much of the prior conversation slowly, gently, and thoroughly roasting her son. And that she wasn't at *all* the person Tej had been led to expect. She allowed herself a moment of crossness— she would have *words* with Ivan Xav about that, later. But right now, she needed to give Lady Alys's serious question the serious attention it deserved.

"We had a place we were planning to go—not here on Barrayar, not in the Imperium, in fact. But we can only go there if we are absolutely certain that we've broken our trail in a way that the Prestene syndicate can't pick up again. Otherwise, it's... it would be worse than getting caught ourselves."

"That would actually come to the same thing," Rish pointed out. "Once they have us, they have..." A blue hand made an ambiguous, if fluid, wave.

Tej nodded grimly. "That was why the balcony, in the end."

"So you protect another," said Illyan, leaning back and tenting his hands together. "One very dear to you." He blinked vaguely. "Must be the missing brother, what's-his-name."

Tej gasped and turned in alarm to Ivan Xav.

He shrugged, and muttered out of the corner of his mouth, "I said he'd lost his memory, not his wits."

"The point was mentioned in Morozov's report," said Illyan, sounding apologetic. "I only read it this morning. It hasn't had time to go fuzzy yet." He took up and emptied his glass, appearing to study the curious absence of his drink before setting it down again. "From the direction and duration of your travel, I would posit that he's hiding on Escobar, with remoter possibilities being Beta Colony, Kibou-daini, or Tau Ceti. Not farther."

Rish had jerked upright in her chair. But there was nowhere to bolt to. Nothing to attack. Or to defend against, either.

"In which case," Illyan continued, "one obvious solution presents itself. The ladies might be conveyed to Escobar as unlisted supercargo in a routine government fast courier, and discreetly deposited downside by the same means by which we used to insert agents. Or perhaps still do; I don't suppose the procedures have changed all that much. The break in the trail from here, at least, would be clean, as our couriers go in all possible directions. And no record of your landing on Escobar, either."

Rish's mouth had fallen open; she leaned forward like a woman contemplating a bakery case. Tej's heart was beating faster. She asked, "Could it really be done?"

"Ivan would no doubt have to call in some favors," said Illyan, a bit blandly.

"Oh, yes, please!" said Rish.

"Er," said Ivan Xav, glancing at Tej. "Is that what you really want?"

Tej sank back in new hesitation. No gifts came without price tags. "What would you want in return for this deal?" She looked in worry at Illyan, at Lady Alys. At Ivan Xav.

Lady Alys finished her drink. "I should have to think about that."

Ivan Xav scratched his nose, frowned at Illyan. "Could you assist me, sir?"

Illyan replied airily, "Oh, I think that's a problem you can solve on your own, Ivan. You know the same go-to men as I do."

Ivan Xav's brow wrinkled. He turned to Tej and said, rather plaintively, "But you just got here. Don't you want to look around a little before running off again—forever?"

"I hardly know," said Tej, wishing she had a net to catch her spinning wits.

Lady Alys touched her brooch again. "Indeed. Ivan's aunt has often remarked on the inadvisability of making decisions on an empty stomach. Shall we dine?"

As she rose, and everyone else followed suit, the smiling woman servant spread wide another pair of marquetry doors at the end of the room, revealing a dining chamber with places for five ready and waiting. Lady Alys ushered them all through.

Ivan Xav had not lied; his mother set a first-rate table. The conversation became general as the discreet server brought course after course, with wines to complement. Rish made no signals regarding subtle poisons in the soup or salad, fish or vat-meat; instead, she bore the blissful smile of a trained aesthete given, for a change, no penance to endure in the name of good manners. It was all as well-choreographed as a dance. If Ivan's mother fed her lover like this all the time, it was no wonder he never left.

"Have you lived here long, sir?" Tej asked Illyan, when a lull in the talk presented an opportunity.

"Say rather, I visit here frequently. I keep my old apartment as my official address, and stay there often enough to make it plausible. And for my mail—letter bombs and such—although I am officially retired, ImpSec still provides a courtesy squad to open it." He smiled quite as if this were not a disconcerting remark. He added a little regretfully, "Just because I have forgotten so many old enemies does not mean they have forgotten me. We set it about that I am more addled than I am, to appease them. Please feel free to add to that public impression, should the subject come up."

"I don't find you addled at all, sir," said Tej, quite sincerely.

"Ah, but you should have met me before the—no, perhaps you should not have. It's far better this way, I assure you."

Both Ivan and his mother shared an unreadable look at this, but it was gone from their faces before Illyan glanced up again from his plate. For all his silences, the man was about as self-effacing as a neutron star; light itself seemed to bend around him.

After dinner, Lady Alys kindly showed Tej and Rish around her more-than-flat, or at least the top floor. Ivan Xav slouched after, his hands in his pockets. The floor below was given over to personal apartments allotted to her servants, of whom she kept four: a cook, a scullion-and-housemaid, who was also the server they'd seen, a dresser-cum-personal secretary, and the driver, Christos. Two rooms she passed over in the tour; Ivan explained in a behind-the-hand whisper that they were Illyan's bedroom and study. They stepped out briefly to a chilly roof garden, designed,

Lady Alys told them proudly, by Lady Ekaterin Vorkosigan, who appeared to be famous for such things. It was past the season for lingering there, though a few late-blooming fall plants still gave up delicate scents, but Tej could see how one might want to, on warmer days or nights. The view was even better than the one from the living room below.

"I do appreciate your welcome," said Tej to Lady Alys, as they paused at the parapet to take in one last look at the light-draped river valley. "I feel so much better about it all now. I wasn't sure what to expect or what to do about—well, anything. I'd never planned to visit Barrayar."

Lady Alys smiled into the dark. "I considered leaving the time and place of your presentation up to Ivan, as a sort of test. Then I considered all the many ways that scenario could go so wrong, and changed my mind."

"Hey," said Ivan Xav, but not very loudly.

"There were two principal possibilities on the table." Lady Alys turned to face Tej. Laying out her cards at last? "First, was that you were an adventuress who had somehow succeeded in entrapping Ivan, and he should be rescued from you as expeditiously as possible. Maybe. After I'd found out how you did it, for future reference. Or possibly he should be allowed to extricate himself from the consequences of his own folly, for a life lesson. I was having trouble deciding which—"

Another inarticulate noise of protest from her son.

Ignoring it, she went on, "But in any case, both Morozov's and Simon's evaluations put that as a low probability. The second main hypothesis was that you were exactly as you appeared to be, the unwitting victim of one of Ivan's less-well-thought-out inspirations, and needed to be rescued from him. My ImpSec consultants were both united in setting that as a high probability." She added after a contemplative moment, "ImpSec men never fail to hedge their bets, I'm afraid. It's most annoying, when one must make decisions based on their reports."

"If anyone needs any rescuing around here, Mamere, I'm perfectly capable of doing it," said Ivan Xav, sounding annoyed.

"So I hope, love. So I hope."

When, at length, they took their departure in the mirrored hallway, where Christos again waited to convey them to the groundcar, Ivan Xav bent and gave his Mamere a rather formal peck on the cheek, which seemed to make her smile despite herself. He really was much taller than her, Tej realized.

Lady Alys turned to Tej with a thoughtful look. "As he may or may not have told you, Ivan's birthday is coming up next week. We always begin it with a little private ceremony, very early in the morning. I hope that he will decide to invite you."

The startled and bemused glances Lady Alys won from both the men for this were the most mystifying yet.

"Uh . . . sure," said Ivan, sounding oddly unsure. "G'night, Mamere. Simon, sir."

He nodded to Illyan, and ushered Tej and Rish out to the foyer. The natural wood inlay on the wide doors that closed behind them made not an abstract jumble, but a mosaic picture, Tej realized in a last look back. It portrayed a dense woodland, with horses and riders half-hidden, crossing through the trees. Her eye had not parsed it at all, her first time through.

In the back of the groundcar, Ivan ran his fingers through his scalp in a harried swipe and moaned, "She makes me crazy." Still, Tej and Rish seemed to have survived the daunting visit, as had he. That it was better to have behind them . . . he was not yet sure.

"You mean Lady Vorpatril?" said Tej. She gave Ivan a peeved poke in the arm. "She was not at *all* like what you led me to believe. From the way you talked, I thought there would be screaming and weeping and carrying on, at the very least. But she's very practical." She added after a moment, "And kind. I didn't expect kind."

"Oh, yeah," said Ivan. "After thirty years of high Vor diplomacy and a few wars, of course she has the chops. This is a woman who knows how to get her way."

Tej cast him a funny look. "Not always, it seems like."

Rish turned her head from a long, thoughtful stare out the canopy to observe, "She reminds me of the Baronne."

"A little, yes," said Tej, with an introspective frown. "Not as tightly focused."

"She's mellowed a lot since Simon arrived in her life," Ivan admitted. "And vice versa, though his was rather imposed upon him by his, um, brain injury." Ivan was put uncomfortably in mind of Tej's alarming response to his mother's first greeting. Tej seemed such a sunny personality, much of the time—these flashes of dark were like a crack in the sky, shocking and wrong. Reminding him that the daylight was the illusion, the scattering of light by the atmosphere, and the endless night was the permanent default behind it all. And *God* that was a weird and morbid thought, but his mother did make him crazy. "Did you, um, love your mother? The Baronne?"

Tej hesitated, her brows lowering. When she spoke, it was slowly, as if she had to grope for truth in a thicket of thorny memories. "I admired her very much. We didn't always get along. Actually, we clashed a lot. She said I wasn't working up to my full potential. Not like my sisters."

"Ah," said Ivan, wisely. "That does sound all too familiar."

Tej looked across at him in surprise. "But you were an only child!"

"Not...exactly. I always had my cousin Miles. And Gregor for an elder brother, but of course it was understood he was in a class by himself." He added after a reflective moment, "All by himself, poor sod."

"So your cousin Miles was like a brother to you?" asked Rish. Glints from her gold earrings flickered in the shadowy compartment as her head tilted.

"Miles...is really hard to explain. He was—is—smart."

"*You're* smart," said Tej, in a tone of indignant protest.

Ivan's heart nearly melted, but he sighed. "Yeah, but Miles was...the thing is, he was afflicted with a severe birth injury. He grew up pretty much crippled, so he poured all his frustrated energy into his intellect. Since the Vorkosigan family motto might as well be, *Anything worth achieving is worth overachieving*, the effect was pretty frightening. And it worked for him, so he did it some more."

"Very like the Baronne," murmured Rish.

Tej said slowly, "Yes...my mother loved being the Baronne, you see. Building the House was her passion. And in her way, I suppose, she loved us, and naturally wanted us to have this great thing she'd found, too. Except...I wasn't her. It was like...if she could just fix me into being her, then she could shower me with the gifts she so valued."

Ivan winced. "Ah." It was kind of appalling, how little trouble he had following that whole line of reasoning. On both sides. Not sure what to say, he slipped an arm around Tej and hugged her in. Warm and soft, why didn't anyone value warm and soft...?

"So will we get to meet your cousin?" asked Rish. Or, possibly, prodded?

"Not sure. He's an Imperial Auditor now—that's sort of a high-level government troubleshooter—so he goes out of town at erratic intervals to find trouble to shoot. I should warn you, if we do go to Vorkosigan House, it's knee-deep in infants these days. Twins, speaking of overachieving. They offer to let you hold one as if it was some kind of *treat*." Ivan shuddered. "And they leak, and make the most horrible noises."

"I never had much to do with infants," said Tej. "Comes of being nearly the youngest, I guess."

"Yeah—only child, here," said Ivan.

"Whereas I," said Rish coolly, "was the baby-sitter." She leaned back and stretched her legs, propping her feet on the seat opposite, beyond Tej. "I expect we'll cope."

Chapter Ten

Tej was plainly distracted and unnerved by her new surroundings, but by diligent efforts, Ivan won back her full attention in bed that night, and a smile when he brought her coffee in the morning. He had not guessed that any of his morning practice placating bleary-eyed admirals would transfer, but that one did. His plans for a post-coffee rematch were thwarted, however, by a call from his mother informing him that she was sending Christos and her formidable dresser-cum-secretary to escort Tej and Rish on a hunting-and-gathering expedition for Barrayaran garb. Granted, the subject had come up last night, but he'd thought it was small talk.

"Is it safe to go out?" asked Rish, both dubiously and longingly. The building had a well-equipped exercise room on the second floor, but being immured inside was perhaps a little too much like being trapped aboard the *JP-9* all over again.

"Gotta be. Mamere and her people enjoy more attentive security than any Jacksonian House lordling could ever hope to buy. On account of what she's done for Illyan, y'know. ImpSec worships her, at least the old guard. And the newbies are all their daunted subordinates."

"I didn't notice the coverage, last night," said Tej.

"You wouldn't. And neither will anyone who attempts to stalk you, till it's too late. You should go," he told the women, wondering why he wasn't more relieved to be let off the hook as sartorial escort. "You won't get a better native guide, except maybe Mamere herself." Who had duties at the Residence this morning or else, she had implied, she would have undertaken the task personally.

The middle-aged and gimlet-eyed dresser expanded upon this. "Clothing is a cultural and social language," she intoned, when shepherding the women out. "And local dialects can be tricky for an outsider to interpret. We must make sure your dress says what you mean it to say, and not something unintended."

Tej and Rish, at least, looked very impressed. If they were like every other woman Ivan had known, he was certain to be treated to a fashion show afterward anyway. This was much easier than tagging along, as all he had to do was approve each garment with suitable compliments, instead of frantically trying to guess which choices they wanted him to endorse, with the distinct hazard of guessing wrong. Much more restful.

He sent them off with a clear conscience and turned to his strangely silent and empty flat. He had three weeks of personal correspondence and other chores to catch up on that had not been urgent enough to be tightbeamed after him to Komarr, which was most of it.

He was half an hour into these tasks when a call came in over his comconsole which, after a glance at the sender ID, he sent to voice delay. After another few moments, the display above his vid plate flickered and gave way to a smiling, or at least smirking, face he didn't especially want to deal with. Damned Imperial Auditor override...

"Hi, Miles." Ivan sighed, and waited. No point in stirring any waters not already roiling.

"Sorry for the interruption"—Miles did not look in the least sorry—"but I must not be behindhand in conveying my thanks for the extremely thoughtful gift you forwarded from Komarr. Ekaterin actually wondered if she should put flowers in it, next time you came over, but I suggested target practice. Or passing it along to the twins, which might be an even faster way to dispose of it. At which point the light dawned, and she looked very relieved."

"Hey, it took me half an hour to find that vase!" said Ivan in mock-indignation.

"Hidden in the back of the store, was it, lest it frighten away customers?"

Ivan's lips twitched. "Yep."

Miles leaned back, his smile stretching in an unsettling way—that is, if you knew Miles. "I also understand some very unexpected congratulations are in order."

"News gets around fast," Ivan grumped.

"I was in on it from the first day the reports started coming in. Your mother called *me* to ask me to explain it to her, as if *I* would know anything—I told her to apply to Allegre, which she did, apparently to more satisfactory effect."

"Yeah, well, that's not my fault," muttered Ivan.

Miles's brows rose, most annoyingly. "You married a woman you'd known barely a day, and it wasn't your fault?"

"Well, it wasn't! It was an accident. And anyway, it's only a temporary expedient. If you've read the ImpSec reports, you know why. She was in danger."

"I heard various recaps, from various people." Miles drummed his fingertips on his comconsole desk.

"My mother talk to you this morning?"

"No, not her. In any case, I have called to invite you to bring your blushing accident and her blue—she really is bright blue?"

Ivan nodded.

"—and her blue companion to Vorkosigan House this afternoon for a get-to-know-you Ma Kosti tea."

Ivan hesitated, concealing the small spurt of saliva that spontaneously appeared in his mouth at any reference to Miles's famous cook. Damned conditioning. "That's bribery."

"As an Imperial Auditor, I am only above taking bribes, not handing them out."

"You've never shown an interest in any of my girlfriends before."

"You've never *married* any of your girlfriends before, Ivan. And in any case, I'm off to Sergyar soon for what may be an extended stay, so I don't want to miss my chance."

"To roast me? You'll doubtless have others." *Get in line.*

"Ah..." Miles took in, and let out, a long breath. "Make that *requests and requires* your attendance. Someone else wants to meet her, in an informal setting. We figured my library would do. Doubling up on my mission planning at the same time."

Ivan paused, his heart sinking. "Oh."

"Sixteen-hundred sharp."

"Uh, right. Sharp."

"See you then." Miles cut the com in his best grandiose My-Lord-the-Imperial-Auditor-dismisses-you style.

There was really no call to whimper. But Ivan wanted to.

Tej sat in the passenger side of Ivan Xav's sporty two-seater groundcar, with Rish balanced awkwardly on her lap, and fumed in terror.

Gregor, he'd said. As if it might be just any Gregor off the street, and not, say, the *absolute ruler of three worlds*, as far above a Great House baron as a baron was above a gutter grubber. Mister Lord Ivan Xav Oh-I'm-not-anyone-important had led her astray, Tej swore, for the last time. And now she was being semi-forcibly carted off to meet Gregor, no, THE Gregor—oh, yeah, no, *he wants to meet you*—in about the most diametrical opposite of hide-and-be-sought-by-no-one as she could have imagined. No, she couldn't have imagined this. Tej felt as if she had laser targeters dancing all over her skin.

And the *Imperial Auditor Coz* was scarcely better. She'd barely had time to look up the definition of the title before having to get ready. The man had the power to order *summary executions*, for pity's sake.

At least she and Rish were dressed well for it. Lady Alys's expert had guided them to a semi-custom shop, the sort of place where one had a personal laser scan and then spent a happy hour poring over the vid catalog and experimenting with various virtual try-ons upon one's three-dimensional holovid replica, before selecting garments to be made up on-demand, to fit exactly, by computerized fabricators. The dresser had dubbed the results "casual," which Tej eventually realized simply meant not suitable for an Imperial function or ambassadorial ball. They had returned burdened with bags to Ivan Xav's flat, where the dresser had reported judiciously to the waiting husband, *The new Lady Vorpatril has an excellent eye for color.* Having experienced the dresser in action, Tej took that as no small compliment. And then Ivan Xav had dropped the news, or bomb, of where they were going next... Had Lady Alys known?

Ivan, with a glance aside at his stacked and glaring passengers, took the next corner with improved caution, and then slowed, thank the hovering fates. A tall stone wall topped with iron spikes sped by, and then he slowed some more, turning in to a short space in front of broad wrought-iron gates. A man in a strange brown uniform with silver embroidery on the collar and cuffs, flanked by a second in black, with silver frosting ditto, emerged from a kiosk and approached the groundcar. Ivan Xav raised the canopy, and they peered suspiciously in. "Ah. Lord Ivan."

Ivan Xav raised a hand in greeting. "And two guests, as per."

The man in black, unsmiling, aimed some sort of scanner at Tej and Rish, then nodded.

"You are expected." The man in brown and silver waved them on as the gates swung open.

A huge archaic-looking stone pile of a mansion—four stories high—rose above the Earth-import trees, almost bare of leaves in this turning season. Ivan drove in under a porte-cochère, parked, raised the canopy, and helped Rish and Tej extricate themselves. The dresser's tutorial on what styles a woman wore for what hours and occasions had been swift but thorough. The Barrayaran-style calf-length afternoon skirts were no more awkward to manage than Komarran loose trousers, Tej was pleased to discover; with some practice, they might even prove more comfortable. The faintest vibration from an invisible force screen shielding the house faded momentarily, carved wooden double doors swung wide, and yet another man in brown and silver motioned them through into a spacious, two-story-high entry hall. An elaborate wooden staircase with a polished banister swept down from a gallery above. Wide archways opened to the right and the left, with a lesser archway under the gallery straight ahead.

Rish stopped short; Tej nearly tripped over her. The hall was stunningly paved in a marvelous colored mosaic like a stone garden underfoot, wildly proliferating with plants and flowers, insects and small creatures peeking from the leaves. The stone-work was so fine it looked at first glance like a master's painting in oils. Tej half-expected the plants to crunch underfoot, giving up strange perfumes. The walls carried the theme skyward, with meticulously hand-painted vines and flowers madly twining, as if the living forest on the floor surged up to reach for the light.

Rish was riveted. "*Oh,*" she said. "I could dance the most amazing dance across *this...*"

A shrill squeal sounded from the right, and a man's light, amused voice, "'Ware escapee!"

Ivan Xav jerked and swung around. He muttered in alarm under his breath, "Oh, God, they're *moving on their own* now." From the archway, a stark naked boy-child not much over two feet high toddled determinedly, as fast as his little legs could carry him. He was pursued by an even more startling figure. The man swinging a cane who limped after the child was less than five feet tall, shockingly short for an adult Barrayaran male, which he obviously was. Dark hair neatly cut, a slightly oversized head set on a short neck, faintly lined face, hunched shoulders, fine white shirt, gray trousers and matching jacket—and if Tej had thought Alys and her Simon had borne a palpable presence, this man's authority filled the hall, drawing the eye away even from the astonishing floor and the happily shrieking child thumping across it.

The toddler stopped dead, staring up at the strangers. No, staring at Rish. "Ooh," he cooed, mouth falling open in flattering wonder.

"Ivan, grab Sasha," the short man ordered, a trifle out of breath.

Ivan Xav stepped forward and gingerly scooped up the child, holding him out well away from his body and handing him off as quickly as possible to the short man. The toddler squirmed like a large pink starfish, reaching out toward Rish and repeating "Ooh, ooh!"

The short man informed Ivan Xav, "Sasha has learned three new tricks this week: how to divest his diaper, how to get lost in Vorkosigan House, and how to outrun me. If only he would take up talking, like his sister, I'd dub him a proper little genius." He then, with difficulty, brought his wristcom to his lips around his unwieldy and resisting burden. "Ekaterin? Found him. Stand down your patrol. He broke cover in the dining room, but was cut off at the pass in the front hall."

"So where is his partner in crime?" asked Ivan Xav, bending to look warily around at floor level.

"Sleeping. They take it in shifts, you know, trying to wear us down. I think they're aiming for unconditional surrender and total world domination. But I can hire shifts too, hah!" He gave up attempting to hold the heavy wriggler and set him on the floor, where the child's attention was caught by a bug in the mosaic; he attempted several times to pick it up and put it in his mouth, without success, and made a moue of frustration.

A tall, breathless, dark-haired woman scuffed rapidly down

the staircase. She said to the short man, "How in the *world* did he manage to get down the stairs without breaking his neck?"

"Crawled backward, I believe. He's actually surprisingly cautious. I broke an arm and a leg on those same stairs, once. Well, sequentially. Different years."

"I remember the arm," muttered Ivan Xav. "Competitive banister-sliding."

The woman gathered up the boy, one arm firmly supporting his little bottom. They made a rather more proportional combination. "Hi, Ivan," she said, and raised her brows invitingly.

Ivan Xav broke out of his infant-induced paralysis, and said, "Miles, Ekaterin, may I make known to you my wife, Lady Tej, and her companion Rish. This is my cousin Miles and his wife Ekaterin, Lord and Lady Vorkosigan." He peered uneasily at the child. "And his heir, Lord Sasha."

"Ackle," Lord Sasha remarked gnomically, reaching up to dislodge a hank of his mother's sleeked-back hair and chew on it.

Lady Ekaterin smiled in distraction. "Welcome to Vorkosigan House, Tej, Rish. I'm so glad you could visit before we have to leave." She added aside to Ivan Xav, "I'm taking the twins to Sergyar to see their grandparents while Miles is about his affairs."

"Nikki, too?" asked Ivan Xav.

She nodded. "He's not too happy about having to do all the make-up work for school, but he's tremendously excited about the travel." She added over her shoulder to her husband. "Miles, why don't you take them on into the library, and I'll join you in a few minutes."

The burdened woman trudged back up the staircase, and Lord Vorkosigan gestured them to follow him through the archway to the left. On the far side of a large antechamber with walls covered in pale green silk, double doors painted white were swung open by an unseen hand. Their host ushered them into a long room lined with antique bookcases. Tej's station-bred eye was briefly shocked by the orange flicker of a fire, burning tamely in a white marble fireplace—no, not an emergency here, just décor. A pair of short sofas and some other chairs were grouped invitingly around the hearth. Upon one of the sofas, a lean, dark-haired, rather hatchet-faced man looked up from his viewer at their entry, stood, and waited with a grave smile. He was dressed in one of those Barrayaran faux-military suits, dark blue and very plain.

"Sire," said Ivan Xav, as they herded up.

"Hi, Ivan. But I'm doing Count Vorbarra today," said the man, his smile turning briefly saturnine. "It cuts down the circus by at least half."

"Right," said Ivan Xav. He was apparently growing introduction-fatigued at the most inopportune time, for he went on far too casually, "Gregor, my wife Tej, her friend Rish. I suppose you read the reports?"

"I had Allegre's précis. And I talked in person with your mother this morning, which was rather more informative." He turned to the women. "How do you do, Lady Vorpatril, Mademoiselle Rish. Welcome to Barrayar."

He said this in the exact same way that Lady Vorkosigan had said, *Welcome to Vorkosigan House.* It came to Tej that he was the one man here who was not a subject. Did that make him an object . . . ? He sat, apparently the signal for everyone else to do likewise. Ivan Xav gathered Tej to him and seized the other sofa, Lord Vorkosigan swung his cane out of the way and dropped into a smallish armchair, and Rish perched gingerly on a similar one.

Rish had to be madly trying to parse the many unfamiliar scents, of which the wood smoke was the strongest and strangest. There were two more men in the black uniforms standing statuelike in the room, one by a pair of glass doors at the far end, apparently leading outside, the other at the wall by their entry. They looked back over the two women like a pair of sleek guard dogs studying a couple of cats that had strayed onto their territory. As if they might grab them in their teeth and break their necks with one sharp shake, if their doggish reflexes were triggered by a wrong move. Tej tried to sit extra-carefully, and not let her fur stand on end.

The emperor of Barrayar leaned back at his ease, one arm stretched out along the top of the sofa, and asked genially, "So, Lady Tej—how did you come to meet our Ivan?"

Tej glanced wildly at Rish, whose stark, stuffed expression returned, *This one's all yours, sweetling.* How far back was she supposed to begin? She swallowed, grabbed Ivan Xav's hand for luck, and started at random: "We'd run out of money, trying to get to—" Wait, should she—but he said he'd talked to Lady Alys, how much of—

"Trying to get to your brother on Escobar, as I now understand it?" said The Gregor.

Tej gulped and nodded. "We were stuck downside on Komarr, dodging what we think were hirelings of the Prestene syndicate. I was working at this grubber shipping store, trying to rebuild our stake, and Rish was in hiding at our flat. Ivan Xav brought in this vase, wanting it packed and shipped—" To *here*, come to think. She looked up at him in belated indignation. "Hey! You bought that horrible thing on purpose just to have an excuse to come into the shop, didn't you?"

He shrugged. "Well, sure."

"We were just closing. He tried to pick me up." Tej scowled in memory.

The Lord Auditor Coz pressed a hand to his lips, briefly. "What, and *failed?*"

Tej nodded again. "Then he turned up on my front steps. I thought he might be a capper stalking me. So I invited him in, and Rish shot him."

The cousin jerked slightly. The emperor's eyebrows went up.

"*Stunned* him, sweetling," Rish corrected, urgently. "Just a little light stun, really."

"And then we dragged him up to our flat," Tej went on.

"*This* wasn't in the ImpSec report," said The Gregor.

"It wasn't relevant by then," said Ivan Xav, in a distant tone. "Forgive, forget..."

"So we tied him to a chair for the night," said Tej.

The Lord Auditor Coz made a strange little *wheeing* sound. He was biting his own hand, Tej noticed. Ivan Xav pointedly ignored him.

"Which proved to be very lucky," Tej forged on, "because when the real kidnappers turned up, we woke up and heard them talking to him and were able to get the drop on them."

"That wasn't luck," protested Ivan Xav. "I engaged them in delay as loudly as I could, till the reinforcements came up. Rather slowly."

"Quick thinking—for a man tied to a chair," murmured the Coz.

"Well, it was!" said Ivan Xav.

"Anyway," Tej plowed on, "he invited us to hide out in his flat for the next few days, which worked fine, till the Prestene contact thought of putting Komarran Immigration onto us, to smoke us out of hiding so they could target us. So Byerly, who came to warn us, and the Immigration officers, and those Dome cops who were trying to arrest Ivan Xav for kidnapping me, which he *didn't*, all arrived at once before anyone had drunk any coffee, and then Admiral Desplains called Ivan Xav, very irate about the Dome cops, I think, and I was so tired and scared, and we—we panicked." She glanced at Rish. Still no help there.

"Quit laughing," said Ivan Xav irritably to the Coz, who actually wasn't, out loud at least, except for the madly crinkling eyes. "It wasn't funny at the time."

Ivan Xav glanced aside at Tej, and his hand squeezed hers. She squeezed back. No, it hadn't been. Not that part, not at the time.

In *retrospect*, though... "So he threw his wristcom into the refrigerator, grabbed this box of instant groats, and asked me to marry him. To keep the Immigration people from arresting me and the Dome cops from arresting him. And I said yes."

"I see," said The Gregor. "I think..."

"It *worked*," said Ivan Xav, sounding stung.

"Why did he throw his wristcom into the freezer?" asked the Coz, diverted by this detail.

"His admiral kept calling back."

"Ah. Makes perfect sense."

"It does?" said The Gregor. The Coz nodded, and he seemed to accept this.

"And then Ivan Xav brought us here to Barrayar, where we are supposed to find this man named Count Falco who will give us a divorce, and then..." Tej ran aground, till she bethought herself of the kind and shrewd Lady Alys. "And Lady Alys's Simon suggested that Rish and I might be smuggled to Escobar on a Barrayaran government courier vessel, if Ivan Xav would ask the right people." She gathered her courage and looked up from her lap at The Gregor. "Would that be you, sir?"

"Possibly." He leaned over and propped his chin in his hand, regarding her quizzically. He had one of those wildly unfair male face-transforming smiles, she noted, even more so than Ivan Xav's; but then, The Gregor's smile was transiting from a much sterner-looking start-point. Ivan Xav had to work hard to look stern, and even then it was more likely to come out just peeved. The Emperor continued, "Where on Escobar is your brother?"

This was not the time to try to deal, Tej realized; this whole meeting *was* a deal. A big one, at that. "Amiri was never happy in the House, never wanted to be involved in the business with my brother Erik and my sisters. He had this passion all his life for biology and medicine, so eventually my parents made a deal for him to go to Escobar to this clinic where they had a special contact, and change his identity and finish his medical education. He's a graduate researcher there, now, under a new name." She moistened her lips and added, "It was always the plan that if something terrible happened, I would go to him, because we always got along best, and my sisters would go to Grandmama."

The Gregor stretched out his arm and drummed his fingers on the sofa back. "Given that Shiv Arqua's Jacksonian parents are both listed as long-deceased, this would have to be your Cetagandan haut grandmother, General ghem Estif's widow, exiled to Earth?"

"Good God!" said Ivan Xav. His hip being pressed to hers on the short sofa, Tej felt him start. "She's still *alive*?"

The Gregor looked across at him in some bemusement. "Didn't you read the ImpSec reports?"

"Didn't figure they'd disgorge 'em without arm wrestling. Besides, I spend all day every day up to my eyebrows in Ops reports for Desplains."

"But there were all those evening—never mind," said The Gregor. Tej wasn't sure if he was looking at her or Ivan Xav or both, but a ghost of that smile went past again.

"But ghem Estif's widow—she was on Barrayar back during the Occupation, and *nobody* still alive remembers that," said Ivan Xav. "She must be over a hundred and twenty years old, at least! Mummified!"

"About a hundred and thirty," said Rish. "If I recall correctly."

"Did you ever meet her?" Ivan Xav asked Rish. But his glance went to Tej.

Tej replied, "After the old general died, she came to live with the Baronne and us for a while. When we kids were all younger. She left almost eight years ago. I haven't seen her since—but she wasn't in the least mummified then. She wasn't *young*, of course, and her hair had turned this fascinating silver color, meters of it, it seemed like, but she was perfectly limber. And tall. And very dignified. It was like—it wasn't that she couldn't move fast, it was simply that she didn't choose to."

A smile of memory flickered across Rish's lips. "That was her."

There was a bustle at the door to the antechamber, and Lady Vorkosigan—Lady Ekaterin?—entered, followed by two maidservants with not so much a trolley as a train of carts loaded high with a bountiful formal tea. *Everyone* came to attention, even The Gregor. The two black-clad guards were already at attention, but every once in a while their eyes flicked longingly toward all the clinking and gurgling going on around the fireplace. It was not until coffee, two kinds of teas, a dozen sorts of little sandwiches and cakes and tarts, freshly candied fruits, marzipan dainties, and miniature and rather messy cream cakes had been served that the conversation resumed, limping around the chewing and swallowing. Rish was nearly mesmerized with sensory bliss.

"Ma Kosti is always especially inspired by one of your visits, Gregor," Lady Ekaterin told the Emperor, who smiled.

"Don't even think about it, Gregor," said the Coz.

"I suppose an Imperial military draft would be cheating," replied The Gregor with a sigh, and homed in on his third cream cakelet.

Everyone was amused. Except for Tej and Rish, who were bewildered. Tej nudged Ivan Xav, but he was chewing, too, and just shook his head. "'Splain later," he mumbled. "Miles defends his cook with his life."

The Coz washed down his bite with a gulp of tea and told his wife, "Just before you came in, Lady Tej was starting to tell us about her Cetagandan haut grandmother, the late General ghem Estif's relict. She was apparently *on* Barrayar toward the end of the Occupation, if you can imagine. She must have been close to old General Piotr's age."

Lady Ekaterin nibbled a frosted cherry, licked her fingers, and nodded. "Oh, Ivan, you'll have to introduce Tej to René and Tatya Vorbretten when they get back to town."

Giving up on Ivan, Tej looked her question at the Coz.

He waved a cucumber-and-cream-cheese sandwich expansively in the air, and said, "Count Vorbretten. Bit of a scandal a few years back, when a gene scan turned up that he was one-eighth Cetagandan ghem. On the male side, unfortunately for Barrayaran inheritance law. Dating back to his great-grandmother and the Occupation, it seemed."

Ivan put in, "They were dubbing him René Ghembretten for a while, but the Council of Counts finally voted to let him keep his countship. A near thing, it was. I was glad of it. Exceptionally nice fellow."

"Exceptionally diligent District count," said The Gregor.

"Now that gene scanning has become widely available," said Lady Ekaterin to Tej and Rish, "quite a few such hidden links are being turned up. Despite huge pressures at the time from both sides against such crosses. The Occupation lasted for two decades, after all."

"Humans will be humans," said her husband. "And so make more humans." They exchanged amused smiles, which fell rather short of private.

"René's case is hardly unique, as far as inter-Nexus romances on Barrayar go," said The Gregor. "Miles's mother Countess Cordelia is famously from Beta Colony, as was Ivan's—and Miles's—great-grandmother who married the celebrated diplomat Prince Xav."

Tej turned in surprise to Ivan. "You're really one-eighth Betan? You never said!" Rish's gold eyebrows, too, went up.

Ivan Xav shrugged. "Can't say as I much think about it. It was a long time ago. Before I was born." He topped this unassailable observation with a marzipan violet, and chewed defensively.

"This medical clinic on Escobar that took your brother the Jacksonian refugee under its wing, the one with the special contact with your late parents..." the Coz said slowly, returning to a subject Tej had hoped was lost in the shuffle.

She stiffened.

"It wouldn't by chance be the Durona Group, would it?" he went on.

Rish gasped, a glazed orange segment dropping from her hand as she stared in horror. "Did ImpSec know all the time?"

"Apparently not," said The Gregor, looking up with a scarily keen interest.

"How did you know?" Tej demanded. It was a secret she'd almost *died* to protect...

"Informed guess."

"*Mark's* Durona Group?" Ivan Xav looked indignantly at Tej. "You could've stood to have said this earlier!"

"What do *you* know about them?" Rish, still tense with alarm, asked the Coz.

"Quite a lot, for my sins. They were once a division of House Fell, a group of thirty-six cloned siblings with extraordinary medical talents. Their progenitor-mother, Lily Durona, who is also on the high side of a century old, I believe, had some special relationship with old Baron Fell that I never did quite understand.

In any case, my clone-brother Mark helped buy them out some years back and arranged for their removal to Escobar, a planet and polity I understand they find considerably more congenial than their House Fell techno-slavery, however much they were valued back in the Whole. Were your parents allies of old Fell, then, Lady Tej? Or of Lily Durona?"

Tej looked wildly at Rish, who opened her hands as if to throw the question back. Tej tried, "My parents were always... I believe they and Fell often found each other useful, yes. There was never a formal alliance, or any question of a merger, though."

The Coz tapped his fingers on his chair arm, his lips pressing together for a moment. "Hm. My brother Mark is a silent investor in the Durona Group, but by no means a secret one. I believe he and his partner Kareen are on Escobar right now, in fact, busy about their affairs. Mark is quite the entrepreneur of the Vorkosigan family. Has several successful—and a couple of unsuccessful—start-ups down in our District, as well."

"Anything worth achieving," muttered Ivan Xav under his breath. "God, even the *clone*..."

"The-Count-our-father approves—the Vorkosigan's District has lagged economically ever since the Occupation, unfortunately. And several of the later civil wars were disproportionately hard on us, as well." He tapped some more. "But the thing is, Lady Tej, this connection of mine is also a connection of Ivan's. If you meant to go to ground secretly with the Durona group..."

"Are you saying now we daren't go?" asked Tej anxiously.

"No. But I am suggesting that your identities and perhaps appearances might need to be rather better laundered than you originally thought." He glanced at Rish.

She glowered back. "You seem to know an awful lot about the Whole, for a Barrayaran."

The Coz shrugged. "I visited it several times in my career. My earlier career, that is, before I became an Imperial Auditor. In any case, Barrayar tracks the five Great Houses that control the Whole's jump points rather more closely than we track the general mob of Jacksonians. House Fell most of all, because of proximity. Less of Cordonah Station, as our interests don't extend much in that direction—we have more economically efficient routes to Earth via Sergyar and Escobar. The fact that the jump point from the Whole into the Cetagandan Empire's backdoor is controlled by House Prestene is, ah...a feature of some interest."

"What earlier career?" asked Tej.

He eyed another cucumber sandwich round, popped it whole into his mouth, and chewed and swallowed before replying. "I was an ImpSec courier for a few years, before I was discharged for medical unfitness. I did a great deal of traveling throughout the Nexus." He looked up and smiled at his wife. "Rather got it out of my system, to tell the truth."

Lady Ekaterin's return smile grew lopsided. "Did you indeed?"

Tej turned again to The Gregor. "But the ride, sir?"

The Emperor rubbed his jaw. "I'll drop a word in Allegre's ear. Ivan and he can discuss the details." He paused, looking her and Ivan Xav over thoughtfully. "Note, it could be some weeks before a place opens up. We cannot delay scheduled or emergency business for this courtesy."

Tej nodded, trying to seem cooperative. Beggars couldn't be choosers.

"Ivan's perimeter has already been notified of the new threat level," The Gregor went on.

"If...if the syndicate's agents track us here, can your people stop them?" asked Rish.

The Gregor's dark eyebrows flicked up. "They're expected to be able to stop much worse."

"If they're not *blindsided*," the Coz put in. "You need to give the poor security fellows as much of a fighting chance to protect you as you can. That means no more withholding information, eh?"

Tej nodded, her throat tight. Ivan Xav felt her hand tremble in his, and frowned at her in worry. She remembered all too clearly the death of their bodyguard on Fell Station. She'd barely known the man, and yet... Among the many, many reasons she'd never wanted power in the House, to play the game as her parents had, was that she'd never wanted her life to be bought at the price of another's. Maybe no one was free of that, really. Or else what were police forces and armies all about, on places like Pol or Komarr? Mass protection, jointly purchased by an entire society, instead of piecemeal by those who could afford it—without even the up-front rewards that Jacksonian enforcers and security people routinely demanded, and were given, for assuming such risks.

The guard beside the door to the antechamber spoke for the first time. "It's seventeen-thirty hours, sire."

"Already?" The Gregor glanced at his wristcom, then looked apologetically at Tej, Rish, and Ivan. "I'm afraid I'm going to have to let you go. I still need to have a few words with my Auditor, here, before we travel our separate ways."

Lady Ekaterin stood up smoothly. "Perhaps Tej and Rish would care to see a little more of Vorkosigan House before you take them home, Ivan. And I could show them the Barrayaran garden."

Ivan Xav's nod endorsed this, and they made what Tej hoped were correct formal farewells and followed their hostess out.

In the front hall, Rish's steps slowed as she stared downward. Her hands twitched, as if she wanted to bend and touch the art underfoot. Or dance across it, pinwheeling. "Is this a recent installation?" she asked Lady Ekaterin. "It's so beautiful. And unexpected. It looks new...?"

Lady Ekaterin smiled, obviously pleased. "When Miles and I were first married, he encouraged me to put some stamp of my own on the house—I mean, besides the Barrayaran garden. It took me a long time to decide what. Then one day my mother-in-law was telling me about some unhappy events that she always associated with the old black-and-white marble tiles that used to be here for, oh, decades, and I thought of this." She gestured in a sweeping arc, from the lavish floor to the lush walls.

She went on, "I was born and grew up on South Continent, where such fine work in natural colored stones is very much a regional art form—the north favors wood as a medium. There was a famous stone mosaic artist whose work I'd adored for years, but could never afford. Miles flew down, quite suddenly one day, and practically kidnapped the poor woman out of her semi-retirement. I worked closely with her on all the botanical details—it took over a year to design and install, not to mention walking the Vorkosigan's District to collect as much suitable stone as could be incorporated. It represents a mixed native Barrayaran and Old Earth ecosystem—just like some places around Vorkosigan Surleau, at the foot of the mountains."

Ivan Xav vented a short chuckle. "When they broke up the old floor, people took the fragments away as historical souvenirs. I saw some of them for sale for an ungodly amount of money, later. If you'd thought to sell 'em yourselves, Ekaterin, you could have funded the whole replacement with the proceeds."

She laughed, too, but said, "I suspect the fresh start suited everyone better." She turned to Tej. "Countess Cordelia Vorkosigan is very close friends with Ivan's mother, you know. Cordelia has frequently mentioned to me how much she treasured having a woman friend, when she first came to Barrayar as a bride and a stranger, to show her how to go on here—all those things the men didn't know. At least there's no war on, this time. Perhaps when Miles and I get back from Sergyar, we can visit again...?"

A heartbreakingly kind offer, Tej thought. She smiled, but shook her head. "We don't expect to be here that long."

"Ah," said Lady Ekaterin, with a curious glance at Ivan Xav. "That's a pity. Well, let's just take a stroll through the dining room wing, and then we can go out the back and around to my garden..."

When Tej had first set foot on Barrayar, she'd felt she couldn't get away again soon enough. Now, after less than two days, even the nebulous plans for their departure in unknown weeks seemed to loom up before she was ready for them. It was as if the whole blasted planet was bent on seducing her.... Odd thought. She shook it from her head, gripped Ivan Xav's anxiously proffered arm, and followed her hostess.

Chapter Eleven

A bit of rest being overdue for everyone, Ivan and his guests spent the day following the alarming interview with Gregor in the confines of Ivan's flat. The women seemed content to limit their explorations of Barrayar to the safety of the comconsole, with meals delivered from some of the large array of providers of provender to bachelors on Ivan's auto-call list. It wasn't till conversation over a late brunch the next noon that Ivan discovered that his ladies' objections to venturing out lay not in mistrust of his security, but in distaste for his groundcar. He then had the happy thought of renting a larger vehicle for the week, an inspiration greeted with applause. They were just discussing his offered menu of places to go and things to see in and around Vorbarr Sultana when they were interrupted by his door chime.

Tej and Rish both jerked in fresh alarm.

"No, no, it's all right," Ivan told them, swallowing his last bite of vat-ham and rising to answer it. "It has to be someone on my cleared list, or the front desk would've called for permission to let 'em come up."

Not that *cleared* necessarily equated to *welcome*, Ivan reflected, when he checked the security vid to find Byerly Vorrutyer waiting in the corridor, looking around and tapping his fingers tensely on his trouser seam. Maybe it was time to review that list, and take certain names off it.... Reluctantly—wasn't this how he'd fallen into all of this trouble in the first place?—Ivan opened the door and let By in, rather like a delivery boy bringing not delicious meals, but bags of snakes. *No tip for you, By.*

By was perfectly neat, tidy, and well-groomed, but he had a harried look in his eye. "Hello, Ivan," he said, padding past his host. "Is everyone all still here? Ah, yes, good. Hello, Rish, Tej." He waved to the women lingering around Ivan's little dining table, who sat up with interest and waved back, and helped himself to a seat, settling in with a sigh.

"If you're looking to hide out from my mother," said Ivan, "this likely isn't the best place."

"Too late for that," said By. "For the love of mercy, give me a drink."

"Isn't this, like, the equivalent of dawn for you? Drinking before breakfast is a sign of serious degeneration, you know."

"You have no idea what serious degeneration is, Ivan. I just had a very long interview with your mother. Worse than my ImpSec debriefing by far, and *that* took a full day."

Ivan balanced mercy against a tempting heartlessness. Mercy won by a hair, so he brought Byerly a clean glass to share out their champagne and orange juice, heavy on the champs. Byerly evidently wasn't in a fussy mood, for he didn't even look at the label till after he'd poured and taken his first sip, not quite a gulp, and raised a brow in belated appreciation.

"I'd have thought you would've had the sense to duck her," said Ivan, settling back into his own chair.

"Wasn't given a chance. I was publicly arrested in the Vorbarr Sultana shuttleport by an ImpSec goon squad as soon as I stepped off the shuttle yesterday, and hauled away in handcuffs."

"Ivan Xav's mother did that?" said Tej, sounding impressed. "She just sent Christos and a car for us."

Byerly appeared to contemplate this. "Much the same thing, I suppose. It was actually my handler's bright idea for getting me to my debriefing discreetly, now that the Vormercier scandal has hit the news. The public tale for me will be that I had no idea that all this brotherly chicanery was going on; I was just the caterer for the party yacht. Drinks, drugs, girls, you know."

"Girls?" said Ivan. "I don't think the term for that is *caterer*, By."

By shrugged one shoulder. "They were actually my co-agents. ImpSec has found that it's often better to recruit from those already in the trade, giving them a step up in the world in return for their loyalty, than to start with a trained agent and persuade them to—well, you see. I called right after I left your wedding, told them to get the hell off Vormercier's yacht, met them on the orbital transfer station to, supposedly, go shopping—that was our code phrase for pulling the plug. We were all three boarding a commercial flight to Barrayar by the time Desplains and your crew descended on the *Kanzian*. Desplains's jump-pinnace passed us by us en route, I suppose—ours wasn't the fastest ship. Nor the best cabin. We had to share." A smile flickered over Byerly's face. "We were commended for our economy, though. ImpSec being in the throes of one of its periodic budget spasms."

"Hot bunks?" inquired Ivan. "What suffering you ImpSec weasels do endure, to be sure. Just you and two beautiful call girls, stuck together for eight days in a tiny room with nothing to do. It must have been hell."

"Not *quite* nothing," Byerly murmured back, taking another sip of champagne and orange juice. "We had all those reports to write..."

"What's a call girl?" asked Tej, her brows crimping in puzzlement.

"Uh..." Ivan sought a translation. "Like a Betan licensed practical sexuality therapist, only without the licensed and the therapy parts."

"Oh." She frowned. "Like a grubber sex worker. That doesn't sound altogether safe."

"It isn't," said By. "It's not a trade that attracts the risk-averse, let us say."

"Like an informer?" inquired Rish, with a small blue smile.

He raised his glass to her, and drained it. "There are parallels. Combine that *with* informer, and you may perhaps guess why I was anxious to extract them before the hammer came down."

"Hm," she said, eyeing him in fresh evaluation.

"So ImpSec released me back into the wild today, supposedly after a grueling night of incarceration and involuntary fast-penta interrogation, which cleared me of complicity in Vormercier's crimes. But left me looking rather a public fool. All good so far." He scowled, and added, "I was also commended for my months of meticulous and, if I may say it, wearing work on the Vormercier case, and raised one pay grade."

"Congratulations!" said Rish. "But...you don't look happy...?"

By's lips twisted. "And then I was promptly reprimanded and docked one pay grade for involving you, Ivan."

"Oh." Ivan almost added *Sorry!* till he reflected that, actually, it *wasn't* his fault. Had he asked By to hand-deliver him a bride? No. Not to mention the *stunned, tied up,* and *threatened with arrest and/or the admiral's sarcasm* parts.

"They did it that way on purpose, you know." By brooded. "If they'd presented it the other way around, it wouldn't have been nearly so stinging. Or just said nothing at all, which would have come to the exact same end. Far more efficiently."

Ivan assured Rish, who seemed taken aback, "Don't worry about it. Byerly's pay grade goes up and down a lot. Think of it as white noise in a general upward trend."

"This marked a new speed record, though," By grumbled.

Tej was still looking thoughtful. "How *does* one become a spy?" she asked Byerly.

His dark brows flicked in amusement. "Thinking of applying? A portion of candidates are filtered in from the Service side of things. Good people in their way, but, let us say, afflicted with a certain uniformity of worldview. Some are purpose-recruited from the civilian side, generally for some special expertise."

"So which way did you get recruited?" asked Rish.

He waved his glass in a what-would-you gesture. "I came in by the third route, recruited piecemeal by a working Domestic Affairs agent. I had arrived in the capital at the age of not quite twenty, bent on going to hell as expeditiously as possible in my own callow fashion—meaning, as like to the other callow, ah, what Ivan and his ilk call *town clowns*, as I could manage. It was not a very original period of my life. I won't say I fell in with bad company—I more hunted them down—but among all the bad apples in my chosen barrel was one who was...not. He used me for a few favors, found me satisfactory, assigned me more small tasks, then larger ones, tested me..." Byerly grimaced at who-knew-what memory—Ivan suspected he wasn't going to tell that one. "And then one day made me an offer which, by that time, did not astonish me—though it illuminated many things in retrospect. I was cycled through a few ImpSec short courses, and the rest was apprenticeship. And, ah...more spontaneous learning experiences." He poured himself more champagne and orange juice. He doubtless needed the vitamins.

"Which brings me to the moment," By went on. "We need to—"

"Wait, you skipped over my mother," said Ivan.

"Would that I could have. She appeared to be remarkably well informed. I tried to explain that my testimony was redundant, but she insisted on the extra angle of view. What I was *about* to say is, that before any of you here go out into circulation in Vorbarr Sultana—I mean, beyond the extremely select company you've already kept—we need to get our stories straight about what really happened on Komarr."

"Ah," said Ivan, unsurprised. "Not a social visit, then."

"Hardly." Byerly glanced under his lashes at Rish. "Well, mostly not, but I'll get to that later. Having, miraculously, not yet blown my cover and lost my livelihood, I would like to keep it that way."

Ivan conceded the validity of this concern with a nod.

"The short version will be that Ivan met you, Tej, on Komarr when he went to mail his package. You indulged in a whirlwind affair, and, when you were suddenly threatened with deportation by Komarran immigration, he married you in a fit of gallantry."

Tej wrinkled her nose. "Why?"

"What, you were beautiful, you were in danger, and I hadn't got laid yet," said Ivan. "Seems simple enough."

Byerly tilted his head. "You know, you were doing well there, Ivan, till that last—never mind. Verisimilitude is everything. Speaking of which, I was told Tej and Rish may as well go on being themselves for as long as they are on Barrayar. Making a virtue of necessity, as erasing them from earlier in the record would be nearly impossible, with all the trail you've left—like an Emperor's Birthday parade, complete with marching bands and an elephant. Highborn but destitute refugees fleeing from a disastrous palace coup—Barrayarans will understand that part, have no fear, even if they remain suspicious of your Jacksonian aspects." His eye fell on Ivan, and he added meditatively, "You spotted me on Komarr by chance, and nabbed me for a known witness when you suddenly needed one. I wonder if you should have been drunk at the time?"

"At dawn?" said Ivan indignantly. "No!" He added in false cordiality, "You're welcome to have been, if you like."

"What, and besmirch my impeccability as a witness? Surely not."

"In other words," said Tej slowly, "pretty much the same tale as we've been telling everyone. Except for Admiral Desplains, Lady Vorpatril, Simon Illyan, Lord and Lady Vorkosigan, Emperor Gregor..." She trailed off, plainly finding it an uncomfortably long list for a closely held secret.

"It's all right," Ivan assured her. "That bunch holds more secrets among 'em than I can rightly imagine."

"Moving on to my concerns," Byerly continued. "In the interests of spreading the correct cover story as soon as possible to as many observers as possible, Rish, I wonder if you would care to attend a select little soirée with me this evening. Dinner beforehand, perhaps?"

"Go out?" Rish's eyes grew wide with both longing and alarm. "On a date? With you? On *Barrayar*?"

Byerly tilted his free hand judiciously back and forth. "Not exactly a date. I need to get out and about to complain, gossip, backstab, and of course curse Theo Vormercier and ImpSec—jointly, severally, and loudly. A tough job, but somebody's got to, and all that."

"What about my"—Rish waved a hand down the slim length of her body—"nonstandard appearance?"

"Some extra distraction for people's eyes and minds while I set about my tedious task of disseminating disinformation seems... useful. Famous foreign artist, enjoying refugee status in the train of a mysterious romance, or possibly scandal, involving the scion of one of the stodgiest of high Vor families—I guarantee they'll muscle past their prejudices for a taste of *that*. And in the company of the Vorrutyer clan's most debonair non-heir, at that. Our audience will be positively agog." He smiled. Ivan bared his teeth. Byerly ignored him, and went on, "Simultaneously, it will begin the process of habituating them to you. Also, it will give you a chance to see a bit of Barrayar *not* in Ivan's stodgy company."

"I am not stodgy! And your company is notoriously, notoriously unfit for... well, unfit, anyway!"

Rish raised her golden brows, and murmured, "Hm!" She regarded Byerly for a long moment through, narrowed, considering eyes. And flared nostrils? "It sounds a small enough task to start on. I think... yes."

"I believe you will find the evening not without elements of interest," By purred in triumph. "And I shall be fascinated by your observations."

"What should I wear?"

"Ah, cerulean on the surface, woman to the bone. Casual-chic and striking would do the job nicely. A touch of the exotic a plus."

Ivan thought the exotic was more of a *default*, but Rish merely said, "I can do that."

Ivan struggled with a formless frustration. Rish was not his spouse, nor did he stand in any way *in loco parentis* to her. But who would be blamed, if something went wrong? Yeah. On the other hand, this would give him and Tej the flat to themselves for the whole evening. They could order in, and, and ... Ivan finally managed, "Well ... well, if you're taking *my employee* out into deep waters, make damn sure you give her a better briefing than you gave me!"

Byerly set down his emptied glass and raised a brow. "Ivan, do I tell you how to run Ops?"

As Ivan sputtered, By grinned, arranged the hour for his return to collect Rish, stood up, and sauntered out, all in fine By style again. About a liter of Ivan's most expensive champagne had relaxed him, presumably.

Ivan returned from escorting Byerly to the door and making sure it was locked after him to find Tej and Rish dividing the last of the fresh orange juice and frowning curiously.

"So ... is By bi?" Tej asked. "Bisexual, that is."

"I have no idea what By's real preferences are," Ivan stated firmly. "Nor do I wish to know."

"What, couldn't you smell him, that first night he came in on Komarr?" said Rish. Addressing Tej, Ivan hoped. "He'd had a busy two days or so. Any lingering scents from prior to that were too attenuated to discern."

"He was pretty confusing," said Tej. "In all ways, including that one."

"To be sure, though I'd call it more compounded than confusing. But whether his contacts were sequential or together, for business or pleasure, enjoyed or endured, even I couldn't guess."

"I *don't* want to *know* this," Ivan repeated, although in a smaller voice. He bethought him of a new caution. "You do realize, Byerly has almost certainly been ordered by his handlers to keep a close eye on you? Surveillance is what he *does*. What could be a more efficient way of keeping you under his thumb than to ask you out himself?"

Rish smirked and rose. "There's nothing that says a man can't enjoy his work." She added over her shoulder, as she drifted out like some exotic blue blossom floating down a stream, "Come on, Tej. Help me sort through this crazy Barrayaran wardrobe."

Tej paused to whisper in reassurance to Ivan, "She adores being seen, you know. She's bound to have a good time." She bounced after Rish with a sort of happy-teakettle chortle.

A more horrid notion occurred to Ivan then. What if Byerly wanted Rish not for a smokescreen, but as bait? What could be a more efficient method of drawing their syndicate pursuers out to where ImpSec could see and nail them than that?

Well, Ivan reflected morosely, *one way or another, at least ImpSec is on the job.*

Rish returned to the flat very late that night; to Tej's secret bemusement, Ivan Xav stayed up to let her in—but not Byerly, who had escorted her to the door, and whom he sent to the right-about with complaints about keeping people awake past their bedtimes. By's ribald return remarks merely made him grumpier. The next night, Rish had Ivan Xav issue her a door remote. Byerly took her out again, although not to a party, but to a dance performance put on by some touring folk group from the western part of the continent, his former and apparently forsaken home. On the third night, Rish called on Byerly's wristcom to tell Tej not to wait up; she'd probably be back around noon the next day. Ivan Xav grumbled disjointedly.

The next morning, however, was his birthday, an event Tej had been anticipating with growing curiosity. They arose in the dark before dawn and dressed rather formally, he donning his green captain's uniform for the first time on his week's leave. They ate no breakfast, merely drank tea, and then he bundled her into his sporty groundcar and they threaded the dark, quiet streets, although to no great distance away. His driving was, thankfully, subdued, though whether because of the bleary hour of the day or the solemn task they were to undertake, she wasn't sure.

He hadn't been very forthcoming about the ceremony, some traditional Barrayaran memorial for his dead father that apparently involved burning a small sacrifice of hair—after it had been clipped from one's head, Tej was relieved to learn. They pulled up in a street lined by older, grubbier, lower buildings, where a municipal guard vehicle was parked, its lights blinking. Two guardsmen were setting up a pair of lighted traffic deflectors on either side of a bronze plaque set in the pavement. The guard sergeant hurried over and started to wave Ivan out of the parking spot into which they eased, but then reversed his gesture into a beckoning upon recognizing the car and its driver.

"Captain Vorpatril, sir." The man saluted as Ivan Xav helped Tej out. "We're just about ready for you, here."

Ivan nodded. "Thank you, Sergeant, as always."

Tej stood on the sidewalk in the damp autumn chill and stared around. "This is where your father died, then?"

Ivan Xav pointed to the plaque, glinting among the amber-and-shadow patterns woven by the street lights. "Right over there, according to Mamere. Shot down by the Pretender's security forces, while they were trying to make their escape."

"Wait, she was *there*? I mean, here? At the time?"

"Oh, yes." He yawned and stared sleepily down the street, then perked up slightly as a long, sleek, familiar groundcar turned onto the block. The municipal guardsman waved it into its reserved parking space with studied officiousness, and saluted its occupants as they disembarked. Lady Vorpatril was accompanied, or escorted, by Simon Illyan, with the driver Christos bringing up the rear and holding a large cloth bag that clanked.

The guardsmen took up parade-rest poses at a respectful distance away, and Christos knelt in the street to withdraw a bronze tripod and bowl from the bag, setting them up next to the plaque. He nodded to his mistress and went to join the guardsmen; they greeted each other and conversed in low tones, then one of the guardsmen went out into the street to direct the growing trickle of traffic safely around the site.

"Good morning, Ivan," Lady Alys greeted her son. "Happy birthday, dear." She hugged him, and he returned her what seemed to be the regulation peck on the cheek. He nodded thanks to Illyan's echoed, "Happy birthday, Ivan. Thirty-fifth, isn't it?"

"Yes, sir."

"Halfway through your Old Earth three-score-and-ten, eh? Incredible that we've all survived so long." He shook his head, as if in wonder. Ivan grimaced.

The War of Vordarian's Pretendership had been more in the nature of an abortive palace coup, as Tej understood it from her recent reading. Shortly after the ascension of the five-year-old Emperor Gregor under the regency of Aral Vorkosigan, the rival Count Vidal Vordarian and his party had made a grab for power. In the first strike, they'd secured the capital city, the military and ImpSec headquarters, and the young emperor's mother, but the boy himself had slipped through their fingers, to be hidden in the countryside by Vorkosigan's gathering forces. It had proved an ultimately fatal fumble.

There had followed a months-long standoff, minor skirmishes while each side frantically maneuvered for allies among the other counts, the military, and the people. Captain Lord Padma Vorpatril and his wife, Lady Alys, relatives and known allies of Regent Vorkosigan, had been cut off in the capital during the coup and gone into hiding. Padma's death rated barely a footnote, less even than the skirmishes. Had it been a chill and foggy night like this?

How much more, not less, surreal the tale all seemed, now that Tej had been in the same room—and shared cream cakes—with the grown-up, forty-year-old Gregor. Not to mention...

The present Lady Alys, composed and commanding, turned to take Tej by the hands. "Good morning, Tej. I'm pleased you came."

Tej considered the significant difference between *husband shot* and *husband shot in front of your eyes.* She ducked her head, suddenly shy before this woman in a whole new way. "Thank you," she managed, unsure what else to say.

"This is the first such memorial service you will have seen, I understand?"

"Yes. I'd never even heard of them before."

"It's nothing at all difficult. Especially not after thirty-five repetitions. Sometimes people perform it on the anniversary of their loved one's death, sometimes on their birthday, sometimes other occasions. As need arises. Keeping the memory alive, or getting in the last word, depending." A dry smile turned her lips. The amber light leached the color from her face, and turned Ivan Xav's uniform drab olive.

Lady Alys and Ivan Xav knelt by the brazier. With a brisk efficiency, Lady Alys pulled a plastic sack of scented bark and wood shavings from the cloth bag and upended it into the metal bowl. She pulled a smaller packet from her purse and shook out a mat of black and silver hair clippings atop. Ivan rummaged in his trouser pocket and unearthed a similar packet, adding a fuzzy black blot to the pile. Parsimoniously saved from their most recent haircuts, maybe? They both stood up.

Lady Alys nodded to the plaque. "This is where my husband was shot down by Vordarian's security forces. Nerve disruptors— poor Padma never had a chance. I'll never forget the smell... burning hair, among other things. This ceremony always brings that back." She grimaced. "Ivan was born not an hour later."

"Where was his uterine replicator?" Tej asked.

Three faces turned toward hers; Lady Alys's twisted in a wry humor. She touched her stomach. "Here, dear."

Tej gasped in new and unexpected horror. "You mean Ivan Xav was a *body birth*?"

"Everyone was, in those days. Replicator technology had barely reached Barrayar, and didn't become widespread for another generation." Lady Alys stared at her uneasy son in reminded ire. "Two weeks late, he was. Nine pounds!"

"Not my fault," muttered Ivan Xav, very much under his breath. He added to Tej, not much louder: "She mentions that every year."

Lady Alys went on more serenely, "The friends who rescued us...me, almost in time, hustled me away to an abandoned building in the old Caravanserai district—very run-down and dangerous, back then—not too far from here. Sergeant Bothari, rest to his troubled soul, played midwife, for lack of any other with the least experience in the task, including me. I was so terrified, but I couldn't scream, you know, because Vordarian's men were still out there looking for us. Bothari gave me a rag to bite...I can still remember the horrid taste, when I think of it. Nauseating. And we got through it somehow, dear heavens, but I still don't know how. We were all so young. Ivan is older now than Padma was then." She regarded Tej in sudden wonder. "I was just twenty-five. Your age, my dear. Now, there's a strange chance."

Half past strange and aiming for very unsettling, Tej thought. But a new, or newly revealed, reason for this aging woman's unexpected sympathy to another young refugee mourning her dead grew very clear, like ice, or crystal, or broken glass, or something else with sharp and dangerous edges. *Oh.*

She knows. She knows it all, and more, probably. Maybe Lady

Alys's glossy surface had to be so thick and smooth *because* it hid so much...?

Simon Illyan's brow furrowed. "Where was I, during all of this? I do wish I could have been there for you, Alys..."

She touched his supporting arm in reassurance. "You were smuggling Admiral Kanzian out, to Aral's great tactical benefit."

His face cleared. "Ah, yes, now I recall." He frowned again. "Fragments, at least."

"Trust me, love, after thirty-five years, fragments are all anyone recalls." She turned again to Tej. "As Ivan's bride, you are now a part of this—however temporarily. Would you care to lay some hair on the fire as well? Since you're here."

Tej was taken aback all over again. That seemed to be happening a lot, lately. "I...is it permitted?" *Not offensive?* Apparently, it was perfectly allowable, because all the Barrayarans nodded. Lady Alys drew a small pair of scissors from her purse—secreted for just this hope, or did she always carry them?—and snipped a curl from Tej's bent head. She handed it to Ivan Xav, who laid it atop the pile and set the wood shavings alight. Little flames crackled up, hot and swift. There did not seem to be any formal words to be recited, because everyone just stood around watching, the flames reflecting in their shadowed eyes as tiny molten glints. The tops of the highest buildings, visible in the distance, sprang into color as the first sunlight reached them, but down here all was yet a pool of damp gray, with the fire a shimmering orange blur in the autumn murk.

Not formal, but words—very low, from Lady Alys; as though she told secrets. "Padma and I were hiding in what was then a cheap boarding house down the street. Just there." She pointed to a building a few doors down, half-concealed by renovation scaffolding. The scent of burning hair was very pungent, now. "When I went into labor, Padma panicked. I begged him not to go out, but he was frantic to find someone, anyone, to take over the terrifying task of delivering a baby that women all over the planet had been doing every damned day since the Firsters landed. Though *I* had the biggest part of the job, and wasn't going to be able to wriggle out of it by any means whatsoever. So he went out, leaving me alone and petrified for hours with my contractions getting worse, *waiting*, and of course he promptly got picked up. Once they brought him back and we'd both been dragged out into the street, he tried to stand up to armed men, all penta-drunk as he was. But I knew, then and forever after, that it wasn't his bravery that killed him—it was his *cowardice*. Oh, dear God, I was so angry at him for that. For *years*."

Illyan touched her shoulder; Ivan Xav stood warily away. Illyan said, "Kou got you and baby Ivan out, didn't he?" Giving her thoughts a more positive direction?

"Yes. Lieutenant Koudelka—later Commodore," she glossed to Tej, "Kou managed to smuggle us out of the city in the back of a grocery van, of all things. His father had been a grocer, you see. Lurching along in the vegetable detritus—Ivan very hungry and noisy, to be sure, and not happy to be thrust out into the cold world in the middle of a war."

The little flames were almost gone, gray ash starting to drift away in the stirrings of air from the passing vehicles. The acrid smell was abating.

"This is a Barrayaran ceremony for remembrance," said Lady Alys, turning to Tej. "It was always my intention, when Ivan married, to turn this task of remembrance over to him, to continue or not as he willed. Because... memory isn't all it's cracked up to be." Her hand reached out and gripped Illyan's, who gripped it back in a disturbed little shake, though he smiled at her.

"Thirty-five years seems long enough, to me," Lady Alys went on. "Long enough to mourn, quite long enough to be enraged. It's time for me to retire from remembering. From the pain and sorrow and anger and attachment, and the smell of burning hair in the fog. For Ivan, it's not the same, of course. His memories of this place are very different from mine."

"I never knew," said Ivan Xav, shifting uncomfortably. "All that."

Lady Alys shrugged. "I never said. First you were too young to understand, and then you were too adolescent to understand, and then... we were both much busier with our lives, and this had all become a rote exercise. But lately... in recent years... I began to think more and more about giving it up."

By every sign, she'd been thinking about this for quite a while, Tej thought. No one built up that much head-pressure overnight. She looked her alarm at Ivan Xav who, belatedly, slid closer and put a bracing arm around her waist.

"It was just something we did, every year," said Ivan Xav. "When I was really little, of course, I didn't understand it at all. We just came here, burned this stuff, stood around for a few minutes, and then you took me to the Keroslav bakery, because we'd not had breakfast. I was all about the bakery, for the longest time."

"They closed last year," Lady Alys observed dispassionately.

"Not surprised. They'd kind of gone downhill, I thought."

"Mm, that, and your palate grew more educated than when you were six." She added after a reflective moment, "Fortunately."

The flames had burned out. At Lady Alys's gesture, Christos came back with the bag and a padded glove, upended the bronze bowl and tapped out the ash, wiped it with a cloth, and put it all away again. He stood up with a grunt.

Lady Alys brightened. "Well. That's all over with, for another year at least. Given that the bakery is gone, removing an occasion for tradition without any effort on our parts, would you both care to come back to breakfast at my flat?"

Tej glanced at Ivan Xav, who nodded, so said "Sure! Thank you, Lady Alys."

They followed the sedate groundcar in Ivan Xav's two-seater. Tej looked over her shoulder to see the municipal guardsmen taking down the lighted barriers and putting them away in their vehicle, returning the street to its normal morning traffic, which was growing notably busier. It was full dawn, now, and the city was awake, eager to get started on another brand-new day. Looking forward, not back.

Thirty-five funerals seemed too many. Yet *none* was not enough. Tej wondered, if Ivan Xav would help them to it, if she and Rish would feel any better for burning some hair in a little pan for Dada and the Baronne, and Erik. Maybe you had to be raised to this.

She turned to Ivan Xav. "What a morbid way to start your every birthday, when you were a child. I mean, most children get presents, and sweets, parties, maybe ponies here on Barrayar— even we and the Jewels all did. Well, not ponies, not on a space station. But you know what I mean."

"Oh, I had all that, too," said Ivan Xav. "Later in the day. Quite ornate parties, for a few years, when the mothers in Mamere's set were competing with each other. All that was damped down by my mid-teens, when we kids were all more intent on moving into adulthood as fast as we could, God knows why." He blinked reflectively. "Not that their teens are something most people would want to linger in." And after another moment, "It felt like childhood came to a pretty abrupt halt when I started the Imperial Service Academy at age eighteen, but looking at some of the frighteningly dewy new-minted ensigns they're sending us these days, I'm not so sure. Maybe that was an illusion on our parts."

And, after a much longer pause, while he negotiated a few corners and dodged incoming traffic: "Sure taught me the price of Vorpatrils mixing in politics, though. I didn't understand much, but I had that down by the time I was eight. I mean—other boys had fathers, most of 'em; even Miles had Uncle Aral, scary as he was—I had a bronze plaque in the street that groundcars ran over. That made Mamere either sad or twitchy or bitchy by turns, but never happy."

"Is—was—she always this, um?" Tej wasn't sure how else to describe Lady Alys. *Desperate for escape?* "When you do this burning thing?"

His brows drew in. "No. She'd never told me some of those crazy details, before. Funny thing, that. I mean, *she's* the one who had that damned plaque installed in the first place, right? Makes me wonder—if she didn't enjoy this, and I didn't enjoy this, and my father, whatever he was or would have been, is decades past caring, why do we keep doing this? She didn't have to wait for me to get *married* to stop. She could've stopped any time."

"Some passing-of-the-generations thing?" Tej hazarded.

"I guess." Following Christos, Ivan Xav turned in at the garage under his mother's building, and offered no more illumination.

Chapter Twelve

The rest of Ivan Xav's thirty-fifth birthday passed quietly, although he did take Tej and Rish out to dinner at an intimate restaurant featuring Barrayaran regional cuisine, where he appeared to be well-known by the staff. Rish drew stares and whispers as they entered, but no overt insults.

"I thought they didn't like mutants, here," murmured Tej.

"Byerly says my appearance goes so far beyond what Barrayarans usually think of as mutants that their categories break down," said Rish. "Although he did warn me to stay out of grubber venues if I don't have outriders. Except he didn't say grubber, oh, what was that Barrayaran term . . ."

"Prole?" said Ivan. "Plebe?"

"Prole, that was it."

"Yeah, probably good advice, till you know the territory better."

To Tej's surprise, they were guided to a five-person table with two seats already occupied. A solid, dark-haired man who looked to be in his forties, not handsome but striking—blade of a nose, penetrating nutmeg-brown eyes—stood up as they approached; a younger, athletic blond woman, taller than her partner, smiled across at them, clearly interested in but not shocked by Rish. This must not be a grubber venue.

"Happy birthday, Ivan," said the man, shaking Ivan's hand. "Congratulations on making it this far alive."

"Yeah, really," said Ivan Xav, returning the handshake and smiling in evident sincerity. "Tej, Rish, I'd like you to meet my friend Duv Galeni, and his wife Delia."

The blond woman waved in a warm way; Galeni bowed Vor-like over Tej's hand and murmured, "Lady Vorpatril," and shook Rish's, "Mademoiselle Rish."

After they were all seated, studied the menus, had the Vorgarin District-style stroganoff recommended, and placed their orders, Tej asked, "How do you all know each other?" Because Galeni was no Barrayaran Vor, certainly; wrapped within that cultured voice Tej heard a faint Komarran accent.

"Delia, I've known all my life," Ivan Xav explained. "Her father, Commodore Koudelka, worked for my uncle, back when. Aide-de-camp and secretary."

Not unlike Ivan Xav's job, this seemed to say. "Wait, was he the lieutenant who smuggled baby-you and your mother out of this city back when it was under siege?"

"Yep, that's the one. Three more daughters, y'know. Where are they all, at the moment, Delia? Because I figured Tej could stand to meet some more Barrayaran women."

The blonde replied, "Martya's down in the Vorkosigan's District with Enrique, working on one of Mark's projects. Kareen's on Escobar with Mark—I'm not sure when they'll next be back. And Olivia's out in the Vorrutyer's District with Dono. Would Count Dono count, do you suppose?"

"*No*," said Ivan Xav, then hesitated. "And anyway, that's a lame pun."

Delia grinned unrepentantly; Galeni hid a smile behind his hand.

"And you and Ivan Xav?" Tej inquired of Galeni.

"I don't go as far back as Delia," he replied easily. "I first met Ivan when I was senior military attaché at the Barrayaran Embassy on Earth, and Ivan, as a wet-behind-the-ears lieutenant, was assigned as one of my assistants. About...has it really been ten years?"

"Eleven," said Ivan Xav, a bit glumly.

"My word." The crow's-feet at the corners of Galeni's eyes crinkled.

As the first course arrived, Galeni and Delia took it in turns to draw Tej and Rish out about their own travels. Rish was describing their time on Pol when Tej, overcome with a sense of Morozovian déjà vu, turned to Galeni and said suspiciously, "Wait. Are you another ImpSec man?"

"Well, yes, but I promise you I am off-duty, tonight," he assured her.

His wife put in proudly, "Duv's been head of ImpSec's Komarran Affairs department for the past four years. He was one of the first Komarrans to enter the Imperial Service, as soon as it was opened to them."

Commodore Galeni, it soon transpired. And another of the Legendary-Illyan's old trainees. But he and Ivan Xav did appear to be friends in their own right, not watcher and watchee. Or not just watcher—as the conversation wended over a surprisingly wide range of topics, Tej had the distinct impression that both members of the couple were testing for the answer to the unspoken question *Is she good enough for Our Ivan?*

That was . . . kind of nice, actually, that Ivan Xav had such friends. Growing up, Tej had enjoyed a string of carefully vetted playmates from among the children of her parents' higher-level employees, but all were scattered now. Or worse, suborned to the new regime. When she tried to come up with a list of *intimate* friends, the sort who might ask, *Is he good enough for Our Tej?*, they all came out family, or at least some of the survivors—Jet, Rish, maybe Amiri. Also all scattered. She hoped Jet was still safe with Amiri.

Galeni's presence did account for the absence of Byerly, she realized a bit belatedly; it would not do By's town-clown cover good to be seen dining out with one of the senior officers of ImpSec.

When they arrived, roundaboutly, at the account of how Tej had met and married Ivan Xav, she was afraid it was going to be The Coz and The Gregor all over again, or at least, Galeni wheezed red-faced into his napkin to the point where his wife stopped giggling long enough to look at him in concern.

Galeni straightened up and caught his breath at last. "At least it sounds better than your last kidnapping."

"I thought so," Ivan Xav agreed ruefully.

"What?" said Tej.

Galeni hesitated, then said, "One of the more traumatic incidents of my till-then remarkably trauma-free sojourn on Earth.

Ivan spent a very unpleasant afternoon kidnapped by, ah, a group of conspirators, who hid him in the pumping chamber of a tidal dam."

"An afternoon?" muttered Ivan Xav. "Try a subjective year. Pitch-dark, y'know? I couldn't have read a clock if I'd had one. Also cold, wet, cramped, and underground. Listening the whole time for the damned pump to start, and drown me, when the tide turned."

Tej, picturing this, felt her throat tighten. "Sounds nasty."

"Yeah," said Ivan Xav.

"Among the several pressing reasons I was kissing my career goodbye about then, that came high on the list," sighed Galeni. "To be handed Lieutenant Lord Vorpatril to look after, and then *lose* him . . . not good on my résumé, I assure you."

"But he was rescued," said Rish. "Obviously. By you, Commodore?"

"Captain, back then. Let's say I helped. Fortunately for my résumé."

"Is your claustrophobia better now?" Delia asked Ivan Xav, more in a tone of curiosity than concern.

Ivan Xav gritted his teeth. "I do *not* have claustrophobia. Thank you very *much*, Delia. There's nothing irrational about it. . . . About me."

"But Miles said—"

"I have an allergy to total strangers trying to kill me, is all. One that Miles shares, I might point out."

Delia's lips twisted. "I don't know, Ivan. I think Miles actually gets rather excited by that."

"You may be right," agreed Galeni.

"Do you suppose it's the attention?" said Delia. "He does like to be at the center."

Ivan Xav choked into his own napkin at this one, and was drawn away from his little moment of irate by uniting with this old friend in trading scurrilous observations about The Coz, none of which, Tej noticed, Galeni tried to gainsay.

At dessert, the commodore pulled a small, flat case from his jacket pocket and pushed it rather shyly toward her and Ivan Xav. It contained a book-disc, she saw. Ivan Xav eyed it warily. "What's this, Duv?"

"Something of a combination birthday and wedding present. Well, perhaps more for Lady Tej than you. A new history of Barrayar since the Time of Isolation. Just released from the Imperial University Press this week, after some years in the preparation. Professora Vorthys is going to teach her modern history class with it, starting next fall."

"How long is it?"

"Ninety chapters, roughly."

"And how many did *you* write?"

Galeni cleared his throat. "About ten."

"I didn't know ImpSec gave *homework*," said Tej faintly.

Galeni smiled wryly. "More of a hobby, in my case. But I do like to keep my hand in, when I can. As much as I can. I have several interesting papers written, waiting for their references to age out of their classified status."

"I should explain," said Ivan Xav, "when Duv said he quit school to go to the Imperial Military Academy, back when the Service was opened to Komarrans, he was a *professor*, not a student. History. He's mostly over it, but sometimes he reverts. Is this thing"—he touched the case with a cautious finger—"written in high academic?"

"I can only speak for my own chapters, but Illyan beat the scholastic prolixity out of me back when I was first writing ImpSec analysis reports for him," said Galeni. "Taught me the ImpSec ABC's—accuracy, brevity, and clarity. Although he did say he was glad to get reports where he didn't have to correct the grammar and spelling."

Ivan Xav laughed. "I'll just bet."

Tej had just enough wits to accept the book-disc with suitable appreciation. This did not seem the time to explain that she wasn't going to *need* to study Barrayaran anything, because she was skiving off to Escobar at the first opportunity. Ditto Delia's offer to hook her up with the array of sisters, when the chances arose. She managed noncommittal thanks.

The Galenis excused themselves soon after dessert—a toddler and an infant evidently waited at home. A vid-cube of the absent offspring was shown about; Tej made suitable complimentary noises. As the couple passed out of the restaurant, Ivan Xav remarked, "No night life for *him* anymore, poor sod." But undercut this by adding, "I expect that suits him to the ground."

Ivan Xav didn't have brothers, but at least it seemed he had brother-officers, Tej reflected. It was something.

❦   ❦   ❦

It wasn't till bedtime, when Ivan Xav was taking his turn in the bathroom and she and Rish were making up the couch, that Tej was able to snatch a private moment to decant the Byerly Report.

"So? Last night. How was it?"

Rish flicked over a sheet and smiled a maddeningly secret smile. "Interesting."

Tej tossed her head. "That's what people say about some dodgy dish that doesn't quite work. Whitefish and raspberries."

"Oh, this combination worked. Delectably."

"*So?*"

Rish touched her lips, though whether to check her words or draw them out, Tej could not guess. "Byerly... I've never encountered anyone whose mouth and whose hands seemed to be telling two such different stories."

"Do I have to *shake* you?"

Rish grinned, and made a rather Byerly-like wrist-flutter. "The mouth ripples on amusingly enough, though most of what comes out is camouflage and the rest is lies—not so much to me, though. But the hands..."

"Mm?"

"The hands are strangely shy, until suddenly they turn eloquent. And then their candor could make you weep. A woman might fall in love with the hands. Though only if the woman were nearly as foolish as my little even-sister—which, luckily, doesn't seem to be possible."

Tej threw a pillow at her.

The next day, the last of Ivan Xav's leave, he spent ferrying them around to see a few locally famous tourist sites, including a military history museum at Vorhartung Castle, the most looming of the old fortresses above the river that were, indeed, lit up colorfully at night. During this outing, he discovered that Tej and Rish not only didn't drive ground vehicles, they couldn't.

"We had sport grav-sleds, at this downside country villa my parents kept, but my older sibs usually hogged them," Tej explained. "And in congested places, towns and cities like this"—she waved around—"even Dada used an armored groundcar with a dedicated driver and bodyguards. Outside the cities it's all toll roads built and operated by assorted Houses, so you need a lot of money to get around."

"Huh," said Ivan Xav. "I bet I can fix that."

His *fix* proved to be a private driver's education service specializing in off-world tourists, whose personable instructor picked them up at the front of Ivan Xav's building the next morning, after Ivan Xav went off to Ops for his day's work.

"It's an excellent choice to learn to drive in our beautiful Vorbarr Sultana," the instructor informed them cheerfully. "After this, no other city on the planet will daunt you."

Tej jumped into the challenge; Rish, claiming distressing sensory overload, opted out after a short trial that left her green, figuratively. In far fewer hours than Tej thought possible or even sane, she was issued a permit that allowed her to practice-drive under Ivan Xav's supervision.

She only froze once, on their first evening's outing, when trying to back the groundcar out of its parking space beneath the building. The pillar made such an ugly crunching noise...

"Don't worry," Ivan Xav told her jovially. "These groundcars are so crammed with safety features, you can hardly kill yourself even if you *try*. Why, I've had half-a-dozen crack-ups with barely a scratch. On me, that is. Harder on the groundcars, naturally. Except for that one time, but I was much younger then, so we don't need to go into it." He added after a moment, "Besides, this is the rental."

Encouraged, Tej set her jaw and soldiered on. They arrived back an hour later without having cracked anything; not even, in her case, a smile, but that changed when she successfully piloted the beast back into its stall and powered down at last. "That wasn't as scary as I thought it would be!"

"Oh, hey, you want scary—the best day I ever had with my Uncle Aral, who usually doesn't have time for me in both senses of that phrase, but anyway, it was the first summer I had my lightflyer permit, and had gone down with Miles to their country place. Uncle Aral took me out, just *me* for a change, over the unpopulated hills and taught me what all you could *really* do with a lightflyer. He said it was in case I ever had to evade pursuit, but I think he was testing his new security fellows, who were along in the back seat. If he could make them scream, cry, or throw up, he won."

"Er...did they? Did he?"

"Naw, they trusted him too much. I got a couple of the veterans to yelp, though." He went on with unabated enthusiasm, "After you're comfortable with groundcars, we'll have to move you on into lightflyers. You need them to get around out in the more remote parts of the Districts, where the roads can get pretty rough. Too bad Uncle Aral is too old now to give you his special advanced course"—he pursed his lips—"probably. Anyway, he's stuck on Sergyar viceroy-ing, which has disappointingly little to do with vice, he claims."

The *That* Uncle Aral, Tej translated this. It was almost harder to imagine than The Gregor. "And your mother encouraged this...coaching?"

"Oh, sure. Of course, neither of us told her what we *really* did. Uncle Aral is nobody's fool."

Ivan Xav next discovered that neither Tej nor Rish, despite their sensory discrimination training, was more than a rudimentary cook. He claimed he was no master, but could survive in a kitchen, cooking a dinner at home for a change to prove it. He then hit on the bright idea of sending them both off to Ma Kosti for formal lessons, on the theory that she was underemployed and bored this week with most of the Vorkosigan household gone to Sergyar.

In appearance, Ma Kosti proved very much their first sample prole, short and dumpy and with a notably different accent and syntax than her employers, and she was at first visibly leery of Rish. This changed when Rish demonstrated her fine discriminatory abilities in taste and smell, plus less of a tendency than Tej to cut herself instead of the vegetables, and Rish was promptly adopted as a promising apprentice. Rish in turn recognized a fellow master-artist, if in a different medium. The days filled swiftly.

Two evenings out of three, Rish went off with Byerly, often not returning till the next day. "By's place," she remarked, "is surprisingly austere. He doesn't bring his business back there much, as far as I can tell. Something of a refuge for him." Tej handed her a pillow, and she punched it to fluff it up. "Not as austere as this couch, though. When am I going to get off this thing?"

Ivan Xav, passing by with a toothbrush in his mouth, removed it to say, "You know, I bet we could get you your own efficiency flat, right here in the building, if I try. Might have to wait for an opening. Or I could put myself on the waiting list for the next two- or three-bedroom unit that comes up. Call the moving service, we could shift digs in a day, no problem. Unless Byerly takes you off my hands." Ivan Xav fluttered his fingers, to demonstrate their potential Rish-free state.

Rish sat up in her sheets and stared at him. "But we're leaving."

"Oh. Yeah."

"*When* are we leaving?" she asked.

"That's kind of up to ImpSec. They haven't called."

"But they could. At any time."

"Well ... yeah ..."

"So what about this divorce ceremony you two have to go through before we can lift off?"

Tej perched on the couch's padded arm, and said, "Ivan Xav said it would only take ten minutes."

"Yeah, but how long do you have to stand in line to get the ten minutes? Is there a waiting list for that, too?"

"And how does it really work?" said Tej, unwillingly prodded into wondering. "I mean, in detail?" He'd never said. But then, she hadn't thought to ask. They'd been *busy*.

"Hm," said Ivan Xav, sticking his toothbrush into his T-shirt pocket and sinking down into a chair. "The thing we have to do is fly up to the Vorpatril's District on one of the days Falco is holding Count's Court in person. He does that at least once a week, when he's in the District, more if he has time. That'll save a world of explanation. We go in, say *Please, Falco, grant us a divorce*, he says *Right, you're divorced. Done!*, bangs his courtly spear butt, and we skitter out."

"Don't you need lawyers and things?" said Rish.

"Shouldn't think so. You're not suing me for support, are you?" Ivan Xav asked Tej.

She shook her head. "No, just for a ride to Escobar, which The Gregor is giving us anyway."

"If it's something this Count Falco only does once a week, for a whole District—how many people are in the Vorpatril's District, anyway?" said Rish.

"I dunno. Millions?"

"How does one man play judge to millions of people?" asked Rish, astonished.

"He doesn't, of course. He's got a whole District justice department, with all kinds of sub-territorial divisions for cities and towns and right on down to the Village Speaker level. But he keeps a hand in for the political symbolism of it, and to sample what his people really have to say. Most counts do, even Uncle Aral when he's home. Which isn't very often, true."

"Hadn't you better *check* his *schedule*?" asked Rish, sounding a trifle exasperated. "In case ImpSec calls with our ride, oh, say, *tomorrow morning*?"

"Um. Yeah, maybe..." said Ivan Xav, and lumbered off reluctantly to his comconsole. He was gone for a long time.

When he came back, he looked sheepish. "In fact, Falco's Count's Court docket is packed for months out. If that fast courier opening comes up sooner, I'll have to pull personal strings. Which I can do, but would rather avoid if I can. Because the thing about me owing a big favor to Falco is, he'll collect. And grin while he's doing it. But I put us on the court's waiting list—they say they sometimes get last-minute openings, which they fill first-come, first-served." He took a breath. "Your protection won't be withdrawn till you're safe on Escobar, anyway, regardless of when we do this divorce deal."

Rish nodded. Tej felt...odd.

They were going to Escobar, in theory, to take up a new life under new identities. *Lady Vorpatril* was certainly a new identity, enjoying a safety that didn't rely on obscurity... *No. Stick to the plan.* Without the plan, they had no anchor at all; it was the last lifeline her parents had thrown to her, as they went down with their House.

Worried that Tej might be a little homesick, Ivan stopped on the way back to his flat one afternoon and found a brand-new *Great House* set, with six player panels. If he'd had any doubt that Rish was Byerly's assignment as well as his hobby, it was put to rest by By's apparent willingness to devote several evenings in a row to a children's game, if, admittedly, a fast-moving, complex, and strangely addictive one. It didn't help that By took to it so well that he was soon giving the born Jacksonians real competition, leaving Ivan to bring up the rear time and time again.

But Ivan found Morozov's *other* way of winning at *Great House* to carry over, too. As one friendly anecdote followed another, in the relaxation and triggering reminders of the old game, Ivan learned a great deal about Tej's upbringing as a real Jacksonian Great House baron's daughter, apparently much doted-upon by her powerful Dada. Ivan traded with a few tales out of school, himself. Only Byerly did not contribute to the exchange, although Ivan was sure he was sucking it all in. But they were in the middle of a round of *Great House* when Ivan finally learned the real relationship of the late Baronne, her children, and her Jewels.

"Even-sister and odd-sister?" said Tej. "We call each other that because we are, more-or-less. Half-siblings, at least. The Baronne used a lot of her own genome as a base to create the Jewels. Although not Dada's, except for the Y chromosome for Onyx. In a way, Ruby was really the first, the Baronne's prototype, so she claims to count as One, in a class by herself. Erik was the next first, and then Topaz, and Star, then Pearl, and then Pidge, and then Emerald, and then Amiri, and then Rish and then finally me, and right after me, Jet—Onyx, that is. Odds and evens, see? It became a sort of family joke." She sighed in memory. "Only now we're all scattered. And Erik...I wish we could get some word about Topaz. I won't say it's worse, not knowing if she's alive or not. But it's...not good."

Ivan stared open-mouthed at Rish, who stared back in somewhat affronted dignity. "So you're my *sister-in-law*?" He sat a moment, not so much in reflection as stunned—like an ox that had just met a mallet. "That sure explains a lot..."

Byerly didn't help by laughing like a loon.

"You could take some other courses," said Ivan Xav a week later, when Tej's ground-vehicle operation training had concluded in triumph, or at least not disaster, and left her with a certification giving her the freedom of the city—if she could, first, borrow a vehicle, and second, wedge through the traffic. Bubble-tube systems were being retrofitted in some areas, but the installation was evidently slow, plagued with problems. It sometimes seemed to Tej as if this entire *planet* was in process of being retrofitted.

"There are three major universities and over a dozen colleges and who knows how many tech schools in this town," Ivan Xav went on. "They have courses for *everything*. Well, maybe not licensed practicing sexuality whats-its, but given the way the conservative crowd complains, that may be next. You're smart. You could pick anything you liked."

Tej contemplated this offer, both uneasy and enticed. "I always had tutors, before. I never chose my own, like, off a *menu*."

"It might be a way for you to meet more people, too," Ivan Xav speculated. "I should really introduce you to more than the Koudelka girls, come to think. All the women I know have women friends—to excess, sometimes." He paused for thought. "There's Tatya Vorbretten, though she's up to her ears in infants right now, as bad as Ekaterin and Delia. Tattie Vorsmythe? She was always fun, despite her strange taste in men. Not sure who all Mamere could suggest, of the younger generation. She used to know lots of Vor maidens, daughters of her cronies, y'know, but they mostly seem to have got married and moved along."

This mental search for names was interrupted when he went to answer his comconsole. When he came back, he looked stricken.

"Bad news?" asked Tej, sitting up on the couch and setting aside her reader.

"No, not...not really. It was the Clerk's office at the Vorpatril District Court. Says they had a case fall off Falco's docket for the first afternoon of next week, and did I want the slot? I, uh... said yes. Because God knows when there'll be another, y'know?"

"Oh, excellent," said Rish, wandering in from the kitchen with a fresh mug of tea in her hand in time to hear this. "One more chore out of the way."

"Oh," Tej echoed hollowly. "Yeah. Good."

It was like some weird sort of honeymoon in reverse, Ivan thought. Taking a personal day's leave from Ops left him facing a three-day weekend, not something to waste. So Ivan seized the chance to show Tej more of Barrayar while he could, outside of the hectic confines of the capital. Rish, upon finding that her witness was not required, elected to stay behind under the loose supervision of Byerly, and just how *loose* that might be, Ivan wasn't asking, gift horses and all that. It left him with a great chance for a real getaway with Tej, just the two of them at last.

It was not the season for tourists in the northeastern coastal District traditionally held by the Vorpatril counts. As his lightflyer beat its way up the shoreline against a cold sea wind, Ivan explained to Tej, "People come up here from the south in the summer to escape the heat. Then go back down in the winter to find it again. If there's time, maybe I could take you down to see the south coast, too."

Time. There wasn't enough time. Yes, the marriage was supposed to have been temporary. But not bleeding *instantaneous*.

He took a detour over the rural territory, to give Tej an idea of the extent of it. A few areas of early snow, just inland, proved no novelty to her, as Jackson's Whole was apparently temperate all the way to the equator, with large and barren polar regions. Happily, the snow covered up the last few biocide blights lingering from the Occupation. But a little way up the coast past the summer resort town of Bonsanklar, *Good Saint Claire* in one of the old tongues, lay a cozy little inn specializing in the Vor trade, fondly remembered from a few visits in Ivan's youth. It was still there, perhaps a little shabbier, but just as cozy. He and Tej managed one walk on the pebbled beach before darkness drove them indoors; the next day it rained, but their end room boasted its own fireplace, food service, and no reason to go out. None at all.

Far too soon the next morning, they were back in his lightflyer, threading their way upriver to the Vorpatril District capital city of New Evias.

"I don't understand what I'm supposed to call him," said Tej, peering anxiously ahead out the front canopy. "Count Vorpatril or Count Falco? And if only his heir is Lord Vorpatril, why are you Lord Vorpatril too, or are you?"

"All right, I'll try to explain it. Again," said Ivan. "There are the counts and their heirs, political heirs. Count Vorwho, Lord Vorwho, Lord Firstname—the firstborn males—like Aral, Miles, and Sasha, all right?"

"That, I got."

"Any other siblings of Lord Firstname, like Sasha's twin Lady Helen, get to stick on a Lord or Lady in front of their names too, as a courtesy title. Whether they drool or not. But those titles aren't inherited in the next generation. So we have a case like By, whose grandfather was a count, whose father was a younger son and so Lord Firstname, and then Byerly, who is just Vorrutyer, the Vor part standing in for any other honorific. So you'd never introduce him as Mister or Monsieur Vorrutyer, just as Vorrutyer. Although his wife, if he had one, would be Madame Vorrutyer, and his sister, before she married, was Mademoiselle Vorrutyer."

"All right," said Tej, more doubtfully.

"Then, just to confuse the tourists, there are a bunch more Lord Vorlastnames running around, like me, who have the title as a permanent inheritance even though we aren't in line for any Districts. My grandfather, who was just a younger grandson of that generation's Count Vorpatril and so didn't even rate a Lord Firstname, was given his when he married Princess Sonia, as some sort of prize, I guess."

"Oh," said Tej, fainter but still valiant. "But..."

"Those are the correct formal titles. Then we come to casual conversation. Falco, or Aral, would be Falco or Aral to their close friends and cronies, wives, and what-not. But I'd never call 'em that; it would be Count Falco or Count Aral, sort of like Uncle Aral. Informal but not so familiar or intimate, y'see? And also useful when there are a bunch of people with the same last name in the conversation, to keep straight which is which. So my mother gets called Lady Alys a lot, because there's another Lady Vorpatril in town, Falco's daughter-in-law, as well as his Countess Vorpatril. Er, and you, now."

"But...I'm not intimate with the same people you're intimate with—so I can't just copy you, can I?"

"Keep it simple," advised Ivan. "Just call him *Count Vorpatril* or *Sir*, unless he tells you otherwise. And still call him Count Vorpatril when we're actually in his court, because that's very formal, see?" He added after a moment, "I sure plan to."

The outskirts of New Evias hove into view, and Ivan had to give over his lightflyer's control to the municipal traffic computer. New Evias was maybe one-tenth the size of Vorbarr Sultana, but perhaps for that very reason, more uniformly modernized. In any case, the control system brought them down neatly into one of the few empty circles painted atop the parking garage next to the assorted District offices of justice. The targeting was accurate to within, oh, twenty centimeters or so. Or thirty. Ivan rubbed his jaw, made sure Tej hadn't bitten her tongue or anything in the hard landing, and escorted her out.

Count Falco Vorpatril sat in judgment, as had several equally stodgy ancestors before him, in one of the few remaining Time-of-Isolation public buildings still left standing in downtown New Evias. The structure's musty legal smell seemed to be ageless. Tej, who had grown very silent, perked up at the dark woodwork and elaborate stone carving gracing the architecture. "Now, this really looks like Barrayar," she said. Ivan was gratified.

In a second-floor corridor, they encountered, prematurely, the count himself, who seemed to be on his way back from lunch.

"Ivan, my boy!" Falco hailed them.

He was still white-haired, stout, jovial—like a sly Father Frost with a hidden agenda. Falco was nothing if not a political survivor, Conservative by inclination, Centrist by calculation. He wore the formal Vorpatril House uniform of dark blue and gold, which adapted itself to his contours much as he adapted himself to the political landscape. A clerk bearing an electronic case filer stamped with the Vorpatril crest dogged his steps, obsequiously. Falco eyed Tej in open appreciation as they stopped and he strolled up.

"Sir." Ivan came to attention. "May I introduce my wife, Lady Tej?"

"Indeed, you may." Count Falco shook Tej's hand, aborting a vague attempt on her part at a curtsey. "I've heard about you, young lady."

"How do you do, Count Vorpatril, sir," said Tej. Loading it all in, just in case, Ivan guessed.

"Talk with Mamere, did you, sir?" Ivan hazarded.

"Quite an entertaining talk, yes."

"Oh, good, that'll save a shipload of time." Ivan squeezed Tej's hand. "See, didn't I say it'll be fine?" Tej smiled gratefully and squeezed back, huddling closer. Ivan slipped a supporting arm around her waist.

Falco smiled benignly. "Countess Vorpatril was very curious about your nuptials, Ivan," he went on, tapping Ivan familiarly on the chest with one broad finger. "She'd like to hear about them from you, by preference. We will both be down to the capital later in the week, note, where you may find her at Vorpatril House at the usual hours. You are behindhand on your courtesy visit, head of the clan and all that."

"It's only a temporary marriage, sir, as I hope Mamere explained? To rescue Tej from some, um, legal complications on Komarr. Which worked fine, all right and tight—got her all fixed up, free of them. Now we just have to get her free of me, and she'll be, um . . . free."

The clerk touched his wristcom, indicating time issues, and Count Falco gave him an acknowledging wave. "Yes, yes, I know. Well, good luck to you both . . ."

Falco toddled off down the corridor to the back door of his chambers. Ivan led Tej in the opposite direction, where they found the waiting area. Another clerk took their names, and left them to wait.

Tej circled the room, eyeing the woodwork and the items decorating the walls, mostly historical artifacts and prints, then stood studying the big wall viewer displaying successive scans of New Evias and rural District scenes since the Time of Isolation.

Ivan, too, rose after a while, because sitting was becoming unbearable, and studied the woodwork, or pretended to. "I'm glad they didn't just knock this old place down like most of the rest of it. Makes it feel like our past isn't just something to be thrown on a scrap heap, now we're all turning galactic, y'know?"

This brought a smile to Tej's lips, one of the few in the past hours. "Is that what you Barrayarans think you're doing?"

But before Ivan could figure out a reply, the clerk returned to say, "Captain and Lady Vorpatril? Your case is up next."

The clerk led them down the hall to Falco's hearings chamber. They stood aside to let a group, no, two groups of people exit, one set looking elated, the other downcast and grumpy. The wood-paneled room was surprisingly small, and, to Ivan's relief, uncrowded: just Falco and his clerk sitting at a desk on a raised dais; a couple of desks toward the front, where a woman lawyer was gathering up what appeared to be stacks of yellowing physical documents dating back to the Time of Isolation, along with her electronic casebook; some empty backless benches bolted to the floor; and, by the door, an elderly sergeant-at-arms in a Vorpatril District uniform. The sergeant received Ivan and Tej from the clerk, who departed again, presumably to deal with whoever next needed to wait, and directed them to the empty tables.

"Um, should be one of you at each of these," he said doubtfully, "and your respective counsels."

"I'll be out of here in just a moment," said the lawyer, stacking faster.

"We're skipping the counsel," said Ivan. "Don't need it."

"And we'd rather sit together," said Tej. Ivan nodded, and they both slipped behind the empty desk. Ivan let his hand dangle down between their uncomfortable wooden chairs, and Tej slid hers into it. Her fingers felt cold and bloodless, not at all like her usual self.

Count Falco lifted his head from some low-voiced consultation with his recording clerk, then made a sign to the sergeant-at-arms, who turned to the room and announced formally: "Next case, Captain Lord Ivan Xav Vorpatril versus Lady..." The sergeant paused and looked down at a slip in his hand, his lips moving. They rounded in doubt; he finally settled on, "His wife, Lady Vorpatril."

The lawyer, about to make her exit, instead turned around and slid onto one of the back benches, her chin lifting in arrested curiosity. Ivan decided to ignore her.

The recording clerk leaned over, grasped an ancient cavalry spear bearing a blue-and-gold pennant that leaned drunkenly against the table edge, tapped its butt loudly in its wooden rest, and intoned, "Your Count is listening. Complainants please step forward."

Tej looked at Ivan in panic; Count Falco leaned forward and encouraged them to their feet with a little crooking of his hands. A charitable pointing of one thick finger indicated where they should stand. Ivan and Tej stood and shuffled to a spot beneath his countly eye, holding hands very tightly.

The clerk observed into his recorder, "Petition for the dissolution of a marriage number six-five-five-seven-eight, oaths originally taken"—he gave the date of that mad scramble in Ivan's rental flat—"Solstice Dome, Komarr."

Ivan wasn't sure whether to think, *Wait, was it only a month ago?* or *Is it a whole month already?* It had not been like any other month of his acquaintance, anyway.

"So..." Falco laced his hands together and stared down at Ivan and Tej for a long, thoughtful moment. Ivan, rendered uneasy by the sheer geezerish Falco-ness of his expression, edged closer to Tej.

Falco leaned back in his chair. "So, Captain Vorpatril, Lady Vorpatril. On what grounds do you petition this court for release from your spoken oaths?"

Ivan blinked. "Grounds, sir?" he hazarded.

"What is, or are, the substances of your complaint or complaints against each other?"

"It was understood from the beginning to be a temporary deal."

"Yet you took permanent oath all the same."

"Er, yes, sir?"

"Do you happen to be able to remember what you said?"

"Yes?"

"Repeat it for the court, please?"

Ivan did so, stumbling less than he had the first time, and leaving out the *of sound mind and body* part because he was afraid the lady lawyer would laugh.

Falco turned to Tej. "Is that as you also remember it, Lady Vorpatril?"

"Yes, sir, Count Vorpatril." She glanced at Ivan, and ventured,

"So what are the usual grounds for divorce on Barrayar, Count Vorpatril, sir?"

Falco folded his arms on his desk, smiling toothily. "Well, let's just run down the list, shall we? Did either of you, at the time of your marriage, bear a concealed mutation?"

Tej's eyebrows rose, for a moment almost haughty. Or haut-like. "I was gene-cleaned at conception, certified free of over five thousand potential defects."

"Mm, no doubt. And the Cetagandan element has undergone recent revision of precedent here, so that won't count either. Besides, I believe Ivan knew of your ancestry?"

"Yes, sir, Count Vorpatril, sir."

"Ivan?" Falco prodded.

"Huh?" Ivan started. "Oh, you know I'm fine, sir!"

"So we all have long hoped," Falco murmured. "Well, that disposes of that issue. Next, adultery. Do either of you accuse the other of adultery?"

"There's hardly been *time*, sir!" said Ivan indignantly.

"You would be amazed at the tales I have heard upon this dais. Lady Tej?"

"No, Count Vorpatril, sir."

Falco paused. "Ah . . . or admit to it?"

They both shook their heads. Tej looked peeved. "Really!" she whispered to Ivan.

"Well, let's see, what next. Desertion, obviously not. Nonsupport?"

"I beg your pardon, sir?" said Tej.

"Does your spouse supply you with adequate food, clothing, shelter, medical care?"

"Oh—yes, sir! Abundantly. Vorbarr Sultana cuisine is just amazing! I've gained a kilo since we got here. Lady Vorpatril's dresser helped me find the right clothes, Ivan's flat is very nice, and medical issues, um, haven't come up."

"We'd cover it," Ivan assured her. "Whatever it was. God forbid, of course."

"And I see you, too, are looking quite healthy, Captain Vorpatril . . . hm, hm. What else do we have here." Falco . . . *made play,* Ivan was sure, of consulting some notes. *Does he do this performance for every divorce petition, or are we special?*

"Abuse—physical, mental, emotional?"

"Sir?" said Tej, staring up in palpable confusion.

"Does your husband beat you?"

"No!"

"Do you beat him?"

"No!" said Ivan. "Good grief, sir!"

"Does he insult you?"

"Certainly not!" Their voices overlapped on that one.

"Does Ivan restrict your mobility, your choices, your access to your family or friends?"

"He got me a groundcar permit, I have more choices than I know what to do with, and my family"—Tej bit her lip—"is out of reach for other reasons. Sir."

"Ah. Yes," said Falco. "Pardon an old Barrayaran's clumsiness."

"Sir." Tej, startled and clearly moved by this apology, returned an uncertain nod. "There's Rish. She's the closest thing to family I have left. She lives with us."

"So, we must cross off abuse, as well. What about denial of marital rights?"

"Sir?" said Tej. "What does that mean, in Barrayaran?"

Falco smiled. "When was the last time you had sex?" he clarified.

"Oh! This morning, sir." Tej thought for a moment, then volunteered, "It was really good."

Two snickers sounded from the back of the room. Ivan did not deign to turn his head.

"*And* congratulations, Ivan," Falco murmured under his breath.

You wily old bastard, why are you yanking us around like this? Ivan thought, but did not dare say it aloud.

"And so, what are we down to, here," said Falco. "Hm, hm. Denial of children?"

Tej looked taken aback. "We've never discussed it."

"It's only a *temporary* marriage, sir," Ivan said. "Children would be, er, rather permanent."

"So we all hope and pray," said Falco.

Tej twisted a strand of her hair in doubt. "Though I suppose if Ivan Xav wanted an egg donation, something could be arranged. My mother sold eggs, when she and my father were first married. To raise venture capital."

Ivan rather thought all of the Barrayarans in the room blinked at this, even the ones behind him. He *would not* look around.

Falco recovered his balance and continued, "So, that one does not hold up, either. I'm afraid we're reaching the bottom of my legal barrel here, Captain and Lady Vorpatril. Do either of you have anything else to offer?"

"But," said Tej, in a confused voice, "it was the deal!"

"Yeah, there you go, sir!" said Ivan. "Breach-of-promise. That's some kind of illegal, isn't it?"

Falco's bushy white eyebrows climbed. "Breach-of-promise, Ivan, is where an expectation of *marriage* is denied, not where an expectation of *divorce* is denied. Also, the complainant has to show palpable harm." He looked them both over and just shook his head.

The clerk passed Falco a swiftly scribbled note. He squinted, read it, and nodded. "Do either of you make any financial claims upon the other?"

"No," said Tej, and "No," said Ivan.

"Now, that *is* interesting. And nearly unique, if I may say so." Falco sat back, sighing. At length, his tapping fingers stilled. He drew a breath. "It is the ruling of this Count's Court that the respondents, Lord Ivan Xav Vorpatril and Lady Akuti Tejaswini Jyoti ghem Estif Arqua Vorpatril, have no grounds for the dissolution of their respective, freely spoken marital oaths. Your petition is denied. Case closed."

The clerk reached over and banged the spear butt in its rest with two loud, echoing clacks.

Tej's mouth had fallen open. Ivan was so stunned he could scarcely suck in air to sputter. "But, but, but . . . you can't *do* that, sir!"

"Of course I can," said Falco serenely. "That's what I come here every session to do, in case you missed the turn, Ivan. Sit, listen to people, form and deliver judgments." His smile stretched, endlessly it seemed. "I do this quite a lot, you know," Falco confided to Tej. "Sometimes I begin to imagine I've heard it all, yet every once in a while there's still some new surprise. Human beings are so endlessly variable."

"But didn't you say you'd talked to my mother?" said Ivan desperately.

"Oh, yes. At great length." Falco leaned forward for the last time, his expression chilling down, and for a moment Ivan was conscious that he stood not before an elderly relative, but a count of Barrayar. "These are some words *not* from your mother. Do not ever again attempt to play fast and loose with solemn oaths in any jurisdiction of mine, Captain and Lady Vorpatril. If you should in the future acquire grounds for your petition, you may again bring it, but my court—which is very busy, I must point out, and has no time for frivolous suits—will not hear you again on the same matter in less than one-half year."

"But," moaned Ivan, still in shock. Even he wasn't sure but *what*.

Falco made a finger-flicking gesture. "*Out*, Ivan. Good day, Lady Tej. Countess Vorpatril hopes to see you both at Vorpatril House in the near future."

Count Falco jerked his head at the sergeant-at-arms, who came forward and grasped Ivan by the sleeve, towing him gently but inexorably toward the door. Tej followed, bewilderment in every line of her body. A mob of people waiting to enter shouldered impatiently past them as they cleared the doorframe and stood, directionless, in the corridor, and the sergeant-at-arms turned his attention to herding the newcomers toward their respective benches. The door closed on the babble, although it opened again in a moment to emit the lawyer, papers and files stacked in her arms.

She twisted around her stack and reached into her case to extract a card, which she handed to Ivan. "My number, Captain."

Ivan took it in numb fingers. "Is this . . . if we want legal advice?"

"No, love. It's for if you ever want a *date*." She trod away up the hall, laughing. By the time she reached the far end of the corridor, the echoes had died, but then she glanced back and her un-lawyerly giggles burst forth once more as she turned down the stairwell.

Holding onto each other like two people drowning, Ivan and Tej staggered out of the archaic building and into watery early-winter sunlight. Apparently, still married.

At least I was right about one thing, Ivan thought. *It did only take ten minutes.*

Chapter Thirteen

Tej paced up and down Ivan Xav's living room. Ivan Xav sat with a drink in his hands, occasionally putting it down in favor of holding his head, instead. Rish perched on the couch with her feet drawn up, listening to their tale; at first with gratifying disbelief, then with increasing and much less gratifying impatience, which was now edging into exasperation.

"I still can't believe that one old man, who wasn't even *there*, could cancel out my deal like that!" fumed Tej. "I thought this was supposed to be all fixed up in advance!"

"It was, it seems—but not by me," said Ivan Xav, sounding morose. "That was my first mistake, going to someone who knows Mamere. We should have taken this to some judge who didn't know me from a hole in the ground, let alone since childhood. Total strangers wouldn't have known what the hell was going on, and might have let us just slide on through."

"So what do you have to do?" said Rish. "To provide these grounds they want."

Ivan Xav shook his head. "Divorce turns out to be a lot of work. Way more than I thought."

"There has to be something. Let's go down your list again,"

said Rish in an annoyingly reasonable tone, squaring her shoulders. "Mutation. Couldn't one of you pretend to be a mutant? Well, not Tej, I suppose. But the captain here is just a natural conception—a *body-birth*, if you can believe it! Run him through an exhaustive enough gene scan, *something* would be bound to turn up that you could pretend to object to."

"No!" said Ivan Xav, incensed. "Besides, it would go down on the court's public record. Think what it would do to my reputation! Dear God, I'd never get laid on this planet again."

Rish tilted her head in concession. "All right, so what about this adultery thing? Which I gather isn't about being a grownup, something we could probably *use* around here, but about sleeping with someone when you're married to someone else. Sounds easy enough. Pleasurable, even."

"Who with, for pity's sake?" said Tej. "The only other male I even know very well on this benighted world is Byerly."

Ivan Xav set down his drink with a thunk that sloshed it over the edge of the glass. "You are *not* sleeping with Byerly."

"Who else have I even met here? Well, there's The Coz and The Gregor, I suppose, but be *reasonable*. Anyway, they're both taken." Tej added after a moment, "And Simon Illyan was very nice, too, but no. Just no. Just...no."

"No," said Ivan Xav. "So many kinds of no, I can't even count the ways."

"That's what I just said." Tej eyed him in speculation. "I don't suppose *you* could sleep with Byerly...?"

"Only if I can watch," murmured Rish.

"*No!*" said Ivan Xav. "*Nobody* is sleeping with Byerly, all right?"

Frostily, Rish cleared her throat.

Ivan Xav waved his arms. "You know what I mean. Neither Tej nor I are sleeping with Byerly. Separately *or* together."

"A foursome, now there's a thought," purred Rish. "You know, I bet we could persuade By to—"

"Stop teasing poor Ivan Xav, Rish," said Tej. He was getting an alarming flush. "If you can't say something to the point, just give over."

Rish looked at Ivan Xav. "Don't you have any old girlfriends you could call on for a favor?"

"Sure, but they're mostly married now. Even Dono, and Olivia would—never mind. Jealous husbands...spouses...I figured I was *done* dealing with that kind of excitement in my life. It's just no fun anymore, y'know? Hasn't been for a while."

Both women stared at him in bemused silence; after a moment, he stirred uncomfortably and took another swallow of his wine.

Rish sat back. "What else was there? Oh yes, abuse."

"I am *not* beating Tej." Ivan Xav glowered at Rish. "You, I'm less and less sure about."

Rish snickered. "You couldn't lay a hand on me if you tried, natural-boy."

Ivan Xav sighed, avoiding conceding the point. "Besides, it'd get me in *so* much trouble with *so* many people—after Mamere, Uncle Aral, and Aunt Cordelia—and Simon—there'd be Miles and Ekaterin and *all* the Koudelka girls lining up to deal with the remains—*and* their mother—*and* Gregor, *and* Desplains— God, there wouldn't be enough left of me to carry to court in a bucket. Hell, a teacup." Ivan Xav sat back in what, had he been of another gender, Tej would not have hesitated to describe as a flounce. A little too large and surly for the term, here.

Rish turned her head toward Tej. "That leaves it up to you."

"But I don't want to hit Ivan Xav! I want to *kiss* Ivan Xav."

"Try it," urged Rish. "Just for the experiment." Her gold eyes glinted.

Reluctantly, at Rish's gesture, Ivan Xav put down his drink and stood up. Tej bunched her hand, drew it back, and poked him in the solar plexus. Her fist made a little *fump* sound, bouncing off his heavy uniform jacket.

Ivan Xav just stared glumly at her. "What was that supposed to be...?"

"It's really *hard*," Tej protested. "When you don't want to. Besides, it would hurt my hand."

"Bloody Falco," muttered Ivan Xav, sitting back down and retrieving his drink, which he drained.

Rish ran her hands through her hair in a ragged swipe. "Look. Think. You're both making this too hard by trying to do the divorce thing first. It's not necessary. Desertion, wasn't that one of the grounds? Tej and I go off to Escobar, change our identities, disappear, you've got your desertion right there. Tootle back to court on your own, get it done. You don't have to drag *us* into it at all."

"There are time limits about that sort of thing," said Ivan Xav.

"Three or four years, or was it seven? Or was that for declaring someone dead...?" He frowned in doubt.

"What does that mean?" asked Tej. "In Barrayaran."

"It means that even though you were gone, I'd still be married to you. For several more years. I couldn't, say, remarry in that time. Or even become betrothed, I suppose."

"Oh," said Tej. "That's right, this place only lets people have one spouse at a time, doesn't it? That wouldn't be a good problem to dump on you, would it? You might meet someone you liked..." A strangely unheartening picture. Didn't she want him to be happy?

Ivan Xav, on the other hand, sat up, brightening a trifle. "That actually could be more of a feature than a bug, come to think. My mother couldn't very well lean on me to seriously court other women if I was already married, huh? Yeah, that docking slot would be all filled up." His brow wrinkled. "Not sure what it would do to my hit rate, though..."

"In that case," said Rish, rolling to her feet, "I hereby declare this a nonemergency, and would appreciate it if you two would clear my bedroom. *Some* of us want to sleep."

Ivan Xav appeared to give this serious consideration. "Yeah, *Miles* goes all frantic and forward-momentum-y when he hits a snag in his plans, but I usually prefer to give it a bit of time. Maybe there'll be a better idea come along, or the problem will change, or, if you wait long enough, even go away on its own, without having to do anything. If people don't keep poking at it, that is."

"Time would certainly do the trick, sure," said Rish cordially. "I figure it would only take, oh, you're a natural—maybe sixty more years? Unless you die sooner in a groundcar crash, that is."

Ivan Xav said, in a faraway voice, "Yeah, that would be the line of least resistance, now, wouldn't it...?"

Rish shook her head. "Go to bed. Screw what's left of your brains out, deal with it again in the morning. Or some other time when I don't have to listen to you two." She departed to collect her bedding from the linen closet in the dressing room.

Ivan Xav stood up and took Tej's hand, warm in his warmer one. "Best advice she's offered all night. Let's just...give it a rest. Maybe something else will come up."

As the week wore on, Ivan contemplated the merits of inertia as a problem-solving technique with growing favor. Desplains kept him only normally occupied during his workdays, there being no real crises at Ops this week, and Ivan being quite unmoved by now by all the synthetic ones, although he did garner some enjoyment selecting snarky return memos. In the mornings, Tej continued her language studies, or games, as she seemed to insist on thinking of them, alternated with afternoon visits along with Rish to Ma Kosti. Even better, they brought back culinary homework. Ivan surreptitiously let his uniform belt out one notch.

Byerly continued to carry off Rish most evenings, a public service to which Ivan could muster no objection. The Creatures of the Night, as he began to think of them, returned at varied hours. He didn't mind it if Rish came in quietly, although he was less fond of stumbling over Byerly at breakfast.

As Ivan was scarfing down his morning groats standing, prior to toddling off to Ops HQ, Byerly, *en déshabillé* in shirtsleeves but slightly less bleary than usual, sipped his tea and remarked, "Interesting chit-chat last night about you and Tej. From Jon Vorkeres, of all people. Countess Vorbretten's little brother, y'know."

Ivan frowned, glad he'd left Tej sleeping. She didn't need to hear anything poisonous. "What was he doing in one of your venues?"

"Hey, not all of my venues are a hazard to the morality of our Vor youth. Else I should have gently steered him out. Jon says that gossip among certain of the more fossilized high Vor dames in town is that your surprise marriage is a disaster for Lady Alys, for all that she feigns otherwise. That Tej's haut genes and connections would render any progeny you two might pop utterly disqualified for the Imperial camp stool, should, God forbid, anything untoward happen to Gregor *et al.* And, presumably, you disqualified along with them, unless you could be persuaded to some second marital attempt, I suppose."

Ivan choked on his groats. "Seriously?"

"Very seriously. Count René Vorbretten is keeping his jaw clamped shut on the discussion, naturally." Byerly eyed him sidelong.

Ivan's brows climbed as the full import of this slowly sank in. "Huh. That's an advantage that hadn't crossed my mind, but you're right!" The corners of his mouth tugged up. "Me and my children, ducking right out of the Vorbarr Sultana political crossfire—oh, *superb.* Have to point that out to Mamere, next time I see her. It would cheer her up no end."

Byerly took a delicate sip, and inquired, "What children?"

Ivan reddened. "Uh..."

Byerly patted his lips—curving in the most maddening way—with his napkin, but did not pursue the point.

It was only as he was entering Ops that it occurred to Ivan that Byerly had been watching his reaction for more reasons than just sly personal amusement. *No, dammit, I have* never *wanted Gregor's job!* He almost turned around right there and then to go find By and a body of water to hold his head under till he stopped *thinking like that.*

Frigging ImpWeasel.

"I bought these bells for my ankles," said Tej to Rish, holding them up and shaking them. They made a cheery chime—tuned to chords, not just randomly dissonant. "If we pushed the furniture back, there'd be room for a real dance practice. I could take Jet's part. Keep the beat for you."

Rish wheeled, sizing up Ivan Xav's living room. "I suppose we could try. I have an hour or so till By comes to get me."

They skinned into their knits and collaborated on shoving sofas and chairs around, clearing a nice, wide space on the carpet. An afternoon without Ma Kosti was an afternoon when boredom and brooding loomed, but Tej had thought ahead, this time. As they began their bends and stretches, Tej asked as-if-casually, "So. By, again. What do you and he *do* every night, anyway?"

Rish's lips twitched. "Really, Tej, you had the same erotic arts tutors that I did. Use your imagination."

"I mean *besides* that." Tej tossed her head impatiently, then had to blow stray hair out of her mouth. "What does he talk about? I mean, when he's not just camouflaging?"

"If his mouth is moving, he's camouflaging," said Rish. But added after a few torso-twists, "Usually."

"Ah?" When this encouraging noise did not pry out further clarification, Tej tried, "Do you still like him?"

"Well...he hasn't stopped being interesting, yet."

Tej dared, "Do you love him?"

Rish snorted. "He's not the warm and fuzzy sort, sweetling."

"Neither are you."

Rish's ambiguous smile crept a tiny bit wider, before she hid her expression in some toe-touches. "I did meet his infamous cousin Dono, in passing. At a party where By had gone to gossip."

"I thought he wasn't on speaking terms with his family?"

"Apparently Count Dono Vorrutyer is an exception to the general trend—he laughed when By introduced me. Delighted, apparently, by a Vorrutyer being even more shocking than himself. Herself. Whatever." A few overhead reaches. "Still, By hasn't spoken to his father for eighteen years, his mother has been estranged from everyone for a decade and barely communicates, and By secretly helped ImpSec put his even more obnoxious cousin Richars in prison. With cause. No love lost there. On the whole, not a close-knit clan."

"How sad."

"Not... really."

"Oh?" Tej raised her arms and her eyebrows, waggling both.

A long pause, while Rish stretched hamstrings. "*In vino veritas*, By calls it," she said at last. "Like some primitive native fast-penta. Except By is almost never as drunk as he appears. If he's slurring and staggering, he's certainly spinning out lines to catch something. When he's *actually* smashed, his diction gets very precise and distant, like... like a scientist reporting the results of an unsatisfactory experiment. It's oddly disturbing."

Tej sat on the floor with her legs out, put her hands behind her head, and bent to touch her elbows to her knees. And waited, not in vain.

Her voice and movements slowing, Rish went on, "We were watching some old vids of the Jewels' performances that ImpSec came up with, and testing out some really dreadful Barrayaran inebriants. Which got us onto the subject of sisters, somehow, which got us onto the subject of *his* younger sister... It seems they were very close when they were teens—By fancied himself quite the brotherly protector. Till their father, as a result of some vile report he had from who-knows-where, accused By of molesting her. And went on believing it, despite the pair of them protesting to the rafters. By says he was more enraged at his father for swallowing the smear than he ever was at the anonymous clown who made it. Which was when he left school and came east to the capital. I'm not sure if you *can* disinherit your parents, but it seems that break was mutual."

Rish stood on one foot, bent backward, and touched the sole of the other to the back of her head, then alternated. Tej merely essayed a few less ambitious backbends, while she thought this through. She finally collapsed to the carpet and asked, "What in the *world* did you trade to him for *that* confession?"

"I'm not at all sure," said Rish, in a tone that frankly echoed this wonder. "But he was enunciating very clearly, just before he passed out."

Tej squinted. "Puts rather a different spin on his choice of careers, maybe?"

"I think, yeah. At first I thought he was in it for the money, and then for the mischief, and then I figured both of those were covers for this crazy Barrayaran patriotism all these Vor fellows go on and on about. Then I thought maybe it was for revenge, for nailing the guilty. Now I wonder if this furtive obsession for sorting truth from lies is actually in aid of clearing the innocent."

"That seems like two sides of one coin, to me."

"Yeah, but it's like the man bets tails, every time."

"Hm."

"In which case..."

"Hm?"

"He won't give it up. No matter how much he despises the work. Or his subjects. Or himself."

"Do you think... this planet. Barrayar. Since this divorce thing snagged up, what would you think of staying here? For a while. Longer." Tej forced herself not to hold her breath.

Rish shrugged. "It's been a more interesting place to visit than I would've imagined, but I wouldn't want to live here. I want"— she hesitated—"what I had."

"You miss the Jewels." It wasn't a question.

Rish stretched like a starfish on her back, then closed her arms and legs in tight. "As I would miss my limbs, amputated. I keep reaching, but they're not *there*."

Tej buckled the bell straps around her ankles, rose, and stamped. The bells sang back in a ragged chorus. "I'll take Jet's part," she offered again. Keeping, somehow, the quaver out of her voice.

Rish rolled to her bare blue feet, kicked once in air, and took up her position. "Do your best." She eyed Tej more closely. "Don't worry, sweetling. I won't abandon you on this benighted world. We'll get out together."

That's not quite what I meant, Rish... Tej bit her lip, nodded, extended her arms, and bent her legs, taking up the complex rhythm at the hub of the wheel, heel-and-toe. The music and motion flowed up through her body and out her spiraling fingertips, as she turned to track her spinning partner around the circle's rim.

Ivan encountered By in the lobby of his building, entering just ahead of him. "Hey, wait up," he called, and By paused. Ivan shifted his dinner bag from hand to hand and asked, "You going up to see Rish?"

"We're heading out for the evening, yes."

"Good-oh."

They entered the up-tube together. Ivan pictured himself demanding of By, *What are your intentions toward my sister-in-law?* in the best paterfamilias style, and winced. Trouble was, By might *answer.* But as they exited to the hallway outside Ivan's flat, his steps slowed nonetheless. By stopped with him, looking his inquiry.

"About Rish. You're not making her, like, fall in love with you or anything, are you? Because you could be reassigned or something, and have to drop her. And I don't want to be stuck in a flat full of weeping, angry women, with no male to take it out on but me."

By tilted his head in appreciation of this concern. "No, I seem to be on the case, at least until they decamp for Escobar. Has your, ah, non-divorce affected the timetable on that?"

"I have no idea."

"Have you asked?"

"Uh . . . no?"

"I see."

By was dressed in casual garb, not evening wear; planning a night in, not a night out, apparently. Ivan went on in covert hope, "So, ah . . . any chance that you'll invite her to move in with you? Save steps and all that. Or that she'll decide to move in with you?"

By's hooded eyes grew amused. "The topic has not come up."

"But you could make it come up. Couldn't you? S'true, I'd rather hug a snake, but there's no accounting for tastes."

"S-s-s-she is amazingly flexible," By agreed. "I expect she could crush my skull with her thighs alone. Very talented thighs. I could be in danger of my life every time we go to bed. Just think of the obituary."

Ivan heroically resisted the straight line, not to mention the spinning visions this comment engendered. "You could make her happy just by getting her off my couch." *Or off on my couch, I suppose.* Except it was possible By already had. *Dammit, I want my furniture back.*

By snorted. "Happy? God, no, I couldn't make her happy. Not in a thousand years."

Ivan's brows rose in surprise. "I don't get it. She seems tolerably amused by you. I mean, you've made her laugh. I've heard her."

By waved a dismissive hand. "She won't be happy till she's reunited with her odd sibs. The other Jewels. They're more than just a troupe or a team, or even a family. I suspect something gengineered."

Ivan's nose wrinkled. "Are you suggesting they're some sort of Cetagandan post-human group mind or, or something?"

"No, not that. Definitely not, by her account of some of their arguments. Something much more visceral. I suspect some sort of kinesthetic biofeedback in play. It's not at all obvious when you see her in isolation. You have to see her with the others."

"Uh, when did this happen?"

"I had ImpSec Galactic Affairs scrounge me some recordings of the Jewels' performances. It's . . . no, it's not clear. But it becomes subtly apparent, if you watch them over enough, that the Jewels were sustaining each other, somehow. But Rish alone is . . . starving isn't the word. I don't know what is." By had forgotten to be smarmy, as his eyes narrowed in memory and thought.

"So what's the difference?"

By's hand reached out and closed, as if trying to grasp something elusive. "Rish with the Jewels looks like a woman with a beating heart. Rish in exile looks like . . . a woman with a muscle in her chest that pumps blood."

Ivan tried to unravel this. "Y'know . . . I haven't the *least* idea what you're on about, By."

By rubbed his forehead and laughed shortly. "Yeah, neither do I. You should watch the vids sometime, though."

"Is Tej in any of 'em?"

"No."

"Ah."

They walked on; Ivan coded open his door. A sound of bells and rhythmic thumping wafted out.

They entered to find Tej and Rish engaged in some sort of vigorous dance practice. Tej spared Ivan a flashing smile, as she turned and stomped. She seemed to dance with every part of her, from her toes to her face; the expressive movements of her arms reminded him, for a moment, of the quaddies. The cadences moved through her generous flesh as though her body danced with itself, joyously. Ivan's lips parted.

Rish, spotting By, glinted a grin like a sickle moon hung in an evening sky, and switched from spinning along around a wide circle like some planetary epicycle, to a kind of precise hand-to-hand-to-foot-to-foot rotation, a blue spider turning cartwheels. Ivan blinked dizzily as the grin rolled upside down with each turn.

"Now...now *that's* just showing off," he muttered to By.

For just a second, By grinned back, though not at him.

Tej, who seemed to be performing the same function as the drummer in a band backing the lead singer, brought the bells and thumps to a graceful closure. The two women stretched and made obeisance to each other, for all the world like two martial arts players completing a satisfactory round. Ivan wasn't sure who'd won.

Rish waved at By and dashed toward the lav. "A quick shower, and I'll be right with you."

Ivan put the dinner bags down on the table and watched as Tej, arrestingly warm and breathless, sat on the carpet and began to unbuckle the ankle bells. By folded his arms and leaned against the wall, till Tej and Ivan drafted him to help pull furniture back into place. Ivan sighed meaningfully at his couch, but he wasn't sure if By got the message. The Creatures absconded without dropping any further hints of their intentions, anyway.

All right, Ivan supposed he was slow. He'd been told so often enough by his assorted relatives, colleagues, and so-called friends. But it wasn't until tripping over the ankle bells on the way back from the lav in the night, and wrapping himself around a warm, squirmy, sleeping Tej, that the thought crossed his mind like a bright, evasive—unhelpful—shooting star.

So...how does a fellow ask his own wife to marry him...?

It took him a long time to fall asleep again, after that.

"Tej? Tej!" A hand shook her shoulder; Tej swam up out of slumber. A dim yellow pool of light from the bedside lamp pushed back the shadows. Ivan Xav was sitting on her side of the bed with his trousers on, his face in that scrunched expression it wore when he'd bitten into something he didn't quite like.

Tej rubbed her eyes and sat up on one elbow. "What *time* 'zit?" She tried a sleepy smile on him, but it won only a return lip-twitch.

"A little after oh-three-hundred. I just got a rather strange call from a Customs & Security officer out at the Vorbarr Sultana Shuttleport. Says they've detained some fellow out there who claims to be a relative of yours. Or at any rate, he was asking for Madame Tejaswini Arqua Vorpatril, which is at least part-right."

"What?" Tej sat bolt upright. "*Who?*"

"Supposedly, some Escobaran tourist named Dr. Dolbraco Dax. Held up because of irregularities, Customs said, although the fellow's documentation seemed to be all in order. I'm not sure what that meant, except that this Dax fellow was insistent that if you would come identify him, you could straighten it all out."

"That's *Amiri's* identity!" Tej cried, scrambling from her covers. "Oh, what's he doing *here*? We have to go out there!"

Ivan Xav prudently ducked out of the way as she lunged for her clothes. "Well, either your brother, or some really clever bounty hunter. Morozov was pretty sure some of those would be show- ing up in due course. Although a bounty hunter would have to be downright crazy to try a snatch in the middle of shuttleport security." Ivan Xav scratched his stubbled chin. "Or maybe just lazy. Not as far to drag you to the exit, after all."

"Most of them actually are crazy, but..." Tej's thoughts whirled, as she shoved her head through her turtleneck and clawed her hair free. "If it's really Amiri, how did he find me? Here, put your shirt on." She crawled back across the rumpled bed in search of her socks. "Did your ImpSec people contact him or something?"

"Shouldn't think he'd have been detained, in that case." Ivan Xav shook his head. "Though I could see... If Miles gossiped to Mark or Kareen about you and me, and he probably couldn't resist doing so, Mark might have told this Lily Durona woman who runs his clinic. Who could have said something to your brother. I can't guess how much information might have been dropped out or added with each link. Or how it was spun. Mark and I, um... don't always get along."

As Tej got him dressed and pulled him toward the door, Ivan Xav added, "I'm leaning toward bounty hunters, myself. I did alert my ImpSec outer perimeter, though I don't much care to talk to those fellows if I don't have to. But at least it'll give the night shift something to do that doesn't involve voyeurism. I expect they'll like that."

"Voyeurism?" Despite her hurry, Tej froze. "I hope that's a joke."

"Well, I hope so, too," confessed Ivan Xav. "Grant you, I gave up asking them questions I didn't want to hear the answers to some time back."

Shaking her head, Tej abandoned this side issue and shoved him into the hallway.

For the first time ever, as his two-seater arrowed out through the wintry margins of the city, she thought that Ivan Xav was driving too slowly. She leaned forward anxiously into her seat straps as the civilian shuttleport at last rose into view. This was her first look at the place, as they'd come downside before via the military shuttleport, where arrangements had been very different. VBS Main looked very much like every other big galactic port she'd ever seen—under construction. Ivan Xav wove handily around worksite barricades. Fortunately, he seemed to know where he was going, and the place was thinly populated at this dark off-hour.

His military ID whisked them past the first layer of security like a magic wand, at which point they were met by a man in a customs uniform, a lieutenant in military undress greens with ImpSec Horus-eyes on his collar, and, hurrying up last, Byerly and Rish, out of breath. The customs man stepped back at the sight of Rish, his lips parting in astonishment, but he glanced at the unreactive ImpSec fellow, swallowed, and carried on.

"I've arranged a preliminary look through a monitor for you, Madame Vorpatril," the customs man told her, and it was a sign of something that Ivan Xav didn't correct the title. "As it seemed to be thought that there could be some safety and security issue." Tej wasn't sure if his irritated glance at the ImpSec officer suggested a conflict of jurisdictions or procedures, or just the accumulated frustrations of trying to get ImpSec to give a straight answer to any question.

The customs man guided them through a code-locked door labeled *Authorized Personnel Only* and threaded a maze of office corridors, mostly with doors shut for the night. Down two floors, through some utilitarian tunnels smelling of dry concrete and machine oil, up again, then to an unlabeled door in a broader corridor. Some kind of satellite security office, judging by the consoles; on duty was only a single clerk, who gave way to the customs officer and gestured to the vid. "Nothing of interest so far, sir."

The plate showed four views of what appeared to be a midsized, private waiting room, brightly lit if a touch shabby, neither luxury lounge nor prison chamber. The ambiguous space was occupied by nine people and many jumbled piles of luggage. The figures were variously sitting up looking very bored, or lying across rearranged chairs and cases, uncomfortably dozing. Three men and six women. Tej's heart seemed to stop beating altogether.

"Can you pick out this Dr. Dax?" asked the ImpSec lieutenant.

She gulped for breath, for rising joy, for hope unlooked-for. "I can pick out *everybody*."

Rish was staring over the vid display with wide, devouring eyes. "The Baronne . . . ?" she breathed.

"And Dada!" said Tej. "And Star and Pidge and Em and Pearl and . . . is that *Grandmama*?"

"What happened to her hair?" said Rish faintly.

Ivan Xav's brows climbed; Byerly looked suddenly very blank.

Tej grabbed the customs man by the front of his uniform jacket. She really hadn't meant to lift him off his feet; it just happened. "Take me to them! Take us to them *right now*!"

Chapter Fourteen

Two armed shuttleport security guards stood alert outside the entrance to the waiting room, Ivan noted at once. The Arqua clan had been sequestered well apart from the usual transients, but, delicately, not yet in criminal detention. That area lay conveniently nearby, though, through those unmarked double doors at the corridor's end, if he was recalling the labyrinthine layout of this place correctly. Ivan decided not to mention this to the frantic Tej. Or to the jittering Rish. Judging from By's narrowed glances around, he was making similar estimates.

The guards made way as the Customs & Immigration officer, a senior shift supervisor named Mahon, coded open the waiting-room door. Tej and Rish nearly fell over him, and each other, blasting through.

"My *parents*, I thought they were *dead*..." Tej squeaked as she elbowed the man out of her path.

A jerk of By's chin invited Ivan to note the vid recorder the customs officer clutched in his hand. Mahon regained his balance and murmured to Ivan, "All those names Madame Vorpatril was rattling off...you do realize, none of them match the documentation these people were traveling under." A thin smile turned his mouth, as of an earnest official contemplating well-honed instincts rewarded.

"Is that going to be a problem?" said Ivan.

"Definitely. I just don't know what kind, yet. Or whose." He and the wary ImpSec lieutenant, Zumboti, exchanged calculating stares.

Ivan twitched, and corrected, "Lady Vorpatril," for the first time. Just in case. Zumboti took the precaution of unholstering his stunner and easing off the safety, though he held his hand discreetly down at his side, before shouldering in ahead of Ivan. A beat, and his glance back gave permission for Ivan to enter.

The chamber was transmuting from sleepy, grouchy boredom to shrieking chaos as various Arquas looked up one after another and saw Tej and Rish. Ivan had just time to confirm that no one was drawing a weapon as Tej flew directly to a stout, gray-haired, mahogany-faced man who barely made it to his feet before catching her in an astonished bear-hug. Ivan had a moment to watch, unobserved, as his eyes squeezed shut, lids glistening with moisture, mouth opening in a huff of an exhalation under Tej's impact; it seemed wrong, somehow, to look uninvited upon a man's face so deeply disarmed, so naked with emotion.

Ivan tore his glance away to see Rish somersault through the air and fetch up kneeling neatly at the feet of the very tall woman with short, dark hair held in a jeweled headband, and crouch to touch the sandaled toes. The woman hastily bent and raised her up into an embrace as well. Her face was vastly more reserved than that of her spouse, but her expression was unnervingly intense for all its restraint.

All hopes delivered...

The pairs parted to share another hug four-about, and then the mob closed in. Ivan's eyes flicked madly, trying to identify them all—if they would only stand *still* for a minute, or better yet, line up, he might have a fighting chance.

Two young women were taller than Tej, although not as tall as their mother—Ivan mentally dubbed them *Fit* and *Fitter*, before memory of the scans he'd been shown kicked in. *Fit* was Pidge, the middle sister, sporting red-brown skin, red-brown hair, and cinnamon eyes, dressed in something blue-green and flowing. Her taller, older, and impossibly even fitter sister Star shared the spicy skin, with sleek ebony hair drawn back in a tight knot, complemented by her utilitarian black pantsuit; her startling ice-green eyes recalled those of her mother the Baronne.

The assorted Jewels were, thank God, color-coded, and much easier to sort out. Ivan barely blinked at Emerald's green and glittering skin and sunlight-on-leaves-colored hair, or the slim woman with pointed ears and white skin laced with silver, her snow-white hair clipped in a similar short pelt—Pearl, obviously. Their pantsuits would probably be travel-rumpled if they dared.

The two young male figures were less instantly recognizable, although Ivan managed to arrive at them by process of elimination. They lacked the Arqua height of their elder sisters, being barely as tall as Byerly. The one had crisp black hair and dark olive skin—he likely could pass for an Escobaran. The second, more thickset fellow had mahogany skin like the Baron's, but weirdly patchy; flecks of onyx-black and silver peeked through here and there. His ears, alone among the Jewels, were round—another change from that old group portrait of Morozov's. Both men were dressed in Escobaran-style street clothes, short-sleeved hemmed shirts worn un-tucked over trousers. Onyx, presumably, and—

"Amiri!" cried Tej, flinging herself on him in turn. "You look so different! Jet!"

The olive-skinned man embraced her, his eyes closing briefly as if in prayer. "You're *alive*. You're both alive, but oh—" His eyes snapped open again in anger shot with joy, crackling with both. "We've been waiting for months! Never heard a word, until—we didn't know if you were alive or dead!"

"I'm sorry, I'm sorry," Tej laugh-cried back, "we ran out of money, we ran out of luck, we ran out of, of nearly everything..."

Rish held out one of the other man's muscular arms, and reached to touch the outer curve of an ear. "You're so big! And your beautiful skin—what's wrong with it?"

"Nothing permanent," he assured her, folding her in a fresh hug. "Just a treatment to blend in on Escobar, wearing off. The extra fifteen kilos is mostly muscle, but I needed some fat to change the shape of my face. The Duronas supplied."

Tej danced in a circle, arms outspread as if to take in everyone. "Oh, how did you find me, how did you get away, why are you all *here*...? And you brought Grandmama, *too*?"

Standing a little aside from the whole show, watching with cool approval, was the tallest woman of all, taller than Ivan. She wore loose silky trousers, shirt, and a light, knee-length coat in an indeterminate planetary style. She was very straight-backed, yet thin and faintly frail. Age-softened skin clad bones of timeless elegance. Her bright silver hair was cut in short wisps around her perfectly shaped head.

Tej bowed before her, hands held palm-to-palm in a respect only enhanced by the pleasure overflowing from her face. A pale hand as delicate as an ice sculpture moved to rest palm-down among her wild curls in a gesture of benediction. "Indeed," the woman murmured.

The customs officer, with another chary look around at all the wildly gesticulating and madly babbling Arquas, edged closer to Ivan. Better the Vor lord that you knew than the Jacksonians that you didn't? He said, not quite out of the corner of his mouth, "Are these really relatives of yours, Captain Lord Vorpatril?"

About to hotly deny any such absurdity, Ivan's mouth opened and hung at half-cock. "Well, er...in a sense. That is, that would be my father-in-law, my mother-in-law"—he nodded variously— "and my, um, siblings-in-law."

"*All* of them?"

"Yeah, pretty much. I know they don't look alike. It's kind of hard to explain..." He took a breath. "Yes." He added after a vaguely shattered pause, "And my—uh—that lady over there would be my grandmother-in-law. My wife's mother's mother. Widowed." Ivan was suddenly profoundly grateful for that. A wizened ghem-general would surely tip this barrel right over.

Wait, no, this wasn't the whole set after all. It seemed the eldest brother Erik was still missing, and a couple of the Jewels—Ruby, and, what was the other one? Topaz, that was it. Maybe it wasn't just jump-lag and umpteen hours in Barrayaran detention that gave the Arqua crew that edgy, exhausted air.

The customs officer looked as if he was thinking hard and fast. Ivan eyed him uneasily.

Tej grabbed Ivan by the arm and towed him over to face the Baron, the Baronne, and Lady ghem Estif. Ivan was sorry now he wasn't shaved and in uniform, instead of stubbled and in wrinkled civvies grabbed off his bedroom floor. Though he supposed it made him even-all with the travel-worn Arquas.

In a voice gone breathless and shy, Tej said, "Dada, Baronne, Grandmother—this is my Barrayaran husband, Lord Ivan Xav

Vorpatril." As if she had several other husbands of various planetary origins tucked away somewhere...? "He's not a lord *of* anything, though."

The three elders swung piercing gazes upon Ivan. Their smiles chilled right down.

"Lily Durona had said as much," said the Baron.

"It all sounded very odd," said the Baronne.

"Not at all illuminating," said Lady ghem Estif.

"The wedding was a bit impromptu," said Tej, "but at the time it saved me and Rish from a world of trouble. I'll explain later."

The Baron's heavy features lightened only marginally. It was the man's height and broad build, Ivan decided, that reminded him subliminally and uncomfortably of Count Falco. And his edginess that recalled, even more uncomfortably, Uncle Aral in a mood. *Yikes.*

"How do you do, sir, ma'am, haut," Ivan managed, belatedly grateful for every lesson in diplomacy his mother had ever tried to inflict on him. The last being the proper form of address to a haut lady, if a touch flattering to one culled and demoted to ghem. Lady ghem Estif's silver brows rose in surprise. In any case, she did not offer to correct it. God, what next? *I am pleased to meet you* was a diplomatic lie of the first order, beyond his scope right now. His mouth moved on automatically to, "How may I help you?" Wait, no...

The Baron brightened a touch more, with a surprised glance under those heavy lids at his daughter. Right answer? "By all means, let's find out. Pidge, come here."

The woman in the flowing blue-green trouser outfit stepped up alertly. "Baron?"

The Baron waved the customs officer forward. "Officer Mahon, I think the time has come for you to talk with our lawyer, the Baronette Sophia Arqua." Pidge's formal name and courtesy title, Ivan dimly recalled. "She will speak for our group."

"Are you oath-bound to practice law on Barrayar, ma'am?" asked Mahon stiffly.

Pidge smiled warmly across at him, eye-to-eye. "I am primarily trained in galactic law and trade law, with some experience in criminal law. I have made a special intense study of Barrayaran law in the past two weeks, however."

Ivan wondered—on Jackson's Whole, how literally did she mean *criminal law*?

"The conundrum would seem to be whether we are still House

Cordonah"—she cast a nod at her father, who nodded back—"and so due all appropriate diplomatic protocol, or whether we are Houseless persons, seeking asylum under the aegis of a Barrayaran Vor relative, and due all assistance as such."

"That's not nearly the only two questions..." Mahon, swinging toward the ImpSec lieutenant, held out a hand in either direction or plea, Ivan wasn't sure.

Zumboti took a neutral pose, not quite parade rest, and observed to the air, "It is ImpSec's mandate to secure the Imperium against threats of violence. I've seen none on offer here, so far. Strictly bureaucratic issues are not normally our department."

What, was ImpSec giving its officers a short course in disingenuity, now? *Probably.*

Mahon rubbed his forehead, and muttered, "Two hours..." It took Ivan a moment to realize he was likely referring to his end-of-shift, when the day officers would be coming on. And, Ivan was reminded with a glance at his wristcom, when he was due at Ops. So would Mahon play this out till then, in order to dump it on his senior colleagues and escape? In any case, he looked marginally happier to be presented with a single Arqua to argue with, rather than all of them at once. And a gorgeous female, at that. A little weakly, he allowed Pidge to glow at him, take him by the arm, and lead him aside, bending her head to murmur at him in an intimate tone.

Shiv Arqua's gaze shifted around to at last snag on Byerly, standing behind Rish. A brow cocked. "And who is this?"

By, with covert reluctance, stepped forward. Rish cleared her throat. "Baron, Baronne, haut, may I present my, um, friend, Byerly Vorrutyer."

Byerly managed a tolerably noncroggled bow. "My pleasure, to be sure." Aye, By was the trained professional liar.

Star, strolling up, sniffed. "*Um-friend?* So it would appear. Really, Rish, your taste in men. He has to be a natural."

"Barrayaran Vor, certainly," said Lady ghem Estif, with the air of an entomologist observing a familiar species of beetle.

"Though not a lord," By put in, with a specious helpfulness.

"But a friend?" said the Baron to Rish. That edge was back. "Truly?"

Rish, put on the spot, shrugged. "Well...friendly. I'll explain later, all right?"

By's stance eased. The Baron's suspicious glower seemed to

slot him into a class by himself, provisionally. Very provisionally. Which wasn't *wrong*.

"So were the news vids all lies?" said Tej. "There were *pictures* of your bodies."

"Yes, that made it rather awkward for Prestene to report our escape, when we followed Star and the girls to Earth," said the Baronne dryly.

"Ruby, Topaz—Erik?" said Rish. "Is everything horrible made not so?"

"Yes and no," the Baronne told her. "Ruby made it to Fell Station, we believe, and is under the protection of Baron Fell for the moment. Seppe is apparently with her, though fallen into contract-debt to House Fell for his medical treatment."

Ivan watched a tremble run through Tej's body. She exhaled and ran the back of her wrist over her eyes.

"That was the yes," said Rish. Her voice was growing quieter.

The Baronne nodded. "Topaz...did not get off the Station when we did. As far as we presently know, she remains hostage."

"Erik—?" said Tej. Her voice, too, had fallen low.

Shiv Arqua grew grim. "It's hard to say. Prestene claims to have his body cryo-preserved. How revivable he may be, we do not know."

Tej swallowed. So did Ivan. Almost worse than death, that boundless uncertainty. In his experience.

Arqua grimaced. "Fool boy—nothing he defended was worth his life, once you girls were away. He should have surrendered!"

"Perhaps he did," murmured the Baronne, and her husband pressed his teeth together.

"Did you get out right after Star's group, then?" asked Rish. Oddly wary, that question. Oddly hopeful.

The Baronne ran a hand through her short hair, almost dislodging the defiantly bright band across her forehead. "No. Not for some weeks. They shaved my head when they took me, among the other things they tried—for all the good it did them." Her eyes flashed in some dark triumph. "It will grow back. We will grow *everything* back, now we've rescued the pair of you."

"Uh, we sort of rescued ourselves..." Tej pointed out tentatively. When no one responded to this, she turned and added, "But Grandmama, what happened to *your* hair, then?"

A muscle jumped in Lady ghem Estif's fine jaw. "I sold it. Back on Earth."

"All three meters of it," confirmed Star. "At auction. It went for a fabulous sum, which we needed at that point. Far more money than I would have believed possible—there are collectors, it turns out. And absolute provenance, since we allowed the winner to cut it himself."

Emerald, at her shoulder, muttered, "I still think he had a fetish." Pearl nodded ruefully.

The Baronne, her own dark hair regrown barely finger-length beneath the red band, said nothing at all. The story under that silence... well, Ivan would doubtless get it later, too. No visible damage marred her skin, but it was not nearly so luminous as in the younger scans. Pallid, almost. *These people are really tired.*

"That was a pretty amazing sacrifice, for a haut woman," Ivan offered, this seeming a less fraught topic. "I once met some of the ladies of the Star Crèche itself, on Eta Ceta, some years ago. Their never-cut hair was a major status-marker."

Lady ghem Estif's expression went rather opaque. "It is long," she stated, "since I left the Star Crèche." She hesitated, looking at Ivan more sharply. "Do the Consorts speak with Outlanders, now?"

"It was a special, um, event. What was your clan, that is, your haut constellation of origin, before you married the ghem general?"

"Rond." Lady ghem Estif delivered the flat monosyllable without emotion. The Rond were one of the mid-grade Cetagandan Constellations, though that was like saying "one of the mid-grade billionaires." But she regarded Ivan with the faintest new spark of... less disapproval. As though he might be trainable, with the right program of exercises and rewards.

Byerly sucked on his lower lip, his expression baffled.

Officer Mahon and Pidge returned from the corner where they'd been talking in rapid under-voices. Mahon's lips were screwed up in something less than joy, but better than hostility. Pidge looked unsettlingly serene.

Mahon blew out his breath. "This is what I can offer tonight, to get you people out of here and into some more comfortable location. If Captain Vorpatril, here, will speak for you as the Barrayaran subject to whom you are related, pledging his word and posting a bond, I can release you into his temporary custody as applicants for asylum. This allows you a two-week limited visa while waiting for judicial review. With an opportunity for extensions should the review take longer."

Kicking the problem upstairs—much the best choice. Ivan would sympathize, except...

"Given the numerous irregularities, not to mention outright falsifications, in your travel documentation, for which you can, yes, plead mitigating circumstances"—a fending gesture at Pidge—"you should not count on your application being finally approved. But at least," his voice dropped, as if talking to himself, possibly as the one sane person here, "I have forms to cover it all."

Tej turned to Ivan, her bright eyes thrilled. "Oh, yes! I knew you could do it, Ivan Xav!"

Ivan tried to point out that he hadn't done anything, yet, but the words stuck in his throat, especially when Tej spared a hug for him. *This is not my fault. Right? Right?* He glanced at By, who blinked back *palpably* unhelpfully.

"Bond," Ivan said to Mahon. "Is that, like, a pledge of credit, or do you need cash down?"

"Cash, I'm afraid, Captain. Times nine, although I may be able to arrange a group discount. And a spoken oath, given your rank."

"Ah." How *many* forms? Multiplied by nine? No, he wasn't going to make it to Ops on time today, was he. Ivan drew a deep inhalation. "In that case, Officer Mahon, I need to make some calls."

Mahon was efficient; documentation hell only ran an hour and a half past the end of his shift. Either conscientious or curious, he stayed to see things through. Ivan read aloud off Mahon's cheat sheet a number of promises to take responsibility for a number of things over which, as far as he could see, he had no control whatsoever, making it official; the Arquas watched this Barrayaran step with the inquisitiveness of metropolitans come down to take in a backcountry show at a District fair.

This dumped Ivan, Tej, the nine new Arquas, and their small mountain of luggage into a rented ground-van headed for downtown Vorbarr Sultana at the peak of morning traffic. By and Rish, who'd come out to the shuttleport by the new bubble tube—in service this week for a change, however temporarily—drove Ivan's two-seater on ahead. Ivan wondered what they were saying to each other.

Conversation in the van had drifted off to a sleep-deprived muttering by the time they arrived at the hotel, just down the block from Ivan Xav's flat. It seemed a middling sort of place, built in a functional mode during the reign of Emperor Ezar with patchy upgrades since, but the location could scarcely be bettered. Ivan Xav saw them all registered, which seemed to involve displays of both his credit and military IDs, then drew Tej aside.

"Now I really have to run to Ops. Don't let them do anything awful till I get back, right? In fact, don't let them do anything."

"I think everyone wants to sleep, first."

"That'd be all right. Yeah, do that." He kissed her and fled.

Surprisingly, Rish managed to scrape By off at the lobby lift tubes; he bade her a fond farewell. Exiting at the seventh-floor lift-tube foyer, Rish paused and picked what seemed to be a piece of metallic lint from under her collar, murmured, "Nice try, By. Love and kisses," and made smacking noises into it, and deposited it in the waste chute. At Tej's sideways look, she merely shrugged.

Ivan Xav had somehow managed to secure rooms all in a row for them. A two-bedroom suite for the seniors with a central lounge connected on either side to bedrooms that absorbed Amiri and Jet, and Star, Pidge, Pearl and Emerald, plus their luggage. They all returned as swiftly as they could to the sitting room, where Tej and Rish were recounting, once more, the tale of their long flight, and took up perches to listen. And, inevitably, to critique.

When Tej came to the part about Ivan Xav's clever marital rescue on Komarr, she glanced at Amiri and Jet and left out the bit about the balcony, saying only, "We weren't thinking too straight by then, I guess. We were both so tired."

"You weren't thinking at all, as far as I can see," said Pidge tartly. "Good grief, Tej, you're as scatterbrained as ever."

Pearl turned to Rish. "And you *let* her?"

"It worked out," said Rish defensively.

Dada held up a thick hand to stem an incipient and well-worn digression into personalities, if adding mildly, "Though really, Tej-love, we could have negotiated you a favorable deal for a House heir anytime these past five years. All those wasted opportunities, just to end up with a Barrayaran?"

This was tolerable only because he had accepted Tej's every *No*— well, *No, thank you, Dada*—on said deals for five years straight with no more demur than an occasional wince and grunt. At least Dada wouldn't complain that Ivan Xav was a natural, being one himself. Nor could the Baronne, without blatant hypocrisy. Not that she couldn't find other grounds.

"This Vorpatril fellow turns out to be quite interesting, for a Barrayaran, I will allow that," said the Baronne. "If I thought it was guile and not blind luck, I would be quite proud of you both. Or—did you know of his high-level connections before negotiating this strange oral contract?"

"For *free*, no less," said Star in an aggrieved undervoice. "*Tej.*"

"No," sighed Tej. "We only found out after."

"Figures," murmured Pearl.

"Did you look him up?" Tej asked the Baronne. "Back on Escobar?"

"Of course. As soon as Lily passed us that—at the time, it seemed a very garbled rumor, but actually it seems correct in more details than I would have believed. Not that we weren't overjoyed to have finally located you two. But how closely does that boy actually stand to the Barrayaran Imperial throne?"

Oh, blast, the Baronne had already stumbled onto that angle. Well, of course she had. She was the *Baronne.* "Camp stool," Tej corrected in a small voice. "When The Gregor has to sit in ceremony. On account of Vor being a military caste." The Baronne waved away this distinction. Tej . . . remembered a plaque in a street that groundcars ran over.

Rish put in, "There are quite a few more bodies between him and that position than when he was younger, apparently—plus he'd have to win a couple of civil wars with rival claimants, to hear him tell it. He was never the only potential heir."

Grandmama lifted a quelling finger. "I would advise against pursuing that direction, Udine, dear. There are many safer approaches you might work in aid of our aims here, and I promise you, you do not want to get bogged down in extended altercations with the locals." She gave the impression of a delicate shudder without, actually, shuddering.

Tej cast her a grateful glance. Dada grunted, not disagreeing.

"Still, he's in their military," said Star. "He can't be totally clueless, in a crunch. Maybe we could use him in our Security. Our new Security, when we set it up."

"Or in Administration," said Pidge. "You say he's a kind of secretary?"

"Or in Hospitality," said Jet, with a snigger. "How well does he strip?"

Tej glowered at him.

The Baronne waved this aside, pursing her lips. "But apparently, he's been kept close confined here in the capital under the eyes of his handlers for nearly the whole of that career. Chained to a desk, which is, I suppose, kinder than chained in a cage. Keeps him out of trouble just the same, to be sure."

"He really works," said Tej, not very loudly. "Admiral Desplains— that's his Ops boss—values him." What Desplains had actually told her was, *Despite Ivan's erratic personal life, he's never once made an error in identifying hidden political stakes. Rare talent, that.* Or had that been *political snakes*? Confusing.

"So I should think," said the Baronne. "This military chief must gain considerable cachet for harboring such a princeling on his staff. Almost a Jewel. I wonder what *his* deal was, behind the scenes, in return for taking on such a charge?"

"He likes Ivan's work," said Tej, though completeness forced her to add, "mostly."

The Baronne sat back and tapped her fingers on the sofa arm. She said unhopefully, "I don't suppose you've had any ideas how best to exploit him, have you, Tej? Having had—or is that enjoyed?—the closest observation."

Really, Baronne, do you have to point that out? Tej twitched uncomfortably. "The Greg—the Barrayarans were going to give us a ride in secret to Escobar. On a government courier ship. It would have given a clean break for Rish and me to lose the bounty hunters. I thought that was enough."

Star sniffed. "There are much more direct ways to dispose of bounty hunters, Tej."

Star had been the understudy of the House Cordonah security chief—a department that had failed signally to stave off the present debacle, Tej was reminded. With a pang of frustration, Tej restrained herself from escalating the critique. The most important part of the takeover had been in behind-the-scenes deals on financial and diplomatic levels anyway—yeah, Pidge's department, wasn't that? Star just liked lots of big guns.

"So what did *you* do about Prestene's hired meat? They must have followed you four, as well," said Tej to Star.

Star lifted her chin, proudly. "They met with fatal accidents, of course."

Dada, with a practiced finger-flicking gesture, suppressed this side-trail as well. "Tej's turn to tell her tale."

Em said, "Still, such a ride—depending on what they wanted you to trade for it—would have saved this expensive side jaunt to collect you two. Too bad you couldn't have brought it off two weeks back."

"Well, there was the divorce thing we were waiting for."

"The what?" said Dada.

With a reluctant sigh, Tej plunged into an account of her and Ivan Xav's trip to New Evias, and Count Falco's strange, archaic court with its unexpected non-result.

Dada rubbed his lips thoughtfully as she wound down, his dark eyes crinkling. "I expect we may simply ignore this local wrinkle when we leave. Alternatively, should you wish to become a widow, you have only to ask. It wouldn't be a first. I'm sure something could be arranged."

"No!" said Tej indignantly, hoping he was joking. She was almost sure he was joking. Despite being a Barrayaran, Ivan Xav wasn't *disposable*.

"Don't be so hotheaded, love," said the Baronne to her mate with a fond smile. "We shouldn't waste our opportunities before we've thoroughly explored them, after all." The double meaning of *waste* might have been intended, because the corner of Dada's mouth twitched up, as it always did when his half-haut queen indulged in Jacksonian gutter slang. The Baronne never could make it come out quite right. Dada could, authentically, when he got on a roll about his old times. But Tej wasn't sure she liked this swing of the Ivan Xav pendulum any better.

Star frowned in doubt. "If your Barrayaran husband wanted to get rid of you, why didn't he just let the bounty hunters carry you off? Problem solved, from his point of view."

"Barrayar's a more complicated place than I thought," said Tej, in a possibly fruitless effort at warning. Was anyone listening to her?

An unexpected murmur of support from, of all people, Grandmama: "Indeed, we should not go rushing in."

"I want some sleep first, before rushing anywhere," said Dada, a yawn cracking his face. "What a dismal shuttleport. Bed next for everyone, I think. Nobody's thinking straight."

"Should I go out and try to scrounge an arsenal, first?" said Star. "We're horribly disarmed, here."

"You have to admit," said Pidge, "Dada was right about not

trying to carry ours along. It would never have survived that second search."

"Would've passed the first one, though," grumbled Star. "Before Amiri insisted on bringing up that Vorpatril fellow's name."

"No, don't you dare!" said Tej, fairly sure that Star out cruising back alleys trying to deal for illegal weaponry fell under the heading of *something awful*. Especially while this short of sleep. And clues, for that matter.

Rish came to Tej's aid: "As far as any unwanted visitors from Prestene go, I think that Barrayaran Imperial Security has us covered for now. I know they're watching out for them. And with more resources than we can command here, right now."

Dada nodded understanding and agreement. "My take as well. *Bed*, chicks and chicklets." He stood and stretched, cracking joints. Grumbling, the Arquas trailed off to their respective roosts.

Dada and the Baronne hugged Tej and Rish a temporary goodbye as they left for Ivan Xav's flat. Their grips lingered, as if reassuring themselves by the most fundamental sensory means of the girls' well-being, and, well, being. "Yes, call us at Ivan Xav's number when you're ready to go down to dinner," said Tej.

Pidge followed them into the hotel corridor.

"We could be halfway through the Hegen Hub by now, if you two had stuck to your original plan," she complained. "This detour is costing us critical resources, you know. Time as much as money. I don't know why they didn't just send Amiri to collect you."

"None of this is anything like the original plan." Tej scowled. "Fortunately, if you want to be honest. If you do. Just for a change, you know."

With a short gesture, Pidge batted this shot away. "We're going back to retake the House. *Everyone* is pitching in—even Amiri. Everyone's expected to help. Even you."

Tej ran an aggravated hand through her hair, which snagged and pulled unhelpfully. "Doing what?"

"Dada and the Baronne for overall strategy, of course. Star's taking Security, I'm taking Negotiations, and the Jewels are doing everything they can. Which is quite a lot. You, well—the *least* you could do is cooperate in making yourself available for a genetic alliance. A bargaining chip—I'll bet the Baronne can slot you in somewhere."

"Dada said I didn't have to! And the Baronne didn't argue with him!"

"That was then, this is now. We don't have the margin for personal indulgences anymore. None of us do."

"Dada wouldn't ask me this."

"Dada shouldn't *have* to ask you this! Isn't it about time you stopped being such a maddening deadweight in the House? You *had* your choice of choices, you didn't take any of them, you've lost your say, I'd say."

"I don't see *you* offering up your body as a personal pledge in some side deal!"

"Who says?" Pidge's voice was grim.

"...Oh."

"So."

"So, um...call us when you wake up, anyway."

"Right." Pidge flung herself back into the suite.

Tej and Rish continued toward the lift tubes. Rish watched her sideways, but for once, offered no comment. Tej loved her family, she really did. She didn't doubt for an instant that they loved her, too, in their way. But she wondered how she'd plunged from soaring elation to glum depression in so few hours.

Chapter Fifteen

Ivan, only slightly out of breath but considerably out of sleep, entered Admiral Desplains's outer office to find one of the senior Ops clerks manning his desk. The morning's first pot of coffee had been made and drunk long ago, he noted from the dark dregs in the bottom of the pot on the credenza and the faint tarry aroma in the air. He checked a desire to scrape out the bottom of the pot with a spoon and eat the residue.

"Ah, Captain Vorpatril," said the clerk, brightening. "The old man wanted to know as soon as you arrived." He keyed his intercom. "Sir, Captain Vorpatril is here."

"Finally," returned Desplains's voice. Ivan tried to read the tone, but from three syllables could only ascertain *not joyful.* "Send him in."

Ivan trod into his boss's inner sanctum, to find the admiral had a visitor—an ImpSec captain, Ivan saw by his collar pins and tabs, as the man twisted in his chair to observe him in turn, frowning. Lean but HQ-pale, salt-and-pepper hair that tried but failed to make him look older than the mid-grade middle-aged man he apparently was. *Raudsepp,* read his nametag. They exchanged the briefest of military courtesies.

Desplains was looking faintly harassed. And, given that the harassment was apparently being delivered by a mere ImpSec captain—bringing the snakes in person?—decidedly irritated. The admiral did not invite Ivan to sit, so Ivan took up a prudent sort-of parade rest and waited. Someone would tell him what was going on shortly; they always did, however little he wanted to know.

Desplains went on, dry-voiced, "Captain Raudsepp has just inquired if, at the time I signed off on your marriage on Komarr, I had known what a curious set of relations young Lady Vorpatril was apparently trailing after her."

"At the time of our marriage on Komarr, everyone thought Tej was an orphan," said Ivan, "including Tej. And Rish. They seemed pretty happy to find out this was not the case, last night. And your interest in this is what, Captain Raudsepp?"

"Until last night, I was the Galactic Affairs officer charged with riding herd on your new wife's alleged bounty-hunter threat. A relatively routine physical security issue that has so far failed to provide much in the way of action, to everyone's relief. I came in this morning to find my mandate had been unexpectedly upped by a renegade refugee Jacksonian baron and most of his extended family, about which the critical complaint is the *unexpectedly* part."

Ah, yes. ImpSec did not like surprises. Too bad; surprises were their *job*, in Ivan's view. He wondered if he ought to argue with the *renegade* tag; how could you tell a renegade Jacksonian baron from any other sort? Refugee, though, yeah, sure. He did put in, "Immediate family, actually. In a sense."

Raudsepp's brows tightened. "My heated memo to Galactic Affairs-Komarr crossed in the tightbeam stream with an urgent heads-up from Captain Morozov, warning us of the party's impending arrival, so it's good to know that they weren't entirely asleep out there. If the alert had arrived six hours ahead of the event instead of six hours behind it, it might have helped. Some-what. And so my routine physical security issue has turned into a completely unassessed political security issue. As I expect my assessment to be requested *very soon*, it behooves me to make one."

Ivan tilted his head in acknowledgement of the justice of this, but resisted being drawn into premature sympathy with a brother officer. After all, ImpSec.

Raudsepp narrowed his eyes at Ivan. "Why did you sign them out of Customs & Security?"

"Well, they looked tired," Ivan offered. "Hours and hours of bureaucrats. On top of jump-lag, you know. The Komarr run is a bitch if you're jump-sensitive."

"Have you managed to find out yet why they're here?"

"They came to pick up Tej and Rish." *Wait, what?* Take them *away?* For the first time, this thought came clear in Ivan's sleep-deprived mind, triggering an unpleasant flutter of panic in his stomach. Though he supposed he could part with Rish without much of a pang. But what if Tej wanted to go *with* her? "Check on them, anyway," he corrected hastily. *Dear God. We need to talk.* "Parents, after all."

"Do you have any other observations to report? Anything of danger—or interest—to the Imperium?"

"All they've done is land and go to bed." Ivan stifled a yawn. "Well, and fill out a lot of forms. You have to have received copies of everything from Customs, and a report from your outer-perimeter night fellow—what the devil was his name—Zumboti, that was it. Which means you know about as much as I do, so far."

"Surely not. You have by far the closest view of the affair, going back the farthest."

I'm not the only one, Ivan wanted to snap back. In fact, he didn't even go back the farthest. *Talk to your own damn people.* What, had By gone off to bed without filing a report, the rat? "In my, what, nine hours of observation, all I've seen is some very jump-lagged people glad to find their daughters alive"—that, without doubt, had not been some show for his benefit—"and grateful to be taken to a hotel." *Hang on...* By was Domestic Affairs; Raudsepp had named himself Galactic Affairs. Was this another fricking ImpSec right hand not talking to the left screwup, again? Ivan was so used to Byerly by now, he perhaps forgot just how high and restricted a level By worked on, however erratically. Should he direct Raudsepp to Byerly, or not? Maybe it ought to be the other way around. *Isn't trying to cover for By how I got into all this trouble in the first place...?*

But Captain Raudsepp was going on. "Looking ahead, then." He rummaged in his uniform jacket and withdrew a card, which he glanced at and handed to Ivan. "This is my secured comconsole code, by which you may contact me directly at any time. Should you find anything suspicious to report, anything at all, please call me at once."

Ivan didn't reach for it. "Uh, you're asking me to spy on my wife's family for you?" Out of the corner of his eye, he saw a slight wince cross Desplains's usually impassive features, although in reaction to just what aspect of this he couldn't guess.

"You *did* take formal responsibility for them, Captain Vorpatril."

As a Vor lord. Not as a military officer. Different chain of command. Oh, crap, that sounded just like one of Miles's arguments, didn't it. Ivan *knew* he was on thin ice if he'd started channeling his cousin. Gingerly, he took the card, glanced at it—code only, no other identifying information, right, one of *those*—and tucked it away in his wallet.

"Although..." Raudsepp hesitated, looking around the admiral's tidy but resource-crammed office—one whole wall was taken up with Desplains's professional library, including a few rare volumes going back to the Time of Isolation. "It does occur to me, nearly everything to do with Ops passes through your comconsole, Captain Vorpatril, one way or another. Until this entire situation is clarified, it might be more prudent for you to take some personal leave. Unexceptionable enough, for a family emergency, certainly."

Ivan's jaw tightened. So, he noticed, did Desplains's. "If my loyalty is suddenly that suspect," he ground out, "that should certainly not be my decision to make, eh?"

Raudsepp's brow wrinkled. "True enough." He looked to Desplains.

Desplains looked back and said blandly, "My aide and I will discuss it. Thank you for your concern, Captain Raudsepp, and for your information and your time on this busy morning."

It was a clear dismissal. Raudsepp must have run out of questions for now, or else he'd decided Ivan really had run out of answers, because he allowed himself to be shifted. The Ops clerk saw him out.

This left Ivan still standing. Studying him, Desplains rubbed his jaw and grimaced. "So, have you become a security risk, Vorpatril?"

"I don't know, sir," said Ivan, as honestly as possible. "Nobody tells me anything."

Desplains snorted. "Well, then, go back to work, at least for the moment." He waved Ivan out, but then added, "Oh. And call your mother."

Ivan paused on the threshold. "I suppose I should, at that." Actually, he'd totally forgotten that little task, in the rush of events.

"I should perhaps say, call your mother *back*." The voice could have dehumidified the room; Desplains was giving him That Look.

"Ah. Yes, sir. Right away, sir." Ivan retreated to the outer office.

He evicted the clerk from his desk, who was glad enough to get back to his own interrupted tasks, settled himself, and tapped in a familiar code. Lady Alys's face formed over his vidplate all too promptly, which suggested she must have been lying in wait for this.

"Ah, Ivan. Finally," she said, unconsciously echoing Desplains.

Dammit, he'd been *busy*. Ivan nodded warily. "Mamere. It's been quite a night. I guess you've heard? Something?"

"In fact, our first word was a copy of Captain Morozov's memo from Komarr, which he had strongly requested ImpSec Vorbarr Sultana forward to Simon. Happily, General Allegre can recognize need-to-know when he sees it. It came in while we were having breakfast. We had a first-hand update a bit later. Not from you, I must point out."

From who, then? Ivan wanted to ask, then realized it would be a redundant question. And Byerly had probably also acquired breakfast *and* bed by now, of both of which Ivan was deprived, and looked to stay that way. "I kind of had my hands full," Ivan excused himself. "Everyone's settled now, though. Temporarily."

"Good. How is Tej taking it? And Rish?"

"Overjoyed. Well, imagine how would you feel to get your family back from the dead, all unexpected?"

"I don't actually have to imagine it, Ivan," she said, giving him a peculiar exasperated-fond look. "And nor do you, come to think."

Ivan shrugged, embarrassed. "I suppose not. Anyway, there seemed to be a lot of family feeling." Of several different kinds, in retrospect. An only child all his life, and his closest cousin the same, Ivan had occasionally wondered what it would be like to have a big family. Mamere's attention would have been more divided, for one thing...

The panic simmering at the back of his brain seeped out. In a suddenly smaller voice, he said, "They, uh... seem to have come here with some idea of picking up Tej and Rish. And taking them away."

Mamere looked back at him. "And how do you feel about that, Ivan?"

A rather long silence fell, before he managed, "Very strange."

Lady Alys's dark brows quirked. "Well, that's something, I suppose." She sat up more briskly. "In any case, clearly we must have them to dinner at the earliest possible opportunity. It's the correct thing to do. And there is so *much* to catch up on."

"Uh, they're all asleep now. Jump-lagged."

"Then they should be both refreshed and hungry by early this evening. Tonight, then. Very good. I'll send Christos with the car—you will of course meet them at their hotel and help escort them."

"Uh, better make that two cars. Or a bus. And isn't this short notice for you?"

"I've put on receptions for hundreds at less notice. My staff is perfectly capable of handling a private family party of fifteen."

Surreptitiously, Ivan counted on his fingers. "I make it fourteen, isn't it? Even including Simon and me?"

"Byerly will no doubt wish to squire Rish."

Thus saving steps for ImpSec, too. Mamere was well aware of *every* angle. Ivan managed not to choke. "Just...don't invite Miles. Or let him invite himself."

On any less-elegant face, that lip-pursing could have been called a retrospective grimace. "I promise you, I am capable of controlling my guest list. Anyway, I believe he's still on Sergyar. Although I shall miss Ekaterin. Another time." She waved a hand that was either airy, or threatening, Ivan wasn't sure which.

Ivan ran beleaguered fingers through his hair. "Yeah, and I came in to the office this morning—*late*, because of last night—to find some ImpSec captain with a stick up his butt giving *my* boss a hard time over all this... It's *not helpful*, I tell you." He drew breath. "Galactic Affairs fellow. Who seemed not to be talking this morning to Domestic Affairs, if you know what I mean. It put me in a quandary. Are they all flying blind over there at Cockroach Central, or does Allegre want to keep his angles of view independent, or what? I *hate* getting sucked into these weasel-traps."

Simon Illyan leaned into the vid pickup, and advised genially, "Call Guy Allegre and *ask*, Ivan. If it's the first, he'll want to know, and if it's the second, you need to know. He'll talk to you.

Briefly, mind." The amused face withdrew out of focal range. The reflective voice drifted back: "Though good for the G.A. man for tackling an admiral, stick or not. It's the backbone one wants to see in an agent..."

Ivan shuddered. *But I don't want to talk to Allegre.*

"Very sensible," approved Lady Alys. "And I'll call Tej and Rish. Carry on, dear. I'll have Christos contact you later with the details for transport."

She cut the com. Ivan sat a moment, gathering his reserves and wondering when, if ever, he was going to get back to Ops business this morning. And whether any of this could be classed as making personal calls on office time, and if he was somehow going to earn a reprimand for it. He sighed and punched in the next code.

"Ah, Ivan," said General Allegre, neutrally, when he'd been gated through by the secretary. Guy Allegre passed as a stocky, middle-aged, normal-looking sort of senior officer, with a normal wife—well, she worked at the Imperial Science Institute—and children in about the same age-cohort as Desplains's youngsters; it took a while knowing him to realize how ferociously bright, and brightly ferocious, he really was. "We may have a place opening up on our fast courier next week—is that request obsolete now, in view of this morning's news? Last night's news, I construe, from your point of view."

"Uh, I think so, sir. It's all very up-in-the-air right now. But this is related. I seem to find myself dealing with two of your people who aren't dealing with each other—" Succinctly, as instructed, Ivan described the conundrum with Byerly and Captain Raudsepp.

"Hm, yes," said Allegre. "I'll have Raudsepp apprised." That, and the general's lack of irritation with Ivan taking up space on his comconsole, was rather a clue that Raudsepp must have been working in the dark re: Byerly. "Good you asked."

Right. "Simon said I should." Just in case Ivan needed a little more shielding.

Allegre nodded. "Vorrutyer does good work, on his level. It may actually have been a bit too much good work, lately. Domestic had been thinking of standing him down for a while, but then this came up."

"How can someone do *too much* good work?"

"Well, irregulars." Allegre gave a vague wave, and adroitly changed the subject: "How is Simon, these days?"

What, *another* family snitch-report? No, that was unfair. Guy Allegre had been Head of Komarran Affairs for some time directly under Illyan, until his promotion into his chief's abruptly vacated shoes four years back. And he'd come up, as a young officer, entirely in Illyan's ImpSec. His interest was personal as well as professional.

"His health seems quite good."

"Glad to hear it. Any new interests? I thought he could use some." Allegre added diplomatically, "No reflection on your lady mother, of course."

"Do you two talk much with each other? Consult?"

"As needed. Ex-Chief Illyan has been very properly circumspect about jostling my elbow, bless his wits. No need to send him to Sergyar like your uncle to get him out of the range of other people's ingrained habits. Although I suppose Simon's medical situation served much the same function of distancing him from his old command." Allegre's eyes narrowed in thought. "I wonder if he'd like to visit Aral? I should suggest it. D'you think your lady mother would be willing to travel? As long as it doesn't create unhealthy excitement among the conspiracy theorists. Although that could be made useful, too..." Something else on the general's comconsole desk was signaling for his attention, Ivan guessed by the shifting of his gaze. "Is that all, for now?"

"Yes, sir." *For now.*

"Thank you, Captain Vorpatril." With a move of Allegre's hand, Ivan was dismissed from his attention and vid plate.

Tej watched Rish, trailing all the younger Arquas, lead them to the hotel lift tubes for what was billed as a short walking tour of the immediate environs, planned to end up in the hotel bar to await their transportation to Lady Alys's. She'd really wanted to give the *whole* family an emergency briefing on Barrayar before they went to dinner—if she would be permitted to get a word in edgewise—but a private talk with Dada and the Baronne and Grandmama would have to do. Rish had promised to fill in the others as best she could.

She touched the door buzzer to the sitting room and was bidden to enter by her mother's voice. She slipped inside to find the elder Arquas-plus-one gathered around a low holovid table that was at present displaying what looked like a large-scale city map. Grandmama touched a control; a dizzy blur, and the map settled again.

"It's just not *here*," she complained, a querulous note in her usually well-modulated tones.

"They can hardly have moved it," said Dada reasonably.

"No, they seem to have moved everything else, instead." Grandmama looked up. "Ah, Tej, good."

"Were you able to arrange the early pickup for us?" asked the Baronne. "Did you explain that Mother wanted to see a bit of the old city that she used to know?"

"Yes," said Tej. "Lady Alys said that Christos would be very pleased. Apparently, as part of his training as a driver he had to memorize every street in Vorbarr Sultana, and he doesn't get to try out the odd bits very often."

"Local knowledge might help," said Dada.

"What are you looking for?" Tej settled herself between Dada and the Baronne, and received, unusually, a welcoming hug from each. The Baronne was not normally physically demonstrative, and would probably get over it in a day or two; she must really have feared for Tej, during their uncertain odyssey roundabout from their lost House to Earth to Escobar to here. Tej would have feared for them, too, if only she'd known they were still alive; it was hard to guess which feeling was worse.

"An old Vor mansion that went by the peculiar name of Ladderbeck Close," said Grandmama, peering once more at the vid display. "At the time of the Ninth Satrapy"—the Cetagandan name for what the Barrayarans dubbed *the Cetagandan Occupation*—"it was where I worked."

"Worked?" said Tej, interest caught. As a child, she had taken her grandmother as she appeared, and hardly wondered about her long past life. "I didn't think ghem generals' haut wives *worked*."

The Baronne's eyebrows flicked up. "Not in some dire little shop, Tej." The Baronne had not approved of that ploy, when she'd heard of it.

Grandmama's fine lips thinned. "You understand, when I was... detached...from the haut, I was already a fully trained geneticist. I simply missed the cut, and not by very much—but it was always harder for us girls from the outer planets to compete with the haut women from Eta Ceta itself. They always had access to the very latest developments, you know. I was matched with General ghem Estif precisely *because* he was being assigned to the Ninth Satrapy, and the ongoing Star Crèche program here wanted a reliable laboratory assistant. The prior woman having been killed in some horrible bombing by those dreadful guerillas. She wasn't even targeted; she just chanced to be in the wrong place at the wrong time." Grandmama sniffed disapproval; Tej wasn't sure if it was of the guerillas, their tactics, or their failure to recognize the significance of their inadvertent victim.

"The *Star Crèche* had a presence on Barrayar? Did the Barrayarans know?" Ivan Xav had never mentioned such a thing, nor had she run across it in her recent reading. "Whatever were they doing here?"

Grandmama waved a dismissive hand. "Just the obvious—assembling a complete gene survey and library of the human occupants of the planet. Barrayar's so-called Time of Isolation was a unique natural genetic experiment, not to be wasted. The hoped-for prize of course would be some novel mutation or set of mutations that might be extracted and incorporated into higher gene bases, but alas in twenty years of survey—sadly underfunded and undersupported for the scope of the task, I must say—we only found some novel genetic diseases. Six hundred years was perhaps too short a time for new strengths to develop and be filtered into the population. It's really too bad the place was rediscovered so soon."

Some Komarrans thought so, too, Tej was reminded, if for rather different reasons. "And you had a—a what? A laboratory in the old mansion?"

"Under it, to be precise. The building had been some count's residence in a prior generation, had fallen to lesser family members, and was appropriated by the satrap government. The haut Zaia, our team leader, was not best pleased with it, but it made a suitably discreet entrance to our actual workplace. The laboratory itself was good enough, for its day. Proper biohazard barriers and all."

Tej hesitated. "If it was just a gene library, why did you need fancy biohazard controls?"

"One never knew," said Grandmama, vaguely.

Tej tried to process this. It stuck, rather. "Huh?"

"That slack-jawed expression does not become you, Tej," the Baronne pointed out. "Do keep up; this is important to our future."

Actually, it all seemed to be about the past, so far. The creakily ancient past, at that. Tej suppressed a sigh and tried to look attentive. She really had to get on to telling them more about Lady Alys before...

"Well, we were dealing with the *ghem*, dear. The haut Zaia kept her own supplies there as a matter of routine precaution." Grandmama pursed her lips, and went on, "What we had here in Vorbarr Sultana was only a regional outpost, mind you. Our main facility was that orbital laboratory, the one that was sent to burn up in the atmosphere during the scramble of the withdrawal. I only visited it once, being too junior to be assigned there myself. Much better equipment than we had downside. Such a waste! Although at least we salvaged all the data out of *that* one."

"Which brings us," Dada rumbled, "back to your young man, Tej."

"What?" Tej managed to close her mouth, this time.

"You've had some time to study him. What are his handles?" said Dada.

"Handles?"

"*Tej*," said the Baronne impatiently, but Dada waved her down.

"For example," said Dada, "does he hanker for power? Prestige? Wealth?"

"I don't know."

"How can you not know something so basic as *that*?" said the Baronne.

Tej shrugged. "I gather that his mother is wealthy—she owns the building his flat is in, and hers, and others besides, and I don't know what-all-else outside of the capital—and he's an only child. And he has some kind of trust fund from his paternal relatives. And his officer's pay, which is what he mainly lives on."

"That's not quite what I meant," said Dada. "Many who are rich want more, perhaps for some purpose or obsession."

And what would Arquas know about *that*, ha. "I think Ivan Xav cares about comfort more than display. I mean, he keeps up with the expectations of his Vor class, but I don't think it's because he's interested in them so much as...it's just easier."

"What about business training? Does he have any? Import, export, trade? Could he, for example, put together a large or complex project?"

"Well, I know he works on military budgets with Admiral Desplains. Those are large and complex projects."

"Hm." Dada drummed his fingers on the sofa arm. "You see, despite the unavoidable need for local partners, I'd like to keep this venture in the family if we can. My old contacts here are...less reliable than I'd prefer. And, in some cases, perhaps a bit too old."

Venture? Tej wasn't sure she liked the sound of that. His eye, nonetheless, had brightened during this conversation, edging out that scary look of weariness and defeat that he'd had when talking about Erik and the loss of the station, so out of place on his broad, beloved face. "What kind of venture do you have in mind on Barrayar, of all places?"

"A mining deal." A flash of grin. "Excavating history. Moira thinks we've found a rich vein of it. Every family should have a lost gold mine, eh?"

"They were current events to *me*," Grandmama objected. "Anyway, the gold is the least of the real value."

"Potentially," said the Baronne, in a voice of caution. "Potentially. This is all still such a long shot."

"Long shot's better than no shot at all," sighed Dada. "Which is what we'll have if the Barrayaran Imperial government finds out about this, so no gossiping about this to anyone who hasn't already been brought inside, eh, Tej?"

Tej wrinkled her nose. "Do you mean that old underground lab? Who'd want an old gene library? I mean, it's all got to have spoiled by now." And what would that *smell* like?

"Actually, anything that was stored sporulated ought to be fully reconstitutable," said Grandmama. "And then there was all that tedious trash the ghem generals and their friends insisted on stuffing in at the last. I suppose some of them really believed they would have a chance to get back to it all, someday."

"Tedious trash...?"

Dada sat back, his grin deepening. "Old records, both Cetagandan and captured Barrayaran. Several art collections, apparently—"

"Mere native objects, for the most part," put in Grandmama. "Though I do believe there were a few good pieces brought from home."

"—Ninth Satrapy currency and coin—that's where the chests of gold come in—"

"The primitives in the Barrayaran backcountry always preferred those awkward gold coins, for some reason," Grandmama confirmed.

"—and, basically, anything that a select mob of Cetagandan ghem lords in a panic didn't have room or time to pack and couldn't bring themselves to abandon," Dada concluded. "I don't think even Moira knows what all might be in there."

"No one did," Grandmama said. "The haut Zaia was quite upset with the incursion on her space, but really, no one could do anything at that point."

Tej had started out determined not to be sucked into any more doomed Arqua clan ventures, but she couldn't help growing a little bug-eyed at this litany. "How do you know...how do you know someone hasn't found it long before this?"

The Baronne rubbed her hands thoughtfully together, and touched her fingertips to her lips. "Even if smuggled out in secret, some of the known objects ought to have surfaced and left a trail. Some of the records, as well. They haven't."

"What—how—how would *we* get at it? In secret?"

Dada flicked his fingers. "Simplest is best. If the building still exists, buy it. Or possibly rent it. If it's been knocked down and built over, buy whatever is atop it, and proceed the same at our leisure. I understand the place wasn't in the best part of the city. If that isn't feasible, buy or rent an adjacent property and penetrate laterally. As always, fencing the stash is where the profit is made or lost—lost, usually, back when I was a young shipjacker. The best value of any item can only be realized when it is matched to the best customer for it. Which will be best done from some future secure base out of this debatable empire."

"Fell Station, to start with," said the Baronne, "if we can present ourselves credibly enough to Baron Fell. Once we attain that leverage point, our options open. *And* I'll have Ruby back."

"Isn't, um, the historical value greatest when things are excavated and recorded on site?" said Tej, tentatively.

"A sad loss," the Baronne agreed, "but in this case, not avoidable."

"How long have you three been planning this, this lowjacking?"

"Since Earth," said Dada. "We had reached the nadir of marketing my mother-in-law's hair, when Moira recalled this place."

"I hadn't thought about it in years," said Grandmama. "Decades, really. But Shiv never did receive a proper wedding gift, when he married Udine. Ghem Estif having wasted the first one on that idiot Komarran he picked out, who wasted it in turn on, oh, so many bad decisions."

"I came to you in nothing but my skin," murmured the Baronne, with a fond look at her mate. "And"—she plucked a trifle mournfully at her short fringe—"hair."

"I remember that," said her mate, with a fond look back. "Vividly. I had very little more myself, at the time."

"Your wits, at least."

"Making this cache into test and wedding gift in one, if Shiv can extract it," said Grandmama. "Does it occur to you two that you are running your courtship backward?"

"As long as we fit it all in somewhere," said Dada, sounding amused.

"Your sudden Barrayaran husband," said the Baronne to Tej, "put several wrinkles in our planning. We had originally intended to arrive here entirely incognito, but your reappearance gave us a second-choice level of plausibility, even as this Vorpatril fellow's unexpectedly high security profile forced the necessity. I hadn't wanted to activate our real identities quite so soon. Not till after the war chest was refilled, and we could prepare some richer welcome for our enemies."

"Flexibility, Udine," rumbled Dada.

"I admit," said the Baronne to Tej, "I was quite frantic about Rish and you, when Amiri reported you'd failed to make any timely rendezvous or contact with him. Lily's roundabout news was the greatest fortune—it made this Barrayar plan seem quite irresistible."

"If we can extract this treasure," said Dada, "it will be the saving of our House. The key to *everything*. It's been a long time since I wagered so much on a single throw. Though if I'm to revisit the desperation of my youth, I want the body back, too." He slapped his stomach and grimaced. His wife snorted. Though Dada looked more stimulated than desperate, to Tej's eye.

"Now all we have to do," said Grandmama briskly, "is find Ladderbeck Close."

Ivan settled his in-laws in the back of Mamere's big groundcar, and took the rearward-facing seat across from them. The canopy sighed shut. He gripped Tej's hand briefly, for reassurance. Of some sort. When he'd sped home to his flat to clean up and dress for this command performance, he'd found Tej and Rish had already gone on. No chance to talk then, no chance, really, to talk now, nor for hours yet, probably. At least, shaved and sharp in the dress greens that he seldom wore after-hours, he ought to look a more impressive son-in-law than last night. He hoped.

Christos began The Tour To Please Grandmama with a spin past Vorhartung Castle. Ivan mentioned the military museum, within, for future innocuous entertainment.

"This place, at least, seems to have survived the century intact," Lady ghem Estif observed, staring out at the archaic battlements. A few bright District flags flew there, snapping in the winter wind, indicating some rump meeting of the Counts in session. "It looks so odd without the laser-wire, though."

A whispered conference with Christos had concluded that the Imperial Residence was best viewed from a distance, this first trip, which they duly did. Christos managed to wedge the groundcar as close to the restored pedestrian alleys and shops of the old Caravanserai area as it would fit.

"Well, *that's* an improvement," murmured Lady ghem Estif, not sounding too grudging. "This part of town was considered a pestilential death trap, in my day."

Ivan decided not to mention being born there, for now. Let someone else tell that story, this round. "The last Barrayaran I knew who'd been alive during the Occupation died, what..." Ivan had to stop and work it out in his head. "Eighteen years ago." When he'd been barely more than seventeen. Was it really more than half his lifetime ago that his ancient and formidable great-uncle General Piotr had passed to his fathers? *Um...yeah, it was.*

A drive past the fully modern Ops building drew no special reaction, a little to Ivan's disappointment, but Lady ghem Estif sat up and peered more avidly as they drew away from the river. The Baronne, seated next to her, and the Baron observed her—pleasure? it was hard to tell, on that reserved face—with interest. "This was close to the edge of town, in the days of the Ninth Satrapy," she remarked.

"Vorbarr Sultana is built out for a couple dozen kilometers more, now," Ivan said. "In every direction. You really ought to see some of the recent outer rings, before you go."

The big groundcar nipped into a rare parking space just opening up, and sighed to a halt. Christos's jovial voice, which had been supplying sporadic commentary throughout the zigzag tour of the Old Town, came over the intercom from the front compartment.

"Here we are, Lady ghem Estif. I had to research back quite a way to find mention of the old place. The Cetagandans had seized it from an old Vor family that had taken up with the Resistance, and used it as a guest house during the time they held the capital, due to its extensive grounds and gardens, I gather. It was occupied again by one of the opposition factions, leveled during the rump fighting, and seized again by Emperor Yuri. The old Vor family never did get the property back, but I guess they were mostly dead by then. But this is definitely the exact site of Ladderbeck Close."

All three senior Arquas—well, two Arquas and one ghem Estif—were staring wide-eyed out the side of the canopy, craning their necks.

"What," said the Baronne in a choked voice, "is that great ugly building?"

At least something in Old Vorbarr Sultana architecture had finally riveted their attention, even if it was one of the most notoriously awful buildings in town. Ivan explained cheerfully, "It's one of the works of Emperor Yuri Vorbarra's megalomaniac architect, the infamous Lord Dono Vorrutyer. He got up five major structures before he was stopped, they say. Not to be confused with the current count of the same name, by the way. Dono-the-Architect was a relative of Byerly's, too, though not a direct ancestor, no doubt to By's relief. By can tell you more tales of him over dinner later. *That* gigantic eyesore is Cockroach Central itself—and it's called that by people who *work* there—ImpSec HQ. Barrayaran Imperial Security Headquarters."

A long silence fell in the back of the groundcar.

"I don't suppose it's for sale," said Tej, in a strange, small voice. "Or rent."

Ivan laughed. "Back when Simon Illyan ran it, he said he'd sell it for a Betan dollar, if only he could find a Betan with a dollar, and no taste. And if only the Council of Counts would build him a new building, which they wouldn't. Mamere says he kept a holo of the Investigatif Federale building on Escobar—tall thing, all glass—on the wall of his inner office for a while, the way some men would keep pinups."

"My, my, my," said Shiv Arqua.

He kept staring back over his shoulder for a long time, as the groundcar eased into the traffic and pulled away.

Chapter Sixteen

I t wasn't till the whole party was rising in the lift tube to Lady
Vorpatril's penthouse that Tej whispered to Ivan, "Um, I didn't
get a chance to explain about Simon yet."

"You haven't . . . ?" Ivan twitched. "What were you talking about
all that time?"

"Not that."

Ivan stepped out into the lift-tube foyer, trailing senior Arquas
like ducklings. "Well, too late." Simon would just have to explain
himself, this round. Or not, as he chose. The marquetry doors
slid open before them—someone had been on the watch. Mamere
and Simon were both standing together waiting in her spacious
hallway. From the wide living room beyond, a clink of glassware
and murmur of voices assured Ivan that Rish and Byerly had
managed to shepherd the rest of the family safely here.

Tej stepped bravely forward. "Dada, Baronne, Grandmama, I
would like to introduce you to Ivan Xav's mother, Lady Alys Vorpatril, and my stepfather-in-law, Captain Simon Illyan, Imperial
Service, retired. Lady Alys, Simon: Lady Moira ghem Estif, Shiv
and Udine ghem Estif Arqua—Baron and Baronne Cordonah."
A slightly defiant tone to that last claim; *retired* was not quite
the word for *their* current status.

Simon cast Tej a strange surprised smile, as he stepped forward alongside Lady Alys to murmur suitable greetings after her to the offworlder guests. The Baronne didn't turn a hair as he bowed over her fingers, nor did Lady ghem Estif, but the Baron, after a startled glance aside at Tej, advanced to shake Simon's proffered hand heartily.

"Ah, *that* Simon Illyan, I do believe—the ImpSec chief with the cyborg brain?" said Arqua, in his deep, carrying voice. "Your fame has reached even to the Whole. Ivan and Tej were just now showing us your ImpSec building. Very, ah, large, isn't it. One of the sights of Vorbarr Sultana, they tell me."

"Not my building anymore, nor my brain either, I'm afraid. My memory chip was removed four years ago," said Illyan. "Upon the occasion of my retirement."

Well, *that* left out a few details. Ivan took note.

"Ah," said Arqua. "Sounds a bit drastic, as exit interviews go. My condolences."

"Hardly that. I was ecstatic, personally."

"Were you." The grip finally loosened, and Ivan wondered if they'd been doing that who-can-break-whose-bones-first thing. Seeing the two men—the two aging fathers-in-law?—face-to-face for the first time was a trifle alarming. Arqua was stout, dark, intense despite his fatigue, openly dangerous. Simon was slight, graying, self-effacing... quietly dangerous. An effect not at all lessened—the reverse, really—by knowing that he wasn't *quite* as mentally reliable as he'd used to be... Ivan was obscurely relieved when, greetings completed and their wraps removed by his mother's efficient servants, they spilled into the living room and the family reunion.

Ivan dropped back to murmur to Simon, "Why did you grin like that at Tej, just now?"

A ghost of that pleased smile flitted over Simon's face. "Because that was the first time I'd been introduced as anybody's stepfather. Oddly flattering."

"Was...that something you'd wanted, sir?" Ivan asked, taken aback. For all the *other* people who'd made assumptions about Ivan's faux-filial relationship with his mother's partner, Ivan realized in sudden retrospect, Simon himself never had. Not once.

"As your lady mother would say, that would not be correct. Which is no one's fault"—*or business* slid past, implied—"but our

own. Although"—a brief, sideways hesitation, surely not *diffident?*—
"I could likely do without all the mumbled *ums.*"

Um, Ivan started to say, then thought better of it. He converted
it to an "Oh." Did Simon *care* about that? *Evidently.* Ivan's mental review of all the awkward, smart-ass ways he'd introduced
Simon these past four years was interrupted, thankfully, by Byerly
sauntering over.

By gave Simon an apologetic nod. It was always a little fascinating to watch By's habitual smarmy irony so thoroughly purged,
not only from his expression, but from his body language, around
the former ImpSec chief. Illyan plainly still unnerved By to the
marrow of his bones, even though By had once worked for him—
or was that, *because* he had once worked for him?

Ivan's glance took inventory of Arquas and Jewels, gathered
around the drinks trolley or gazing out the windows into the
softening winter dusk. "I see you managed to get them all here.
Mamere find a bus?"

"A luxurious sort of ground-barge, yes. We didn't lose a single
Arqua overboard," Byerly said, with mock pride. "Not for lack of
their trying. You have a *lot* of new in-laws, Ivan."

"Yeah, noticed that." Ivan nabbed a drink, with a smile of
intense gratitude to his mother's servitor, a regular from that
catering service Lady Alys called on for very-high-end governmental receptions, when she wasn't using Imperial Residence
staff. The woman smiled back in a motherly manner. Simon
and Mamere were tag-teaming, Ivan saw out of the corner of
his eye, Mamere escorting the Baronne and Lady ghem Estif
to the wide windows to point out the highlights of Vorbarr
Sultana, Simon doing the same for Shiv, both covertly watching
the senior Arquas' interactions with their very assorted children.
Very adult children, but did any of the oldsters really see them
that way...?

Tej was drawn into conversation with her brother Amiri,
and his apparent jeeves-shadow Jet, or Onyx; did each of the
full-blooded Arqua children rate his or her own Jewel, or what?
This was a family dynamic that Ivan's acquaintance with the
Barrayaran historical precedent of acknowledged bastards did
not quite seem to cover. He made the rounds of the rest of the
clan, inquiring politely after their hotel, their naps, and their trip
to his mother's flat, all of which were reported as tolerable, then

drifted over to join Simon and Shiv in time to hear Simon say, "So how *did* Prestene get the drop on you?"

Shiv heaved a sigh. "In part, it turned out to be an inside job. Some trusted subordinates—shouldn't have been."

"Unfortunate. But that can happen to the most supposedly secure bastions." Simon touched his forehead in a frustration-gesture Ivan hadn't seen for a while. "That was how the bastard took down my chip."

"Your eidetic memory chip that was removed upon your retirement? Was this not ordered by your Imperial masters? I don't follow."

"The other way around, I'm afraid. First the chip was bio-sabotaged, quite thoroughly—Ivan would doubtless remember that part better than I do"—a sharp glance under his lidded eyes Ivan's way—"then the slagged remains surgically excised, happily before and not after the ugly side-effects killed me. *Not* the way I would have chosen to retire from the Imperial Service, for all my daydreams of doing just that, after forty years."

"Ah. I *quite* see," said Shiv, sounding entirely sincere.

The two men toasted each other ironically with their nearly empty glasses, and drained them. The drinks-trolley elf appeared magically to refill them, then vanished into the mob again.

The marquetry doors on the end of the living room parted like the curtains on a play, revealing the stage, or at least the table, now pulled out to a spacious oblong and invitingly set. Mamere and her minions smoothly guided the guests to their places. Shiv seized the moment to murmur something in his daughter Pidge's ear, before they were separated.

Ivan was unhappily parted from Tej, seated opposite her father who was placed at the foot of the table on Simon's honored right. Alys, at the head, had Moira ghem Estif on her right, and Udine Arqua on her left—the usual protocols had plainly broken down in the face of the Arqua challenge, or things were being let to go a casual sort of family-style, or else Mamere had devised place-ments by some plan of her own, possibly with advice from ImpSec (retired). Ivan found himself plunked between his mother-in-law and his senior sister-in-law Star, with Byerly beyond her, sepa-rated from Rish by Emerald. Jet, Pearl, Amiri, and Pidge filled the opposite side of the table between Lady ghem Estif and Tej. The table was too long to maintain a single conversation except in spurts; most likely the talk would fragment into two or three parts. By, in the middle, was placed to either hear everything or be utterly distracted, depending.

A hearty Winterfair-style soup appeared, appropriate to the season—Ivan recognized the recipe on the first heavenly sniff. His mother had apparently kidnapped Ma Kosti for the evening, and he trusted Miles wouldn't find out. Rish, down the table, was assuring her fellow-Jewel Emerald that everything was going to be *just fine*, and the genetically sense-enhanced portion of the table, which was most of it, raised their spoons in bliss.

Lady Alys diplomatically began the conversation with the most neutral topic available, inquiring of Lady ghem Estif how she had enjoyed Earth, and drawing Ivan in with a few leading remarks about his career-polishing stint there as an assistant military attaché, a decade—no, *more*—ago. A glance under her lashes warned Ivan to leave out the Interesting Bits, hardly necessary; it would take more drinks than this before Ivan would want to expand on his lingering feelings for *those*. Anyway, Lady ghem Estif relieved him of the necessity by being willingly led, describing her past eight years of residence on humanity's homeworld in unexceptionable terms. To Ivan's surprise, it seemed she had not spent her time there in a cloistered retirement, either rich or straitened, but in some sort of genetics-related consulting business, "To keep my hand in," as she explained. "My original training is sadly out-of-date by Cetagandan standards; not so much by Earth's. Though I have kept up." She smiled complacently at her assorted grandchildren, ranged along the table.

Star, who in Ivan's estimation had been drinking pretty heavily, unless she had some sort of gengineered Cetagandan liver, looked up and said, "How *did* you and the old general come to have the Baronne, anyway? Did your old Constellation order it? Must have—it's said the haut keep their outcrosses tightly controlled."

"That is incorrect, dear. Although by then my Constellation and I had long parted ways. It's the haut-haut crosses that are meticulously planned. It is precisely the outcrosses that are loosened, so as to permit the possibility of genetic serendipity."

Udine smiled rather grimly across the table at her mother. "Did you find me so serendipitous?"

"In the longer view—ultimately. I admit, at the time, my motivations were more short-term and emotional."

Star's brow furrowed. "Were you in love with Grandfather ghem Estif, back then?"

Moira ghem Estif waved away this romantic notion. "Rae ghem Estif was not a lovable man, as such. I did feel, strongly, that he—that all of us who chose to stop on Komarr rather than return to the Empire—had suffered our efforts to be betrayed by our respective superiors. It was Rae's one loss to the Ninth Satrapy that I could make up."

Jet, next to her, looked confused. "What loss was that?"

Udine sipped her wine, smiled affectionately across at her son-and/or-construct, and said, "What, you never heard that tale?" Jet, Ivan was reminded, was the last Arqua, even younger than Tej.

Conversation had died, all along the table, as those at the far end strained to hear. Tej leaned forward and peered around the line of her seatmates, alert for some new tidbit. Their *materfamilias* must not often bore them with accounts of her youth, Ivan decided.

"It's a very Barrayaran story, all waste and aggravation and futility, which I must suppose makes it appropriate to tell here," said Lady ghem Estif, with a glance down the table at her presumed host. Simon smiled distantly back, but his eyes had gone quite attentive. "The general's son by one of his prior wives was lost in the Ninth Satrapy."

"Blown up by Ivan Xav's ancestors?" Rish inquired brightly from her end.

"We initially thought so, but our best later guess was that he was killed by what is so oxymoronically called friendly fire. Captain ghem Estif vanished while on a three-day leave. Normally this would have been put down to his being murdered by the guerillas or having deserted—desertions were a growing problem by then—but Rae insisted it could not be the second and there was no sign of the first. It was only much later—we had already reached Komarr, as I recall—that one of his son's friends spoke privately with us, and we found out that the captain had taken a Barrayaran lover."

She paused to sip soup; fourteen people refrained from interrupting, in unison.

She swallowed delicately and went on: "The captain had apparently penetrated enemy lines to the most dire and notorious nest of guerrillas on the planet in search of his young man. It is entirely unclear if he had found out the city was secretly slated to be destroyed by the ruling ghem-junta—of which General ghem Estif was not a part, so he could not have had the news that way—and was trying to get him out, or if it was just bad luck and bad timing. For all the ironic horror of his son's immolation, Rae did seem to take some consolation in the assurance that it was not desertion."

The four Barrayarans around the table were not, actually, *quieter* than the rest of the audience, Ivan thought—but maybe he was getting a worked demonstration of the difference between *attentive* and *choked* silence. The infamous nuclear destruction of the Vorkosigan's District capital had been the act that had galvanized the war-torn and exhausted planet into its final push against the Occupation.

"My cousin Miles actually owns the site of Vorkosigan Vashnoi," Ivan put in, affably. Pseudo-affably? Even he wasn't sure. "It's finally stopped glowing."

"Has it?" said Lady ghem Estif, unruffled. "Well, salute the brave ghem-captain and his beloved for me, next time you fly over. I assume you do not land there."

"No," said Ivan. "Not even now."

Lady Alys, with thirty years of diplomatic experience under her belt, looked as if she was discovering a whole new meaning for the term *conversation pit*. But she made a valiant effort to recover. "Is that why you and the ghem-general took up Komarran citizenship?"

"I believe Rae's motivations for that were more practical—he had been given access to a large block of planetary voting shares."

Bribed, did that translate as?

"I did not actually apply for Komarran citizenship myself, merely claiming umbrella residency as a spouse," Lady ghem Estif went on. "Later, when I lived with Udine and Shiv, the question of governmental loyalties was, hm, locally moot. I have actually managed to remain a stateless person for the better part of a century, which, I can tell you, is not something the Nexus generally makes easy to do."

"Indeed," said Illyan from the other end of the table, staring at her in fascination, "not."

The next course arrived and the conversation broke apart, the female-dominated end of the table going on to Cetagandan genetic techniques as applied to Jacksonian outcrosses, with a side-order of current Barrayaran techno-obstetrical fashions, the other end to military history and its financing. Ivan was maddened by not *quite* being able to hear the details when Simon and Shiv began to compare-and-contrast, or possibly one-up, anecdotes of brigandage and covert ops in the Jackson's Whole system, presumably heavily edited on both sides.

Ivan decided to let someone else explain the provenance of the mouth-melting maple ambrosia served for dessert, but to his relief no one inquired; Lady Alys's description of it as 'a traditional Barrayaran confection' seemed to cover it. The menu item was likely inevitable, given the cook; Ma Kosti was collecting royalties on the recipe, Ivan understood.

Dinner ended without disaster, despite Lady ghem Estif's little wobble into ancient angst. With the seniors setting the pace, it was clear the evening was not going to run late or turn raucous. Ivan followed when Simon drew Shiv off to his study, an unusual postprandial honor; he normally only permitted the most select guests into this private space, such as Gregor or Miles, or Uncle Aral when he was on-world. The honor was underscored when Simon rummaged in his credenza and emerged with a bottle of the even more select brandy, the one from the Vorkosigan's District so rare that it didn't even have a label, being distributed solely as a gift from the Count's own hand.

And two glasses. Simon studied Ivan with his most annoying blandness, and murmured, "I expect Lady Tej will be wanting your support out there, eh, Ivan?"

They eyed each other; Ivan tried not to let his gaze fix on the bottle gently dangling from Simon's hand. "I'm very concerned for Tej's future, sir."

"I am aware, Ivan. It's one of the things in the forefront of my mind."

Ivan couldn't say, out loud in front of his putative father-in-law watching this play with keen interest, *Dammit, I need to be dealing with Shiv! Wait your turn!* Nor, as Simon chivvied him firmly to the door and evicted him, *Don't forget!* Just how many things could Simon keep in the forefront of his mind these days without losing track? The very soundproof, not to mention projectile-, plasma-, and poison gas-proof, door slid closed in front of Ivan's nose, exiling him to the hallway.

Byerly wandered up, looking faintly frazzled. "Have you seen where Arqua and Illyan disappeared to?"

Ivan jerked his thumb at the study. "Private conclave, evidently. Discussing Vorkosigan brandy, and I'm not sure what else."

Byerly stared at the blank door with curiosity second only to Ivan's own. "Well...Illyan. Presumably he has things in hand."

"I'm not so sure. You were closer to that end of the table than I was. Did you get the impression that Shiv was *hustling* Simon? I mean, subtly, of course."

By shrugged. "Well, of course. Arqua has to be hustling every possibility he sees, right about now. Trying to get support for his House in exile, in the interest of making it not in exile. It was less clear"—By hesitated—"why Simon seemed to be hustling him back. Even more subtly, note. Unless it was just habit, I suppose."

"That's a disturbing thought. The two of them, hustling each other."

"Yeah. It was...rather like watching two women trying to make each other pregnant."

Ivan contemplated this arresting, not to mention distracting, metaphor for a moment. "That's done. Technologically. Even on Barrayar, these days."

Byerly waved a dissociating hand. "You see what I mean, though."

"Yeah." Ivan nibbled his lip. "Are you outed, by the way?"

"By Rish? I'm not yet sure. Do you know if Tej has told her family anything?"

"About your line of work? Not a clue. No one has given me any time to *talk with my wife* for the past day." Ivan hesitated. "She has talked with them about something."

"Well, try to find out, will you? Both," By added in afterthought.

Ivan growled. "Spying is supposed to be your job."

"I'm *trying*," By bit out.

"Hey. You're the one who outed yourself, back on Komarr. Surprised the hell out of me at the time. Were you trying to impress the pretty python with your daring dual identity, or what?"

"*At the time*, there were only the two of them, and I never imagined they'd ever get closer than five jumps to Vorbarr Sultana. It seemed a fair deal, and they seemed to agree. They weren't going to blab to their enemies. Never pictured it lasting more than a couple of days before we went our separate ways. Or Rish having to choose me over her family, for God's sake."

Or Tej having to choose me over her family? Ivan had just time to think, before a door slid open down the hall, and By's teeth snapped shut. Tall and cinnamon Pidge emerged from the guest lav, began to stride back toward the living room, spied the two of them lingering, and hove to with a smile. Snazzy heels on her shoes positioned her to look Ivan directly in the eye, and down on Byerly, very Baronette Sophia Arqua. Strange courtesy title, that. Ivan kept hearing it as *bayonet*, which . . . might not be so wrong.

"Oh, Ivan Xav." A nod included Byerly in the greeting. "What a very pleasant evening this has been, after the tensions of our travels."

"I'm glad," said Ivan. "Do tell my mother. Entertaining is an art form, to her."

"I could see that," said Pidge, with near-Cetagandan approval. "Your mother's partner is an interesting fellow, too," she went on. Yes, she had been closer to Simon's end of the table, through dinner. In the place next to Tej that should have been Ivan's, eh. "*Illyan* is a, what do you call your grubbers, a *prole* name, though, isn't it? Not one of you Vor."

"No twice-twenty-years Imperial Service man need yield to any Vor for his place in our military caste," said Ivan firmly.

Pidge looked to Byerly for confirmation of this cultural detail; he nodded cordially.

"Still, a captain. Even after, what, forty years—why do you call it twice-twenty, I wonder? But isn't that the same rank as you?"

"No," said Ivan. "Chief of Imperial Security, which was his job title, technically isn't a military rank at all, but a direct Imperial appointment. He froze his military rank at captain because his predecessor, Emperor Ezar's security chief Captain Negri—the man they called Ezar's Familiar—never took a higher rank, either. A political statement, that. It was, after all, a very political job."

Pidge tilted her head. "And what did they call your Illyan?"

"Aral Vorkosigan's Dog," By put in, lips quirking with amusement.

"But . . . Vorkosigan wasn't an emperor. Was he . . . ?"

"Imperial Regent for sixteen years, you know, when Emperor Gregor was a minor," Byerly charitably glossed for her outworlder benefit. "All of the work, none of the perks." Ivan wondered if that was a direct quote from Uncle Aral. Or Aunt Cordelia, more likely.

"And what do they call the current Chief of ImpSec?"

"Allegre? They call him the Chief of ImpSec." Byerly cast her the hint of an apologetic bow. "I fear we live in less colorful times."

Thank God, Ivan thought. "Allegre was already a general at the time of his appointment. They didn't make him give it back, so I suppose that's the end of that tradition."

Pidge's generous mouth pursed, as she puzzled through this. "It seems quite odd. Are Barrayaran captains very well paid, then?"

"No," said Ivan, sadly. He added, lest she think less of his um-stepfather, "Illyan was given a vice-admiral's salary, though, which makes more sense considering the workload." Or perhaps it didn't—26.7 hours a day for thirty years, all-consuming? Such a pyre wasn't something a man entered into for *pay*. "Half-salary, now he's retired."

"How much would that be?"

Ivan, who dealt with military payrolls regularly and could have recited the wage ranges for every IS-number/rank ever invented, current or historical, said, "I imagine you could look it up somewhere." Byerly smiled a little; the sweep of his lashes invited Ivan to carry on.

"Then . . . is he rich independently?" Pidge persisted.

"I have no idea."

Pidge tossed her head in surprise; the amber curls gathered in a clasp at her nape, far more controlled than Tej's cloud, failed to bounce much. "How can you not know?"

"I expect he has his savings," Byerly put in, stirring what imagined pot Ivan barely wanted to contemplate, but was probably going to have to. "He couldn't have started out with much, as a young prole officer, but that social class tends to be frugal. And he had no visible vices."

"Nor secret ones, either," Ivan put in. "He wouldn't have had *time*." Not that Illyan hadn't been good at secrets . . . many years of unrequited and largely unsuspected prole pining for Lady Alys, for example. Which had escaped Ivan's attention entirely, till the shoes had dropped—both pairs . . .

Well, all right, *one* secret vice. They had both been *very* drunk at the Emperor's Birthday celebration a couple of years ago, Ivan by habit and tradition, the retired Illyan because he'd always been on ImpSec duty before and had never, he said, had a *chance* to. Through a progression of subjects that were soon a blur in Ivan's mind, they had somehow got on to just what Illyan did and did not recall or miss from his memory chip, at which point Ivan had learned just *where* the largest and most arcane pornography collection on Barrayar had been secreted...

It's not as if I acquired most of it on purpose, Illyan had protested. *But the damned chip didn't allow me to delete anything, whether I picked it up inadvertently or in a moment of bad mood or bad judgment or bad company, and then I was stuck with it forever. Or in the line of work, oh, God, those were the worst. Do you have any* idea *how many truly appalling surveillance vids I had to review in forty years...?*

There were some things, Ivan reflected, that no man should know about another, not even or perhaps especially his um-stepfather. People had occasionally—in Ivan's hearing or even buttonholing him directly—speculated about just how long this matter between Illyan and Lady Alys had really been going on, since Illyan's retirement when it had become...overt? Public? Not *flaunted*, Lady Alys didn't *flaunt*, that would be tasteless. More like...they wore each other with well-earned pride. But it had occurred to Ivan then that the physical danger Illyan trailed from his work might not have been the *only* thing he'd been loath to take to bed with his esteemed Vor lady. Ivan had decided he was thankful when Illyan appeared to have forgotten the conversation the next day—hangovers were definitely for the young, the man had moaned—and didn't remind him of it in *any way*.

And when Ivan had got over his own hangover, and the generational whiplash, and the unwanted lurid-but-maybe-not-even-lurid-enough imaginings, he'd finally decided that what it had mostly sounded like was *lonely*, actually.

Being married to a wife beat being married to a job, it seemed increasingly clear to Ivan.

"Captain Illyan is—or was—a clever man, was he not?" said Pidge. "I should have thought that a position as a security chief would have lent itself to considerable personal acquisition, in three decades. If not directly, then through clever use of inside information."

It was a measure of...something...that this thought had never crossed Ivan's mind till now. If nothing else, Illyan had spent vast tracts of time and wells of energy dealing with corrupt people and the effects of their corruptions; really, there could hardly be anything he hadn't learned about the depravity of the human condition. And yet...just because Illyan took confessions didn't make him a priest.

"No," said Ivan after a moment, grabbing for his tilting certainty. "ImpSec *was* his passion; he didn't need another. If he had a drug, it was adrenaline."

Byerly's brows rose. "Really?"

"God, yes. He only looked normal by contrast because he hung around with a pack of the biggest adrenaline-junkies on three worlds. All the great men have to be, to ride the Imperial Horse. I mean, think who Illyan used to *run* in covert ops. And at *whose* request."

"That," said Byerly, "is a point."

"But he's retired from all that now."

"A modest frugal retirement for a loyal Imperial bureaucrat?" said Pidge. "And yet your mother so wealthy."

"Doesn't bother her," Ivan said stoutly.

"But does it bother him?"

About to deny this with equal vehemence, Ivan realized that among the many things he didn't know about Simon...that was another. "I am sure he has more important things on his mind."

Pidge smiled at him. "Fascinating." With a little Shiv-like wave of her fingers, she trailed away toward the party; Byerly, with one of his less-comprehensible grimaces, promptly trailed after.

Ivan gave the blank study door one last look of frustration, and followed.

Ivan still hadn't had a chance to talk alone with Tej when the party broke up an hour later. Simon and Shiv had at last emerged from Simon's lair. Byerly was fidgety from having been excluded from a long, all-female confabulation amongst Lady Vorpatril, Lady ghem Estif, and Baronne Cordonah, from which they'd emerged as *Alys*, *Moira*, and *Udine*. Wraps were produced in the hallway, even its generous proportions elbow-jostling for this crowd. Christos reappeared to guide everyone back to their respective groundcars.

Simon and Shiv parted with another of those disquieting handshakes. As the mob thinned, Simon gazed thoughtfully at the broad departing back, but turned with a slight smile to take Tej's hand.

"Intriguing fellow, your Dada, Tej. The man could sell elephants to circus masters."

She gave him a puzzled, gratified, and alarmed smile back. "I'd think circus masters would *want* to buy elephants, sir."

Illyan's smile stretched. "Quite so."

Tej had successfully avoided Ivan Xav all evening, while the party swirled around her spinning head. A bass beat of *Cetagandan gold, Cetagandan gold, Cetagandan gold!* had thumped in her brain, with an occasional descant of *Buried treasure!* and discord wail of *But ImpSec...!* Dada, despite the lack of stepfather-in-law intel for which he had shot her that pointed look—and it *wasn't her fault* that no one had let her explain earlier—seemed to have made a swift recovery and hit it off just fine with Simon. That had to be good. Didn't it?

Normally, she looked forward to pillow talk with Ivan Xav, and what followed, for sheer aesthetic reasons if nothing else. It had become a very *comfortable* time of the day, something to anticipate with pleasure. Not this day. As they dodged around each other and Rish in and out of the bathroom, the conversation was utilitarian. Tej made it under the covers first. She didn't have to pretend to be exhausted—if she just rolled over and closed her eyes...

"Tej..." The other side of the bed creaked and dipped as Ivan Xav sat down, but then he sighed, got up again, padded to the bedroom door, opened it, and called through, "Hey, Rish!"

"What?" Rish's tired, irritated voice called back.

"Have you outed Byerly yet? About what he does for a living, I mean?"

"Of course not! That was the deal. Tacitly. I assumed."

Ivan Xav's tense shoulders relaxed. "Ah."

"—just to my family, of course."

The shoulders went from relaxed to slumped. "Of course," Ivan Xav mumbled. He raised his voice again: "That would be, like, nine more people, yeah?"

"Great, the natural-boy can count."

Ivan Xav growled, and let the door slide shut.

He returned to the bed and sat up against the headboard, looking down in the soft lamplight at Tej, who, under the press of the stare between her shoulder blades, rolled over onto her back.

"Tej," he began again, hesitantly, "could your Dada possibly imagine that he could *suborn* Simon?"

How to deal with this... "Suborn, what a word, *suborn*. You'd only need to *suborn* someone for something, like, treasonous, or evil. Something political or military, bad for Barrayar." *Financial wasn't* *political or military*, right? "Of course Dada wouldn't do something like *that*."

"*Couldn't*, I'd say. You do realize—Shiv must realize—Simon's had thirty, forty years for his probity and loyalty to be tested by, by more pressure than anything your Dada could possibly bring to bear—maybe more than you or I can even imagine."

"Yeah, so?"

"So..."

"Look, Dada's not *stupid*."

"Neither is Simon." Ivan Xav's face managed peeved, not his best expression. "They're up to something, aren't they. You—the Arquas."

"They came to Barrayar to get Rish and me."

"Yes, and that's something else we need to talk about—I mean, that's the conversation I've been rehearsing all bloody *day*, before all this came—Tej, *what do you know?*"

She scowled up at him, looming on her left. Ivan Xav wasn't stupid, either, of course. "Then are you in or out?" And was it even worth probing? He was Barrayaran to the bone, seven-eighths, anyway. He'd be bound to want to grab everything for his empire, his own gang—that was what the uniform he wore every day *meant*.

"Of *what*? I can't say till I know what I'm in or out *of*. Though it's got to be trouble, or you'd just be telling me. There's some kind of Jacksonian deal going on under the table. Yeah?"

"I can't tell you unless you're in. Or you decide you're out, and then I really can't tell you."

"Married people," said Ivan Xav austerely after a moment, "shouldn't keep secrets from each other."

Tej rolled up on her elbow, annoyed. For once, this move failed to distract him. "What, you keep secrets from *me* all the time. All that classified stuff at your work."

"That's different. That's... it's assumed, no, it's not just assumed, they make it quite explicit that fellows don't babble about Ops business at home. Or anywhere else. It's not like I keep those secrets from you *preferentially*."

"It would probably be really boring anyway."

"Most of it," admitted Ivan Xav, almost diverted.

"Except maybe that stuff you mumble about in your sleep."

Ivan Xav stiffened, and not in the good way. He was, in fact, quite limp in that region at the moment. "I talk in my sleep? About classified...?"

"It's kind of hard to tell." Tej composed her mouth into Ivan Xav's accent and cadences, and recited, "'Don't eat that avocado, Admiral, it's gone blue. The blue ones have shifty eyes.'"

"Don't remember *that* dream," Ivan Xav muttered, looking vaguely horrified. "Fortunately..."

"I actually guessed it was a dream. Unless Barrayar's running some sort of military bioengineering experiments, I suppose."

"Not as far as I know. Not like that, anyway. The avocado didn't... *meow*, did it?"

Tej stared. "I don't know. You only said it looked shifty."

Ivan Xav appeared inexplicably relieved. But then, alas, went on: "If it's something benign, there's no reason to keep it a secret."

"Sure there is."

"Like what?"

"Like, oh, to keep other people from stealing...whatever."

"It's a thing, then."

It was a bit hopeless to tell herself *Wake up!* when her head was so filled with fatigue-fog. Tej tried anyway. "Not necessarily. People steal ideas."

"So it's a thing, and...and Shiv and your family think it's something that can somehow help their cause, I suppose. That would make sense. Well, really, By is right; it's the only thing that would make sense. Something that would help them, something they need to take back their House. So, more power to them—but not *here*. What can they be up to *here*?"

"I am not playing fast-penta interrogation with you at this time of night. Or at any other time."

"That's...actually a party game. Fast-penta or Dare. People take turns asking questions, and you have to either tell the truth, or take the dare. Not with real fast-penta, of course. Unless it's a pretty dodgy party. By would know..."

"Barrayarans are *strange*."

"Yes," Ivan Xav agreed with a pensive sigh, then seemed to belatedly decide this might be considered a slur on his homeworld and revised it hastily, "No! Not as strange as Jacksonians, anyway.

Or Cetagandans." He added something under his breath that might have been, *Frigging mutant space aliens*, but swallowed it before Tej could be sure. She did not ask him to repeat it more loudly.

"It's not just the House," Tej tried, after a minute of silence stretched unpleasantly. "Prestene has Erik and Topaz. Held hostage or... or worse."

"So..." Ivan Xav's voice went uncomfortably uncertain. "Erik may well not be revivable. And Topaz is... just a Jewel, right? No genetic relation to Shiv. You said."

Tej frowned. "Dada never made any distinction amongst us kids. Or else when he was yelling at us, he wouldn't have kept mixing up our names." Those cadences came easily to her mouth and memory; her voice deepened automatically. "'You, Rish, Pidge, Jet, Em—no—Tej, you're the one—you, stop that!'" Her lips turned up despite herself. "I suppose you could think of him as a stepfather to the Jewels, but since he didn't bother to sort us, we never bothered to sort him. Of course, he was a busy man. It might have just been equal inattention, but the point is..." She'd lost track of the point.

"And your mother? With all the names?"

"The Baronne," sighed Tej, "never mixed up anything." She paused. "Simon seems a funny sort of stepfather to you."

Ivan flapped his hands. "If I'd been five. Or fifteen. When he took up with Mamere. Things might have been different. I'd *wanted* a father, then. At thirty, we could only be adult acquaintances, and him Mamere's... husband. Sort of. Um-husband. Partner. Whatever." He hesitated for a longer time. "Leaving aside the thirty years he'd watched out for me before that. But then, Simon Illyan watched out for *everybody*. Not... not making a distinction amongst us. But Simon—" Ivan Xav stuttered, and went on, "Do you realize that—no, I can't say that. Or *that*, I suppose. Or... or that..."

Tej, irate and exhausted and not *just* by the day, snapped, "Well, then, *stop talking* and go to sleep."

Ivan Xav *humphed*, sounding like... a lot like Count Falco, really.

They rolled over with their backs to each other.

Chapter Seventeen

Ivan's first thought on waking was the same as the last that had plagued him before he'd—finally—got to sleep. Could Simon be herding Shiv into a sting? Such a move was likely as instinctive as breathing to the former ImpSec chief. It was as plausible—a lot more plausible, really—as the idea that Shiv could be suborning Simon.

In that case, would Shiv lumber blindly into the trap, or would he guess this, and set a counter-pitfall for Simon before Simon could do him . . . ?

Neither vision was appealing.

It was maddening to suspect something was in the Arqua works, but have no idea what. Did Simon know, by now? The comforting notion that, in that case, Simon would surely be on top of it ran aground on the reflection that Shiv could well be stringing Simon along with heavily doctored information. In which case, the former ImpSec chief would likely let things run a bit to see what turned up. Giving the former pirate time to get the drop on him in turn . . .

This cannot end well. Ivan clutched his hair and stumbled to the shower.

Tej and Rish were still asleep when he let himself out of his flat. The routine of the morning rush at Ops was calming, almost.

Admiral Desplains inquired after Ivan's evening, in a perfunctory sort of way, and was evidently much reassured by the news that Lady Alys and Illyan had welcomed the refugee visitors diplomatically and without incident.

"Ah, Illyan, of course," murmured the admiral, gathering up his coffee mug. "*That* should cover everything."

"Mm!" said Ivan brightly, and turned to his comconsole.

He was still sorting snakes when a call came in over his secured channel from ImpSec HQ, the stamp informed him. Ivan mustered a faint, practiced smile of welcome when Captain Raudsepp's face materialized over the vid plate.

"Good, Captain Vorpatril." Raudsepp returned the nod. "General Allegre thought you should know, your case seems to be warming up. About a day ago, ImpSec Komarr picked up a team of four individuals at the main orbital transfer station who proved to be freelance bounty hunters out of the Hegen Hub, looking to collect your wife and her companion and deliver them to a contact back in the Hub."

Ivan lurched in his chair. That was . . . fast? Slow? Expected, unexpected . . . unfortunate? "Just Tej and Rish? Not the rest of the clan?"

"Apparently. The reward for the two women's delivery to the Hub station was substantial. A reward for their delivery all the way to the Whole is even more substantial. The source of what the Jacksonians are pleased to call an *arrest order* is confirmed to be this Prestene syndicate that took over House Cordonah eight months ago."

"That's not a surprise, by now. Were these rental goons arriving or departing when Morozov's people caught up with them?"

"Boarding ship for Vorbarr Sultana, in point of fact."

"That's . . . a bit late."

Raudsepp shrugged. "They were quite professional. And while we now have red flags on anything related to the new Cordonah consortium, their damned bounty system puts a natural break in any connection. Anyone at all—who is in the trade, that is—may pick up an advertisement of the bounty, and the first thing the Jacksonians who posted it, let alone us, may know of them is when they pop up on their doorstep ready to deliver and collect. Personal motives not required."

"Crap," said Ivan. "Then they could come out of the walls anywhere."

Raudsepp nodded glumly. "The charge of conspiracy to kidnap a Barrayaran subject will hold this crew for the moment." He added in a more reflective tone, "One does wonder what we will do with them if they accumulate. Some special holding pen for galactic human traffickers might have to be devised. Not that we aren't happy to have them identified and pulled out of circulation, but... well, perhaps it's premature to look so far ahead."

Ivan pictured it. What the hell was the Barrayaran government supposed to do with dozens and dozens of bounty hunters? They'd make a slippery bunch to hold on to, too, as well as some of them being seriously crazy. *Miles* would know what to do with a sack of rabid weasels, but that might be a cure worse than the disease. And anyway, Miles wasn't here. It was perhaps unworthy to think *thank God.*

"I suppose," said Ivan slowly, "they'll keep coming as long as this Prestene consortium is still out there offering the booty. And for a while after, as people fail to get the updates. Speaking of updates, is there any sign that the Arquas' enemies have found out that the rest of them are now all here?"

"Not yet," said Raudsepp. "But I shouldn't think that it will improve the situation once they do. This could get expensive for my department."

Ivan grimaced. "I suppose you fellows can think of it as a live training exercise."

Raudsepp appeared unamused. "Do you have any idea yet how long your, ah, relatives-in-law are planning to stay?"

"Their initial emergency visa runs thirteen more days. I don't know if they'll succeed in getting an extension."

"Hm." Raudsepp frowned. "Were you able to discover if they have any further plans? Otherwise, I don't see any impediment for them to take their family members and decamp promptly. Which would remove them from *my* work queue, at least."

"One of them is married to a Barrayaran subject. That's an impediment."

Raudsepp waved this away. "I was told this marriage of yours was a temporary ploy. Not one that anyone takes seriously."

I do. Did he? Did Tej...?

Raudsepp mused on, "One would think a notorious Vor womanizer would have a less drastic seduction technique." *Losing your touch?* hung implied in Raudsepp's eyebrow twitch.

Ivan wondered irately what pruney prole ImpSec analyst had him down in reports as *a notorious Vor womanizer.*

"In any case, did you learn any more about their intentions last night?" Raudsepp sat up straighter, preparing to record Ivan's snitch-report.

General Allegre had said—implied—that Galactic Affairs-Raudsepp had not formerly been in the need-to-know pool about Domestic-Affairs Byerly, in the interest of preserving By's valuable cover. By's valuable cover, in Ivan's view, was beginning to resemble a lace fig leaf. He'd wanted to ask, *But what if they try to shoot each other?* Well, Byerly wouldn't shoot the uniformed Raudsepp, probably. Accidentally.

So had that *apprising* taken place yet, and this a mere triangulation? *Bloody ImpSec.* Ivan fell back on: "Simon Illyan was there. The Spook's Spook. Can't you ask him?"

Raudsepp was taken aback. "Oh, of course." A daunted look came over his face. "I should not like to bother him in his retirement. His medical retirement. But certainly, no one's observations could be keener." Doubt colored his voice. "Once..."

So, that's what dithering looks like on Raudsepp. Under other circumstances, Ivan would have found it mildly entertaining.

"If Chief Illyan had spotted anything critical, he would certainly have reported it. Though maybe not on *my* level..."

Simon might have, at that. But to whom? *So why aren't I in that need-to-know loop? I bloody need to know!* "Ask around," Ivan suggested, shrugging. "Ah, excuse me. Admiral Desplains is paging me. Gotta go."

Raudsepp, reluctantly, parted with him for now. That line about Desplains would have been a good lie for cutting himself loose, Ivan thought, if only it had been a lie. Wasted for now, but perhaps he could file it for future reference. He turned to hastily muster the requested files. Another, God spare Ops, interdepartmental meeting in forty minutes. Wormhole jump station Logistics versus Budget & Accounting with spreadsheets at twenty paces at dawn, aiming to kill unless someone—and Ivan knew just what someone would be expected to pitch in—could persuade them to delope. He rose to report to the inner office.

Tej and Rish arrived, yawning, at the Arqua hotel suite to find everyone else up betimes. Even, it appeared, Byerly, just exiting in tow of Jet, who had drafted him for a local guide. By spared Rish a grimace of a smile; she spared him a grimace of one back. Tej thought, *Why don't you two just kiss each other and get it over with?* They so obviously wished to. But they exchanged greetings and farewells in nearly the same breaths, and parted at the lift tubes both looking back over their shoulders in dissatisfied ways.

Inside the suite—should she start thinking of it as House Cordonah HQ in Exile?—everyone seemed to be pursuing a different project at a different comconsole terminal, Star and Pearl at one, Pidge and Em at another, Dada at yet a third. Grandmama sat in the center and regarded it all benignly.

The Baronne greeted her directly with "Tej! Do I understand correctly that you can drive in Vorbarr Sultana?"

"Yes . . . ?"

"Excellent. We will have work for you shortly. Don't run off. Rish, Star needs you."

Rish, with another grimace, went off to join the little subcommittee at Star's terminal in the next room.

"But I don't have a vehicle." Ivan had taken his sporty groundcar to work, and besides, it would only hold one other Arqua at a time. Although that might not be a disadvantage.

"Then you can also take charge of obtaining rentals as needed. Good, I had been wondering what to do with you."

As if Tej were a spare puzzle piece that didn't fit in anywhere, perhaps accidentally included from another set. And here came another. Amiri wandered in with a coffee cup in his hand, looking vaguely at a loss, but he brightened when he saw Tej.

"Is there more of that?" asked Tej, nodding at the coffee.

"Yes, right this way . . ." He guided her to the credenza.

"What's Jet up to? I saw him going out with By." She poured, added cream, and drank. Mere hotel coffee, but the cream had that extraordinary mouth-filling taste that told of a real organic origin, not from a biovat like Station dairy products. Having now seen pictures of the organic origin, Tej wasn't sure she wanted to think too closely about it, but she had to admit that the result was amazing.

"Decoy. Sort of. Whichever of us Vorrutyer is with, or who is with Vorrutyer, is supposed to switch to decoy mode. With eleven of us, Dada figures we can keep him occupied. What *was* Rish thinking, to pick him up?"

Tej, remembering the exchange of scents at that first historic meeting in Ivan's Komarr flat, wasn't sure that *thinking* had had as much to do with it as either Byerly or Rish would likely claim. "He found us first, really. But it was a different situation then. We were both looking for cover."

"Not the way I should have preferred my sisters to obtain it, but done's done, I guess. Gods, Tej!" He shook his head, his crisp hair moving with it. "I'm so relieved the Baronne and Dada have found you two. Maybe, if they can bring off this damned treasure hunt, they'll let me go back to the clinic on Escobar."

"Is that what you want?"

"Of course it is. I was just getting my teeth into my first big postdoc project. It broke my heart to be dragged away. I'd thought I was *done* with House Cordonah and all its works, I thought I'd made my escape. All right, I can understand that Dada and the Baronne have just had this big scare, and why they want to keep us all collected under their eyes for a time, but I do not want to be drafted as a replacement heir for Erik. Not only would either Star or Pidge be better, they'd *want* it."

Tej wrinkled her nose, and lowered her voice. "I'm not sure of the dynamics of that. Star and Pidge both accepted Erik as heir. Do you think either of them would accept the other?"

Amiri looked as if he took the point. "Well...in either case, it wouldn't be *my* problem." He drank again.

"How long have the rest of you known about the treasure hunt?" Tej asked.

"Just since last night. After we got back from Lady Vorpatril's. Dada and Grandmama and the Baronne called a family meeting and told us the new scheme. They'd really kept it tight before then—I suppose because they weren't sure yet that the bio-bunker-thing would still be here. I thought we were just coming here to get you two, and I'd wondered why we all had to be dragged five wormhole jumps when we could have just sent one rep. And *much* more discreetly."

Tej wondered what she and Rish would have done if just one Arqua had turned up, demanding they depart at once. Might have depended on which one...

"Why *did* they haul you along?" Tej asked.

"That was the big mystery to me, too, till last night. They seem to have some idea of fencing any interesting old Cetagandan bio-stuff out through Lily Durona. I wonder if they'd told her about it all? That would explain why she was so ready to let me go, at least. Makes me feel a bit better." Amiri paused, then countered, "How long have you known?"

"Only since yesterday afternoon, when Rish was briefing the rest of you on local terrain. But did they tell you what the Barrayarans have planted on *top* of Grandmama's old place?"

"Yeah, that sounded a bit...challenging. But Dada seemed to think he had it all under control." An uncertain tone entered Amiri's voice. Dada and the Baronne had presumably thought they'd had Cordonah Station under control, once, too.

Amiri turned to Tej with more urgency. "But you *have* to help make sure this comes off, Tej, you *have* to. My whole life is riding on it."

What about my *whole life?* Tej stemmed the rebellious thought. Of course Amiri's life was more important. Amiri *did* things. Tej, as her family never seemed to tire of pointing out, didn't. She sighed. "I'll try, Amiri."

"Don't just try, *do*," he urged. "It's really important to me. To everybody, really, but especially to me."

"Yes, yes..." said Tej, distracted. *I was prepared to jump off a damned balcony for you. Shouldn't that be enough?* She was beginning to rethink that balcony business. True, it had been as much to escape the exhaustion and the being-afraid-all-the-time as it had been for imagined family heroism. None of which had been a problem since...since Ivan Xav, really. He was not the balcony *type*.

I like that in a man. She was just beginning to realize how much.

The Baronne was calling her away to consult on local transportation logistics with Dada. She sighed and trudged off to do her Arqua duty.

Ivan woke, not as late as he'd have liked, on his first day off after the Invasion of the Arquas to an unexpectedly empty bed. A gulping moment of panic was quelled, as he sat up, by the sound of voices from the next room and someone rattling around in the bathroom.

Ivan had needed to work yesterday; Tej had spent all the long day and into the evening driving assorted Arquas around town on mysterious errands which she'd barely talked about. From years of practice with his cousin, Ivan could recognize evasion both when he heard it, and when he didn't hear it. He wasn't reassured by either mode. He'd held her attention briefly with Raudsepp's account of the intercepted bounty hunters, which she'd assured him she would pass on to her folks, but with unfeigned tiredness she had slipped—*away,* perhaps?—into sleep shortly thereafter.

Yawning, he dragged on trousers and went in search of caffeine. Tej was in the comconsole niche, talking to someone—a Barrayaran, a commercial clerk of some sort, apparently. She switched to Barrayaran Russian in mid-sentence; the man brightened and became more voluble. And cooperative? In any case, her business was concluded by the time Ivan came back with a steaming mug in his hand.

Ivan nodded at the comconsole. "How did you know that fellow's mother tongue? He had a pretty urban accent."

Tej gestured to the now-blank vid-plate. "I can hear it in their voices. Can't you?"

"Accents, sure. But he sounded pure Vorbarr Sultana to me."

"Not really. I haven't got all the District dialect variations sorted out yet, though. Sixty-times-four plus South Continent. I have to pick up more local geography."

"Do you expect to? Sort them all out?"

She shrugged. "If I'm here long enough, they'll sort themselves."

"Tej..." He wanted to follow up that ambiguous-sounding *if I'm here long enough,* but stuck to his first thought. "How many languages do you *speak*?"

"I dunno." Her nose wrinkled. "Since I came here—nine?"

"That's a lot."

"Not really. Good translator earbugs will handle hundreds. Why bother making work out of it, when the ones you need likely won't be the ones you learned anyway? I never even *heard* of Barrayaran Russian before I came here. Or your local Greek dialect, which is pretty corrupt—well, altered—see, I didn't say *mutated.* I mean, learning them yourself isn't a *practical* hobby. The earbugs do it better." A crooked smile. "Kind of fun, though. I like fun."

"Fun," said Ivan, bemusedly reflecting on all the lack of fun he'd had in his school language drills.

Rish emerged from the bathroom, fully dressed. "Tej, did you get the ground-van and the big speakers? Are we ready to go now?"

"Yes and yes." Tej popped up and offered Ivan a placatory kiss on the cheek. "Gotta run."

"Where are you going?"

"The Jewels wanted a place for some dance practice, since this is the first they've been together for ages, and Simon found us this nice park. There wasn't any place big enough in the hotel. I'm doing tech on the music."

"Outdoors? In this weather?" Ivan wandered to a window and peered blearily out. All right, the angled winter sun was shining brightly, and it was windless and well above freezing, but still.

"It's really pretty nice out today. Supposed to change tomorrow, though, so I really have to go now..."

She and Rish blew out.

Ivan munched groats, a little later, with his uneasiness growing. He shaved, dressed, and, with extreme reluctance, called his mother.

"Mamere," he said, when her impeccably groomed features appeared over the vid plate, wearing an expression of surprised inquiry. "Do you know anything about some dance practice place Simon recommended to the Jewels? A park or commons, outdoors." Vorbarra Sultana had dozens of such nooks.

"Oh, yes, he mentioned that. He's gone off to watch. I thought it was good for him to get out. I'd have loved to go with him, but I'm running a diplomatic luncheon at the Residence today for Laisa, as she had to go down to that Vorbarra District economics conference in Nizhne-Whitekirk."

"Where? The dance practice, I mean."

"He suggested the little park across the street from ImpSec headquarters. Hardly anyone ever uses it, you know. Except those poor fellows with that seasonal affective problem, who come out to eat their lunches sometimes. Simon *did* make full-spectrum lighting an allowable requisition, years back."

"Um, yeah. Thanks." About to sign off, he hesitated. "Mamere— has Simon told you anything about what Shiv had to say to him? Or vice versa?"

Her smile never shifted. So why did he get the impression of her putting on her most diplomatic poker-face? "He said they had a very enjoyable exchange. I was pleased. I quite liked Udine and Moira, you know. Such adventurous lives! Earth! I've never been farther than Komarr." She sighed.

"You should get Simon to take you," Ivan suggested. "Or take him. Lever him out of his comfy rut. Four, pushing five years since his retirement, all the really hot stuff in his head—whatever's left of it—has to have cooled off some by now. Doesn't he think it's safe to travel out of the Empire yet?"

Her brows rose in a thoughtful way. "He's never suggested travel farther than the south coast. He was really... extremely exhausted, immediately after all that—" a flick of her hand summed the nightmare weeks of Simon's chip breakdown. And nightmare decades of its full function, before that, Ivan supposed. "More so than I think he let on."

"He always was pretty closed," said Ivan, in what had to be the understatement of the century. "It's not like you could tell the difference from the outside."

"No, I suppose you couldn't."

Ivan heard the faint emphasis on that *you*. Which presumably did not include *her*. Her thirty years of working with Simon hadn't exactly been like one of those long marriages where people started finishing each other's sentences, but it did perhaps partake of some of the elements. Ivan tried to remember what had been the longest time he'd ever stuck with one girlfriend. *Or vice versa.* Surely at least one of them had been more than a year? Almost a year? More than a half-year...?

"Delightful for you to call, but I must go," his mother said firmly. "Tomorrow, we really must come up with something else to do with your visitors. Properly, it would be their turn to invite us to dinner, but they may not like to do so in that hotel."

"Um, right," said Ivan, and let her cut the com.

It being the last weekend before the start of Winterfair proper, parking around ImpSec HQ was not as impossible as usual. Ivan only had to walk about a block before the bare little park, and the great gloomy building across from it, came into view.

The security headquarters had an imposing façade, utterly windowless, with the wide stairs leading up to the front doors deliberately designed to be higher than most people could comfortably step. The great bronze doors were, as far as Ivan knew, rarely opened—everyone with business here went around to the human-scale entrances on the sides or the back. The stone face of the building was severely plain, except for a stylized bas-relief frieze of pained-looking creatures that Miles had once dubbed *pressed gargoyles* which entirely circled the edifice.

At the time of the reign of Mad Yuri, the gargoyles had possessed some political/artistic/propagandistic metaphorical meaning, which had once been explained to Ivan, but that he had promptly forgotten. Ivan thought the poor things just looked constipated. The people of Vorbarr Sultana, over time, had named them all, and endowed them with varied personalities; there were running jokes about the conversations they had up there, frozen in their frieze, and some of them regularly appeared as editorial cartoon characters. And in a short-lived children's animated show, Ivan dimly remembered from his youth.

The whole was surrounded in turn by a cobblestone courtyard and high stone walls topped with iron spikes not unlike the ones around Vorkosigan House, though already archaically outdated for actual defense even at the time they'd been built. All the real defenses were electronic and invisible. The wall was pierced fore and aft by two gates, the gate guards armed with energy weapons. Muskets would have seemed more in-period.

The park was indeed sunny, if only because ImpSec had never permitted trees, kiosks, bathrooms, or bushes installed to impede the line of sight, or fire. Grass, a little brown after the first frosts but neatly groomed, held up well due to the small number of pedestrians who ventured to cut across it.

Five brightly dressed people were milling about on the turf—Rish, Jet, Em, Pearl, and Star—while Tej knelt at the side messing with a portable comconsole and some wireless speakers. Under Star's direction, Tej stood up and shifted one of the speakers a few meters. Tej saw Ivan and waved, but didn't come over to greet him. Star, with Jet consulting, also shifted around a couple of brightly colored sticks topped with sparkly pom-poms; counting off strides, taking a line of sight, and sticking them back in the ground.

Simon, wrapped in an aged military greatcoat, was sitting on a bench at the grass's verge benignly overlooking the show. Hatless—Mamere would have had words—with his thinning, graying hair making him look very much like some retired old man watching youngsters at play. Which Ivan supposed he was. Sort of. In some pig's eye somewhere.

A uniformed ImpSec officer without a coat—a major, Ivan saw

as he approached—was standing talking to Simon, looking back and forth from his former chief to the dance practice that was just getting rolling again. Bright music blared. Jewels were suddenly in motion, swaying, stomping, gesturing, rising and dipping. Jet, in a bravura moment, suddenly began a series of back-flips that ran in a straight diagonal all across the park, and ended with him balanced first on one hand, and then on one foot.

"That's impressive," the major said to Simon, as Ivan came up. The fellow's eyes shifted from Jet to check out Ivan, in civvies because this was his day off dammit; his face cleared. "Captain Vorpatril, is it? Ops?"

Ivan granted him a nod, in lieu of a salute. "Yes, sir."

"So you would know what all this is in aid of...?"

"A rather high-energy galactic dance troupe who have been cooped up on jumpships for too long, celebrating their reunion, is the tale I was told," said Ivan easily. Did Simon *smile*, there, into his lack of a beard?

"I had never seriously watched dance," Simon remarked to the major, "before my retirement. Lady Vorpatril has her own box at the Vorbarr Sultana Hall, you know. She has been kind enough to invite me to escort her there, many times since. It's been a real artistic education. Of a style I'd never had time for, earlier in my life. Old dogs, new tricks, who knows where it could all end?"

"Hm. Well. If they're with *you*, sir..." The major, with a restraint that practically seemed to break something—perhaps his heart—visibly kept himself from saluting his former chief, managing a mere curt farewell nod before turning away to dodge traffic across the street and slip back through the front gate.

Ivan slung himself down on the bench beside Simon, who had twisted a bit to watch the fellow retreat.

"That's the fifth man who has come out so far to check this out," Simon observed, turning back. "The ranks keep getting higher."

"Have they?" said Ivan, neutrally.

Star, all slicked-back hair, green eyes, and long leggings, bopped out and moved the sparkly pom-poms again. The music started up once more, a slower beat this time. Jewels glittered, in an eye-grabbing and athletic whirl. Jet repeated the astonishing back-flip routine, on the park's other diagonal.

"I had always considered," Simon mused after a bit, "that for a building housing a cadre of men whose insignia"—he touched his civilian shirt collar, where no Eye-of-Horus pins now hung—"proclaimed to the Imperium, *sees all, knows all*, to have *no damned windows allowing them to see out*, to be some sort of cosmic irony."

Ivan leaned forward slightly to glance around Simon at the looming façade. "I expect they were more worried at the time about windows being blown in." The techno-eyes were mostly nonobvious, but for some antennae and reception dishes peeking over the crenellated roof edge. "They have electronic surveillance, surely."

"Of a redundant redundancy. It was like working in a granite spaceship. Hermetically sealed."

"So, um . . ." Ivan considered how to phrase this. "How far up does the rank have to go before someone in your parade of concerned officers comes out and says, *What the hell, Simon?*"

"I wait with some fascination to find out."

Star shifted markers. The four Jewels began to dance another pattern.

"Granted," said Simon meditatively, "the half-dozen men that I'm sure would begin their inquiries in just those words either have the day off or are out of town. Which seems like cheating, but then, it was often much about cheating. On all sides."

Ivan considered this. "What the *hell*, Simon?"

Simon flashed a thin slice of grin. "Make that seven. Don't you see?"

"No."

"Neither can they." He glanced across the street. "No windows, y'see. I'm sure we still have some analysts in there somewhere who specialize in the arts, but they're probably kept in a box in the basement, poor lads. Keep watching, then."

The Jewels set up once more, for a longer pattern this time. Frowning, Ivan got up, pulled one of the pom-pom sticks out of the ground, and examined it. It wasn't very heavy. The surface featured swirling candy-colored stripes. It had a metal ferrule; Ivan tilted it up to peer in the end, which was not solid, but which was dark. Star, frowning more fiercely, came up and twisted it back out of his hand, shook it vigorously, and reset it. "Don't screw up our stage marks," she chided him. "Someone might have an accident." It was hard to tell, but Ivan suspected the stripes were not the same as before. He trod back to rejoin Simon.

The music this time seemed to mix a cheerful march with a winding wail, like women lamenting the departure of their city's valiant militia. Jet produced another bravura set of flips. Again.

So...what was so different about Jet? He certainly wasn't any more athletic than Rish or the others. Why weren't they doing flips?

He said aloud, before he could stop himself, "Jet's the heaviest."

Simon glanced aside at him, that disturbing faint smile again turning his lips.

More music started up. Rish had portioned out the ankle bells Ivan had seen on her and Tej the other day among the three female Jewels. They began another dance, or dance section—they seemed to be practicing movements rather than whole compositions. This time the mood was merry, the timing—the frequency?—different yet again.

Jet began his run-up, and bounced over the ground in a quick succession of thumps.

Ivan blinked. And blurted, "Sonic mapping."

Simon's smile deepened. "You're wasted in Ops, you know. I have increasingly thought so. If not, I admit"—some grimace of memory Ivan *certainly* wasn't going to inquire after—"earlier in your career."

"*I* don't think so. More to the point, Admiral Desplains doesn't think so. I'm *happy* in Ops."

"Well, there's that. And your mother is happy to have you there"—another lip-pursing—"*relatively* safe."

"Nobody's tried to blow up Ops for ages. They always went for you fellows first."

"One of ImpSec's many unsung public services: human shields for Ops. But did Ops ever say *thank you*?"

Ivan had no idea. Most Ops commentary on ImpSec reports that he'd heard was prefaced by swearing, but maybe that was just habit. "Has anyone tried to bomb Ops lately? Or ever? Since our new building went up after the last one was leveled in the Pretendership, that is."

Simon huddled down in his coat. "I wouldn't recall the details now. Nor the main points, in some cases."

I can't remember was Simon's all-purpose response to any question he didn't want to answer, Ivan had suspected for some time. It almost always daunted the hell out of the inquirer, who sheared off.

Except that Ivan was getting *used* to Illyan, in some strange domestic way. All those little tricks of expression, inflection, reminder, that he used to defend his dignity. It had been a horrifically beleaguered dignity, during the chip breakdown, in some ways Ivan had witnessed and didn't wish to dwell on. Still—the Spook's Spook had also been the Weasel's Weasel. For all that Simon had forgotten, Ivan didn't think he'd forgotten all of that.

Ivan scrambled back up the conversational diversion to the last knot. "Mapping. Underground mapping. What the hell, Simon? I would think you fellows would have had every cubic centimeter of underground Vorbarr Sultana mapped to the limit. *Especially* right around this place." *Underground, ugh.*

"Indeed, one would think that. I certainly did." Simon scratched his neck. "Although most people don't realize how incredibly complicated and ill-documented it can get, under the Old Town. Old sewers. Abandoned utility tunnels. Freight access. Built-over foundations. A couple of outdated, bankrupted attempts at public transport, before the bubble-tube system was planned or even thought of. Streambeds, drainage. Assorted Vor mansions' personal bolt-holes and escape hatches—and the same for some less savory prole venues. And a rat warren of other covert passages dating back mostly to the Occupation, but some to other wars. Several centuries of forgotten secrets down there, dying with their possessors."

Ivan glanced again at the six skewed floors and several subbasements of paranoia piled across the street. "Why aren't they picking anything up? Of this, over there?"

"What would you guess?"

"I dunno..." He considered the odd stage-mark stick that he'd held in his hand. "Passive analog data collectors, I suppose, with nothing electronic about them?"

"I understand the color-gradient has a biological base that sensitively responds to vibrations, yes. Dancing microbes of some sort."

Ivan wiped his hand on his trousers, nervously. "Oh. You're in on this, then." *Whatever this is.*

"I wouldn't say that, exactly."

"What would you say, exactly?"

"At this juncture, not much."

"Simon." It took a bit of effort to make the name come out low and commanding, and not a reproachful wail.

It was effort wasted; Simon just twitched the damned deadly eyebrows at him, as if he'd heard the wail in his possibly-telepathic mind anyway and *don't even think about that, boy.* "There is nothing illegal or even immoral about looking, Ivan. I'm sure I've even seen those old gentlemen with the metal detectors right here in this park, searching for ancient coins and the like. Retirement hobby or destitution, I was never quite sure."

"Your guards ran them off, surely."

"Not always. They might, after all, have found something *interesting.*"

"And have the Arquas found something *interesting*?"

"We don't, of course, know yet. Till Shiv and Udine analyze their measurements."

"And what will you do then?"

"Flowcharts, Ivan. I'm sure I've heard you go on at length over some meal or another with your lady mother about the warm, fuzzy feelings you get from flowcharts. This is only the first bifurcation in the decision-tree, not the last."

Whatever Ivan was feeling right now, warm and fuzzy wasn't in it.

The sun was climbing toward noon, though not overhead, as high as it got this time of year. From the ImpSec gates there issued a gaggle of pallid men, officers and enlisted both, clutching lunch sacks and drinks of various sorts. They split up and spread out to take over the benches in a practiced-seeming way, with some of the enlisted ending up sharing their lunch picnics on rolled-out ground sheets. They all gazed in suspicion at the Jewels; some gazed in suspicion at the two civilian-clothed men on the last bench, especially the group displaced from their usual perch, till apprised by some of their older colleagues. Then they just stared.

Tej grinned across at Simon and at Ivan, almost the first *his wife* had acknowledged his existence since he'd sat down, and went into a brief huddle with the Jewels. Star opted out, looking mildly bored; she had collected all the stage markers back into a bundle, and seemed to be loading things up.

The group of Jewels split up again and took positions in a circle, or square, or imaginary four-pointed star. Tej bent and started the music once more, louder than heretofore; a very traditional Barrayaran mazurka, if with a livelier, updated beat and flourishes. The Jewels began to move, grandly leaping and kicking, in a version that recalled traditional Barrayaran men's dances without in any way being one. It was by far the most athletic performance yet. Even Jet, usually the thrower, took his turn being thrown into the air—if by two of his sister-Jewels in cooperation—and somersaulting to daring landings. All the men around the perimeter of the park stopped eating to goggle. Tej watched as if hypnotized with pleasure.

When the dance finished in a whirl and a shout, all the Jewels were breathing heavily, sweating despite the chill. Quite spontaneously, the ImpSec men scattered around their impromptu stage broke into applause; the Jewels grinned and bowed back, in one cardinal direction after another, concluding with an especially low sweep toward Simon and Ivan.

Simon rose, with one of those my-back-hurts sounds made by the aging, whether sincerely or for audience effect. There had been a deal of audience effect running in several directions here this morning, Ivan was pretty sure. The Jewels and Tej finished packing up their scant props, or gear, hauling it to the ground-van parked on the far side of the grassy space.

"You talk to Guy Allegre about all this yet?" Ivan nodded toward the late outdoor stage. "Or was he one of your six men?"

"Not yet."

"Or him to you?"

"I set it as a high probability that we'll be talking to each other sometime."

"Ah . . . Gregor?"

Simon's eyebrows mocked him. "And what is Gregor's favorite motto?"

"*Let's see what happens,*" Ivan recited glumly. "I always thought that was an appallingly irresponsible thing for an emperor to say."

"There you go."

Tej came over, to inquire rather breathlessly of Simon, but not Ivan, "Did you like the show, sir?"

"Yes. I did. Street theater of the highest order."

"Complete with audience participation?" Ivan muttered. Wait, right—Simon hadn't answered his last question. Or his first, for that matter.

"You should take your wife to lunch, Ivan," Simon suggested genially. He asked Tej to convey his thanks to the Jewels for the show, excused himself, and walked off down the boulevard, just as though he had been some ordinary passerby who'd stopped to watch the rehearsing dancers.

But Tej, still elusive, claimed chauffeuring duties, and fled in the opposite direction.

Ivan, feeling at default if not fault, sat back on the bench and stared at the blank landscape, trying to imagine how far was *down*.

Chapter Eighteen

Ivan woke the next morning to an empty bed, again, a depopulated flat, and a note on the coffeemaker: *Gone driving. T.* Which was better than no reassurance at all, but wouldn't *Love, T.* have been a better closing salutation? Not that he had ever ended any note to Tej with *Love, I.,* so far, but then, he hadn't ever gone out and left her with just some laconic, uninformative scrawl. She'd come in very late last night, too, after some family thing, and gone straight to sleep, with no talk and scarcely a cuddle.

He buttered his instant breakfast groats, which made him think back to the emergency impromptu wedding on Komarr, and wondered if the gelid grains would taste better with a shot of brandy poured over them instead. *No.* No drinking at dawn, that was a bad sign, not that this was dawn—merely midmorning. He tried Tej's wristcom, without reply, and was dumped to her message bin. *Dumped,* that wasn't a good word, either. Nor—memory intruded again, albeit not one of Tej—a good sign. When his would-be-breezy *Hey, Tej, call me. Ivan, your husband, remember?,* produced no response by the time he had shaved and dressed, he steeled himself and walked down the street to the Arqua-occupied hotel.

Shiv himself admitted him when he buzzed the door of their

suite. "Ah. Ivan." He called over his shoulder, "Udine, Tej's Barrayaran is here." He gestured Ivan in and to one of the sitting room's upholstered chairs, and fetched coffee from a credenza; Ivan accepted it gratefully.

The Baronne shut down her comconsole, joined her husband on the small sofa facing Ivan, and cast her provisional son-in-law a cool smile of welcome.

"I just popped in to ask where Tej had gone," Ivan explained. "She left me a note, but it didn't say much."

Udine answered, "She has kindly taken my mother and Amiri out for some touring. I don't believe they had a set destination."

Well, all right, that sounded pretty safe and benign, compared to yesterday's...odd performance. Lady ghem Estif was not wholly alarming, for a haut woman, or ex-haut woman, and Amiri was surely the least Jacksonian of this crew. A doctor, after all, aspiring unworldly researcher to boot. But Ivan was beginning to regret getting Tej all those driving lessons. "Couldn't you hire a driver?" Wondering if that sounded rude, he added, "I could help you find one." *Or Captain Raudsepp could, no doubt.*

"Perhaps later on," said Shiv. "But this gave Tej a chance to catch up with her favorite brother."

"Ah," said Ivan, unable to argue with that. Dead end. He cast around for another topic. One came up readily. "So, ah...how long are you folks planning to stay on Barrayar, anyway?"

"I expect that will rather depend on Pidge's success in obtaining our emergency visa extension," said Udine.

"Oh, yeah," said Ivan. "How's that going for you?"

"Moving along," said Udine. "She thinks it may prove advantageous to hire a local lawyer; she said she'd know by tomorrow or the next day."

"My, um, mother might be able to put you in touch with a good one," Ivan suggested. Not that he necessarily *wanted* their stay extended. With one exception.

"Lady Alys has already made that offer," said Udine brightly. "So helpful, your mother."

"What will you all do if the extension is—" he started to say, *denied,* but switched on the fly to, "granted? You wouldn't be planning to stay permanently, would you? Apply for immigration status, take oath as Barrayaran subjects? I should probably warn you, they take oaths pretty seriously around here."

Udine smiled slightly. "I am aware."

"It wouldn't be my first choice," said Shiv, gem-black eyes narrowing in his dark face in some unreadable emotion, "but if there is one thing my life has taught me, it's the need to stay flexible. Barrayar is not a place I would ever have gone voluntarily, but I must say I've been agreeably surprised by what I've seen here. They do say travel broadens the mind. If none of our first-choice plans work out, we may simply have to develop some new... enterprise." His carved lips drew back in a smilelike expression.

Ivan tried to imagine how a Jacksonian who had *already* once fought his way to the top of a major House defined that last term. *Plus wife, don't forget*—they did seem to be a team. The only comparison he had was Miles's Jacksonian-raised and relentlessly entrepreneurial clone-brother Mark, which was...not especially reassuring.

Ivan wondered if it was better to lay his cards right on the table—*Just what are you people after under that park in front of ImpSec?* Or let them assume him oblivious? Presumed obliviousness had served Ivan well many times in the past, after all. Perhaps he should split the difference. Just how close to tapped out *were* the Arquas, anyway? Could he ask Raudsepp? Morozov?

Hell, why not ask Shiv?

He leaned back and tented his hands, remembered where that gesture came from, almost put them down, but then left them up. "So...just how close are you folks to being tapped out, anyway? It's been a pretty long run for you to get this far." He just barely stopped his mouth from going on and apologizing for such a rude question, as Udine, at least, was nodding in rare approval.

Shiv's eye-flick caught it, too. His thick shoulders gave a little shrug. "How much is *enough* depends on what you want to do with it. Venture capital—I believe you planetary agriculturalists would call it *seed corn*, ah, yes, that's the term—if a man is reduced to consuming his startup stake, he has nothing to hazard for the next round. What do you people call your currency, *marks*—well, Barrayaran marks, Betan dollars, Cetagandan reyuls, doesn't matter, the principle's the same. There's a saying in the Whole: it's easier to turn one million into two million than it is to turn one into two."

"The effective break-point for us," put in Udine, "is *enough* to fund a credible attempt to retake House Cordonah. We are, shall we say, not without hidden resources and potential allies back in the Whole, but not if we arrive appearing to be disarmed, destitute, and desperate."

"Whether you can climb up to success or are forced down to grubberdom depends on making your break-point," said Shiv. "Both success and failure are feedback loops, that way. Me, I started as a gutter grubber. I don't plan on going back down to that gutter again alive."

Jacksonian determination glinted in Shiv's eye, reminding Ivan, for a weird moment, of his cousin Miles. People for whom failure was psychologically tantamount to death, yeah.

Ivan had a few clues as to what forces had shaped Miles that way, putative child of privilege though he was. The chief of whom had been named *General Count Piotr Vorkosigan*, though Barrayar's endemic hostility toward perceived mutations had certainly provided an ongoing chorus to that appalling old man, whose every grudging grain of approval had been won by his mutie grandson by an equally appalling achievement, or at least some bone-cracking attempt at it. On Ivan's personal youthful list of people to avoid, Great-uncle Piotr had been at the top. Not a ploy available to Miles, poor sawed-off sod.

So what had shaped and wound that same tight spring in Shiv? And Udine as well? Ivan wasn't sure he wanted the tour.

"Isn't enough to fund a small war also enough to, say, buy a nice tropical island and *retire*?" Ivan couldn't help asking.

"Not while those Prestene bastards hold two of my children hostage," said Shiv grimly.

"Not to mention my hair," said Udine, plucking at her fringe. Shiv caught the nervous hand and kissed it, looking sideways at his wife, and for the first time Ivan wondered, *What else besides the hair?* Yet whatever had been done to her, in the unsavory hands of her enemies, Ivan was pretty sure the hair was going to be the only part ever mentioned aloud.

"Ah. Yeah," said Ivan. No, it wasn't just about money; there was blood on the line as well. Ivan understood blood, well enough.

But it did give Ivan a notion as to what the Arquas thought was under that park: enough to fund a small war. Or buy a tropical island, depending on one's tastes in such things. And these two didn't look to be going for the drinks with fruit on little sticks.

"But, ah—Tej wouldn't really need to go back with you for

that, would she? Surely it would be *safer* to leave her here on Barrayar." *With me.*

"With you?" said Udine, raising an eyebrow and making Ivan twitch.

"I do, um . . . like her a lot," Ivan managed. He wondered if *So does my mother and sort-of-stepfather* would be good to add, or if that would just up the bidding on the deal.

Udine sat back. "So you . . . *like her* enough to want her to forsake her family and stay with you—but do you *like her* enough to leave your family and go with her?"

Shiv, too, stared narrowly at him at this. "It's true, he does have that Barrayaran military training. It is unclear how much he also has Barrayaran military experience, however."

Ivan gulped, unnerved. "I'd be delighted to leave my family and go somewhere with Tej, just not . . . not Jackson's Whole. Not my kind of place, y'know."

"Hm," said Shiv, opaquely. He eased back in his seat, though Ivan hadn't noticed him tense.

Ivan said, "Look, I can support a wife here on Barrayar. And I know my home ground. On Jackson's Whole, I'd be, what . . . destitute and disarmed. Not to mention out of my depth."

"As Tej has been, here?" Udine inquired sweetly.

Shiv gave him the eyebrow thing. "A man should know himself, I suppose," he said. "Me, I've been face flat, sucking gutter slime, three times in my life, and had to start again each time from scratch. I'm getting too old to enjoy shoveling that shit anymore, but I can't say I don't know *how*."

This was not, Ivan sensed, a remark in Ivan's favor, oblique though it sounded.

"I, as well," murmured Udine, "though only once. I do not mean to let this present contretemps stand as twice."

"But you left your original family," Ivan tried. "To go with Shiv. Your new husband. Didn't you? Anyway, left your planet."

Udine's voice went dry. "More evicted than left, in the event. We were fleeing the Barrayaran military conquest of Komarr, at the time."

"Although that worked out surprisingly well," Shiv murmured. "In the long run." That passing hand grip again, on the sofa between them.

Her eyes grew amused, and turned back on Ivan. "Yes, I

suppose I should thank you Barrayarans for that. Ejecting me out of my rut."

"I wasn't born yet," Ivan put in, just in case.

Dare he ask them, straight out, *Are you planning to take Tej away?* What if the answer was *Yes, certainly?* Did Tej think she had a vote? Did *they* think Tej had a vote? Or Ivan?

No, Jacksonians didn't have votes; they had deals. For the first time, Ivan wondered uneasily what he had to offer at the Great House scale of play. His personal wealth, though doubtless impressive to some prole or grubber, would barely tweak their scanners. His blood was more hazard than hope, the main question being how far it would splash in a crunch. And he wasn't a candidate for conscription into *their* system, as they had hinted, not under any circumstances. Which left—what?

Udine's gaze strayed to her abandoned comconsole. The suite was awfully quiet, Ivan realized. Where were all the rest of the clan this morning, and what were they doing? "Well, don't let us keep you, Captain Vorpatril."

From what? But Ivan took the hint, and stood. "Right-oh. Thanks for the coffee. If you hear from Tej before I do, ask her to call me, huh?" He tapped his wristcom meaningfully.

"Certainly," said Udine.

Shiv saw him back to the door. "As it so happens," he said, eyeing Ivan shrewdly, "we do have a little side deal in progress here on Barrayar. If it is successful, it will certainly aid our departure." *And if you want to see the back of Clan Arqua, maybe you'd better do your bit to see it is successful, huh?* seemed to hang in the air, implied.

"I sure hope everything works out," Ivan responded. Shiv merely looked amused at that manifest vagueness.

Ivan retreated down the hotel corridor.

He rather thought he might also see the back of Clan Arqua by just waiting and letting nature, or at least Customs & Immigration, take its course. Deportation, that was the ticket. And he, personally, wouldn't have to lift a finger. And Tej would not be included in the roundup, because she had, what had Lady ghem Estif called it, umbrella residency as a spouse, all right and tight and no argument there.

If she chose.

Yeah.

It seemed to Ivan that he needed to court his wife. Promptly. In the next, what was it, ten days. If he could catch her in passing, in this spate of Arqua chores. *But how can I court her when no one even gives me a chance to see her?*

Tej parked the rented groundcar and stared dubiously around the dim underground garage. After yesterday's dance in the park, and some sharp debate over city maps, Pearl had found this place—by the simple method of walking around and looking—under one of the few commercial buildings near ImpSec HQ, which was otherwise mainly ringed by assorted stodgy government offices. This building housed mostly offices as well: attorneys, a satellite communications company, an architectural firm, a terraforming consultant, financial managers of various sorts. The two layers of garage were packed during the day, but relatively clear after hours and on the Barrayaran weekend, which this was.

This commercial building lay on a corner across the street from the backside, as it were, of the security headquarters. The far side, unfortunately, from the little park that had indeed been found to top Grandmama's old lab site, or most of it; some of the lab had been mapped to run under the street fronting the headquarters. If ImpSec's subbasements had been dug two dozen meters farther southeast, back in Mad Yuri's day, they'd have cut right into the lab's top corner. Tej didn't see how they could have missed detecting it, but the Baronne claimed they must have. Dada...was perhaps persuading himself to believe.

As Tej, Amiri, and Grandmama exited the groundcar, Pearl detached herself from the shadow of a pillar and waved them over. Amiri removed a hefty valise from the trunk and followed.

"It's looking good," said Pearl. "Seems to be a storeroom for garage maintenance, in use, but no one has been in or out since I've been monitoring. I've adjusted the lock for us."

She glanced around and led the way into a small, utilitarian chamber lit only, at the moment, by a cold light set on a metal shelf. The chamber and shelves seemed to contain stacks of various traffic barricades, buckets of paint, a ladder, and encouragingly dusty miscellanea. Pearl cracked a second cold light, doubling the eerie illumination.

"We need to leave it looking like no one has been in or out, too," said Amiri. "At least for now. Where should we start?"

"Let's shift these two shelves," said Pearl. "We can shift them back, after. Here, Tej, take one end."

Tej dutifully lifted her half of the grubby thing. When they were done, a large patch of concrete flooring lay exposed in the chamber's corner.

From the valise, Amiri handed out breath masks, all marked with logos from the jumpship line the Arquas had traveled in on. Tej was under the impression that such safety devices were supposed to be handed back at the end of the voyage, but oh well. Waste not. He then donned biotainer gloves and removed a bottle from the valise; everyone else stood well back as he squatted and trailed a line of liquid in a smooth circle about a meter in diameter over the concrete, which began to bubble.

While the cutting fluid worked, he laid out other objects, including a long, mysterious padded case. Then they all stood back and stared for a while.

"All right," he said at last, and he, Tej, and Pearl combined to lever the concrete slab out of its matrix and shove it aside. Revealed was a layer of pressed stones.

Pearl trundled up a waste bin, and she and Amiri and Tej then knelt and began prying up rocks—by hand. "You might have brought a shovel," Tej grumbled.

"There should only be about a half a meter of this before we hit subsoil," Amiri said. "Maybe less, if the contractor stinted."

"Many hands make light the work," Grandmama intoned, watching. At Tej's irritated glance over her shoulder, she added, "It's an old Earth saying I picked up."

"No wonder everybody left the planet," muttered Tej. Hired grubbers with power tools seemed a better deal for lightening a load to her.

"I would feel more secure if we could have found a place to rent or buy," said Amiri. "Really proof against interruptions."

"But this leaves no data trail," said Pearl, perhaps defending her find.

This squabble continued intermittently until Tej found herself at the bottom of a half-meter-deep hole levering rocks out of identifiable dirt. Grandmama leaned over, shone the light down, and said, "That's probably enough." At least Amiri gave Tej a hand out. She pulled down her mask and sucked on a bleeding fingertip where her nail had broken.

Amiri brought the long box to the lip of the hole, took a deep breath, and knelt to open it.

"You don't have to handle it like a live bomb," Grandmama chided. "It's quite inert until it's activated."

"If the stuff eats dirt, won't it eat us?" said Amiri.

"Only if you are foolish enough to get it on yourself while it's working," said Grandmama. "Which I trust no grandchild of mine would be, especially after how many years of expensive Escobaran biomedical education?"

Amiri sighed and redonned his gloves. Tej ventured nearer to look more closely into the box.

It bore a label reading *Mycoborer, experimental, GSA Patent Applied For. Do not remove from GalacTech Company premises without authorization, under penalty of immediate termination and criminal prosecution.* Inside the box were layers of trays holding an array of thin, dark sticks, each about fifty centimeters long.

"How deep should we go for the first vertical shaft?" asked Amiri.

"Since Pearl's location has given us the first two stories down for free, I think eight meters should be enough to start," said Grandmama judiciously. "We may have to dogleg down more later, depending on what we find between, but that should put us approximately level with the top floor of my old laboratory bunker."

"What diameter? A meter may not be very roomy, if we have to bring much stuff back up and out."

"Mm, we may be able to drive a parallel or diagonal shaft later. For the moment, the chief urgency is to get someone inside to inventory what's still there as swiftly as possible."

If anything, Tej couldn't help thinking.

"Right," said Amiri, and gingerly took up a pair of cutters, measured eight centimeters along one of the sticks, and snipped it through. He then took a half-meter-long drilling rod, descended to the hole, and began twisting it down through the hard-packed soil. Everything still all by gloved hand.

"If we're doing this," said Tej, "then why do I have to spend all day tomorrow driving Star around to engineering and plumbing supply places?"

"To give your nice ImpSec people something to look at, dear," said Grandmama. "They will be happier that way, I'm sure."

"By the time they think we're ready to start, we should be

done," said Pearl. "How did you find out about this"—she bent
to peer at the label—"Mycoborer product, anyway?"

"I did some consulting a few years back for GalacTech Bioengineering, and struck up an acquaintance with one of the
developers."

"Did you steal it out of their labs?" asked Pearl, with an air
of incipient admiration.

"By no means," said Grandmama, with a bit of a sniff, possibly
at so crude a concept. "But when I and your mother and Shiv
thought of this possible resource, I remembered Carlo, and went
to see him. He was happy to give me a large supply. I *thought* it
might be needed." Her tone was a touch smug.

Amiri slipped the stick down his new hole, eyed it for straight-
ness, climbed out, and drew from his valise a liter bottle of perfectly ordinary household ammonia, apparently purchased from
some local grocery. He descended again and gingerly poured about
half of it in around the stick. It disappeared into the dark with
a bare gurgle, only its pungent aroma rising, along with Amiri,
from their little excavation. Tej hastily readjusted her mask.

Four people stood around the pit, staring.

"Nothing's happening," said Tej after a minute.

"I thought you said this would work fast," said Pearl.

"It's not instantaneous," chided Grandmama. "Macrobiological
processes seldom are." She added after a while, as anything visible continued to not happen, "The Mycoborer was developed as a
method of laying pipe without having to dig trenches; the genetic
developer hopes it can be trained to build its own custom pipe as
it goes, but that seems to lie in the future. For the moment, they're
happy to have it proceed in a straight route with uniform diameter."

"Pipes," said Tej, trying to picture this. "Will they be big
enough for people to get through?"

"Some pipes are quite large," said Grandmama. "For civic water
tunnels and underground monorails, for example."

"Oh," said Tej. "Um . . . if it's really alive, what stops it from
just growing forever?"

"The tubular walls, which are composed of its own waste products, eventually choke it off," said Grandmama. "Failing that,
there is a suicide gene built-in after it loses enough telomeres, and
failing that, there is ordinary senescence. And failing *that*, it can
be sterilized by heat. Really, I was *entirely* in sympathy with poor

Carlo over his frustration with the delays about the scaled-up out-door testing. Those Earth regulatory agencies are so obstructive."

Amiri blinked. "Wait. This stuff has never been tested?"

"Outdoors, no. It has been tested most extensively in Carlo's laboratory." She added pensively, "It is supposed to penetrate fairly swiftly through soil, subsoil, and clay. So-so through sand. Poor in limestone, stopped by granite and other igneous rocks and by most synthetic materials. It is possible we may be compelled to reroute a few times, if the Mycoborer comes up against unexpected subsoil inclusions."

Amiri was staring downward, looking disconcerted. "Never been tested...and we're betting the House on it?"

"It's being tested *now*," said Grandmama, in a voice of utmost reason. "And in a very tidy legal isolation from its Earth-based parent company, too. Biological isolation as well. Although I have promised to send Carlo a full report of the trial, sub rosa of course. That was, as dear Shiv would say, our deal."

She took the cold light from Pearl, knelt, and squinted. "Ah," she said, sounding suddenly satisfied. "Now you can start to see something."

All Tej saw was what appeared to be a foam of black goo forming around the lip of the borer hole, but Amiri seemed vaguely impressed.

"No noise, no vibration, no power surges of any kind," said Grandmama. "Silent and stealthy as a fungal filament. Nothing for sensors to detect, until we start to walk about down there. I trust you all can contain your chatter, when the time comes."

"Great," said Pearl. "Now can we go to lunch?"

"Excellent idea," said Grandmama. "Certainly."

"Is it safe to leave this stuff alone?" asked Amiri.

Grandmama shrugged. "If it's not safe to leave, it's not safe to stay with, now is it?"

"That's...a point," said Amiri reluctantly. He didn't say what kind.

Tej helped shift the slab back, move the shelves, and tidy up. When they finished, there was no sign of their intrusion but a new crack in the concrete, which, since the floor had a few others, ought to pass visual inspection. They exited the garage into a cold afternoon rain, and then she had no attention left for anything but getting them all through Vorbarr Sultana traffic alive.

∽   ∽   ∽

As a first step toward re-seducing Tej, Ivan had a splendid dinner waiting her return that evening. And waiting, slowly drying out. About two hours after she'd said she'd be home, the door at last slid open, and voices sounded. Ivan arose grumpily from the couch, schooled his face into a smile, and lost it again as not only Tej, but Rish and Byerly strode in. In the middle of a raging argument.

"—and stop putting bugs in my hair!" Rish snarled to By. "You'd think you were twelve!"

"If you would just *talk* to me, we wouldn't have any *need* for this roundabout method of communication," said By, his normally suave voice slipping a bit.

"And where do you get the *we need*, anyway? If I need to talk to you, I will, believe me!"

Tej rubbed her temples, as if they ached. "Hi, Ivan Xav," she said in a dull voice. She did not advance to kiss him or, as had been her even more charming habit considering her fetching build, hug him. "Sorry I'm late. Things ran on."

"What things?"

"Just things."

"Well, dinner?" said Ivan brightly. Yeah, it looked to be hypoglycemia city all around, here.

"I had a late lunch," said Tej.

"I'm going back to the hotel," said Rish. Ivan didn't even get out an *Oh, good*, before she went on, "Are you coming with me, Tej? Or do you want to stay here and be *interrogated*?"

Tej cast Ivan a grimace that had little in common with a smile, and a tired wave. "Yes, all right..."

"Wait!" Ivan called as they reversed direction, shedding By. "When will you be back?"

"I don't know."

"Well, will you be back here to sleep? Should I wait up?"

"I don't *know*."

"*I* won't," said Rish. "I'm going to bunk in with Em and Pearl. I suppose the hotel can give me a gel-mattress or something." She glowered at Byerly, and padded past him without looking back. Tej trailed disconsolately. The door slid shut once more.

Silence fell. Ivan and By stared at one another.

Ivan said, "Weren't you supposed to be the glib, debonair ImpSec agent, here?"

Byerly said a rude word. "Or not, as the case may be. She's

cut me off, she says. I suppose I shouldn't have tried to slip in a few subtle questions during sex. She didn't like it."

"Ah," said Ivan, and mentally edited his own planned ploy for later. If there was a later.

"But I am half *maddened* with curiosity. Arquas have been handing me off one to another for the past three days, all the same runaround going nowhere. They wouldn't be working so hard if they didn't have something to hide. Unless it's a practical joke, I suppose." He let out his breath in a huff and sloped over to fling himself on Ivan's couch.

Ivan stuffed his hands in his pockets and followed, reluctantly. "Can't you call for backup?"

"Did." By put his head back, eyes closing. "ImpSec, it seems, is busy this week. Galactic, Domestic, Komarran, all the Affairs. That high-level diplomatic conference going on at the Residence, the big comconsole-net security convention downtown, prep for dear Laisa's upcoming excursion with the crown prince to Komarr to see the grandparents—yes, they promise me help. At the end of the week. Or next week. Maybe. Meantime, I'm on my own. Just me and this ungodly herd of *your in-laws*." His eyes opened, and shot a look of unmerited blame Ivan-ward. "To whom I am *already outed*."

Ivan had seldom seen By emit so much emotion at one time. Granted, it was all *one* emotion, frustration, but still. Byerly-the-Smooth was decidedly ruffled.

"I've cozied up to every Arqua," said By, closed-eyed and addressing the ceiling once more. "Staked out the hotel. Planted bugs, which have either yielded nothing but rubbish, or gone fuzzy altogether. They're spotting them, all right. God. What haven't I tried?"

Ivan hesitated. "Simon?"

By made to raise his head, but it fell back. He did open his eyes again. "Are you nuts?"

"No, listen..." Ivan described his excursion yesterday to the park in front of ImpSec, the dance practice, Simon's security street theater, and what seemed the pertinent bits of his strange conversation this morning with the Baron and the Baronne. By sat up and clasped his hands between his knees, listening hard.

"Simon and Shiv have some deal going on, I'd swear it," said Ivan. "Or something. Going back to that first night in Simon's study."

"And they think there's something buried, where, under ImpSec HQ? What, for God's sake?"

"I don't know. Something big enough to fund a small war. And old enough...I hesitate to guess how old, but what say a hundred years? Occupation, maybe? Or should I say Ninth Satrapy?"

"That's before ImpSec was *built*."

"Simon ought to know." But did he remember?

"If Simon Illyan is up to something, we shouldn't bump his elbow," By declared firmly.

"I'm...not so sure."

By's eyes narrowed. "I thought he was just *playing* befuddled."

So, By had spotted that. Good on By. "He does do that. He's got half of Vorbarr Sultana believing he's as addled as an egg, and my mother his caretaker. *And* the people they report to."

"Right..."

"But sometimes he...shorts out, just a little. You can tell when it's real, because it's the only time he tries to hide it."

"Oh." By frowned. "I suppose you would know. Seeing him close up and all."

"Mostly it's seeing my mother. She gets this kind of brittle look around her eyes, when she's covering for him."

"But that's just little memory lapses, right?"

"It's Illyan. You want to try to guess what goes on in his head?" Ivan gave it a beat. "Or do you want to go ask?" That's what Simon had once told Ivan to do, after all, in so many words. If Barrayar's Foremost Former Authority gave you advice...

"No," said By frankly. He hesitated. "But I'll go if you'll go with me."

"What are we, a couple of women getting up a posse to go to the lav?"

"Why *do* women travel in herds like that, anyway?"

Ivan said glumly, "Delia Galeni, back when she was Delia Koudelka, once told me they go together to critique their dates."

"Really?" By blinked.

"Not sure. She might have just been trying to wind me up, at the time."

"Ah. Sounds like Delia." Byerly waved a limp hand. "All right. Lead on."

Ivan sighed, and pulled him up.

Then made him help eat the dehydrated dinner first, because Ivan had cooked it himself, dammit. But definitely without the seducing part. He left the dishes in the sink.

Chapter Nineteen

Ivan drove By to his mother's building in his two-seater; despite, or perhaps because of, the heavy rain, the city traffic was relatively light. To Ivan's secret relief, they found Simon alone for the evening. Mamere had gone off to the Imperial Residence to help coordinate some sort of feed, hosted by Gregor and Laisa, for those galactic diplomats By had complained of—a crowd guaranteed to clear a buffet table much the way Time-of-Isolation cavalry charges had cleared street riots. Ivan was only surprised neither of them had been roped in as native Barrayaran décor, as Mamere frequently did unto them for these things.

"Huh," said Simon, looking them both over when they were guided into his study by the maidservant playing porter tonight. "You two again." He set aside his reader, and took his slippered feet down from the hassock that had supported them in extended comfort. He was dressed in shirtsleeves and a sleeveless sweater, making him look in the lamplight like someone's retired schoolteacher-uncle. "Close the door, would you please, Marie?"

"Yes, sir. Should I bring drinks?"

By looked briefly hopeful, but Ivan said firmly, "No, thank you, Marie."

"Very good, Lord Ivan." She withdrew, and the door shut rather more than firmly. It was extraordinarily quiet in this chamber, once that lock clicked. Byerly swallowed, and Ivan thought irritably, *Welcome to Chez Vorpatril. Please, take a seat. I will be your spine for this evening . . .* Not his favorite role under any circumstances.

"Well, gentlemen." Simon waved genially to chairs, and tented his hands above his lap. "What brings you to me this rainy night? Why aren't you out squiring your young ladies?"

By grimaced and barely shifted the comfy chairs; Ivan dragged them closer to their host, on whom he felt an unwanted responsibility to keep an eye. By sat on the edge of his.

"Sir," By began, atop Ivan's, "Simon . . ." They both stopped and waved each other on.

Ivan began again, since By seemed determined to outwait him. "Simon. What do you know that we don't about what the Arqua clan is up to in front of ImpSec? Or under ImpSec, as it may be?"

Simon's eyes crinkled, just slightly. "I can't guess, Ivan. What *do* you two know?"

"That they think there's something under there, probably Cetagandan and probably dating back to the Occupation, and Shiv and Udine Arqua think it's valuable enough to fund their attempt to retake their House, which has got to be a high-end hobby. How the *hell* they think they can extract whatever it is right under ImpSec's collective nose, not to mention get it out of the Empire, defeats me. But I think not you. Want to give me a clue?"

Simon murmured something under his breath that might have been, *But you're so much more amusing without one*; Ivan didn't ask him to repeat it. Simon went on, "Well, that's proving more interesting than I thought at first glance. How do we know what we know? It's really a very philosophical question."

"Yeah, but I'm a practical kind of guy," said Ivan, recognizing Simon-diversion. The man could keep interrogators going in circles for *hours*, at parties. All that practice, Ivan supposed. On both sides of the table. "And I'm tired and my wife's stopped talking to me."

"Oh, I'm sorry to hear that. Was it something you said?"

"*Simon.*"

Byerly mustered his nerve and got out, "Sir, did you make some kind of *deal* with Shiv Arqua? Or does he just think you did?"

"Mm..." said Simon, in a judicious tone. "I believe it was more in the nature of a bet."

Ivan rubbed his face. "Just how drunk *were* you two, the other night?"

Simon...smirked. "Perhaps a little. But it was my favorite sort of bet, very rare in my experience—one I can't lose."

It was By's turn to wail: "*Sir.*"

Simon held up a hand, abandoning, thank God, his sport upon his juniors. "To answer your first question first, Ivan, what the Arquas appear to be after is a Cetagandan bunker, built during the Occupation under the mansion that formerly stood on ImpSec HQ's site. It was first mapped and marked cleared at the time the foundation for the headquarters was excavated. Under Mad Yuri's and Increasingly Disturbed Dono's civil engineering aegis, you know."

"You mean I've been running in circles for a week chasing *nothing*?" said By indignantly.

"Not quite that," said Simon.

"But ImpSec *knew* it was there, all this time?" said Ivan.

"Once again we return to the subtleties of the term, *know*. Or perhaps—*remember*. ImpSec's records have been damaged many times, in the intervening decades. And even without that, people who know things transfer or retire or die, to be replaced with... people who know different things, let's say. A kind of cumulative organizational amnesia. It's possible there might be some half-a-dozen men in ImpSec now alive who have personally examined those original historical documents, but that's likely a generous estimate."

"Are you one of those men?" asked Ivan.

Simon shrugged. "I may have been. I did a great deal of such homework, when I was just taking over the place three-and-a-half decades ago and cleaning up after the Pretendership. And Negri, dear God. Almost *worse* than...anyway. All I can tell you now is that the information didn't make enough of an impression upon me for much detail to be retained in my organic memory alongside my artificial one. Of course, there was a great deal of competition for my attention, back then."

"That's the old records," said Ivan. "What about the bunker itself? Surely it has to still be on ImpSec's own current site maps."

"Oh, certainly it is."

"And it's just been left sitting there ever since Yuri's day?" said By.

"More or less. *My* plan for that park was that it was to be the site of the *new* ImpSec building which, as you know, I never got. Whenever they excavated the foundations, the bunker would have been revisited, and after a quick check by us for safety issues, turned over to the University historians to get what they could, after which my contractors would continue. I had the archeological dig boss all picked out, in my mind." Simon sighed.

Simon remembered quite a bit, apparently, along certain odd lines.

"Did Shiv promise to cut you in?" demanded Ivan. "For a percent of . . . um . . . nothing?"

"So who was doing who?" By muttered.

"And then—what?" Ivan continued, growing perturbed in a whole new way. "Just let them go on, falsely hoping? Watch them while they try to break into an empty vault? You're a cruel bastard, Simon."

"I always had to be. This time, however, the future of the Imperium and millions of lives don't seem to be at stake, making it all much more relaxing. Not to mention the quite standard procedure of letting a suspect run to lead the observer to other contacts, which I should not have to explain to *you*, Byerly."

That probably worked a lot better when the observer hadn't been outed to the suspects, Ivan thought glumly.

Simon added after a reflective moment, "Also, I was extremely interested to see how far they would get. Something of a private test."

"For Guy Allegre?" *What did he ever do to you?* "In that case, was it fair to cover for that damn mapping dance, yesterday morning? You know the Jewels would've been run off if you hadn't been sitting there, nodding benignly."

"Mm, not so much cover as catalyze, in my view. Speed things up." Simon frowned, and added, "Although my presence should *not* have caused an alteration in security procedures. I mean to have words with Guy about that, later." He added after another moment, "Mind you, my personal evaluation is that the civil engineering problems of tunneling in secret around ImpSec will defeat them, as they have the many who have tried before. And a smash-and-grab approach, say, driving down through the park dirt with a plasma beam some, what, some twenty or thirty meters and boiling a hole through the roof of the bunker, is simply not on. Nevertheless, *if* they manage some way through those challenges, and *if* they finally break in...then will be the right psychological moment to make *my* deal."

Ivan's eyes narrowed. "What are you playing for, Simon?"

"Wider strategic concerns."

By made a kind of weak, inquiring, throat-clearing noise.

Simon cast a head-tilt his way. "Jackson's Whole has always been a problem disguised as an opportunity, for ImpSec and the Imperium. Too far away for direct intervention, but sitting astride a major wormhole route out of the Cetagandan Empire, which gives the Cetas roughly similar strategic interests to our own. And the same problem with working through local contacts—they tend not to stay bought.

"House Fell has always been dangerous, but determinedly independent. Morozov believes that House Prestene has strong Cetagandan contacts—and it now controls two out of the five wormholes in a possible first move on a monopoly. The loss of House Cordonah was originally judged to make little difference in that count, as they were thought to be technically neutral but with personal ties to the Cetagandans through the Baronne. Having now met Moira ghem Estif, I am...rethinking that."

"I, uh...Shiv Arqua doesn't strike me as material to be anybody's puppet," said Ivan. "Still less Shiv and Udine. Ours *or* the Cetas."

"Puppet, no. Ally...perhaps. Even just having a reliable safe house for our agents in the Whole would be a tactical improvement over the present confusion."

"So you're thinking of offering him—them—what?" asked By.

"At present, nothing, till I've had a bit longer to evaluate the man."

"Word in your ear, Simon," Ivan put in uneasily. "The man and the woman. Evaluating Shiv without Udine would be like, like...trying to assess Uncle Aral and leaving out Aunt Cordelia. They seemed that tight, to me."

Simon's brows climbed. "Really." His attention on Ivan was suddenly sharper. "How do you come by that impression?"

Ivan stirred uncomfortably. "Not any one thing. Just the way they add up."

"Hm." Simon's lips pursed. "Not that I, in my capacity as a mere retired Imperial subject, am in a position to promise anything to anyone, of course. Shiv kept...not noticing that."

Ivan refrained from blurting a raspberry through his lips at this disingenuity. It would have disturbed By.

"So," said By slowly, "what is all this, then—an IQ test for a future ally?"

Simon's smile flashed. "Nothing so simple, alas. Or unidirectional. The one other thing I would point out—but did either of you notice? I handed it to you, a few minutes ago."

By shot Ivan an agonized look. Simon playing mentor sometimes reminded Ivan of his worst moments from his school days, or maybe one of those nightmares where you found yourself running to a test naked. And he'd been *Miles's boss* for years; maybe that, too, explained something about his cousin. Simon sat back, clearly willing to wait till the coin dropped. For hours, if need be. And no end-of-period bell to save them.

Simon had always been very precise in his speech, a habit that had survived the chip-removal; his current pauses for memory-searches were hardly distinguishable from the old ones for—the same thing, only more reliable. He'd said, he'd just said...

"Marked cleared," said Ivan. "Would that be the same thing as, um—*was* cleared?"

Simon's smile at him grew briefly genuine. "It was not only before I took over ImpSec, it was before I was born. Who now knows?"

"Moira ghem Estif?" Ivan hazarded. "It's plain she does think there's something there. One of you has to be wrong."

Simon nodded. "As for the *marked cleared* problem, I have someone looking into that. With suitable historical expertise. Privately, on the side, when he gets a spare moment."

Ivan blinked. "You got Duv Galeni running inside searches for you? Won't he get in trouble? And it's not his department."

"For all I know, it's all declassified and stored in the Imperial University archives by now," said Simon, "but in either case, Duv's the man to most efficiently put his finger on it."

"I should report this," said By. "Er...should I report this...?"

"I don't know, Byerly, should you?" Simon said.

"That's...not fair, sir."

"Not especially, no." Simon took in By's harassed look and

measured out a small drop of mercy. "You have some time to meditate upon it. Shiv can only have started to tackle the tunneling problem. They need to line up local equipment, perhaps local contacts—if I were you I'd keep a close eye on Shiv and Star as the most likely to possess the technical expertise. The problem was always what to do with the telltale dirt, and the longer the shaft, the bigger the pile . . . well."

Ivan admitted reluctantly, "Tej drives everyone everywhere."

"And isn't talking to you, you said. That's actually rather convenient, right now. At least you know it's not personal."

Ivan wasn't so sure.

"Which means the Arquas are under the gun to solve their visa extension problem, or they'll never make it to the engineering ones. I am so tempted to help with that . . ."

Afraid your game will be over too soon, Simon?

In any case, Simon had apparently decided that it was time for this chat to be over, for he slid the conversation into amenities, and then somehow, a few minutes later, Ivan found himself and By being amiably escorted to the door. Ivan, calculating how soon his mother was likely to be back, allowed the eviction without protest.

"That was reassuring," said Byerly, as they settled themselves in Ivan's two-seater once more. "Illyan *is* on top of it. Might have known."

Ivan's lips twisted. "Eh . . ."

By glanced aside at him. "I didn't notice anything addled about any of that. Did you?"

"No," Ivan admitted. *Addled isn't exactly the problem, here.* Where would Tej fall, if things played out the way Simon pictured—or if they didn't, for that matter, but in any case, if she was forced to take sides? If she and Ivan each were?

By buckled up in a pointed manner; Ivan aimed his car out of the garage and turned into the street, and said, "Where do you want me to drop you? Your flat? Or back to the hotel?"

"No, I shan't put any more Arquas to the trouble of finding new circles to lead me in tonight." By sighed. "My flat, I suppose."

Ivan took the turn that would lead on to the shabby-trendy parts of Old Town Vorbarr Sultana. By put his head back and closed his eyes, although, given the lack of any white-knuckled grips anywhere, presumably not at Ivan's driving, which if not sedate was at least equally fatigued. After a few minutes, apropos of some unguessable chain of thought, By remarked, "I don't usually get attached to my surveillance subjects."

"Considering your usual crowd, I can see why," said Ivan.

"Mm," said By, not disagreeing. And after another minute, "Ivan, you've had a lot of girlfriends—"

Byerly Vorrutyer is about to ask me *for relationship advice?* Ivan didn't know whether to be flattered or appalled. Or to distract his passenger with a few evasive lightflyer moves, somewhat impeded by being in a ground vehicle.

"—seems like every time I saw you, you had a different one hanging on your arm."

"They weren't all girlfriends. Mamere always made me do a lot of diplomatic and social escort duty." Actual real take-to-bed girlfriends had been less abundant, though Ivan wasn't about to explain this to By.

"You made them all look like girlfriends."

"Well, sure."

"How did you keep them all happy?"

The light-spangled night rain flickered by outside the canopy. The wet streets wanted background music, some soulful lament to urban loneliness . . . "You know," and somehow, probably because of the damned rain, Ivan's mouth went off on its own: "I've always wondered why nobody ever notices that lots and lots of girlfriends entail lots and lots of breakups." Enough to learn all the road signs by heart, yeah.

By's eyes opened; his brows climbed. "Huh. You never seemed to point up that part."

"No."

A lot of his troubles had seemed to start, come to think, with oblique or not-so-oblique pressure for a high Vor wedding, even from a couple of the women who were *already* married, which Ivan had naively thought would put a sock in the issue. He'd never had those troubles with *Tej*, hah. If he'd known how relaxing being married—as opposed to *getting* married—could be, he might have done this years ago, except then it wouldn't have been with Tej, so it wouldn't have been like this, now would it? He contemplated this paradox glumly.

By leaned back in his seat with a tired sigh. "Well, at least parting with Tej should be no challenge for you."

Ivan could not, he supposed, stop his car in the middle of traffic and strangle an ImpSec agent, no matter how personally annoying the man was. Fortunately, By's block came up before temptation overcame prudence. By bade him thanks and farewell with his usual boneless wave.

Ivan wondered whether Tej would be home yet. Or not. And then couldn't decide whether to speed up or slow down, an irresolution that kept him tepidly at the speed limit all the way back to his building's garage.

Ivan spent the next two days chasing Tej around the clock. She returned from the hotel very late, Rishless, when Ivan was already half comatose and shrinking from the thought of tomorrow morning's alarm. The workweek resumed; Ivan's shift ran over due to what seemed an unending stream of minor Ops cockups and stupidities eliciting a return of memos running a short range from the tart to the sarcastic, and had Ivan mentally composing a whole new level of the latter, *searing*. In any case, he missed dinner, and Tej, who was out doing *more driving*.

Ivan's preemptive strike for the next evening—dinner reservations at a restaurant for Tej and her family, for which she'd have to show up if only because she'd have to ferry the rest of them—resulted in less than a quorum of Arquas, but still more than enough to prevent any serious personal discussions. Vapid tourist talk dominated the table. The public venue had been a bad idea. Ivan should invite them to his flat for the sort of intimate conclave he wanted—preferably with fast-penta served with the soup. Or maybe the predinner drinks. Alas that the truth drug could not be administered orally.

No private talk with Tej that night, either, nor even sex as a substitute, an evasion for which Ivan was beginning to think he might be willing to settle. Since the evening ended with Rish back on Ivan's couch, presumably By's bed-luck was equally dire, but it seemed an insufficient consolation. And in the morning, Tej let him oversleep too much—deliberately?—so that he had to rush off for his day of arm-wrestling with Ops's finest idiots without talk, kisses, breakfast, *or* coffee.

This can't go on.

The Mycoborer was misbehaving.

Tej adjusted her mask—a simple hospital filter mask, without electronic components, acquired by Amiri from who-knew-where—yanked on her plastic gloves, and prepared to follow Amiri, Grandmama, and Jet on the none-too-solid flex-ladder down the meter-wide black shaft. The chemical cold lights hooked to everyone's belts bobbed as they descended, making a bright but unsteady illumination.

She had to admit, the results of the first three days of Myco-borer penetration were impressive. After that initial visit, Amiri and Jet had found their way to the garage on their own, by different routes each time, for once-a-day checks and repositionings of new myco-sticks as the old ones successively pooped out. But Tej was afraid Grandmama was going to have to report to her Earth friend that his *straight route and uniform diameter* goals were still a hope for the future. The black walls of the shaft wavered—and not just from her wobbling light—widened and constricted irregularly, and bent away. Tej arrived at a kind of foyer Amiri had made at the bottom of the shaft to store the bulk of their supplies, straightened, and caught her breath.

Amiri held a finger to his mask. "As little talking as possible, from here on," he whispered. Jet and Tej nodded dutifully. They'd left their wristcoms in the locked utility room, and traded shoes for soft, muffling slippers. Tej's had bunny faces on the toes, and Grandmama's had kittens, which was what they got for letting Em do the shopping, she supposed. The floor felt odd, through them—rubbery, not solid.

The tunnel leading away toward the park was just wide enough to stand upright in, though Grandmama had to bend her head, except where it occasionally constricted, and they all had to duck through. Worse, it turned, randomly. Twice, they had to sit and slide around complete bends. It seemed less like traveling a tunnel than like crawling through a giant intestine.

Continuing the comparison, the tube also seemed to be growing appendixes. Most were no larger in diameter than Tej's arm; she felt no impulse to stick her hand in, glove or no, but Jet, having taken a possessive attitude toward it all, demonstrated that one could. Tej made a face at him. Jet stopped at another irregular wide spot, his eyes bright over his mask.

Amiri was leading Grandmama on toward an inspection of the working face; he cast a look of irritation over his shoulder, but could not, of course, yell at them. Their lights bobbed away.

"Here!" Jet whispered, pointing with his light to his prize, or surprise, as he'd resolutely refused to tell his sister what the wildly wonderful thing that he'd found was.

A pale, skeletal foot was sticking through the wall, at about waist height.

Tej jumped back, and glared at her odd-brother. Even-brothers, odd-brothers, all brothers were the same. He apparently found it hilarious that she wasn't allowed to scream, choking instead. She drew a calming breath, deciding that an unruffled front would be the best revenge. "Well, that's one Barrayaran who won't be bothering us."

Jet snickered, and drew a long, folding steel knife from his jacket pocket. He opened it and held the point to the rubbery wall beside the foot, leaning in. After a moment of resistance, it poked through.

"What are you *doing*?" Tej demanded in a tight whisper, as he began to saw.

"The walls harden up after a couple of days, as they cure," he whispered back. "Won't be able to do this tomorrow without making noise. It's now or never."

Tej could see the logic of that, though she didn't see the problem with *never*. Or at least, *somebody else, much later*. Jet, finding that he couldn't pull the foot out of the wall even after he'd cut a small circle around it, started on a much larger circle. When he peeled that away, entirely too much dirt came through, and Tej wondered if she should run, and which way, but the stream trailed off. Jet dug a bit more, then stood up with his hand stuck through out of sight and a surprised expression on his face. "There's space past here!"

"Another tunnel, maybe?" asked Tej. "That poor fellow has to have got all the way down here somehow."

Jet knelt again, digging with canine enthusiasm. And style. After too much more dirt, he bent and wriggled through his opening. His voice came back after a moment: "Wow, you should see this!"

Tej wasn't sure that was true, but... she couldn't let her little brother go off exploring in a dangerous place on his own, now, could she? She nearly had a *responsibility* to follow him.

She stuffed her hair down her jacket collar, donned her knit hat, and wriggled after Jet.

He was crouching in a small, smelly space seemingly held

upright by some bowed-looking timber supports. Not very much farther along, some other supports were crushed very flat. Had a cave-in trapped their corpse?

A long time ago, or the space would smell much worse. About half of the body was uncovered, face-down, skeletal arms out as if clawing. A tiny wisp of hair still clung to the skull, but otherwise most of the organics seemed to have decomposed, including some of his clothing. The synthetics still held up, shabbily; some woven straps, most of a backpack of some sort, flung out before him as if by his bony hands. Some metal bits were blobs of corrosion or rust, others still shiny, including those eye-pins she'd seen on the ImpSec men and a strange necklace around the skeleton's neck. Tej worked it loose, to find a metal tag at the end with incised letters: an unfamiliar prole name, *Abelard, V.*, the rank of sergeant—assuming that was what the abbreviation *Ssgt.* translated to—and a long alphanumeric string. "It looks like he was a Barrayaran soldier," murmured Tej. "So what was he doing down here?"

She looked up to find Jet opening the backpack.

"Don't touch that!" she said in a fierce whisper.

"Why not?" asked Jet, folding back the cover.

"I think it's a bomb."

Even Jet paused at this. He brought his cold light closer to reveal a wad of corroded and uncorroded but in any case dead electronics, and an even more mysterious gray mass. "Er," he said, and backed up a little.

Tej pocketed the necklace and crawled over to look more closely. The gray mass, several kilos' worth, was slumping, and old wires led into it. "Plastic explosive of some kind?" Tej hazarded.

Jet's brow wrinkled. "Some really old kind. Maybe it's deteriorated by now."

"Maybe it's not."

"Um."

A frightened whisper, Amiri's voice, came from their hole. "Tej? Jet?"

Jet rolled over, stuck his head down, and whispered back, "Amiri, you have to come see this!"

"I *told* you to leave that damned foot *alone*."

"Yes, but it's attached to a whole guy! You're the doctor—you might be able to tell how old he is!"

Some muffled swearing was followed, a few minutes later, by Amiri wriggling through their makeshift passage. Anger at his more adventurous siblings warred with curiosity, in his expression; with a visible mental IOU, curiosity won, temporarily. Amiri's gloved fingers danced over the visible portions of the corpse, probing, pulling, checking.

"Can't be sure without knowing more about Barrayaran soil ecology," he whispered. "But it's not very dry down here. Not less than twenty years. Not more than forty. A local forensics expert could likely date it more precisely." His eye at last fell on the backpack, stretched out beyond the skeletal fingers. "Oh, *crap*. Don't even touch that!"

Jet tried for an innocent grin, defeated by his medical mask.

"Told you," whispered Tej.

"It might be too old to go off, though," Jet suggested. "Maybe we should, like...try to take a little sample to analyze."

This approach plainly appealed to the researcher in Amiri, but he did stick his head down their hole to whisper, "Grandmama! You're more of a chemist than I am. Do plastic explosives deteriorate over time?"

"Some do," her voice came back.

"Ah." Amiri unceremoniously plucked the knife from Jet's hand, knelt, and gently tried to carve out a few grams of gray blob. It had apparently hardened with the decades.

"...some become unstable," Grandmama's voice continued.

Amiri abruptly desisted.

"I vote we leave it alone," said Tej. "Or at least come back later when everything else is done. If there's time."

"Yes," said Amiri, reluctantly folding the knife up. He didn't give it back to Jet.

Jet didn't protest.

From the same pocket, Amiri withdrew a child's toy compass, a very simple analog tool indeed. He held up his cold light and squinted at the quivering needle. "I wonder where he was heading?"

"Depends on if he was coming or going?" said Tej.

Amiri sighed, and pocketed the compass again. "I need to get down here and hand-draw a meter-by-meter map, so we don't waste time sending the Mycoborer in the wrong direction. Some more."

They wiggled after him back through their unauthorized hole to find Grandmama waiting, scowling at the pile of dirt.

"Jet, you will have to clean this up," she said, pointing. "Thoroughly, or everyone will be tracking it all over. And put something over this hole you made. The idea!"

"But Grandmama, it was a dead body!"

"Barrayaran graveyards are full of them, if you want more," she said unsympathetically. "And very unsanitary they are, too. Cremation is much better."

That was the Cetagandan custom, certainly.

Leaving the two boys to clean up, Grandmama gestured Tej back along the tunnel. Amiri didn't deserve the chore, but it was plain someone had to watch Jet.

As they went along, Tej studied the ceiling more warily. Was it bending down, at any point?

They arrived back in the vestibule and doffed their masks and gloves. "What was wrong at the tunnel face?" Tej asked.

"The Mycoborer split around an inclusion. Went off in four perfectly useless directions. We started another."

"What kind of inclusion?"

"Mm, storm sewer, I would hypothesize. It was a cylindrical pipe, anyway, and we could hear water running on the other side."

"This deep?"

"We are actually close to level with the river, at this stratum. Though it wasn't Barrayaran work—far too well made. I think it probably dated back to the Ninth Satrapy."

"Grandmama—could our tunnel collapse? Like on the poor Barrayaran..." *bomber?* Tej tested that word-string in her mind, trying to decide if it made sense. Yeah, probably. Even if the fellow had been a suicide bomber, that had to have been a horrid death. She fingered the identity necklace in her pocket, and wondered if Ivan Xav owned a similar one. She'd not seen it among his things.

"Certainly, in due course." Grandmama frowned back down their tunnel. "You have to understand, a perfectly circular pipe is in effect two arches supporting each other—an extremely strong shape. I saw such arches back on Earth, built only of simple stones, that have survived three millennia, and that despite it being such a tectonically active planet."

"But our tunnel isn't perfectly circular. It's more sort of... intestinal."

"Yes, pity. Fortunately, it doesn't have to last the ages, only a week or two."

But what if it collapses on *somebody?* Tej wanted to ask, but Grandmama was already climbing the rickety flex-ladder. She sighed and followed the carefully moving kitty-slippers.

That night, by some miracle, Ivan found himself and Tej both awake and in the same place at the same time; and better yet, it was his bedroom. Tej was restless, though, wandering about the place. She opened the top drawer of Ivan's dresser, into which he swept all his miscellaneous junk, and peered curiously, turning an item over now and then.

"What are you looking for?"

"I was just wondering ... do you have any kind of military identification necklace? I've never seen you wear one."

"Necklace? Oh, dog tags."

"What do dogs have to do with it?"

"Nothing, that's just what they're called. I dunno why. They've always been called that. Plural, though they only issue you the one. I suppose that's what they are, but *necklace* probably sounded too girly for the grunts."

"Oh."

"I think mine are hung with my black fatigues in my closet."

"Do Barrayaran soldiers only wear them with the fatigues?"

"They're not for everyday, at least not at HQ. Just if you're out in the field. Going into some dicey situation, say. There was an argument going around Ops for subcutaneous identity inserts, with electronic trackers, but the troops didn't like it, and then somebody pointed out that if we could find our guys with a ping, so might an enemy, and the idea died in committee." Not to mention the possibility that the bad guys could *be* their guys, in some civil fracas. It had happened before.

"So ..." She hesitated, looking over her shoulder at him, where he waited in what he hoped was a good tactical position on what had become his side of the bed. "So if you were going into danger, that's how I'd know?"

"I would *hope* you would know because I'd *tell* you."

"No ..." Her gaze on him grew thoughtful. "I'm not sure you would."

He cleared his throat. "Anyway, why do you ask?"

"I, uh ... saw one today, and I wondered. About you."

"Where?"

"I—found it on the floor of a parking garage. Here, wait..."
She padded out, and padded back in again a minute later, a thin
chain that clinked and winked dangling from her hand.

Ivan rolled up and received it, turning it over and reading
the inscription. "This is a really old style. Mine look different.
Somebody must have saved it for a souvenir. Maybe it dropped
out of his pocket." Ivan's imagination flashed another, sadder
picture. "Or hers."

"That would make sense."

"I bet they'll want it back. Which garage?"

"Um, I don't remember. There were so many."

"Maybe I can look this fellow up tomorrow, in the Ops archives."

"Oh! Can you?" Tej looked briefly cheered, then alarmed. "But
maybe...I'd like to keep it as a souvenir myself." Her hand
reached uncertainly after the relic.

"If you want *that*, I can give you my old set. From when I
was a lieutenant." Ivan's even older set, from when he'd been an
ensign, had gone with some girlfriend or another and not come
back, Ivan suddenly remembered. Proving that, as a girl-leash,
they didn't work, despite the name, though it seemed as if they
ought to.

Tej at last sat on the edge of the bed, still looking abstracted.
His stretch for her halted in midair when her next question was,
"Ivan Xav...do you know anything much about old Barrayaran
military plastic explosives?"

He sank back, flummoxed. "I hope you didn't find any of *that*
on the floor of a garage!"

"No, no."

"How old?"

"Really old. Twenty years, maybe more?"

"I had a munitions course back at the Academy, but that was
all about current stuff."

"How long ago?"

"Er...seventeen years?"

"But that's almost twenty years."

Ivan blinked. "So it is. Um." He remarshaled his forces. "Anyway, if you ever run across anything that looks the least suspicious, what you do is call a bomb squad. Or call me, and I'll
call a bomb squad."

"Is that what you'd do?"

"Of course! Well, except for that old guerilla cache Miles and Elena and I found up in the Dendarii Mountains when we were kids. But we were being very stupid kids, as everyone from Uncle Aral on down explained, very memorably, after the—never mind that now. Anyway, the point is, people can still find old, dangerous stuff lying around on this planet, and civilians shouldn't fool with it." Untangling himself from this digression, Ivan finally got back to the important question, which was, "Why do you *ask?*"

"No reason," Tej said airily.

Right. *Avocados* probably did shifty better than Tej. It was most un-Jacksonian of her.

"It was just something I was reading about," she added, finding who-knew-what in his expression. Consternation, belike.

"How's about," said Ivan after a minute, "I take some personal leave?" And to hell with whether any busy-ImpSec-body thought he was admitting to being a security risk. "If your family's only going to be here for a while, I should seize the chance to get to know them better. It only makes sense."

"Oh!" She looked briefly pleased, then dismayed. "I wouldn't want to interfere with your work. I know your career is very important."

"We're not at war. This week, anyway. Ops can suffer along without me for a few days without collapsing, I expect. They always have before."

Her eyes were bright, like those of an animal in the headlights. "Good, that's settled. Let's make love!"

It was a patent diversion. Dammit, she'd be faking orgasms, next.

. . . But not, it appeared, yet.

This means she likes me, right? some awkward young Ivan who still lived at the bottom of his brain urged, just before the physiologically induced lights-out.

Surly old Ivan could only think, *Ivan, you idiot.*

And not one Ivan on the whole pathetic committee had yet been able to muster aloud the only question that mattered. *Tej, will you stay?*

Chapter Twenty

On the next morning's drive Tej found herself threading through a new part of the city, an unexpected suburban sprawl north of the ridges that cradled the river valley and the Old Town. Barrayarans seemed to date all their activities in terms of famous military events—before the Occupation, during Mad Yuri's War, after the Pretender's War—but in this rare case, by a peaceful one: the area had mostly been built up *since Gregor took the reins*, or in other words, in the past two decades.

Tej turned in at a modest industrial park, and found a slot for the rented groundcar in front of what was soon to be a rather bewildered minor pipe-laying firm. Star took her notecase and headed purposefully for the door, but for a change Dada did not go with her, nor instruct Tej to stay with the vehicle. Instead, he gestured Tej after him, and walked off toward the street. Tej turned up the collar of her coat against the thick, chilly fog—a change from the recent rains—and followed.

"Where are we going?"

"To see a man I know."

"Does he expect us?"

"Not yet."

No appointment, no comconsole contact, and the rental car, which had a mapping system that also served to precisely locate the vehicle for anyone who might be wanting to follow its movements, had a legitimate place to be. Well, faux-legitimate. Tej found herself growing unwillingly alert.

Dada added, "I'm not keen on bringing in an outsider, but we're now expecting and in fact counting on our visa not being extended. Time grows tight. A reliable contact said she'd used him as a carrier, not long back, and found the results satisfactory. He'll be open to our business. And, if he has his wits about him, future business."

They walked two blocks and crossed over to another utilitarian building, and through a door with a sign over it reading *Imola & Kovaks, Storage and Transshipping*. A harried-looking human receptionist presiding over a cluttered counter, which gave Tej a small, unwanted flashback to her days at Swift Shipping, looked up and said, "May I help you, sir, ma'am?"

"Would you please tell Ser Imola that an old friend is here to see him."

"He's very busy this morning, but I'll ask." Standard clerk-speak prep, Tej recognized from experience, for greasing an unwanted visitor back out the door. "What name should I say?"

"Selby."

A brief intercom exchange, and the clerk was escorting them upstairs to another office, also cluttered. A man on the high side of middle age, dressed in relatively unmilitary Barrayaran casual business garb, looked up over his comconsole desk, frowning; his frown changed to an expression of astonishment. A touch of his hand extinguished the current display. "Thank you Jon," he said. "Please close the door." The clerk, disappointed in his curiosity, did so. Only then did the man surge up and around his desk to grasp both of Dada's hands and say, "Shiv Arqua, you old pirate! I heard you were dead!"

"An exaggeration. Again. Though not by much, this time." Dada smiled without showing his teeth, and turned to Tej, but then turned back. "And what name are you going by, these days?"

"Vigo Imola."

"Vigo, meet my daughter, Baronette Tejaswini Arqua."

Tej shook hands, wondering. Formerly, on these business stops with her sisters or mother, she had been named *our driver*, or not introduced at all, or left with the car. "People usually call me Tej." Or *Lady Vorpatril*, but none of her family had used her new name yet. She stifled an unruly urge to trot it out here; Dada was plainly going into dealing-mode.

"Delightful! I would guess she gets her looks from her mother?" Imola's gaze swept her up and down; he scored a point, or two, by not lingering on her chest. "Mostly."

"Fortunately," said Dada, with his low laugh. Their host pulled up a pair of serviceable chairs, gesturing them both to sit.

"Where do you two know each other from?" asked Tej. Sometimes she got an answer, after all.

"In a former life, Vigo was my planetary liaison officer when I was a captain in the Selby Fleet," said Dada. "Just before I met your mother."

"And weren't those the days," said Imola, planting himself comfortably behind his desk once more. "Was old Selby insane, to take that defense contract with Komarr?"

"We were young. And probably thought we were immortal," said Dada.

"Yeah, I got over *that* about then," said Imola. Imola's underlying accent was Komarran, Tej judged, overlain by a long residence on Barrayar; in this urban environment, very blended. "Who would've thought that a backward planet like this could field such an aggressive fleet?"

"Not your Komarran comrades, it seems."

"Huh." Imola shook his head at some old military memory. "So what the devil are you doing on Barrayar? I thought House Cordonah had suffered an extremely hostile takeover. Prestene, wasn't it?"

"Yes, the bastards." At the name, Dada bit his thumb and made a spitting gesture. "It's a long story, very roundabout. I'll tell you the whole tale at some more leisured moment. So, you ended up in the transshipping business."

"As you see." Imola waved around at his unpretentious company offices.

"Ah... *all* of it?"

Ser Imola smiled, reached under his desk, and turned something off. Or on. "Sometimes. If the price is right. And the risks are low. The second being more important than the first, these days." He heaved a sigh. "I'm not as ambitious as when we were younger. Nor as energetic. Nor as crazy."

"Your end should be low risk. The price... we'll need to discuss."

"So what do you have for me?" Imola inquired. "Weight and volume? Perishability? Live or inert? Live costs more."

"Inert, as it happens. Weight and volume to be determined, though it won't be high bulk. But you ship live cargo? How does that jibe with *low risk*?"

Imola smiled in satisfaction. "We solve the perishability problem by shipping all such consignments cryo-frozen. The new generation of portable cryochambers being much more reliable, with longer service cycles. Shipping deceased expats or ill-fated tourists who want to be treated or buried back home is a legitimate part of the business, see. I have a contact on the medical side who sends clients my way, or sometimes helps prep them, and if we occasionally slip in a few extras on the manifest, the documentation is all in order."

Dada's brows twitched up. "The cargo takes a risk."

"For voluntary cargo, well, they're willing. For involuntary cargo, their shippers are usually even more willing. Our losses in transit are actually lower. And it's vastly cheaper, since they don't have to send handlers along to thwart escapes en route. The method does depend on having adequate cryorevival facilities on the far end, but that's not my problem." Imola waved a didactic finger. "The trick, as always, is not to get greedy—not try to ship too often, or too many at once. There are only so many tragic accidents to go around. We reference real ones, whenever we can."

Dada nodded approval. "Very clever. I see you're not too old to innovate."

"It was my son-in-law's idea, to give credit where it's due. My daughter married this Barrayaran boy, some years after the annexation. I wasn't thrilled at first, but he's come along. Junior partner. He's the *Kovaks*. Our medical contact is his brother."

"Glad to hear you're keeping it in the family. That's...almost always safer." Another brief grimace of a smile.

"Heh, daughters getting married—that's a crap shoot to make the old days look sensible. You don't know *what* they'll drag in. My other one married this Komarran fellow, who is completely useless but at least lives five jumps away. You folks've got the right idea out in the Whole, Shiv—pre-vetted contracts, money and considerations up front."

"Oh, well..." Dada did not follow this up, to Tej's relief. "Can you get local ground transport—a mid-sized cargo van, say?"

"I have vans. And loading crews."

"That aren't traceable back to you?"

"That could be done, too." Imola's eyes narrowed with interest.

"We would do our own loading. Could you get it by this weekend?"

"Probably."

"And very private storage?"

"Could be made available."

"Deal would be, park your van overnight in a certain underground garage in the Old Town. Send someone in on foot to drive it away in the morning. We might need a second night, in which case best have a different van. One of us will meet you separately to oversee the unloading—some of the cargo may be delicate."

Tej tried to picture the implied scene. A bucket brigade of Arquas spaced along the Mycoborer tunnel, silently hand-carting contraband all night? They might just about do it. Heavy loads that could not be broken down might have to be regretfully abandoned—happily, this did not include gold coins. Nothing inside the old lab could be very large, though, or its original owners could not have squeezed it down through the elevator shaft, the one Grandmama had said she'd once been responsible for blowing up, as last haut woman out.

"Once our target location is cleared and the goods safely stored," Dada went on, "the transshipping arrangements could be completed at leisure, more carefully. Possibly in small batches."

"Where to?"

"Not known precisely yet. Out of the Barrayaran Empire; some towards the Hegen Hub, some to Escobar."

"Makes it hard to calculate a price. You thinking percentage or flat fee?"

"Until the items reach their final destination and are disposed of, they're solid, not liquid. I think you might prefer flat fee, now, rather than an unknown amount decanted off an unknown amount, much later."

"Why not both?" said Imola. "Flat fee up front, to be sure all possible expenses are covered, and the percentage after success. Say, fifteen percent. That's pretty usual."

Dada winced slightly. "Could be. We need to move quickly and quietly."

"For a percentage, I can do quickly and quietly. So do we have a deal?"

After a short hesitation, Dada rose and reached across the desk; a brief handshake. "Deal."

Imola leaned back and prepared to make a note. "So what's the address of this garage of yours?"

Dada named it. Imola's hand froze. "Shiv, do you know what's across the *street* from that building?"

"Oh, yes," sighed Dada. "Hence our discretion."

"You may not have spotted the scanners, but I guarantee any vehicle that parks within three blocks of ImpSec headquarters gets scrutinized somehow. And recorded."

"Quite thoroughly scanned, entering that garage, yes. But—not leaving it. That one's cursory, just to be sure outs match ins. We checked."

"Ah." Imola frowned, obviously thinking this through. His anonymous van would be arriving empty and innocent, yes. The driver would know nothing… "One of the ways I stay in business around here is that I don't get involved with local politics. Strictly commercial, I am. Vorbarra District Guard and Imperial Customs are all bad enough. ImpSec—that's too high up for me. Give you a nosebleed, those boys will."

"I have no interest in local politics, myself."

"Strictly commercial, is this?"

"I certainly hope so."

"Hm." Imola stared at the address on his autofiler, evidently memorizing it, then deleted the screen. "You might have said."

"You didn't think I'd pester you with something trivial, did you?"

"No, I suppose not. You always were a beat ahead of the rest of us, back when." Imola sighed. "Do give my best to your lady. She's still with you, I suppose?"

Dada nodded.

"And the rest of the clan?"

"All safe with us, for now." Dada, Tej noticed, did not go into the distressing details about Ruby and Topaz and Erik.

"Mustering for a fresh move on Prestene, are you? Or something?"

"More or less. Or something." Dada's lips twitched. "Or we might buy a tropical island."

Imola looked nonplussed at this last, but said, "Eh, good luck on that. People just don't keep up with each other, these scattered times. Does Udine still have her fancy dance troupe? Quite the show, I heard, when you were all on Cordonah Station."

"Her Jewels, yes. And they will dance again," said Dada firmly. "You'll have to stop by, next you get out that way."

After a few more anecdotes about the Good Old Days, which sounded like the Repulsive Old Days to Tej, Dada rose and they extracted themselves, and exited to the street once more. The fog was thinning, or perhaps just condensing into a cold drizzle.

"Let's wait in the car," Dada directed, when they'd made their way back to the pipe-layer's building. "No point in stepping on Star's script."

She slid into the driver's side, and Dada into the seat beside her. He turned to face her.

She eyed him sideways. "You weren't quite straight with that man. Imola. Do you trust him or not?"

"The limits of trust depend much on whether you mean to do business more than once. But it's just good practice never to show all your cards in the first round of a deal. One must maintain reserves. Besides, what he doesn't need to know he can't tell, not even under fast-penta. Speaking of sound practice. He knows that game."

"I suppose." Tej sighed.

"You don't seem happy, honey."

"None of us are just now, I expect."

"True. Well, we'll all be home—soon enough."

He's leaving out a few steps. And the new House Cordonah was going to be unavoidably different from the old, Tej suspected. Home would be changed. *Or I will be.*

"You know," Dada went on, "you were Udine's special gift to me. All the other kids, I was happy enough to let her play the haut geneticist, but you were merely gene-cleaned. Unmodified her, unmodified me. My almost-natural offspring."

"I knew that." Star had once called her *the control child*; it hadn't been a compliment.

"I always wanted to see you do well."

To prove what for you, Dada?

"I meant to hold out for something really special, when it came to your marital contract. Still could, you know."

"Mm," said Tej.

"But... there's another possible deal in the air, now. How well do you like that Barrayaran boy?"

"Ivan Xav? I like him fine." And one of the things she most

liked about him, she realized, was that he'd had nothing whatsoever to do with any Arqua deals, ever. He was surrounded by
his own Barrayaran style of crazy, true, but surprisingly little
seemed to have rubbed off on him.

"Should a deal emerge that did involve him, would you be
willing to be party to it?"

"What kind of a deal?" she asked automatically, then said,
"Wait. Do you mean a marriage contract? We're kind of a done
deal that way, I thought." *Count Falco said so.* And they'd made it
themselves, with their own breath and voices—funny Barrayaran
phrase, that. Their own breath and no one else's. "The only way
that deal could change is to be *un*done."

"Which could happen in so many ways. I can't help but notice
that you've not been pursuing any of them."

"We've been *busy*. And then you all arrived, and we've been
busier."

"Does your Ivan Xav know that you think it's a done deal?
Or your stepfather-in-law?"

"I . . ." *don't know*, Tej realized. Did she even know herself, for
real, for sure?

"Because if they don't, I can certainly see no reason for you
to tell them. *That* could be slick. Trade them something they
already have, for . . . heh. *Considerations*, yes."

Tej tried to keep her face from scrunching up in dismay. "Has
this got anything to do with that private talk you had with Simon?"

He looked cagey. "Might."

Her heart chilled. Ivan Xav had seemed very sure that his
um-stepfather couldn't be suborned by threats or bribed by wealth.
But what about love?

In more than one form. It was plain that the strange, reserved
man wanted some better relations with his stepson than he had
yet been able to construct, if only to please his high Vor lady.
And more: Simon liked Ivan Xav in his own right—in his own
quietly awkward way—though Ivan Xav didn't seem to see it. The
late great Captain Illyan had been superb with security, it was
said; maybe not so deft with family. He'd evidently never had
one before, in all his long adult life, or was that only . . . his long
adult career? But surely the man couldn't be compromising his
peculiar Barrayaran honor just to secure his stepson's marriage.
Simon was a mystery; how could you tell what he was thinking?

Although it was bad enough that Dada wanted to use her as a counter in his deals. Dada at least was *Dada*, Baron Cordonah for real. *Simon* had no right...

"Have you already made some kind of a deal with Simon about me?" she demanded in alarm.

"Mm, I wouldn't go so far as to call it a deal. More of a bet."

"That's *worse*."

"Oh, it didn't involve you. Yet. Though it was clear that you and Ivan Xav weighed in his calculations."

"What did it involve?"

"Step One of our program here—the site mapping. Simon bet we couldn't do it in any way. Undetected by ImpSec, that is, on ImpSec's doorstep. I bet we could." He added after a moment's reflection, "As long as one doesn't count Simon himself as ImpSec, of course. We won."

"What did we win?" she asked suspiciously.

"Round Two. Which Simon thinks Star is pursuing as we speak. The Mycoborer, fortunately, still remains outside the realm of his otherwise far-reaching imagination."

"Oh. So—every round you win buys us another round?"

"Yes. But we only need two. Simon's thinking three or four."

Weasels, that was the term Ivan Xav kept using. But which old weasel was the, the weaseliest?

Maybe Simon simply wanted Lady Alys all to himself. Was Ivan Xav's protracted bachelorhood holding up Simon's own marriage, the way it had evidently been holding up Lady Alys's longed-for release from the burning ritual? Maybe he thought he was trading not Tej, but Ivan Xav—to be carried off by Clan Arqua to the Whole as a prize, or what? Would the The Gregor allow that—or applaud it? The Emperor had his own sons now—maybe Ivan Xav was reclassified as redundant, an heir in excess of need. An embarrassing leftover, and everyone relieved to have him be shunted out of the way.

Tej didn't know whether to be distressed or really, really annoyed. With the whole lot of them, Arquan and Barrayaran both.

Dada, watching whatever parade of emotions was passing across her face, said a bit plaintively, "I'd do my best for you, honey, but you have to give your old Dada a clue."

"If I get one," she sighed, "I'll share."

His belly jumped in a muffled, pained laugh that didn't make it out his mouth. *Women, eh*, didn't quite appear as a caption over his head, but it might as well have. She wanted to return, *Men, ugh!*

And if it would help Clan Arqua to sell what was already given away, didn't she have an obligation to allow that much? . . . Especially as it might get her off the hook for further demands. It wouldn't make any *practical* difference to her and Ivan Xav— would it? *Damn it, now I'm all confused. Again.* It was hardly a help that Ivan Xav didn't make her crazy when everyone else around them was doing so good a job.

Star emerged from the door of the engineering firm, looking self-satisfied. She and Dada slid into the back for a short report on her fake tunneling bid. Tej started the groundcar again and pulled into the street.

"Oh, about Ivan Xav," Tej called over her shoulder. "He was going to ask Admiral Desplains for some personal leave. He hopes to get tomorrow free. To join us."

"Oh, hell," said Star. "Rotten timing. Why couldn't he have waited till next week? What will we do with him?"

"The same drill as with his friend Byerly," Dada assured her, unmoved. "Not a problem."

Speak for yourself, Dada.

Tej did her best to slip away without him, the morning of Ivan's first day off, but he cornered her in the kitchen.

"Driving again?" he asked amiably, sucking coffee. "What say I go with you?"

"It'll be boring," she told him, drinking her own coffee faster. "Who would have thought I'd ever be saying that about Vorbarr Sultana traffic? Live and learn."

"I'm never bored with you."

She flashed him a nervous smile. "And there wouldn't be room."

"I don't mind squeezing up."

He wondered how many rounds she'd go on this hedging, and had a brief insight into Simon's fascination with the clan, but she gave over the argument and let him follow her down the street to the Arqua hotel. There, he discovered, she'd cannily sited reinforcements, and he somehow, without intending it, found himself assigned to drive another set of Arquas around on an assortment of errands that extended into a lingering lunch.

They were joined in this meal by Byerly, trailing Emerald and looking thwarted. As diversions went, Ivan supposed it displayed a certain efficiency.

The polite runaround continued all day in this vein. It was only by chance, miscalculation, and a couple of social lies that Ivan managed to cross paths with his wife in his flat once more, at nearly bedtime. She was dressing—not for bed, which more usually involved undressing—in some casual, sturdy clothes that looked more suitable for a walk in the woods than a night on the town.

"Oh," she said, looking around in surprise as he came in.

"Hi, beautiful." He kissed her hello; even her return kiss felt evasive. "What's up?"

"Just a few more chores for my family. Don't wait up for me."

"At this hour? You should be in bed. With me." He nuzzled her neck; she slipped out of his grasp, which he just managed not to let become a clutch.

"We might not have much longer together on Barrayar. Pidge is having trouble getting the visa extension."

Good. Wait, not good. "That doesn't include you, you know. Lady Vorpatril."

"Uh . . ." Her evasiveness was shading into panic, in her eyes. It wasn't all that amusing.

"Tej," he sighed. "We need to talk."

"Next week. Next week would be good for me. I have to go now, or I'll be late."

"Not next week. Right now." He captured her hand—it jerked in his grip, but didn't jerk away—and led her to sit on the edge of the bed with him.

She offered him only a tight-lipped smile; she, clearly, wasn't going to start. Up to him, eh.

"Tej. I know a lot more about what's going on with you and your folks than you think."

"Oh?" she tried. Leading, not conceding.

"In fact, I bet I know something you don't."

"How can you know that you know something I don't when you don't know what I know in the first place? I don't see how you can. I mean, logically. Or you wouldn't be asking."

Simon had recently tricked him into going first with much the same turn of phrase, Ivan was wearily reminded. Or at least the gist of it. "Tej. I know that your family is after a certain Cetagandan bunker dating back to the Occupation, or at least, after something in it. And it's sitting under that park in front of ImpSec. You mapped it during that dance last weekend."

She froze for a moment, and then came up with: "Well... so? Simon was watching us."

"Simon's onto you."

"He has an, an understanding with Dada, yes. You might have figured that out."

"I did, yes. But Simon knows one thing that you—you Arquas—don't."

He waited, to by-God *make* her say something. Anything. Her face screwed up in the effort to contain her words, not to mention her curiosity, but lost the fight: "*What?*"

Ivan felt like a lout. No, this wasn't going to be fun at all. "The bunker was found and emptied decades ago, when ImpSec HQ was first built. The bunker's still there, yes, but there's nothing inside. Simon's setting you all up for a fall." *The weaselly bastard.*

"*No,*" she snapped. And, a tiny doubt creeping into her voice, "Can't be. Grandmama would have known, and the Baronne."

"Is so. Empty." *A trap without bait.*

"Isn't." Tej could look remarkably mulish, when she set her mind to it.

"Is."

"*Isn't.*" Her jaw unset just enough for her to say, "And I can prove it to you."

"How?"

"I won't tell you." She was getting better with *shifty*; maybe it was all the recent practice. "But I'll make you a deal for it. A... a bet. If that's more Barrayaran."

"What kind of a deal? Or bet."

"If the lab—the bunker is empty, I'll do what you want."

Might that include *stay on Barrayar*? Could he twist this into a ploy to make her stay? He just kept that thought from falling straight out of his mouth; he didn't know if she'd think it was a jewel or a toad. "And if it's not?"

"If it's full, then you'll do what *I* want." She frowned in reflection. "That seems balanced, doesn't it?"

"Which would be... what?" Ivan was learning caution around Jacksonians bearing deals.

"Uh…" She'd been caught short, but was thinking fast. "To start with… help carry stuff. You're big and strong. And, and go on keeping your mouth shut. About everything you see or hear. And no cheating by giving people *hints*. And after that… there might be more."

"This deal seems to be getting a bit open-ended."

"So what do you care? If you really think the bunker is empty."

So… should he bet on Simon? Ivan had a lot of trouble fitting *Simon Illyan* and *wrong* into the same sentence, although Aunt Cordelia claimed it was historically possible. And she should know. *Not often* wasn't, after all, the same thing as *never.*

And he'd just be following Simon's own example, with that bet. He wondered how well that might work as a defense, later. *Not sanguine*, was that the phrase? Which had something to do with blood. No, this was not a helpful line of thought.

"All right," Ivan heard his mouth saying. Because Tej wasn't the only person in this room being driven to insanity by curiosity, it seemed. "It's a deal."

He'd rather have sealed it with a kiss, but she offered him a firm Arqua handshake instead.

"Oh," she said, turning back at the bedroom door. "And bring a pair of slippers."

Tej made Ivan Xav park his two-seater a good five blocks from ImpSec Headquarters, just to be sure, which then entailed a long trudge through a cold drizzle. He had grown more and more silent, on the short drive over, as she'd explained about the Mycoborer. But his tone grew irate when she led him to the lower level of the garage—quiet, deserted, and shadowy at this late hour. "Why couldn't we have parked *here*?"

"Shh," she hissed back, equally irate. A bulky ground van was sitting directly across from the utility room; evidently Ser Imola had done his part. She tapped gently on the door.

It swung open; Star's hand shot out to yank her inside. A couple of bright cold lights cast conflicting green shadows. "Tej, you're late." Star looked up in consternation at Ivan Xav, shouldering in after her. Her hand went to the stunner holster riding her hip. "Why'd you bring *him*? Are you crazy?"

"He's going to help. He… volunteered." *Sort of.*

Ivan Xav stared around the little chamber in deep suspicion, and Tej wondered belatedly if she should have demanded that Vor-name's-word thing on their deal, or bet, as well. The access well to the Mycoborer tunnel was uncovered; a pulley was set up on a frame above the hole, with ropes descending into the dark.

Star scowled at Ivan Xav, who scowled back. She said, "I'd stun him where he stands, but we can't let off energy devices."

"Then why are you even *carrying* that?" asked Tej, gesturing to the stunner.

"Last resorts. Come on. Everyone's in ahead of us, and I doubt they'll wait."

Tej walked around the pulley. "That's new."

"Yes, Dada's idea. He says it'll speed getting things up the shaft, and make it safer, too. No hand-tractors or grav lifts allowed, either."

Tej considered their flimsy telescoping ladder, and nodded in relief.

Star stepped back to lock and block the outside door, then said, "All right, everybody in."

Tej led the way to the ladder. Ivan Xav stopped short at the lip of the hole.

"Wait, we're going down there?"

"Yes?"

"Underground?"

"Most tunnels are underground. Oh, no, Ivan Xav—I forgot about your claustrophobia thing. Why didn't you say something? I'm sorry!"

"I do *not* have a claustrophobia thing. I have a *perfectly rational dislike* of being locked up in small, dark, wet spaces by people trying to kill me."

"So you won't, like, panic down there?"

"No," he said curtly.

"Are you sure? Because you could stay up here and help by manning the pulley—I'd count that—"

Ivan Xav growled and swung down the ladder.

Tej followed; Star brought up the rear.

The vestibule was quite a bit larger than when Tej had last seen it. A bench had been added, now piled with assorted Arqua wristcoms, audiofilers, and something she was afraid might be a very illegal plasma arc. Star divested her own wristcom and stunner; Tej followed suit.

"Everything electronic or that has a power cell has to be left here," whispered Tej. "And our shoes." A long row of Arqua footgear was piled along one wall. Tej counted the pairs; *everyone* was here for the big moment. She could hardly blame them. Despite everything, her own breath came fast with excitement and anticipation.

She watched Ivan Xav, an unjoyful expression on his face, pull his slippers one by one from his jacket pockets and let them drop to the floor, which seemed much firmer underfoot than it had the other day; evidently Jet was right about the curing rate for the Mycoborer tubes. After a long hesitation, Ivan Xav pulled off his wristcom and emptied his pockets of forbidden gizmos, including his car and door remotes and that neat military stunner that Tej had first met on Komarr. Tej and Star each picked up a spare cold light from a box at the end of the bench. Ivan Xav followed their example, then, after a narrow glance at Tej, proceeded to stuff his pockets with more.

Tej bit her tongue on any comment. It wouldn't hurt anything. He could return the unused ones later.

Star handed out hospital masks and plastic gloves all around.

"What the hell?" said Ivan Xav.

"It's all right," said Tej. "You just don't want live Mycoborer stuff to rub on your skin. Or get in your lungs, I guess."

"And you people turned this crap loose on *my planet*? That is not my definition of *all right*. If it's that nasty, I'd want a full biotainer suit."

"Well, this is what Grandmama said to use, and she should know. And we've been running in and out of here for days with just this, and nothing's happened to us."

Ivan Xav stared at Tej with new alarm, as if he expected to see flesh-eating fungus start spreading all over her skin on the spot. His gaze flicked to Star with equal curiosity, if somewhat less concern.

"You don't have to come along," added Star. "Nobody invited you."

Ivan Xav donned the gloves and yanked the mask up over his face. His deep brown eyes, Tej discovered, could glower quite fiercely all on their own, without any help from his mouth.

Tej held up her cold light and started down the tunnel. She whispered over her shoulder, "From this point on, as little talking as possible."

"Right," Ivan Xav whispered back.

The tunnel, too, seemed slightly larger in diameter than before. Ivan Xav didn't even have to duck his head, although he did anyway. He was very careful not to touch or brush the walls in passing. He plainly did not like the sitting and sliding around the two bendy parts at all. He held up his cold light to the occasional random appendix-holes, his brow furrowing in disapproval. Tej tried not to feel defensive. *She* hadn't invented the Mycoborer.

A wide place in the passage was impeded by a big pile of dirt, a few pale bones, and a tattered backpack with electronic parts spilling out of it.

"I thought Grandmama was going to make Jet and Amiri clean this up," Tej whispered to Star, stepping carefully around it.

"They did," whispered Star back. "But something shifted when we were out today, and this all came spilling out of the wall again. Dada says Jet has to come back and clean it up again before we start hauling goods out."

"What the *hell* is this...?" whispered Ivan Xav sharply, holding his cold light down to illuminate the pile. The bones sprang out in harsh relief.

"It's poor Sergeant Abelard," Tej whispered back. "I didn't actually find that dog-tag necklace on the floor of a garage. He was wearing it."

Ivan Xav knelt, staring wide-eyed, not touching.

"He was in a collapsed tunnel that our tunnel crossed. Or at least his foot was; Jet made the hole. I didn't think that was such a good idea, but, you know, brothers. Well, I suppose you don't know brothers. Guys, then."

Ivan Xav's hand turned up a flap of backpack, then drew back.

"I do not have claustrophobia," he...well, it was still a whisper, but it had a lot of snarl in it. It seemed he actually *did* possess emotional range beyond *peeved*. "I do, however, have a quite active *unexploded bombs* phobia. This could be—anything. Unstable, for example. Are you people *insane*?"

"It can't be too unstable," said Star, unsympathetically. "It didn't go off when it fell in here, and it didn't go off when Pidge tripped over it and kicked it a bit ago. I wouldn't *play* with it, mind, but it's not going to do anything spontaneous, I don't think."

Unlike Ivan Xav, who looked quite close to something spontaneous, possibly combustion. But he just stood up and waved them on.

Their next check was at a point where the Mycoborer tunnel split into five channels. Three of them wrapped around a large-diameter pipe, from which the sound of rushing water filtered faintly. Ivan stared at it, listening, then shook his head. He muttered something that sounded like, *Oh, sure, of* course *there's water*, but didn't expand.

"Uh, which way?" Tej asked Star. She hadn't made it quite this far the other day; but neither had the Mycoborer.

Star counted, then pointed. "That one."

They trudged after her, slippered feet shuffling. After a number of meters and a few kinks, but no more loop-the-loops, a faint viridescent glow showed up ahead. They rounded one more bend and climbed a slope to find a new vestibule, brightly lit by wavering cold lights, dead-ended against a flat wall and full of silent, milling Arquas.

Dada and the Baronne looked around and spotted Ivan Xav. "Tej!" whispered the Baronne, with a shocked gesture at her Barrayaran.

"It's all right," Tej whispered, coming over to them. "He's with me."

Dada scowled. "But is he with *us*?"

"He will be," she promised. Ivan Xav smiled tightly behind his mask, but did not gainsay her. Yet.

Amiri was just fitting some sort of hand-pumped suction device to an oval in the wall showing signs of work by cutting fluid and maybe something more physical. He motioned Jet forward; shoulders straining, they shifted the slab out of the wall and let it down slowly and silently.

Amiri tossed in a couple of cold lights—Tej could hear them hit something and roll to a stop—adjusted his mask, and stuck his head through. Nine other Arquas, a ghem Estif, and one Vorpatril held their breaths. Or was that, eight other Arquas, one ghem Estif, and two Vorpatrils...?

"What can you see?" demanded Dada. His hand reached out to clasp the Baronne's. She gripped back just as hard.

Amiri's voice floated back: "Marvelous things!"

Chapter Twenty-One

Ivan had never thought of his nightmares as being insufficiently imaginative, before tonight. *Dark, wet, constricted, underground,* check. How had he left out *biohazards*? After all that, the frigging *unexploded bomb* just seemed a . . . a redundant redundancy. And the stray corpse a mere decoration. *How did I get into this mess? Miles isn't even* here.

Though the labyrinthine results of the Mycoborer were impressive as well as alarming, he had to admit. The discovery of the supposedly empty Cetagandan bunker had been interesting, though Ivan wouldn't have been human if he hadn't found its transmutation to a ghem-generals' lost treasure vault riveting, as irresistible to him as to any Arqua. But the belated news of its original provenance as a Cetagandan haut *bio-lab*, which Tej hadn't let drop till they were *almost here*—had to make it the most entirely resistible temptation he had ever encountered.

And that idiot Amiri was *going inside*. Ivan hadn't had cause to dislike his new brother-in-law before now, but this was just *wrong*. Amiri turned to politely help his haut grandmama over the threshold of the oval they'd cut into the wall, incidentally compromising any biohazard containment integrity the old lab had still held, but hey, who cared about that? Not the intent Arquas, it seemed. The tall woman bent her head and twitched her long coat through the aperture, as dignified as an aged queen returning to her country after some long exile. Other Arquas filed through eagerly after her. Tej glanced back over her shoulder as she followed, bright-eyed with triumph.

Ivan was not going to be able to get through the rest of this night without inhaling, alas. And Tej had just slipped out of his view, even though he edged closer and craned his neck. He drew a long breath through his filter mask, squeezed himself down, and ducked in after them all.

Arquas were spreading out through the chamber, their bright green-white cold lights held aloft. The place wasn't huge, about eight by ten meters, though Ivan spotted a stairway going down to another level. But it was crowded with crates and boxes and covered bins: on the floor, under and upon benches and desks and chairs, some in neat, tight stacks—those against the walls reaching the ceiling—others seemingly flung atop the rest in a scattered hurry. A faint plume of dust had settled over the array, fanning from a rubble-filled aperture on the far end, but on the whole the place looked as pristine as the day it had been sealed off. Ivan wondered if he was now breathing hundred-year-old air, a few molecules of which might have passed through the lungs of Prince Xav, or not-yet-mad Prince Yuri, or other famous Barrayaran ancestors.

Lady ghem Estif was staring around with satisfaction; she stepped up on a crate and pulled down her filter mask. Most of the others followed her example. Ivan left his in place as, he noticed nervously, did the biologist Amiri. "We should be able to speak to each other in normal tones, inside here," she announced to the Arquas at large. "No loud thumps or shouting or screaming, of course."

No screaming, eh. Good she'd reminded Ivan of that. It was dawning on him that he'd just lost the biggest wager of his recent life; the ramifications were spinning out beyond his boggled imagination. But at least he wasn't running around the room mad with greed like the Jacksonians...

"This one's heavy." Emerald lifted a plastic box atop a pile, and shook it a little. Something slid inside. "Think it could be the gold?"

Tej, Rish, and Pidge crowded around; drawn, Ivan looked over their shoulders as Em pried open the top. Inside was another large, rectangular box, of fine polished wood. The gold clasp yielded to her green fingers; the velvet-lined lid swung up.

"Oh," said Rish in disappointment. "It's just a bunch of old knives."

Tej held one up. "Kind of elegant, though..."

Ivan, getting a good look into the tray of cutlery at last, reached out and plucked it from her hand with trembling fingers. "This is a Time-of-Isolation seal dagger. Count's sigil on the hilt... dear God, they all are." The first tray of twenty knives lifted out to reveal another, and a third. Ivan's eye decoded the arms, Vorinnis, Vortala, Vorfolse, Vorloupulos... holy crap, Vorkosigan as well, and yes, there was a Vorpatril... it was like a roll-call of the old Council of Counts. "It's a *complete set*. A complete set of seal-daggers from all sixty Counts-palatine in existence a hundred years back." Some brilliant connoisseur ghem-officer's collection...

"Do they have any value?" Tej inquired ingenuously. "They don't look all that fancy."

"Ordinary Vor seal daggers from the Time of Isolation can go for ten thousand marks up. Way up, if it's from anyone famous. Ten times that, from a count or prince. My cousin Miles has one that's literally priceless." Which he used as a letter opener, Ivan recalled. "A *complete* set... *with* provenance..." Ivan tried to do the multiplication in his spinning head. "Six to ten million?"

"Barrayaran marks or Betan dollars?" Shiv inquired, coming over.

"Either," said Ivan, shaken. Very belatedly, he realized he *should* have said, *Oh, it's just a bunch of dusty, rusty old knives. If you don't want them, I'll take them off your hands...*

And that was only the first crate. This place held *hundreds* of them.

He suddenly wanted to run around the room madly breaking open bins. *And* screaming.

Jet pried open the top of another crate and peered within. "What's this?" he asked the air, looking nonplussed. Ivan craned his neck; it looked like a pile of old electronics, and some slate slats.

Lady ghem Estif, crossing from one side of the room to the other by threading her way through the piles, stopped to look over his shoulder. Her frown echoed his. After a long pause, she pronounced, "Artwork." And after another, "Or perhaps a weapon. Not sure. Just set it aside, for now."

Ceremonial objects, wasn't that the catch-all term? Ivan thought wildly. He turned to find himself looking through the faded plastic side of another bin; it seemed to be packed tightly with flimsies. Or maybe papers, back then. He lifted it down from its pile of brethren, popped the top, and was retroactively relieved not to have the contents turn to dust—someone ought to be being *careful* with all this stuff—but, remembering he was already wearing gloves, tried to thumb through the top layer. Real, old-fashioned paper, yes. Some of the pages stuck together. His eye picked out the salutation on a handwritten letter, faded brown ink, *Dear Yuri,* but of course no saying it was *that* Yuri...gingerly, he wriggled it out. His wildly skipping glance caught only some talk about requisitions, and the closing salutation, *Your brother in a better grade of arms, Xav.*

...Duv Galeni would have a *stroke.*

"What's that?" asked Shiv, at his elbow. Ivan flinched. His brain finally catching up with his mouth, he said airily, "Not much. Just some old papers and letters." Hastily, he tucked the page inside his jacket in trade for the knife and closed the lid of the bin, tapping it sealed again, firmly. And, just for luck, returned it to the top of its stack. "Probably not worth hauling out. Go for the gold, eh?"

"Oh, that as well," said Shiv.

On the other side of the chamber Pearl had found another stack of small, heavy cases, locked and with some Ninth Satrapy seal incised on the tops. Star brought over a flat metal bar looted from a lab bench drawer; together, they pried the top case open. Pearl held up a cylindrical roll that gleamed through its plastic wrapper. "Ah, here are the gold coins. You were right, Grandmama."

Lady ghem Estif was now moving around to all the cupboards and old, dead refrigeration units in the lab, examining their insides intently; she waved blasé acknowledgement of this. "That's nice, dear."

Tej and Rish bopped over to see; Ivan replaced the dagger in its velvet slot, controlled an urge to slip the Vorpatril blade into his pocket, reverently closed and latched the lid, and followed.

Pearl broke open the wrapper and let the coins spill out in a bright clinking stream, handing them around for closer examination.

"Those Ninth Satrapy coins are worth way more than their face value on the collector's market," Ivan observed. "Most of them were melted down after the Occupation, and the currency was burned. Although..." He noted the stacks of cases, and gave up on the multiplication, "You might not want to let all those out at once, or you'll crash the prices."

Shiv's paw descended on his shoulder in an approving grip. "Good thinking, Ivan Xav. We'll make a Jacksonian of you yet." Though he, too, rolled a few of the coins around curiously in his hand. *His* sample went into his pocket when he was done.

Shiv stepped up on a couple of crates and looked over the room with a calculating eye. "I know you're all excited to be opening presents, children, and so am I," he called out over the stacks. "But work before pleasure."

That seemed an un-Jacksonian sentiment, but it was perhaps how Shiv had become a top-dog Jacksonian, Ivan reflected.

Shiv went on, "We'll need to save the complete inventory for later, in some more secure space. Time is as much of the essence as treasure tonight. Location, location, location, they say; and this is not one to linger in."

A faint, disappointed-but-not-disagreeing moan from his progeny scattered about the room acknowledged this pronouncement.

Shiv's eye fell on his eldest daughter. "Star, you're supposed to be guarding the entrance."

"I locked the door, Dada. And I wanted to *see*."

"Yes, yes"—he waved an understanding hand—"but now you have. Back to your post. You, Jet, Em—no, Rish, you go with him, you can keep him on task—go clean up that mess in the tunnel. Each of you carry something with you as you go—we don't have time for wasted trips tonight. Off with you!"

They each grabbed a coin case—even Jet gave a little grunt, lifting it to his shoulder—and, stepping over the high threshold, filed out the oval hole in the wall.

"Some of it is bound to be trash," murmured Udine, giving her husband a steadying hand as he stepped down off his makeshift podium. "Those would be wasted trips as well."

"Mm, true. Well, if the next room down is like this one, we're going to need more than one van. And more than one night. We can take the obvious items tonight, and leave some of us in here tomorrow during the day to triage the rest."

She nodded.

Shiv herded more of his children into shifting the coin cases from their stack through the hole in the wall to a staging area in the Mycoborer vestibule. Lady ghem Estif, meanwhile, straightened up from a cupboard on the far side of the room with an "Ah!" of surprised satisfaction. Both Ivan's and Udine's heads swiveled around.

"What did you find, Mother?" Udine inquired, zigzagging over to her. Ivan and Tej followed.

Lady ghem Estif held up what might have been a really, really elegant combat utility belt. "My old biotainer girdle. I wonder if it still works?" And, in a bemusing womanly addendum, "I wonder if it still *fits*?" She slipped out of her coat and cinched it about her waist, and a sincerely delighted smile illuminated her face as she found that yes, it did still fit. One hand went up to fluff her short hair, and the smile twisted.

Her long fingers danced over what was evidently a control panel on the left side. Ivan jumped back as a flickering force-field abruptly sprang out around her, shoving over a stack of boxes, which slid and fell with a few dull thumps; she touched another control, and its spherical shape became a more form-fitting tall oval. She looked as if she were standing inside a narrow, translucent egg.

"Hey, what about no electronic signatures?" Ivan cried in panic. Wait, no, wrong. He *wanted* them to be surprised by ImpSec, didn't he? In some way that he had nothing whatsoever to do with, in order to keep his word to Tej. This could be perfect.

Lady ghem Estif glanced upward. "Oh, no one will pick up anything through *these* walls."

Crap, thought Ivan. Nonetheless, she turned the sputtering field back off.

Ivan narrowed his eyes in belated recognition. "Wait. I saw something like that before, back on Eta Ceta. When Miles and I had to go as the Barrayaran diplomatic representatives to the late Cetagandan empress's funeral, twelve, thirteen years ago. The haut-lady bubbles. All the haut women traveled around in these float chairs, with personal shields a lot like that one."

Lady ghem Estif looked at him in surprise. "Indeed. The biotainer girdles were made a symbol of haut status. Personally, I disapproved of fitting them onto the float chairs—robbing them of their original purpose in pursuit of display. Really, I do sometimes wonder if my old caste is becoming effete. I begin to believe I was well out of it. Young people these days, no sense of the right robust relation of form and function. And they call themselves artists!"

"So," said Ivan, taken aback to have the formerly settled insides of his head so abruptly rearranged, "the haut-lady bubbles actually started as biotainers? But they don't work as suits anymore?"

"Oh, of course they still do *that*," murmured Lady ghem Estif, and headed purposefully for the stairs.

Udine shrugged and picked up the nearest case, turning toward the hole in the wall. "Tej, Ivan Xav"—a warmer drop in her voice at his name acknowledged his volunteer status—"time to start hauling. Quickly, now."

Tej dutifully picked up the next crate down, and Ivan, more dubiously, followed suit—its weight tried to pull his arms out of their sockets. What the hell *should* he be doing down here? It had been all too easy to get sucked into the general excitement and forget that, no, his aims were *not* those of the rest of the people in this place. Maybe some opportunity would come as he helped lug all this stuff through that damned twisty tunnel—dark and confined, true, but he'd hardly be alone. They'd be just like a line of ants, or termites, or one of those other Earth social insects in their little burrows. But once he'd carried his first load to the access well, he might lay hands on his wristcom again, and then—his eye fell on Tej—then he would have a *real* dilemma.

Amiri, pausing at the new doorway, called over his shoulder to his sire, "Do you think it will be more efficient to each carry these all the way, or pass them along?"

"Pass along," Shiv replied without hesitation, also now lugging a case. "Space yourselves evenly as to time, though, not distance. Those switchbacks are going to make slow spots."

Amiri nodded and stepped through.

Hell, thought Ivan. But he might still work his way back to the access well, just not as directly. Ivan was now almost as reluctant to leave this treasure vault, so barely explored, as he had been to enter it. If he could just—

Amiri stepped backward through the ragged oval aperture, his empty hands reaching out above his head. What was he doing, stretching? No one had yet had time to become that fatigued—

A total stranger with a stunner in his hand, trained on Amiri's midsection, stepped through after.

Ivan's heart jumped in his chest; he stumbled to a halt.

Then Pearl, who'd also stepped out to the vestibule, came through likewise walking backward. And then another stunner-armed man, much older, and a third.

Not ImpSec in plainclothes—Ivan wasn't sure what subliminal signs his backbrain was processing, besides the general absence of Byerly Vorrutyer, though God knew he'd looked up close at enough ImpSec men in his life—but he was sadly sure of it. Ordinary garage security guards? No, they wore uniforms. Very gently, Ivan set down the case he was carrying on the nearest stack, to free his hands, and eased in front of Tej, who had stopped short in shock.

"Do you know what this is?" Ivan murmured to her, almost voicelessly.

"Ser Imola. Dada just hired him to be our carrier. But..."

But the stunners, right. Not a whole lot of doubt about which way they were aimed, either. With only the briefest hiccup, Ivan translated the Jacksonian *carrier* to the more forthright Barrayaran *smuggler*. It was a measure of the night's distractions that Ivan hadn't even begun to wonder how Shiv had planned to shift all this treasure off-world. The question would have occurred to him eventually, he supposed.

"Oh, hell," said Shiv Arqua in a tone of boundless disgust, slowly setting down his own case. The stunner in the older man's hand swiveled to point at him. "Imola, you damned fool."

"I think not, Shiv," the older man said affably.

Shiv rolled his eyes. "First of all, your timing is terrible. The least application of thought might have told you that the time to go for us would be tomorrow night, after we'd emptied the vault for you. And you could have caught us and the cargo both. I've wondered about you Komarrans ever since the Conquest, really I have."

"Got the drop on you all, didn't we? Tomorrow night, you'd have been more on your guard." Imola glanced around the chamber. "Although I begin to think you were holding out on me after all. Maybe, after we send you on your way, we'll come back and clear this place out by ourselves."

"Oh," breathed Shiv, his anguished glance darting over their assailants' power weapons and wristcoms, "you won't be by yourselves. I guarantee it."

"What a *sinful waste* of an *opportunity*," mourned Udine, sliding up behind her husband. "I could just *cry*." Or spit, it looked like. Venom.

"Hello there, Udine," said Imola, with a nod of greeting and a slight, prudent shift of his aim. "You've held up well, I must say. Shiv said you were along. He probably shouldn't have mentioned you. It was just cruel, to tempt a man like that. Do you have any idea what House Prestene is now offering for Arquas, delivered to their doorstep? Individually or in bulk?"

"Less than your fifteen percent would have been," said Shiv growled. "Now you'll get nothing. And so will we."

"Oh, no," whispered Tej in Ivan's ear. "I bet he wants to *cryofreeze* us. That's how he smuggles people, to keep them from fighting back. Horrid!"

Ivan could see that temptation; Arquas all over the chamber were shifting about, trying to look unthreatening and not succeeding.

Pearl said uncertainly, "Should we make them stun us, to slow them down?"

"By all means," said Imola, grinning. "Then we won't have to listen to you complain. Your transport awaits—my ground-van will hold you all with room to spare. So convenient of you to arrange it for us."

"That won't be necessary," said Lady ghem Estif, in a loud but quavery voice. "All of you, just hold still. Someone might be hurt." She emerged from the stairwell and made her way in a newly tottery manner toward the doorway. Her hand, held out, trembled like that of a frail old woman on the verge of collapse.

"Who's that?" muttered one of the big goons backing Imola— a few cuts below even budget ninjas, in Ivan's quick appraisal, but dangerous nonetheless when they were armed with distance weapons and you weren't. One of them, he saw with indignation, held Ivan's own good military stunner, no doubt lifted off the bench in the entry vestibule in passing. The grip of the cheap civilian model he'd traded up for peeked from a pocket.

"My grandmother," said Amiri, suddenly watching hard. "She's a hundred and thirty years old. You don't need to hurt her *or* kidnap her—I bet Prestene doesn't even have her on their list. She's of no value to you! You leave her alone!"

"They don't," Imola began, then his eyes narrowed suddenly. "Wait, is that Udine's haut-woman mother—"

His caution fell a moment too late. Ivan poised on the balls of his feet as Lady ghem Estif meandered up to the men and her shaky hand wandered to her belt. With a deep, spluttering snarl, her force-field sprang out at full power and spherical diameter, knocking one man off his feet and pinning the shrieking Imola up against the wall by the door.

Ivan had his target all picked out, the big bastard who'd stolen his stunner. The man tightened his finger on the trigger and fanned the room; nothing happened, except for Ivan hitting him with all the force of his full weight in launch mode and knocking him back through the doorway. The fellow was strong and nasty and...kind of slow, compared to Ivan's usual sparring partners. Some knuckles to his windpipe, a few nerve jabs; Goon Two willingly gave up the useless stunner to Ivan's wresting fingers in order to gather himself for a lunge that would put his outweighed opponent on the bottom of the pile, and was thoroughly, if briefly, surprised when the stun beam hit his head at point-blank range instead.

Ivan pushed himself up, breathing, well, not *too* hard—it was more the adrenaline than the exertion—to find Tej looking down at him with vast approval. The metal bar gripped in her hand was redundant to need, but might have proven a very well-chosen accessory to a Vor lady's evening garb. He grinned back in sudden exhilaration. His filter mask had been torn off in the struggle; he didn't bother to try to reaffix it.

"And you said you were just a desk pilot," murmured Tej.

"But it's a *Barrayaran* desk," he murmured back, and scrambled to his feet. Together, they looked over Ivan's victim, lying on his back with his legs bent over the jagged doorway. They each took an ankle and dragged him through into the chamber, and out of the path; Tej did not concern herself unduly with his head thumping over the threshold, Ivan was proud to note.

"That was either really brave or really stupid," said Tej, her admiration tinged by faint doubt, "jumping him unarmed like that."

Ivan was tempted to claim the first, but was afraid of being tarred with the second. Sheepishly, he admitted the truth instead: "Neither. I could see he had filched my stunner. It's one of the new issue, with the personally coded grips. Only the upper ranks have theirs so far. They're still arguing over whether to give them to the grunts or not."

"Oh, good," said Udine in passing. "Your mother told me she didn't think you could be an idiot."

Imola and his other partner had been overpowered and disarmed. Imola was still whimpering from his contact with the force-field. It must have been just like running up against a really *big* shock-stick. Driven by a really *angry* haut woman. Her teeth bared and tight, Lady ghem Estif turned off her antique biotainer field again; with a last blurt of protest, it powered down.

Pidge, now in possession of one of the other stunners, bent to give the struggling Goon One, whom Emerald and Amiri together were barely holding down, a buzz to the back of his neck; he jerked and lay still. Em and Amiri then combined to haul up the shaking older man that Tej had named Imola and push him to the wall.

"I'd be delighted to test the Mycoborer on him," said Lady ghem Estif in a precisely measured voice, "but I suspect the results would be too slow. Perhaps I can find something faster downstairs."

"No need," said Shiv, padding closer to this old friend-enemy. "We'll do something lower tech."

Imola watched Shiv approach him with fearful fascination; he realized his new mistake when the taller Udine whirled, grabbed him by the neck, lifted him off his feet, and pressed him to the wall with all her half-haut strength.

"Where are my children, you worthless sack of greed?"

"Glp!" he replied, eyes bulging.

Shiv's voice in his other ear dropped to a tiger's purr. "Star, Jet, Rish. You have to have passed them, coming in. What did you do with them?"

Ah, a quick round of good-Cordonah-bad-Cordonah, Ivan recognized. Or bad-Cordonah-worse-Cordonah. He suspected the roles were interchangeable between the two at need. He wouldn't have interfered for worlds.

"How many more men do you have out there?" Shiv continued.

Udine permitted Imola a breath of air. Prudently, he used the exhalation to gasp, "Only saw one! Tall girl!"

She waited a little, and permitted him another.

"Really! M'boys took her down—put her in the van!"

Another long pause.

"Four, waiting on stragglers! Crossfire, no escape!"

Udine, after another pause that Imola no doubt found quite lengthy, let him drop. He crumpled to the floor, frantically rubbing his neck.

"If that's so," said Em in doubt, watching all this, "where are Jet and Rish?"

Tej's hand had found Ivan's, during this show; it tightened in alarm.

"And how do we get out, if they're laying for us at the only exit?" asked Amiri a bit plaintively.

"Oh," said Shiv sadly, "I imagine all we have to do is sit down and wait a bit. Ivan Xav's stepda will be along. To collect on his bet." He added after a tight-jawed moment, "*Dammit. We were so close.*"

"Who the hell is Ivan Xav?" said Imola, clearly bewildered by these additions to the play list. "Or his stepda?"

Ivan hunkered down in front of the man. "I am," he told Imola, with false geniality. "My stepda used to run that big building"—not being quite sure how the lab was turned in relation to ImpSec HQ, or which side the erratic Mycoborer had put them in on, Ivan made his wave vague but generally upward—"full of humorless men whom everybody *but* you has gone to great pains to not attract. But that's all right. I'm sure you'll be getting to know them really well, really soon. And vice versa."

Ivan thought Imola had processed the *ImpSec is coming for you* part of this, which really wasn't much of a stretch at this point, but not the rest. He stared at Ivan in personal bewilderment, then back at Shiv.

"In that case," he croaked, "maybe we should team up again, huh?"

Shiv just snorted.

"I don't know, Dada," said Pidge, tapping the captured stunner thoughtfully in her palm. "Perhaps we should reexamine our op—"

It felt as if a giant's hands had cupped Ivan and pressed inward at all points at once. He didn't exactly hear the boom, because his hearing had gone wonky in that instant, but he felt it in his bones. Tej may have yelped; in any case, her mouth moved.

Ivan fell back on his butt. A couple of cases thudded to the floor, knocked off their stacks.

And it was over.

All the Arquas were working their jaws, trying to get their eardrums to pop back. Imola cried, in a voice that sounded as if it were coming from a great distance, "What the hell was *that*?"

Ivan climbed back up as far as his knees. "Sergeant Abelard's time bomb," he managed to get out, over the ringing and hissing and rumbling, most but worryingly not all of which seemed to be coming from inside his own head. "Running thirty-five years late."

Chapter Twenty-Two

Tej drew breath against the appalling concussion that had seemed for a moment to crush her lungs, and pushed herself upright from the stack of cases she'd stumbled against. She braced for an aftershock. But except for the humming in her ears, only silence came from the dark, open doorway into the tunnel.

"*Rish*. Jet!" she gasped, and bolted for the aperture. She held up her cold light, making dull gleams race over the uneven black walls, and ran down the slope. Around the first, or last, bend.

Behind her, she could hear Ivan Xav's strained shout, "Tej, no!" and the thump of heavy, slippered feet. She didn't look back.

She dodged through the kink. Another straight, descending stretch. The next kink. She was almost back to the storm sewer pipe; the breach and the bomb hadn't been much beyond that. What if Rish and Jet were trapped under some fall of dirt, tons of dirt, like the poor sergeant? Could they dig them out before they suffocated—if they weren't crushed already—and were there any tools back in the lab for—she skidded to a halt.

Filling the tunnel before her feet was a flat stretch of roiling, dark water. The downward slant of the tunnel, here, brought the roof to its level; the water lapped at the tunnel top. A sort of water seal—she could not make out any dirt- or rock-fall beyond it. Though the blast must have both broken open and collapsed the pipe, to dam and back its flow up into the Mycoborer maze. She put one foot into the icy water. How deep did it go? Could she swim through to the other side—or was there no other side, the tunnel over there flattened?

Ivan Xav's hand grabbed her arm and yanked her back. "No," he gasped. "Don't you dare!"

She gulped, and tossed her cold light out as far as it would go. It bobbed a moment and sank slowly; but its glow was quickly occluded in the opaque brown murk of the bubbling water. She could see nothing through it. Scum rings twisted on the moving surface.

As they stared, aghast, Grandmama jogged up—Tej had never seen her move faster than a dignified stride, before, and finding her breathless was weirdly jarring. She stared with them, then, hesitantly, stepped back and put a hand to her belt. The pale oval force-field sprang out around her, buzzing and sputtering.

"No, Lady ghem Estif!" said Ivan Xav. "That bloody thing is shorting out already. It won't hold, and once the water gets in, it'll kill you outright."

Reluctantly, her hand fell once more, and the field died away. Her lips moved numbly in her carved face. "I'm afraid your evaluation is correct, Captain Vorpatril." She looked . . . old.

"What can we do?" Tej's whisper was not, now, for secrecy.

Ivan Xav glanced down where the waves nibbled at his toes. "Back up. Water's still rising." They all did so, peering uneasily downward.

"We must return to the lab, and stay inside," said Grandmama, with a glance around. "The freshest areas of the Mycoborer tunnel have a certain amount of flex and rebound, but that concussion may have cracked the more cured sections. Very unstable, very unsafe."

"It was pretty hardened around the, the bomb," said Tej. "What if it collapsed on Rish and Jet? What if they're buried?"

"Or drowning," muttered Ivan Xav. "Or buried and drowning, oh God."

Grandmama hesitated. "If they were close to the explosion, I don't expect they'll have survived to experience either. If they weren't." The last sentence fragment stopped rather than trailed. She didn't finish the thought aloud.

Ivan Xav was swearing under his breath, or praying—it was hard to tell which. But, his hand still gripping Tej's arm too hard, he turned her around, and they all started back.

"It was a squib," he said after a minute.

"What?" said Tej.

"Sergeant Abelard's bomb. If it was originally intended for ImpSec, it should have turned this whole city block into a crater. The explosives *were* deteriorated. Just...not quite enough."

"But I saw those eye-pins on his collar," said Tej. Because otherwise she would start talking about Rish and Jet, and saying stupid, hopeful, unlikely things, and the spinning words would hurt like razors. "Would an ImpSec man have been trying to blow up ImpSec?" Maybe he'd been a bomb-disposal man, instead...?

"I looked him up," said Ivan Xav. "Yesterday. Maybe it's day before yesterday, by now." His stricken gaze darted around the tunnel, permanently night but for the jerking cold-light beams poking between his and Grandmama's tight grips. "He was one of Negri's boys, but all his records say is that he disappeared during the Pretendership. He could have been on the Lord Regent's side, trying to take out the building when Vordarian's troops held it. Or he could have been one of Vordarian's—they had men inside all the corps, the whole military was divided—either before or after. Once..." He swallowed. "Once Simon might have known. Which. Offhand."

They stepped back inside the lab, where, apparently, some argument between Dada and Ser Imola had just ended; at any rate, Imola was sitting on the floor clutching his jaw and moaning, and Dada was rubbing his knuckles and being very narrow-eyed. He looked up at them, gaze widening. "Did you find—" he began, then, seeing their faces, cut himself off. "What did you find?"

"We can't tell how much of the tunnel is collapsed, if any, because evidently the blast cracked that storm sewer," said Grandmama. "Water was pouring in. It had filled the portion of the tunnel nearest the pipe already."

"We can't get past," said Tej.

"It's rising," said Ivan Xav.

"Can it get this high?" asked the Baronne, coming up behind Dada in time to hear this. Her hand clutched his shoulder; his hand rose and pressed hers.

"It might," said Ivan Xav. "I suppose it depends on how many of those damned random Mycoborer branches lie below our level. And how hard it's been raining out there tonight."

Dada moved quickly through the doorway, and bent down to examine the oval slab of wall that had been removed. "Hm." He called back over his shoulder, "Amiri made most of his cuts angled inward, good boy. If we can find something for sealant, we should be able to boost this back up in place; the pressure of the water on the outside will hold it. If it comes to that."

"I guarantee," said Ivan Xav, "that we have ImpSec's full attention right now. I expect they'll find that access well in the garage pretty quick. If anyone can get through from that side...well, they'll get to us somehow. Sooner or later."

"Does—I hate to bring this up—but does anyone out there actually know we're in here?" said Pidge, joining the circle collecting around the aperture.

"Star," said Tej after a minute. "Ser Imola's men."

"If they didn't just toss her in the back of their van and all take off, when the job went up," said Emerald. "If they had half a brain among them, that's what they should have done."

"They likely just about did have that," sighed Dada. "Damned cheap rental meat."

"Ivan Xav," said Amiri, looking around at him in fresh hope. "Surely they'll miss *you*."

"When I don't show up at work in a couple of days, sure," said Ivan Xav. Then stopped. And said, "Ah. No, they won't. I'm on leave. Nobody's expecting me." He walked over to the still-unconscious man he'd stunned, bent, and stripped him of his wristcom. Stepping out through the aperture, he looked up, then began trying to punch through a call. Nobody tried to impede him.

Unfortunately, no one had to. Nothing went through. He came back and parted the protesting Imola from his fancier one, and tried again.

"We're pretty far underground..." said Tej, watching over his shoulder.

"Cheap civilian models," he growled, shaking it and trying again. "*Mine* would have worked here." Still no signal. "Damn."

"Simon will figure it out," said Tej, trying to inject a note of confidence as she followed him back inside. "Wouldn't he?"

"Simon," said Ivan Xav, rather through his teeth, "for some reason—you might know why, Shiv—is under the impression that you all haven't even started to tunnel yet. Let alone arrived at your goal. All the Arquas suddenly disappearing off the face of Barrayar... might have more than one hypothesis to account for it. In Simon's twisty mind."

"And you, too? Without a word?" said Amiri.

"I've been kidnapped before," said Ivan Xav. "You would be *amazed* how many memories tonight is bringing back to me. All of them unpleasant."

Tej would have held his hand, but she wasn't sure it would be taken in good part, just now. He was looking a bit wild.

They all were. And maybe she was, too, because Ivan Xav reached out and gripped hers, and gave her a tight grimace that might have been intended for a smile.

"No sign of Rish and Jet?" said Em, in a constricted voice.

Tej shook her head, throat too thick to speak.

"They might... maybe they were on the other side of it, when that explosion went off," Em tried. "Maybe they got out. Maybe... ImpSec will find them over there. Or—Imola said he didn't see them, and they can't have got past him, so maybe they went to hide up one of the other branches."

Or down one. Tej had an instant and unwanted flash of it, freezing water pouring into some Mycoborer side-channel, knocking the two off their feet, making the slope too slippery to scramble up...

"Or maybe..." Em ran down, which relieved Tej of the urge to slap her silent. But for a snap decision on Dada's part, it would have been Em out there with their youngest brother, Tej reminded herself.

Ivan Xav hesitated, then said, "Couldn't you use the Mycoborer to tunnel *out*?"

Tej was briefly thrilled with her Barrayaran husband's simple genius, but Grandmama frowned; she said, "It consumes oxygen as well... at a rate of... hm."

"Don't bother trying to calculate it," sighed Amiri. "The box is back at the entryway with the rest of our supplies."

A sickly silence. All around.

"How many cold lights do we have?" asked Pearl, patting her pockets. She came up with a single spare.

This triggered a general inventory. Most of the Arquas were carrying one or two extras; Ivan Xav harbored a double-dozen, plus a couple he quietly palmed to an inside pocket when almost no one else was looking.

"Rather a lot," the Baronne concluded. "But space them out. Don't start any others till the ones we have run down."

The eight cold lights presently providing their bright chemical glow made the lab seem a well-lit workspace. Tej imagined it with only one or two, and the word that rose in her mind was *haunted*. And not just with all the history.

"Water?" said Pidge, and gestured inarticulately when Tej gave her a *look*. "I mean water that's safe to drink."

"I might find something to filter some," said Grandmama. "Boil...no, likely not."

"We brought plenty of food to keep everyone going all night," said Pearl glumly. "Too bad it's all back at the entrance with everything else."

Em swallowed, and said, "Air...? These walls are pretty tightly sealed."

Perfectly sealed, as Tej understood it, except for their new door and maybe the old one, filled with rubble.

"The rooms are rather large," said Amiri, his voice thin with a worry that undercut the actual sense of his words. "And there are two of them."

"And the tunnel," said Tej. "And...there might be some oxygen exchange through the surface of the water out there?"

"Works till we have to seal the door on it," said Pidge. "But there are twelve of us in here breathing."

Quite a few Arqua gazes swiveled to Imola, still sitting on the floor beside his unconscious hirelings and listening in growing horror.

"Nine would last longer," said Pearl, tentatively.

"Premature," growled Dada, "though tempting. Very tempting."

"Yes, but if we were going to do it at all, sooner is better than later," argued Pidge, in a tone that attempted to simulate lawyerly reason. Tej was almost glad that she quavered a little.

"Nevertheless," said the Baronne. Her tone was cool; her gaze calculating; her word mollifying; yet Imola shrank from her more than he had Pidge. No quaver there.

"Those two," choked Imola, with an abrupt gesture at his snoring followers. "You could have those two." He contemplated the inert forms, then offered, as if by way of a selling point, "They'd never know..."

"I'll be sure to mention you said so," purred Dada, "when

they wake up." He strolled away to look over the contents of the chamber some more; scouting for ideas, Tej suspected, rather than treasure. Dada had never run short of ideas that she knew of; he merely made more.

Ivan Xav looked at Imola and just shook his head. He leaned over and murmured to the man, "Look on the bright side. With all these other constraints, it's unlikely we'll have time to work around to the cannibalism." He bared his teeth in an unfriendly smile.

Imola flinched.

"Still, probably better not to indulge in, um, too much heavy exercise," Amiri offered. "Just... sit or move quietly."

"Mm," said Pearl. She and Pidge moved off to poke, quietly, though a few more boxes. Opening presents seemed a lot less riveting now than it had been at first.

Tej was watching Ivan Xav running his fingers along the side of a bin, lips moving as he estimated the number of papers packed inside, when a sharp scrape, a loud pop, a dull yellow flash of light, and a yelp rising to a screech whipped her head around.

Pearl had pried open the top of some ornately enameled bottle that she'd unearthed, which had exploded. Whatever liquid it contained had splashed upon her black jacket, dancing with blue and yellow flames. She recoiled, flung the bottle away, and leaped aside.

"Pearl, don't run, *don't run!*" Ivan Xav bellowed. Pearl, mouth open and astonished, only had three steps to do just that before Ivan Xav brought her down. "Drop and roll, roll!"

His cry pierced Pearl's shock; she overcame her flight reflex as he shoved her to the floor and pressed her flat, smothering the acrid conflagration before it could do more than lick her face. Tej jerked toward them, her world gone slow-motion and fast-forward all at once.

Momentarily unwatched, Imola shot to his feet, ripped off the lid from another bin of papers, flung them toward the spreading oil-or-chemical fire, and pelted out the door.

Ivan Xav lurched to his knees and took in this new hazard with eyes sprung wide as Grandmama hastened toward Pearl, sweeping off her coat. The narrow-necked bottle had not broken, but it had spun, trailing the lethal liquid it contained in a flammable spiral. He lunged, grabbed the emptied bin, and upended it hastily over the wobbling bottle, the scribble of oil, and a few fluttering papers that had just reached it. With an ugly flicker, the flames trapped underneath sank, smoked, and died.

Tej took her second breath. By the time the flush of adrenaline racing through her blood threatened to blow off the top of her head, it was all over.

Ivan Xav, holding the bin down as if it would fight him, shoved himself up, wheezing. He climbed to the top of this new pedestal and stood glaring around the room at the various Arquas, frozen with surprise or hurrying. Grandmama wrapped her coat around Pearl, finishing the job of containment, and a frightened Amiri knelt at her side, checking for damages.

Ivan Xav drew a long breath, and—goodness, he *could* yell. "Could you people *stop* trying to come up with *novel ways to kill me* for just one hour? Or maybe the rest of the night? I would so like that. Just the rest of the night. Just *sit down*. Just *stop doing anything*. Sit down and *wait sensibly*. Earth, water, air, fire—you're running out of elements, here!"

Amiri looked very impressed by this ringing baritone rant. Grandmama...looked less impressed, if perhaps sympathetic. Rising from Pearl's side and helping her up, she observed, "In some Old Earth mythologies there was imagined to be a fifth element—metal, as I recall."

Ivan Xav said through his teeth, "That was a rhetorical remark, not a bloody *suggestion*." But he stepped down off his podium and his ire into Tej's frantic clutch, nonetheless. None of the horrific stuff seemed to have splashed onto him, her shaking fingers found. His hand covered hers, closing it to his chest and stilling the shakes. His jaw unclenched, and he buried his face in her hair.

Dada and the Baronne had clambered through the obstacle course of boxes and crates from the other end of the room. The Baronne's face was gray; Dada's, more greenish. The Baronne went to Pearl, and Dada to the aperture to stare out angrily into the utter darkness where his enemy had vanished. Ivan Xav and Tej came over to his side.

Dada ground his teeth, muscles jumping in his jaw. "You were down there. Dead end, you said. Should we chase him?" he inquired of Ivan Xav.

"I wouldn't bother," said Ivan Xav, mouth almost equally stiff.

"Either he'll come back on his own, in which case we may as well save our breaths, or he'll drown himself trying to get out. Thus saving the exertion of cutting his throat, or whatever. I'm for damn sure not willing to sacrifice any more oxygen for *his* sake."

"Well, if he doesn't come back before we have to put the door up, I vote we don't go look for him," growled Amiri. Tej could only nod in dark agreement.

Dada gave Ivan Xav a sideways look. "You were very quick, there. And . . . correct."

"Training," said Ivan Xav shortly. He added after a reluctant moment, "And training accidents. You learn these things. One way or another."

"I see you do." Dada gave him a short, approving nod.

"What was that stuff?" Tej asked Grandmama, who had run her gloved fingers across a stray splash on the floor and was now sniffing them in chemical inquiry.

"Scent, at one time, I believe. Now merely stink. I don't think it was supposed to do that." She glanced around the room. "Kindly do not open anything more that you cannot identify before I've had a chance to check it," she instructed her descendents.

"Or at all," grumbled Ivan Xav. "*Humor* me."

Pidge, eyeing him in a subdued and wary way, sank down on a crate and sat with her hands folded tightly. Pearl, eyeing him more favorably, joined her. She seemed to have suffered only a light sunburn and singed white eyebrows. Pidge put an arm around her, calming her lingering shivers. Tej assisted Ivan Xav in picking up the scattered antique papers, very dry and crackling, and carefully repacking them in their bin. A little inconsistently, he scanned them in covert curiosity as he reordered them.

The chamber grew *really quiet* when everyone stopped talking. Tej was half-tempted to start another argument just to drive back the heavy silence. Instead, she and Ivan Xav followed Grandmama back downstairs, Tej because she hadn't seen that level yet, Ivan Xav evidently with some notion of sharing his light to improve the general visibility down there, or thinking that one wasn't enough. Or just to keep an eye out for the next emergency.

"As long as we don't run short of lights before we run out of air," he muttered.

"I suppose the ideal would be to have them both run out together," Tej mused.

"I'd rather have the light last longer."

Tej decided not to try to argue with the illogic of this. It wasn't as if they had a choice anyway.

The room below was similar to the one above, except for a few separated office cubicles on one end. Grandmama commenced trying cabinets and former freezers once more.

"Something special you're looking for, Lady ghem Estif?" Ivan Xav inquired politely. "Can we help?"

She waved away the suggestion. "Just...memories, so far. With which you cannot aid me, I'm afraid, Captain."

Ivan Xav shifted a few crates into a makeshift sort of sofa; he and Tej sat, and he eased back and put his arm around her. She leaned into him, wondering how many tens-of-millions-worth in anybody's currency they were sitting on—for that much money, it should have been more comfortable. The old lab was cool, not cold, the steady temperature of deep underground, and not especially clammy, but his warmth was welcome nonetheless. For some reason she was put in mind of that night back on Komarr, not-quite-cuddling on his couch and watching the vid of the unexpectedly graceful legless dancers in free fall. She'd been more afraid then than she was now. Strange.

"Ah!" said Grandmama from the other side of the room. "Filters!" Clutching her prize, she made her way back up the stairs.

"There's a help," Tej said. "At least we'll have something to drink."

"But then we'll have to piss," said Ivan Xav. "I suppose we can go out in the tunnel. Pretend we're camping, or on maneuvers."

"Or we might find some pots in here."

A smile moved his lips for the first time since the near-fire. "Priceless porcelain vases from the Time of Isolation, perhaps? Did they make porcelain back them? Not sure. Or carved jadeite bowls, those were popular once, I think. Worth thousands, now. Hell, maybe some ghem-general collected old Barrayaran Imperial chamber pots. I know they had *those*, seen 'em in the Residence. For all I know, still used by the more conservative Vorish guests."

A little laugh puffed her lips.

It was quiet for a time. "Now what?" she said after a while, wondering if it would help any to breathe less deeply. Likely not.

"Now what what?" He sounded, if not sleepy, very tired.

She was exhausted, she realized. What time was it? So late it was early, it felt like. Some cusp of night. "What did you do the last time you were stuck in a hole like this? To pass the time?"

"It wasn't a hole like this. It was a lot darker. And smaller. And wetter. Though air was not an issue. This is practically a palace, by comparison."

"Still."

"Well. First there was a lot of screaming. And pounding on the walls. And more screaming."

"I don't think that would help, here."

"It didn't help there, either. Screaming back at death doesn't help. Pounding on the walls till your hands bleed...doesn't help."

She captured one now, and stroked it till it unclenched, releasing the memory. "What does help?"

"Well, Miles. Eventually. Though I note that he's on another planet right now. Mind you, he wasn't *much* help—the first thing he wanted me to do was hide from the bad guys by going back down in that bloody hole."

"Did you?"

"Well, yes."

"Why?"

"It...was the right thing to do. At the time. It all worked out, anyway."

"And then?"

"Huh?"

"You said first. What was next?"

"Oh. When I was still trapped. I actually got, um, a little strange after a while. I tried to sing myself all the old Imperial scout camp songs that I could remember, from when I was a spotty whelp. And then the rude versions. Except I couldn't remember enough of them, and then I ran out." He added after a minute, "But then, I was alone." And after another minute, "Don't take this the wrong way or anything, but I kinda wish I was alone again. And you...back in our bed, maybe. Sleeping dreamlessly."

She returned his apologetic hug. "Same to you."

"Let's be sensible and wish for both of us there, while we're wishing. I mean, it's not like wishes are *rationed*."

"Good point." Except...she was glad he wasn't alone to face this unnerving reminder of what sounded, despite his making light of it, like the most terrifying hours of his younger life. It was not an erotic moment; imminent death by suffocation was a bit of a mood-killer. But it was good to just sit, not going anywhere, cuddling contentedly.

"Tej..." he said, and his voice was oddly uncertain. "There's a question I've been meaning to ask you for a while."

She blinked into the crowding shadows. "Now would probably be a good time to get it in, yeah."

He drew a long, long breath. It must be important; they'd both been breathing shallowly, when they'd remembered to. "Tej. Will you stay with me for the rest of my life?"

At the little jump of the laugh in her chest, his encircling arm tightened, heartened and heartening. He'd intended her to laugh, she guessed. Ivan Xav was good at that, it occurred to her. Making light in dark places.

"That... might not be too hard a commitment, I suppose. Right now."

"Well, it's not the sort of question a fellow wants to take a chance with, you know." His voice was rueful.

They were both, she noticed, holding on harder. How much courage had that question taken? More than the first time he'd asked, she suspected. She turned her head to watch his profile, looking out into the shadows of the chamber. "Where would I go? Upstairs?"

"I would follow you to the ends of the bunker," he promised.

Which kind of was the ends of their universe, currently. Who could promise more?

She, too, drew a long breath, because he was worth it. "Do you know what the third thing was I was going to ask you if I'd won our bet? Which I did do, just pointing that out."

"Tell me, my little wheeler-dealer."

"I was going to ask if I could stay with you. When my family left."

"Ah." His voice brightened; his lips curved up. "Now, isn't that a happy coincidence."

"*I* thought so." She hitched around and pillowed her head on his shoulder; he stroked her tangled curls.

If it seems too good to be true, her Dada had used to warn Tej, *it probably is.* A much lesser man than Ivan Xav might have appeared to offer escape enough from her beloved, overpowering, constricting, maddening family. Not quite *anyone with a pulse,* but such a choice had been scarily close a few times. And then she wouldn't have *this*. Maybe only love gave you *more* than what you'd dealt for.

Oh. So that's what this is. Oh...

So...if you spurned a miracle because it seemed to come too easily, would you ever get another? She suspected not.

Hang on to this one, then. Hang on for all you're worth.

Their breathing slowed in their shared warmth; that was good. "You know what I like best about you, Ivan Xav?" she asked, newly shy in her illumination.

He turned his chin into her hair in an inquiring sort of way. "My shiny groundcar? My Vorish insouciance? My astounding sexual prowess? My...my mother? Dear God, you're not taking me for the sake of getting my um-stepfather?"

"Well, I do like them both very much, but no. What I like best about you, Ivan Xav, is that you're *nice*. And you make me laugh." She smiled now, into his shoulder.

"That...doesn't seem like much." He sounded a bit taken aback.

"Yes," she sighed, "but consider the *context*."

He stared out into the dark room. "Ah," he said after a minute. "Oh."

Ivan Xav makes light for me. Even here. To the ends of their universe...maybe even to the ends of their lives. Where light would be wanted, she was pretty sure.

They both fell silent for a time, conserving heat together.

Tej stretched the crick in her neck, and said, "Remember the first thing you said to me?"

His face scrunched up. "*Hi, there, Nametag, I have this vase to go to Barrayar...?*"

She giggled. "No, after that. Do you recall that entire—never mind. But you made an indelible first impression."

"So did you—you *shot* me."

"No, Rish did." Her breath caught at the name, and Ivan Xav went still; they both looked up toward the face of the lab with the tunnel entrance. But it remained very quiet on the floor above. Tej controlled her wobble; tried to recapture their fragile moment of peace, but maybe all such moments were fleeting. *If the good ones fleet, so must the bad ones. If you don't pack them up and carry them with you, like...like anti-treasures.* "Well, we couldn't let you get away. That would have been...a huge mistake." *Speaking of understatements.* The greatest mistake of her life, and she wouldn't even have known it. The chill of that thought was like some predatory shadow passing overhead...and passing on. *He saved my life. In more ways than one.* "No. It was about your first rule of picking up girls."

"Don't remember that," he—lied prudently, she suspected.

"You said you'd never give up till I laughed." She hesitated. "*She laughs, you live.*"

"I'd be willing to take that for a prophecy, right about now," he admitted.

"The *never give up* part sounded good, too."

"Yeah," he sighed.

They rested, and waited.

Ivan thought he might have dozed off for a little, but biology ruled all things; thirst and a need to pee drove them both back upstairs all too soon. Together. Tej had said together. She had *meant* together, hadn't she?

This time, yes. Thank God for do-overs.

Team Arqua, under the Baronne's capable direction, had addressed biology's most immediate demands. Several large plastic bins had been emptied of old clothing.

Some were now filled with turbid water, slowly settling. One was set up in a corner behind a stall made of yet more priceless boxes, adequate camp toilet and with a tightly fitting lid that they might have cause to be grateful for later. A drip-filter was measuring out drinks, rather slowly for the crowd, but sips were shared around in fine antique glassware, its gold leaf showing sigils suggesting the—alas, incomplete—set had been the personal property of the infamous Count Pierre "Le Sanguinaire" Vorrutyer. Ivan didn't even attempt to mentally appraise it.

Imola had returned, trousers soaked to his thighs; he sat back in his surly huddle and didn't say much. The water was now lapping the outer wall of the bunker.

Shiv, Amiri, and Ivan then combined to switch the vacuum-handle to the other side of the door slab, and heave it back up into place, just beating the rising tide. The jagged seam around the slab grew dark and wet at a steady pace, creeping upward, but only a small dribble leaked through, to be captured by some mats found downstairs.

Ivan was impressed by Shiv's level-headedness in this emergency, which set the tone and the example for his whole family, bluntly curbing the potential chaos. But then, anyone who had once suffered defeat by Admiral Aral Vorkosigan in a pitched space battle likely had much higher standards for emergencies than most mortals.

The thought of his uncle caused stern lectures on prisoner-of-war regulations to rise to Ivan's mind, so he supervised the waking of Goons One and Two to allow them to piss and drink. He didn't argue, though, when Shiv put the woozy men back to sleep with another stun shot, along with Imola, who had started to restively complain again, for good measure. Unconsciousness would slow their metabolisms and breathing, right? It was all for the common good.

The younger women in the crowd, including Tej, then began to sort through the piles of clothing that had given up their containers to the drinking water reserves. No new lethality sprang from the benign diversion, and Ivan slowly relaxed. It was almost all fine court wear, in both Cetagandan and Barrayaran styles, including some old military dress uniforms that Amiri, and in a bit Ivan, were compelled to somewhat sheepishly model, ghem and Vor respectively. The Cetagandan garb was challengingly complex, with a non-obvious fastening protocol that Lady ghem Estif was drawn into advising upon.

It was while they were engaged upon this enterprise that Pearl picked up and shook out a long outer-coat, and something fell out of the folds to the floor with a clink. Ivan controlled his flinch.

"Oh!" said Lady ghem Estif. She bent and swept it up into her palm, and stared avidly. "I certainly didn't expect to find this there!"

"What is it, Grandmama?" Tej inquired; the females gathered around to look.

"My old brooch." The old haut woman smiled. "I thought it was lost."

Ivan, stiff in some dead Barrayaran prince's uniform that was a trifle too small for him, wandered over to see. It was not a very pretty piece of jewelry; an array of beads that looked more like ball bearings, set in a symmetrical array. Cetagandan then-modern art? But it seemed to mean a lot to the old lady, for she instantly fastened it to the inmost layer of her clothing.

"Very good, Pearl!"

The fashion show was brought to a close by the gradual fading of the cold lights. Ivan skinned out of the scratchy wool and heavy, rather greenish gold braid, roused to a new and unexpected pity for his military ancestors, and gratefully redonned his weekend civvies, manky as they now were with the night's exertions. The Baronne cracked a new light and set it up on a central box. People drifted away in small groups to the edges of the chamber, to make bedrolls of sorts out of the fine fabrics. Sleeping was encouraged, on the basis of slowed breathing all around.

The confiscated but otherwise useless wristcoms of Imola and his minions at least allowed them to track the time; about three hours before the late winter dawn, Ivan judged. If it had been a work day, he'd be getting up in about an hour. He and Tej cuddled in by one wall; Shiv and Udine by another. The remaining Jewels, Pearl and Emerald, made themselves a bedroll, and Pidge and Amiri anchored close by, not quite intruding on their space. Lady ghem Estif alone sat up, her eyes gleaming in the shadows, watching who-knew-what parade of memories pass before her mind's eye.

Ivan snuffled up around Tej, using her as a comfy body pillow, and let his face hide itself in her hair. The scent of it was soothing. He had an edgy relationship with darkness, just at the moment, but maybe letting his eyes close would make it seem more natural. He was certainly too keyed up to sleep...

Ivan shot awake into a deep thrumming noise that seemed to come from the very walls, reverberating directionlessly around the room. The cold light propped on the box fell over and rolled to the floor. Another cold light snapped into existence from Shiv and Udine's side of the room; Ivan added one of his own and sat up, raising it high. Tej was awake and on her feet already, looking sleep-shocked. Ivan clambered up after her.

"What the hell is *that*?" shouted Amiri, as the thunder continued unabated. It shifted, changed pitch, stopped for a moment, then started up again.

Ivan moved around, trying to get a bearing; he eventually decided *up* by process of elimination.

"Either Vorbarr Sultana is undergoing a surprise bombardment from space," he shouted back, "or some engineers are shifting a hell of a lot of dirt in a hurry with a heavy-duty grav-lifter."

Welcome as this sign was, it occurred to Ivan that being directly *under* a big grav-lifter at work was not the healthiest possible location, especially if the operators were working blind. "Stay away from the middle of the room!" he shouted. Were there any stronger places, like doorways, to cluster under? No, not exactly. Would downstairs be safer? Maybe... He was about to suggest this when the noise stopped.

He couldn't decide if the thunder or the silence was more unnerving. Everyone around the room was staring upward now, with a range of expressions ranging from hope to fear, with a few side jaunts—Lady ghem Estif's expression was bland in its haut mask; Shiv's was blackly ironic. Tej... stuck tight to Ivan. That worked for him.

The uproar started and stopped again a dozen agonizing times in the next hour. It was getting louder... closer... the vibrations took on a strange, whiny, lighter timbre. Weird thumps followed from the ceiling—roof—however you wanted to think of it.

An ear-splitting shriek; dust began to sift down from a circle slowly being drawn over the center of the room. Ivan darted forward and rescued the seal-dagger box, then skittered back to Tej's side, trying to calculate the weight of a two-meter-wide disc of very thick, very peculiarly reinforced plascrete, and its probable momentum after a three-meter drop. Would it go right through the floor to the chamber below? Possibly...

But in the event, when the circle completed itself, the slab hung suspended and then, miraculously, fell *up. Hooray for grav-tractors!*

Cold gray light filled the room, and a whoosh of chilly air that made Ivan realize just how much of a damp reek of exhalation had been starting to accumulate down here, accounting for his growing headache if it hadn't had a dozen other probable causes. Their tunnel door slab groaned, shifted, and abruptly blew out into the Mycobore vestibule, wet but now empty of water. The draft increased, whistling wildly for a moment, then faded to a steady flow.

A soldier in groundside half-armor dropped through the hole on a rappelling line; his dramatic entrance was spoiled when he landed askew on a pile of boxes, which fell over, and him along with it, though he found his feet at once. A number of Arquas around the chamber prudently held up their hands palm-outward, clearly empty of weaponry. A second man dropped beside the first, as the point man began shouting in excitement into his wristcom, "We're through, sir! We've found them!"

The third man in was the last individual Ivan would ever have expected to see dangling at the end of a rappelling harness: Byerly Vorrutyer, and looking vastly uncomfortable, too, with a few pieces of military gear slapped over his rumpled civilian suit. Ivan handed Tej the precious seal-dagger box and advanced to catch him, and incidentally protect the crates he was in danger of kicking over in his awkward landing.

"I hate heights," By gasped, as Ivan guided him down to his feet.

"Well, I hate depths," Ivan returned.

"To each his own, I guess."

"Evidently."

Chapter Twenty-Three

Tej tore her gaze from the gray circle of heaven, or at least Barrayaran sky, now visible through the roof of the lab and being crossed by banking military grav vehicles. She set down the box of those daggers Ivan Xav was so taken with and hurried to his side in time to interrupt the start of some *What took you so long?* exchange with Byerly.

"Have you seen Rish and Jet on your end?" she demanded.

Byerly jerked around to her. "No. They're not safe with you? Star hoped they might be."

Star is rescued? That's one . . . Tej shook her head. "They were in the tunnels when the old bomb went off." Tej pointed toward their entry. "We haven't seen them since. We were trapped on this end by the rising water, and they—we don't know."

"I've only seen Star," said By. "She's in a state, or she was—she's waiting now above with, er, everybody." He freed himself from his harness and hurried to the aperture.

The second soldier, now kneeling by the tunnel door and laying out equipment, flung out a stern hand and said, "Wait, please, sir." He picked up and aimed a remote probe: "Go, Rover!" The little grav device blinked on a brilliant headlight and flew away into the shadows. The soldier became intent upon his control panel.

Ivan Xav took Byerly by the shoulder and pulled him back. "Corps of Engineers," he said, mystically. "You just have to get out of their way."

"But," By sputtered, "if she's still in, uh, if they're in there—"

"Then we'll find out in a couple of minutes, without having to send a second rescue team to rescue the first. Lady ghem Estif thinks the tunnels are very unstable, after the explosion and the immersion."

By stood and jittered a moment, then wheeled about and made a quick head count of people in the chamber. He had to start over at least once, lips and fingers both moving. "Then all the Arquas—and you, Ivan—are accounted for except Rish and Jet? And who are the three spares?"

Imola and his brace of goons were just waking up, groggy and disoriented.

"Ser Vigo Imola," Tej put in, "a very bad man whom ImpSec should arrest at once, and his two unfortunate employees. At least, I'd think he was a bad boss. I bet they will, too. And that's not his real name."

"Oh. Good. We were looking for him."

By went to consult briefly with the first soldier, who had gathered all the Arquas together and was inquiring in a not-unfriendly military bellow, "All right, to start with, are there any medical emergencies here...?"

When By came back, Ivan Xav asked, "So, while we've been sitting around in the treasury all night contemplating the true nature of wealth, what have you been doing?"

"Going mad in white linen, pretty much. By midnight, when I realized that all my surveillance subjects, plus you, had simultaneously vanished, I knew something was up. When the first garbled news came through of someone trying to incompetently bomb ImpSec, I didn't connect it instantly. Because, you know, I'd thought Simon and Shiv had a pretty *friendly* rivalry going, till then. Also, I thought Shiv would have done a better job."

"Probably," allowed Ivan Xav.

"It had started when an ImpSec ground patrol went to check out some excess energy signals coming from that garage on the next block, and they surprised a quartet of thugs dragging an unconscious woman into a van. Municipal Guard work, but, you know, Allegre's boys don't mind a little live-fire practice on a dull night. Plus—one told me later—there was a chance she might be grateful. They took down two of the thugs, but the other two disappeared into your tunnel, and the ImpSec patrol chased them in. There was an exchange of stunner fire—"

"And then the surprise," said Ivan Xav. "So *ImpSec* set off the bomb!"

"It would be hard to calculate whose fire did it," said By, a bit primly, "the scene of the crime being presently buried under some ungodly number of tons of mud. But someone's energy beam apparently intersected the old explosive. At *this* point, the flare went up big-time. One of the patrollers and one of the thugs had to be dug out—"

"Was anyone seriously hurt?" Tej interrupted.

"Both, but not critically. It really wasn't at all clear what was going on for a couple of hours, till the medics finally got Star woken up. Then, of course, all hell broke loose. Especially after some fool—somebody finally thought to call and wake up your mother and Simon."

"Ah," said Ivan Xav, uneasily.

"Star swore there would be survivors in the bunker, even though the sensors were picking up nothing from it. The rest of the night was setting up the engineering, as soon as the search-and-rescue boys figured out it would be impossible to go in from the garage end. It's a real circus up there."

Ivan Xav glanced upward, his lips twisting. He walked over to the first soldier and advised him, "Let your command post know to treat this as a Class Two Biohazard Area. At least."

The soldier wheeled. "And you are...oh. Captain Vorpatril. Yes, sir." He spoke into his audio pickup.

Overhearing this, the engineering tech crouching at his control panel stopped inhaling, but, after a minute, gave up and continued his task.

Coming back to Tej and By, Ivan Xav said, "I'd want to dub it a Class Five, myself; but my grandmother-in-law would probably correct me. But that should discourage too many tourists till someone can get the appraisers down here for inventory. This place is going to need guards, and guards on the guards."

"Well, they've certainly come to the right place..." By mused. "Is there really a fortune down here, or was Star exaggerating for fear we might not dig you out?"

For answer, Ivan Xav took him over and showed him the box of seal-daggers, in which he seemed to have taken a possessive interest; Byerly sobered considerably. "And that was just the first crate we opened," said Ivan Xav. "You should see some of the rest. Not to mention the half-ton or whatever it is of Occupation gold."

Byerly, looking spooked, stared out over the sea of crates, then went aside and spoke into *his* audio pickup.

Tej went back to hover over the engineering tech, hovering over his control panel, so was the first to hear him say, "*Good girl,* Rover!" He looked up with a grin that made him suddenly look his real age—well, no, he probably wasn't fourteen—despite his military garb. "Found 'em. They're following Rover home now."

She and Byerly both leaned through the door, watching anxiously, as a bright light appeared in the throat of the tunnel. Scrambling after it, two exhausted, muddy, chilled figures...

Byerly reached out and dragged Rish over the threshold, and was suddenly plastered all over with lithe blue woman, a somewhat darker shade than usual. "You rescued us!" Rish cried, a view that unfairly left out the rest of the army that seemed to be involved, but which Byerly did not bother to correct. Jet stumbled into a welcoming committee of Arquas, and it was *several minutes* before the critique began.

"We were just working on the dirt pile," Rish told them all, "when we saw lights coming down the tunnel that weren't ours. We retreated all the way back to the storm sewer, then ducked up the biggest blind alley. There was a ruckus down on the other end, shouts and stunner fire, and we drew back—just in time, I think—we were both near-deaf for an hour, after the blast. When we looked, the entry end was collapsed, and the other was already filling with water. We retreated...and kept retreating...and the water kept rising. Then our cold lights gave out—"

Ivan Xav, listening, shuddered in vicarious horror, then went over and gave her a quite spontaneous and perhaps not altogether appreciated hug.

"Uh, thanks, Ivan Xav," Rish said, extracting herself and giving him a bemused stare; she went on with her narrative. "We were down to this little air pocket, when this weird noise and vibration started. It went on forever, starting and stopping. Then it was like someone pulled the plug on the drain. The water went down...we followed it. We were trying to decide whether to attempt to wade the tunnel when the lovely robot probe found us." She smiled at the engineering tech, who smiled back a bit uncertainly. Beautiful blue-and-gold ladies with pointed ears were not in his prior experience, Tej guessed, nor very many other ladies of any hue. Byerly, who certainly did not share this deficiency, took Rish's cold hand and rubbed it.

In any case, when the medical evacuation floater arrived—a small one, to fit through the roof hole—Rish and Jet were sent up in the first load. Imola, Inc. were sent up next, each individually with an armed guard with him. The Baronne and Grandmama followed, then Dada and Amiri, then Pidge and Em. Pearl went next, Byerly joining her to keep an eye on his subjects; Tej waited to go with Ivan Xav.

They watched Pearl and By's floater rise. "You know," he said, in an oddly faraway voice, "the *other* thing I wanted to do was take you dancing. We'd never got to it. Thought about that, last night. All the things we'd never got to do, yet."

Years of things. She began to suspect they would never run out. "I would like that." Their hands found each other. "I'd like that a lot."

"It's a deal, then." His grip tightened.

When the floater came back, he helped her into it with all the panache of a Vor lord of old handing his fine Time-of-Isolation lady into his carriage. *Lady Vorpatril. I could get used to that...*

The medevac floater was little more than a glorified stretcher, designed to hold one patient lying down but, in a pinch, two sitting up, plus its operator in the control saddle. Ivan, sitting cross-legged opposite Tej, stared through the canopy as they angled out the lab roof and ascended through the new access well, which was shaped like a narrow cone, widening at the top. More engineers on floaters were spraying some kind of fixative on the walls to stabilize the dirt, as they rose past.

Circus was an understatement, Ivan realized with a sinking heart as they cleared the lip of the well and briefly gathered more height. The new hole was dug down through what had been the lower end of the little park; the opposite side was now occupied by a conical mountain of what seemed, inexplicably, twice as much dirt, spilling over the park boundaries, the sidewalks, and, on two sides, into the streets beyond, which were blocked with barricades; municipal guards were rerouting traffic, fortunately still sparse on this early weekend morning. The pavement shone with a wet gleam, but it had finally stopped raining.

Heavy military engineering equipment was parked seemingly at random all over the place; soldiers hurried about, or stood and gawked. Portable floodlights on stands, not yet turned off in the pale dawn, shone everywhere. A command post under a temporary tarp roof was set up just beyond the corner of the ex-park, overlooking the excavation and blocking more street. Several medical ground-vans waited beyond it, their emergency lights blinking in a thumb-twiddling sort of way. Above, security vehicles circled; out beyond them, what Ivan guessed were news aircars also circled, telephotos no doubt trained on the bizarre scene.

Even as he watched, a biohazard team arrived, half suited-up, along with a group of older and less-fit fellows, a couple of whom Ivan recognized as senior functionaries from the Imperial Accounting Office, looking a bit out of place on this active, outdoor site. They all went to argue precedence with the engineers.

Beyond its walls and courtyard, the looming ImpSec building overlooked it all. In addition to an increased complement of patrollers at the gate on this side, quite a few officers with, Ivan suspected, no actual reason to be there sat on the upper steps or lingered outside the walls, watching the show. Ivan spotted one companionably sharing a breakfast rat bar with his fellow before the floater descended between the command post and the waiting med-vans.

When the canopy opened, Ivan helped Tej out and waved off a medtech trying to descend on them. When he turned toward the command post, he realized that might have been a premature gesture; a little tactical malingering could have been a better ploy.

A mob of people were approaching. Mamere and Simon, who was looking very gray and strained, led the wave, but Ivan spotted General Allegre and Commodore Duv Galeni right behind them. Both were in full uniform, their military greatcoats flapping about their knees in the raw air, but neither was shaved, and Ivan could only wonder at what wee hour each had been booted out of bed to scramble for this. In any case, he had to extract himself from the frantic maternal hug before turning to not-salute, since he was in civvies, but at least present a suitable acknowledging nod to his grim superiors. Tej was next in line for the hug, Ivan was glad to see. Simon just gripped his hands, a weird troubled expression on his face, and said nothing, though he also took the opportunity to embrace Tej, as what man would not? Ivan thought he heard him whisper in her ear, "Tej, I am so sorry," but he wasn't sure.

Allegre caught his eye. "Vorpatril," he bit out, "are you responsible for this mess?"

"God, I hope not," said Ivan fervently. An uneasy memory of all the documents he'd so blithely signed off on, back at the shuttleport about a subjective year ago, rose in his mind. The transition from *brave rescuee* to *court-martial accusee* might be just a slip of the tongue away; despite his fatigue and pounding headache, Ivan tried to come alert. He could only pray that the discovery of the immense treasure waiting below would pacify everyone, eventually, once they got it all sorted out.

Meanwhile, spread the blame... Ivan turned to Allegre, and asked, "Did you ever find out anything more about Sergeant Abelard and his bomb?"

"What?" said Allegre, startled. This gave Ivan the opportunity to tell that tale, and present the dog tags, happily still in his pocket. Star had only evidently got as far as conveying the *skeleton* and *old bomb* parts; Ivan could see Allegre was gratified to have at least one answer to his high-piled heap of morning mysteries presented, as it were, on a platter, especially as it didn't seem like anyone would be doing any DNA work on the poor dead bastard any time soon, even if any body fragments could be found after the blast. Also, it punted the ball back into ImpSec's lap, if at a thirty-five-year remove, which could only be to the good.

"Is there really a treasure worth millions of marks down there?" Simon demanded next. Galeni was right at his shoulder, for this one.

"Simon, there were millions in the first crate we opened. Hundreds of millions down there, at the least guess." Ivan turned to Galeni. "And crates of hundred-year-old documents packed to the ceiling, Barrayaran and Cetagandan. They're going to take *years* to sort. I found a holograph letter from Prince Xav to Prince Yuri in one of them." He pulled the folded letter out of his jacket and handed it across to Duv, who took it; one glance, and his mouth, which had opened to say something—probably about correct document conservation starting with not folding up rare items and stuffing them in one's pocket—just stayed open. Ivan had never seen Duv's eyes go so wide.

Across the road, a stressed-out-looking Captain Raudsepp finished loading Imola and his followers into a security van with the assistance of a couple of burly patrollers, then turned and plowed back through the crowd to Ivan.

"Lady Vorpatril is safe? Thank God! But I swear, those clowns didn't slip in through any shuttleport on the planet!"

"No, they probably drove downtown from the northern suburbs. What Shiv would call local rental meat. That Imola fellow has a shipping company out there."

As Raudsepp continued to look unsettled, Ivan added charitably, "Both the District Guard and Imperial Customs are going to be very pleased with ImpSec in the person of you for nailing him. Smuggling, conspiracy to aid kidnapping—seems he's been up to his neck in sneaking people off-planet in the form of cryocorpses, all very nasty. Imola's affairs'll keep folks busy digging for weeks, I expect. Commendations all round at the end."

"But I wasn't—but I didn't—"

"He's all yours now. Finders keepers, I say."

Raudsepp perforce had to dash back to the security van, flashing its lights and ready to leave, but Ivan was satisfied he'd given the man lots to think about besides, or with luck instead of, Captain Vorpatril's peculiar lapse in providing timely snitch reports on his in-laws.

Byerly appeared at Ivan's side, aiming for Tej. He had evidently been trying to herd Arquas into the waiting medical vans; Shiv and Udine had broken from the pack and followed close on his heels.

Tej stared across apprehensively. "Are they arresting us?"

Allegre looked as if he thought this would be a good idea, but Byerly reassured her, "No. Or anyway, not yet. They're just taking everyone to ImpMil—the Imperial Military Hospital—for trauma examination. And there're those unresolved biohazard issues."

"Are you going along?" Ivan asked By. "For the love of God, get someone who speaks old-high-medical onto Lady ghem Estif as soon as you can. She's a woman who knows where all the bodies are buried if anyone does."

Byerly nodded understanding, and turned. "Tej, are you coming with your family?"

Udine cut in: "Your Dada and I think you should stay with your husband—Lady Vorpatril."

Tej, Ivan could see in her expressive face, took a moment to process the full implications of this. Her parents might only be thinking of distancing their daughter from whatever legal entanglements were about to engulf the rest of the clan. But he rather thought Tej meant something more when she lifted her chin, threaded her arm though Ivan's, and said, "I think I should stay with my husband, too."

Ivan slipped his other hand over hers, pressing it warmly. *Yes, stay right there. For the rest of my life.* Which was looking hearteningly longer than it had mere hours ago, but he wasn't about to suggest amending his last-night's proposition.

Shiv gave a short nod, and looked up to meet Simon's searching gaze. He stuck out a big hand. "Well. It's been an adventure dealing with you—Captain Illyan. Excellently played."

Illyan, as if compelled, took it and shook it. "Thank you. Though I fear you were mainly ambushed by mischance. And—we may not be done dealing yet. Baron Cordonah."

Shiv's brow furrowed at this, but he allowed Byerly, now looking like a sheepdog on the verge of a nervous breakdown, to chivvy him and his spouse off to the waiting med-vans. Udine glanced once back over her shoulder, her eyes narrowing in new curiosity. The vans pulled away in a convoy, without sirens, to Ivan's relief. He wasn't in the mood for sudden, loud noises just now.

At some high-priority ping from his earbug, Allegre stepped aside. "What? Here? No, wave him off!" After another moment, his back straightened in an involuntary brace. "Yes? Yes, he's right here. No...I must protest... Yes, sire." That last was delivered with a somewhat defeated sigh, and he strode away to the covered command post.

Ivan was therefore less than surprised when, a few minutes later, Imperial armsmen outriders in their black-and-silver winter uniforms appeared around the corner, their float bikes bracketing a long silver groundcar. It sighed to the pavement. Armsmen and ImpSec guards exchanged codes with one another, and, gleaming even in the dawn murk, the rear canopy rose. Gregor, in a Vorbarra House uniform, rubbed his face and handed off the cloth to an urgent fellow whom Ivan recognized as his faithful valet—this was one Commander-in-Chief who was not going to appear at the scene of any emergency unshaven, if his man had anything to say about it—and exited the groundcar under the anxious supervision of his senior armsmen.

Everyone braced as he approached, except for Lady Alys who granted him a chin-dip that evoked a curtsey; Allegre and Galeni saluted. Gregor returned a fitting Imperial nod.

"Ivan!" This was one Voice that seemed unapologetically glad to find him; Gregor's embrace was sincere. "They told me you were drawn up from the tomb alive, but I had to see for myself. Lady Tej. I'm so glad." He bowed over her hand; she managed a reasonably graceful obeisance.

His eye fell on Simon, watching this with his mouth gone wry. "And Simon. What the *hell*?" The *Why was I blindsided?* look was very clear in the Emperor's eye, which Ivan could only be grateful was not turned on him. Yet.

Simon gave him a beleaguered head tilt. "You know that long lunch appointment I made with you for tomorrow?"

"Yes . . . ?"

"I should have made it for yesterday."

Gregor accepted this with an extremely provisional nod. "We'll discuss that. Later."

Gregor's gaze swept over the disrupted landscape. "General Allegre . . ." Allegre steeled himself. "Good work." The general let out a pent breath as Gregor went on, "I'd like to have a personal word with your commander of engineers, if you please."

Allegre went over to the command post and fetched the man, who'd been directing the platoon of engineers spread all over the site through the portable comconsoles there. Ivan recognized him: Colonel Otto, one of the top men in the Vorbarr Sultana local command. Like Galeni, he had a doctorate tucked away under his military rank. He, too, was in uniform—sensible black fatigues under his greatcoat, with proper engineering mud splashed about, thick on his engineer's boots. He accepted his emperor's personal congratulations on his night's work with a pleased but slightly distracted expression.

Released from the Imperial Attention, Otto took Ivan aside. "Vorpatril. What can you tell me about this so-called Mycoborer shit we're dealing with? That woman, Star, wasn't too helpful."

"It eats big holes right through dirt. Branching semi-randomly. I think it turns the inorganics into its tunnel walls, but I'm not sure. You need to catch up with Lady ghem Estif, before noon by preference, and don't let her snow you—requisition a high-powered biologist from the Imperial Science Institute when you go. She has more samples—be sure to confiscate them and get them into the hands of the I.S.I. As a construction application, it could be worth millions."

"As a tool? Or as a weapon?"

Ivan sighed. "As a tool—it needs development. As a weapon—it seems good to go. But you *really* need the I.S.I. boffins on it."

Otto's mouth twisted up in joyless understanding.

Allegre, his hand to his earbug, came over to them. "Otto. There's a Captain Roux at the security perimeter, one of your boys. Do you need him now?"

The new security perimeter, added due to Gregor's, Ivan hoped temporary, complicating presence. Gregor was over having some possibly stern words with Simon and Lady Alys; Tej was listening intently, and putting in a brave gloss now and then.

"Yes, I do! Let him through," said Otto.

If mud made the engineer, Roux had to be some sort of boy genius, Ivan thought, as the captain cruised up and quickly dismounted from a float bike. Otto looked merely artistically flecked, by comparison. The salutes exchanged between Roux and his superior were almost as perfunctory as those of ImpSec analysts, as they got down quickly to business. Gregor, noting this arrival, strolled near enough to eavesdrop, but not enough to force an interruption.

"We finally traced that damned storm sewer, Colonel," Roux reported, slightly out of breath. "It empties into the river about a kilometer below the Star Bridge. It was blocked way the hell up; but it became unblocked in a hurry about an hour ago. We lost our remote probe—swept out in the mudflow. Thank God we hadn't sent any men in yet. We were estimating efflux at one to three cubic meters a second."

Allegre, coming over in time to hear the tail end of this, said, "One to three cubic meters a minute are going to drain the water backup fairly quickly, yes?"

Roux glanced up, took in the eye-pins and the general's rank tabs, and managed a normal salute, courteously returned. "Not per minute, sir. Per *second*. And not rainwater. Mud. It's like—it's like a *mud cannon*. The stream was still shooting straight out about ten meters before it arced into the river, when I left."

Gregor, edging closer at this fascinating word-picture, stopped and looked at something across the street, his head tilting slightly.

Allegre's brow wrinkled. "So where is it all coming from?"

"That's a good question, and we'll address ourselves to it as soon as we've dealt with your last five urgent requests, General," said Colonel Otto, looking harassed. "Now, if you'll just let my people get on with their jobs..."

"Guy," called Gregor, still staring. "Has ImpSec HQ always been sort of...tilted up on one side? Or is that an optical illusion?"

Allegre looked around; his gaze grew arrested.

Gregor went on, uncertainly, "I'd not seen it before from this angle of view. Maybe it's just more of Dono Vorrutyer's subtle disproportions devised from his cracked theories on the psychology of architecture."

Ivan wheeled around as well. So did everyone else. Simon, Alys clutching his arm, and Tej came over to Ivan's side.

Ivan blinked. He squinted. Gregor wasn't wrong; the left side of the ImpSec building did look slightly higher than the right. Or...the right side lower than the left...?

In the courtyard, visible through the open iron gates, a lone cobblestone erupted out of its matrix and bounced, clacking. In a moment, a few more followed, looking and sounding like popcorn just starting to pop. Big, granite chunks of popcorn. A soldier crossing the courtyard yelped and dodged this unexpected, knee-capping bombardment.

A loud crack; a visible fissure propagated up the unclimbable front steps, zigzagging. With a horrible, grinding shriek, the bronze doors topping the high front steps twisted slightly apart.

"What the hell...?" said Allegre, starting forward.

Otto grabbed his arm and held him back. "Wait, sir...!"

"Oh, it's straightening up," said Tej. "Or...not..."

"No..." said Otto, his engineer's eye sweeping the crenellated roofline. "The other side is sinking. Too."

From both side doors, an efflux of men in green uniforms began, at a rate, Ivan guessed, of about a cubic meter a second.

"They're leaving their posts?" said Allegre, caught somewhere between approval and anguish.

Simon, his teeth pressed into his lower lip, released the stress to say, "At a guess, those would be the fellows who grew up in earthquake country, Guy." And after another minute, under his breath, as the evacuation continued more sporadically, "The ones still inside, you'll want to commend. The ones outside, those are the ones I'd promote..."

Allegre moved away, speaking harshly into his pickup, pausing to listen to his earbug. Colonel Otto, after one more wild-eyed stare, ran for his bank of comconsoles.

Simon's lips parted and his eyes grew big as the building continued, very slowly, to sink. It went as a unit, nothing collapsing; old Dono-the-Architect had been deranged, not incompetent. But inexorably, in the course of the next few minutes, in a silence only broken by under-voiced swearing nearby and a few cries from beyond the spike-topped walls, its first story was entirely swallowed by the earth. The bronze doors hit ground level and kept going. The frieze of pressed gargoyles above them sank from view as if being dragged down to their old hell. The descent finally slowed at a point where occupants on the third floor could have stepped out of their windows to the ground, if there had been any windows. A few men rappelled off the roof, instead.

"Well," said Gregor, in a choked voice. "There's...a surprise."

A startling cackle broke from Simon's lips. He clapped a hand over his mouth, and managed in a more measured voice, "My God, I hope no one has been injured." Except then he cackled again, louder. Lady Alys gripped his arm in worry.

Gregor's fretful armsmen finally managed to drag him away from this riveting show and back to his groundcar. Surrounded by its black-and-silver-clad outriders, it rose on its fans and slowly pulled away. Ivan thought he saw a familiar face pressed to the canopy, looking backward in still-stunned fascination, as it rounded the corner on the route back to the Residence.

"We aren't doing anything useful here, Simon-love," said Lady Alys, after a few more silent, staring minutes. "Perhaps we should go home. Ivan—now you're rescued—Tej, will you come with us? We want to hear more about your, your ordeal. And I'm sure anyone who wants us will be able to find us there." She cast one more astounded glance back over her shoulder at the...the upper half of ImpSec Headquarters. Emergency teams of every description were thick on the ground now, arguing with each other about access.

Said Simon, faintly, "I'm sure they will," and allowed himself to be drawn off.

Chapter Twenty-Four

Tej had the impression, that afternoon, that ImpSec would have preferred to drop a giant, concealing tarp over their whole two-block area of Vorbarr Sultana, but it was much too late. Between the dramatic—not to mention noisy, muddy, and public—engineering rescue, the rumors of almost-stolen treasure, crime lords, off-world invasion, secret bombings, ugly kidnappings of beautiful women, smugglers, and much, much more, all playing out in the Eye of the Imperium that was the Old Town capital—and all of it overtopped by the swallowing of one of the most notorious structures on the planet *by* the planet—about the only thing the Barrayaran government managed to keep a lid on was the details of the Mycoborer itself.

"The Arquas had better hope Gregor's damage-control people succeed, on that one," Ivan Xav advised Tej. "All the rest could just get them jailed. Barrayar is still traumatized from some of the Cetagandan weaponized biologicals and chemical warfare experiments during the Occupation. The news that you all have managed to release a mutant alien fungus into *our biosphere* could get you torn limb from limb. The Dismemberment of Mad Emperor Yuri would be nothing to it. The angry mobs would fill the city. They'd tear the *pieces* to pieces. And the military couldn't stop them because most of the military would be *joining* them."

"But the Mycoborer was from Earth," Tej offered hesitantly. "Not Cetagandan at all. Old Earth is practically the definition of *not alien*. And Grandmama *said* it was safe."

"Big, big heaving mobs," said Ivan Xav. "As far as the eye can see."

Simon Illyan nodded in reluctant agreement.

The Arqua clan was released from ImpMil that evening with clean bills of health, and returned not to their hotel but to an empty apartment a few floors down from Lady Alys's penthouse. Uniformed ImpSec guards stood at the foyer doors, with more patrolling downstairs. The Arquas' things, minus all communications devices, arrived much later, transported from their hotel after a detour for close examination by whatever high-clearance security people could be spared at present. Ivan Xav wondered aloud just how many Winterfair leaves had been summarily canceled over this, and indicated that this grudge, too, would be added on the debit side of the House Cordonah ledger, at least in the dark matter column.

They were not yet officially arrested, though Tej heard that Ser Imola had been, satisfactorily. The legal phrase for their own state was *detained at the Emperor's pleasure*, a term that had Pidge wrinkling her nose and, conducted by an impassive sentry, ascending to Lady Alys's flat to look it up. Ivan Xav explained, morosely, that it would more accurately be described as *detained at the Emperor's displeasure*. But it seemed it trumped, at least temporarily, their visa termination, though Tej gathered that deportation on that point could be brought back into play at any time.

Requests for media interviews penetrated despite all the sequestration.

Pidge said hesitantly, "It might be a way to start to put a good spin on all this. Pave the way for our defense."

"I," said Lady ghem Estif austerely, "would be more than *happy* to give this benighted world a piece of my mind."

Baron and Baronne Cordonah looked at each other.

"No interviews," said the Baronne. "Not one word."

"Right," sighed Dada.

Evacuation of critical equipment and files continued out the roof of ImpSec HQ, under tight military escort, to be temporarily relocated in an assortment of nearby government buildings appropriated for this emergency. Illyan, wincing at the pictures in passing, muttered only, "God, but the evidence rooms are going to be a bitch. When they get down to them."

The edifice's ongoing descent, it was said, had slowed to an almost imperceptible rate. But by midnight, Lord Dono the Architect's masterpiece had sunk to the fourth floor.

Simon kept his appointment the next day with Emperor Gregor. He returned over an hour late.

"It is not often," he remarked, either to Lady Alys or the air generally, it was hard to tell, "that Gregor permits himself the self-indulgence of sarcasm. I could see that it was very relieving for him." With an added mutter of, "We live to serve," he disappeared alone into his study and did not come out till dinner.

When the Imperial Accounting Office auditors inventorying the old Cetagandan bunker—under the general direction and command of Commodore Duv Galeni, pulled off his departmental duties for the special assignment—reached an estimate of eleven hundred million marks, they stopped publicly reporting.

"What," said Pidge, peering over Ivan Xav's shoulder, "is an *Imperial Court of Inquiry*"—she squinted—"*most secret*?"

"You could think of it as a subpoena," said Ivan Xav. "With fangs. But it would be...be..."

"A charming understatement?" suggested Tej, peering over his other shoulder.

"No," said Ivan Xav, in a distant tone, "not charming..."

Ivan had looked forward to escorting Tej on her first trip to the Imperial Residence, but not under these circumstances. She stared up apprehensively at the sprawling pile, a great irregular rectangle of four-to-six-story-high wings with odd inner links, in style a bit like Vorkosigan House bloated by a factor of four but with modern additions dating back to one postwar rebuild or another. The East Portico was one of the older, more ornate and impressive entrances. Mamere's groundcar was just finishing disgorging her and Simon and the senior Arquas (and one ghem

Estif) as Ivan pulled up behind it in his two-seater; they caught up with the group at the double doors, to be herded through by Gregor's own majordomo. The man's expression this morning was grim and suspicious, though as he caught sight of Simon it took refuge in very, very blank. Ivan won *grim and annoyed.*

Followed by a pair of Residence guards, to pick off stragglers presumably, the majordomo led around and, unusually, down. Ivan had not often seen this subterranean section of the Residence, devoted to a pocket of practical conference rooms, as it was never open during the assorted public ceremonies or festivities, such as the annual Imperial Winterfair Ball coming up soon. The chamber into which they were gated felt more like a small, if unusually well-appointed, university lecture hall than a courtroom. At the front was a lectern and a comconsole table, and more seats were arrayed in a semicircle of gently ascending rows. It might have held forty people in a crush. Which this was apparently not to be, despite the milling other-Arquas-plus-Byerly who had arrived just before them. A table at the side was set up with, mercifully, coffee, teas, and an assortment of pastries; Ivan wasn't sure if it represented hospitality or a sign that this was going to be a very long session.

Ivan made certain Tej had coffee with cream—she declined the pastries with a wan smile, not a good sign—and edged over to By. "Did you get a personal invitation, or are you here as an ImpSec plainclothes guard?" he muttered.

"Both," By muttered back. "Courtesy of Gregor *and* Allegre. Though I've had my own debriefings with ImpSec."

"Plural? They had time?"

"Oh, I'm special this week." By grimaced. "And not in a good way. I *told* them I needed backup—never mind."

And then it was time for everyone to hastily put down their drinks and swallow their last bites as the majordomo announced simply, "Your attention, for Emperor Gregor Vorbarra."

Ivan, after much dithering, had chosen a good suit instead of his military dress greens for this; Gregor, curiously, had made a similar choice, severe in dark blue. He was trailed by his senior armsman and his chief secretary, who went to set things up at the lectern. Gregor accepted assorted uncertain head-ducks with a wave of his hand that seemed to say, *Yes, but not yet;* the armsman hurried to supply him with coffee and, Ivan saw with a twinge of guilt, a couple of painkiller tablets, which he swigged down before turning to take command of the front of the room. The rest were directed to seats: the seniors in the front row, along with Pidge, Tej, and Ivan at the end where he could see everyone without craning his neck, much; and Byerly and the remainder—Rish, Star, Pearl, Emerald, Amiri and Jet—in the next. The armsman took up a parade rest at the side of the room where he could keep an eye on everyone; the secretary seated himself at the comconsole table, preparing to record everything.

Gregor set down his coffee on the lectern and turned to stare unamiably out over his captive audience.

"There are a number of interlocking jurisdictions and issues, legal and practical, involved in last weekend's events in my twice-capital. First are the questions of crimes, misdemeanors, and the creation of public hazards in the city of Vorbarr Sultana and the Vorbarra District. For this, the highest legal venue is the Vorbarra District Count's Court, of which I am, as Count Vorbarra, senior judge and final arbiter. Next, what might be construed as an attack on a critical Imperial military installation, for which, as Commander-in-Chief of the Barrayaran Military Service, I am again the ultimate authority. And finally, there are matters involving the welfare of the Imperium as a whole, for which, as Emperor, I am—again—finally responsible.

"It is my intention to stack up all of these jurisdictions"—he didn't say, *in one big heap*, but Ivan fancied he could hear it—"and get through the major issues this morning all at once. In short, I offer you a Star Chamber. You have a choice whether to accept this offer and my authority, and abide by the outcome, or not. You may have a moment to consult among yourselves before you reply."

Pidge rose and darted to the senior Arquas; Gregor went aside for more coffee and a bite of pastry. Ivan could only think, *Yes, for the love of mercy get your blood sugar up, sire.* He joined the huddle. Simon and Mamere, he noted, stayed seated.

Pidge was saying, "If we want to hold off retribution for as long as possible with delaying actions, now is our chance. You know I had the sequence of court fights all mapped out—"

"If I may advise?" said Ivan, pitching his voice low. Shiv put out a hand to quell Pidge, who scowled at the interruption.

"Please do," said the Baronne.

"About ten thousand people are lined up behind you competing for a slice of Gregor's time, but he's offering you this morning on a platter. He won't make that offer twice. Also, his clothes."

"What about them?" asked Shiv, his heavy face dark in bafflement.

"Signal. If he'd planned to go after you about the local issues—including that damned Mycoborer—he'd have come dressed in his Vorbarra House black and silver. If he meant to crush you for what you did to his ImpSec headquarters, he'd be in his Service dress greens. But he's wearing his politician-suit, instead. That means he wants something he doesn't already have. That means there may be the offer of what you might call a deal, depending. If you don't waste his time, and if you don't piss him off."

"How does one piss him off?" asked Shiv, eyes narrowing.

"Well, wasting his time would be a good way to start."

"And how can you *tell*?" asked Tej, with an anxious glance past his shoulder at the podium. "If he's pissed off, I mean."

"Um..." Ivan hesitated. "You all probably can't. But ask me."

He backed away, to give the Arquas one last chance to confer privately. To his intense relief, Shiv turned and stated, "House Cordonah chooses to abide by the authority of this Star Chamber."

Lady Alys didn't say a word, but her hand pressed to her lips looked to Ivan like hope rewarded. Which made him *really* wonder what all those all-senior-female confabs among Moira, Udine, and Alys had covered, these past few days.

The secretary glanced at a signal from his wristcom, then rose to go to the chamber door and receive from the majordomo a new delegation of men. Ivan recognized them all.

Duv Galeni was wearing his dress greens, all the polished Imperial officer this morning; General Allegre likewise, as was Colonel Otto, too secure in his expertise to be daunted by his surroundings, and entirely mud-free. Equally secure in his expertise, not to mention his ego, was Dr. Vaughn Weddell from the Imperial Science Institute, one of their major bio-boffins—molecular, xeno, genetic, all of the above. He was followed by I.S.I. Senior Administrator Susan Allegre, possibly there as his handler, as he usually needed one, possibly to track and gate any other demands on the Institute that might emerge this morning; at any rate, when they were directed to seats, she went with Weddell and not her husband.

When the room had settled once more, Gregor continued, "There are two possible approaches to solving a dilemma, in justice or elsewhere; begin with the facts, and follow out their logic where it leads one, or begin with the desired outcome, and reason backward to the necessary steps to achieve it. We shall see if it is possible to do both, and meet in the middle. To begin at the beginning, with some anchoring facts—Commodore Galeni, were you able to find out how the information about the Cetagandan bunker and its contents were first lost to ImpSec? And the source of Sergeant Abelard and his bomb? We know his fate."

"Yes, sire. I made considerable progress on both questions yesterday and last night."

Since his last report, in other words, so some of this was going to be new to Gregor as well. A wave of the Emperor's hand directed Duv to the front; Gregor leaned on the podium, and Duv took up a practiced lecturer's stance beside the comconsole table. His eye took in his audience almost as curiously as his audience's eyes took in him.

"In examining what documents and records remain from the construction of ImpSec Headquarters, almost eighty years ago, I was able to trace the officer who signed off on the bunker inspection, a Captain Geo Pharos. He was ImpSec: he had as his listed assistant a sergeant of engineers, Vlad Norman. One month later, both men, along with three civilian employees, were killed in that on-site construction accident where, according to the subsequent engineering reports, two floors in progress collapsed due to incorrect-to-spec sizing and improper installation of the bracing connectors. *Buggered to fit*, was the, er, engineering term underlined in the holograph report. Twice."

In the third row, Colonel Otto, brows rising with keen interest, nodded; Galeni cast him an acknowledging sort of analyst's salute.

Galeni continued, "For which unauthorized shortcut Emperor Yuri, on his architect's recommendation, had the construction boss hanged, and bracing on the girders and connectors throughout triply reinforced, but that's another tale."

"Ah, those were the days," muttered Otto; Ivan couldn't tell if it was with irony or approval.

"There are two possible explanations for the lapse at the time in revealing the, if I may say it, extraordinary contents of that bunker. One, Pharos and Norman may have simply blown off the

inspection, due to laziness or time pressures, assuming that the
then-thirty-year-old bunker held nothing of interest or danger. The
project was already over budget and late—hence, apparently, the
business with the girder connections—so this hypothesis cannot
be totally ruled out. Or two, they discovered the contents but
chose to conceal the news, hoping to come back secretly later and
make some private profit for themselves. Norman's prior military
records are unexceptionable, but the temptation, as we have discovered, was large. Pharos has possibilities in this direction—things
around Yuri were already getting worrisome by then, which he
would have been in position to see at close range, so he might
have been driven to this alternate method of providing for his
future by either greed or fear. Or both, of course."

"Do you have a favored explanation yet?" inquired Gregor.

Galeni shook his head. "The most interesting question of history
is always, *What were these people thinking?* But I'm afraid it's often
also the most elusive. Unless some new documentation surfaces in
my searches, that's as far as I can honestly take the tale."

"Very good," said Gregor, meaning, probably, a slightly disappointed *Very well.* "And Abelard? I should mention, in a personal
communication I received from the Viceroy of Sergyar last night,
Aral says he doesn't remember ever ordering anyone to blow up
Vordarian's ImpSec building. Such a decision ought to have made
it up to his level, he said, but in the confusion of the times, it's
perfectly possible it didn't. And, ah, a few other remarks about
excessive initiative in subordinates, but they're not pertinent here."

Galeni had come alert, but now his shoulders slumped slightly.
"I was hoping he could clarify—oh, well. At least we know it
couldn't have been ordered by Negri against Vordarian, because
Negri was dead on the first day."

Illyan cleared his throat, and spoke up. "Actually, some such
beyond-the-grave sleeper order from Chief Negri would have been
perfectly possible. Back then." His hand and Lady Alys's found
each other, down between their seats.

Galeni appeared to suffer a brief pang from having what might
have been his only certainty plucked from him. "Ah. Well. In that
case. Abelard had an exemplary record prior to the Pretendership.
That . . . gets us no forwarder, because it's quite clear that many
officers and men at the time did honestly think Vordarian might
be the best thing for Barrayar."

"Hence Regent Vorkosigan's generous pardons, after," Gregor put in.

Galeni nodded warily. "Abelard was a senior guard on ImpSec HQ itself; he certainly knew the territory he was, er, under. His records break off abruptly at the start of the hostilities, and don't take up again till after, during the cleanup, when he was finally listed as missing. Missing, period, mind you—neither 'in action' nor 'absent without leave.' He's certainly not accused of desertion. At this point, I would want to turn his remains and those of his equipment over to a forensic pathologist, to look for any other physical clues—the nature of the bomb or the construction of the tunnel in which he was found might have helped—but, ah."

"Indeed," sighed Gregor, with a less-than-pleased glance at the Arquas assembled.

"Is that pissed?" Tej whispered in Ivan's ear.

"Not yet," he whispered back. "Sh."

"So what's your best guess?" said Gregor. "As a former ImpSec analyst."

Galeni suppressed a pained look. Ivan wondered if he was reciting, *Accuracy, brevity, clarity* to himself, possibly with an added, *pick the best two out of three.* "My *feeling*"—and his emphasis suggested his low opinion of that word—"was that he was probably one of the many men cut off from their units, who re-sorted themselves as they could find each other, and prosecuted the war as best they could on their own. That still doesn't prove for which side. Given more time, my next suggested direction of inquiry would be to send field agents to locate as many of his old mates still alive as we could, and interview them."

Ivan glanced back at Allegre; his slight wince suggested he was praying, *Please Gregor, not this week.*

Gregor may have heard that prayer; in any case, he went on. "And how is emptying the bunker coming along?"

Pidge shot to her feet. "May I note a point of purely Barrayaran law. Your, er . . . sir." She'd at least retained Ivan's hasty instruction, *No, don't call him sire; he's not your liege-lord, so he's not your sire.* In any case, Gregor granted her a curt nod. She went on, "Barrayaran law supports the claim of a ten-percent finder's fee for lost items, including historical artifacts confiscated by District or the Imperial governments."

"Hell, Pidge, that's meant for *lost wallets*," muttered Ivan, under his breath. He thought only Tej heard him, by the squeeze on his arm, but Pidge glanced his way in irritation before she went on more firmly.

"House Cordonah, jointly, wishes to put in such a claim upon the contents of Lady ghem Estif's old workplace. Because without us, it would never have been found."

"At this time," said Illyan, not quite in an undervoice.

"Intact," countered Pidge. "Given yet more time, who knows who else might have found and raided it before you people ever got around to looking?"

Gregor held up a palm. "I am aware of the precedent, Baronette. We will return to the point later."

Collective or Imperial *We*? In any case, Pidge, in a moment of blessed acumen, nodded and sat down.

Gregor said, "Continue, please, Commodore."

Galeni gave a short nod. "I've placed Professora Helen Vorthys and her picked team of conservators in charge of all papers, documents, and data devices, the last of which we cleared out yesterday and sent to a secured location at the Imperial University. Sorting and preservation has only just started."

Gregor waved a hand, *And...?*

"Our best guess of the value of the rest of the items inventoried and removed so far—as of this morning; I checked on the way here—is"—Galeni cleared his throat, unaccountably dry—"three point nine billion marks."

Make that *accountably dry*, Ivan corrected his observation. Gregor, who had hitched himself up on the edge of the comconsole table, nearly fell off it. Shiv Arqua rubbed his forehead, his face screwing up like a man suffering from the sharpest twinge of existential pain in history.

"Almost four billion marks, Duv?" choked Gregor. "Really?"

"So far. We hope to have cleared the upper floor by the end of the week. I have absolutely no idea what we'll find on the lower one."

"More of the same, as I recall," murmured Lady ghem Estif.

Silence fell throughout the room, as everyone present paused for a bit of simple arithmetic.

"I would note in passing," observed Duv, recovering his driest professorial tones, "that the current value of the art and artifacts is very much higher than the, what one might call street value, would have been a hundred years ago. Appreciation, in both senses. Yet quite a number of people must have known what was in there, because it certainly took more than one man to fill it up. I really have no idea why no Cetagandan entrepreneur has been back since."

Lady ghem Estif gave a muffled sniff, dulcetly, and waited.

Gregor opened his hand to her, a bit ironically. "Enlighten us, milady, if you please."

"Because most of the items were the property of the ruling ghem-junta, and most of the ghem-junta were executed upon their return to Eta Ceta," said Lady ghem Estif. She added, "They *had* planned to be back in person, of course."

Ivan had no idea if it was the historian or the security analyst ascendant in his hungry tones, but Duv said, "I *do* hope you'll have time to chat with me later, Lady ghem Estif."

She held up her own hands, palms out, in a gesture that had little to do with surrender. "That will not be up to me."

"Thank you, Commodore Galeni, that will do for now," said Gregor. "Colonel Otto, do you have a, perhaps, fuller and more detailed account than your preliminary one of why my Imperial Security building is now largely an underground installation? From a technical perspective."

Since Ivan recalled, among the cries coming from the command post the other day, some anguished engineering bellows of *It sank! It sank! The sucker just sank!* he suspected Otto did.

Galeni stood down and Otto came up.

"Sire." His nod to Gregor was very respectful; his glower at the Arquas, not. "We're still modifying details of our picture as new data come in, but I think what I have here is a correct general outline." He shoved a data chip into the read-slot on the com-console table; a large-scale, three-dimensional image in outlines of colored light sprang into view above the vid plate.

Otto gestured with a lightstick. "Ground-lines in dark brown, surrounding buildings in light brown. ImpSec building in green." All six floors and the several subbasements, a boxy cage of cold-light-hued lines. "The bunker." Another short stack of boxes in blue, catty-corner to the one in green. "The old storm sewer." A translucent tube of red light, running at a diagonal far under the street. "We suspect Sergeant Abelard's old tunnel might have had its start-point from the storm sewer, by the way. It's possible that a patch there might have provided a weak point"—a darker red blob, with uncertain dotted outlines—"that blew out when the bomb"—an ominous purple pinpoint, accurately placed as far as Ivan could tell—"went off."

"As much of the remaining Mycoborer tunnels as we could map." Starting as a solid yellow tube descending from the garage under the office building across the back corner; a second, solid end snaking back from the vestibule hugged up next to the bunker.

"Our current best guess of what existed in between the two ends prior to the bomb blast." Dotted yellow outlines, branching and rebranching directly under the ImpSec subbasements.

"The Mycoborer walls appear to cure very hard, strong in compression but weak in tension, and brittle. At some point during the firefight between the criminals and the ImpSec guards who pursued them underground, someone's stray stunner beam struck the old bomb on the tunnel floor, setting it off." Scrupulously, Otto's picture did not suggest whose stunner this triggering energy pulse came from. A flare of purple light filled the tunnel network. "The air and gases in the tunnels transmitted a strong concussion to the walls throughout; we don't yet know if there was further chemical reaction. The stretching in tension cracked and in some places shattered the walls, both visible and micro cracks. At the same time, the weak portion of the storm sewer abutting or closely abutting the Mycoborer tunnel blew out, a section of the drain just down from the breach collapsed, the water so dammed diverted through the breach, and the shattered tunnel began to rapidly fill. Water not being compressible, this actually helped keep the network from collapsing for quite some time. Water from the ongoing heavy rain drainage further penetrated and weakened the cracked walls, and began mixing under considerable pressure with the formerly dry and solid subsoil. In effect, the branching Mycoborer tunnel turned into a giant sponge under the ImpSec Headquarters." A bulky, irregular region under the green cage filled with red light. "The pressure mounted." The red light grew more intense; the sponge swelled.

Both Illyan and Allegre had exactly the same expressions of horrified fascination on their faces, Ivan noted in a brief look around.

"At the time that my engineers dug down to the bunker roof with grav-lifters"—a white circle appeared on the ground level of the park, and grew downward to the blue box in a neat cone—"possibly at the moment that we cut through the roof, the storm sewer unplugged itself. I suspect, but can't prove yet, that the vibrations from our rescue work might have helped that along. In any case, the sewer unplugged and began draining the Mycoborer tunnel network of what was now a hell of a lot of liquid mud. The ImpSec building directly above acted as a giant weight, compressing the sponge and expressing its contents out the newly opened exit channel."

Pulses of red light marched down the storm sewer.

"And the rest"—Otto sighed—"we all witnessed." Slowly, as the red sponge flattened, its filaments collapsing, the green cage began to sink below the brown ground lines.

"How far down d'you think we'll end up?" asked General Allegre, from his back row.

"Not much farther, I think. A man should just about be able to jump off the roof to the ground. Without breaking his legs, that is."

A little silence followed this word-picture. If Allegre contemplated suicide over all of this, he was going to have to find another method than the traditional parapet, Ivan reflected. Gregor stirred himself and broke the hypnotized hush with, "Thank you, Colonel Otto, that was very clear."

"Thank you, sire. But the big question I want answered"—he pointed to the sewer line—"we know damned well that bits of Mycoborer tunnel walls had to have been mixed with the mud. Which has mostly ended up in the river. *What's it doing downstream?*" His glare at the Arquas was impartial, but far from impassive.

"For the answer to that question, I *hope* Dr. Weddell will have more information than this time yesterday. Doctor?" At Gregor's gesture, Otto stood down and Weddell took his place.

Weddell was a distinguished-looking researcher in his sixties. His past, Ivan had reason to know, was considerably more speckled than his appearance would suggest, but that didn't make him less able to do his job. Possibly the reverse.

Weddell cleared his throat, nervously. "Well, sire. As we all know, absence of evidence is not evidence of absence. Nevertheless, my field teams have not *yet* found live Mycoborer cells downstream from the capital. We have, on the other hand, positively identified a few fragments of former tunnel wall, and if the one is present, the other should be, too. One bright spot—the live cells we've been studying do not appear to like an environment of salt water. So if any reach the sea, it is unlikely they will survive there."

"Told you *that*," murmured Lady ghem Estif. "Three days ago." Weddell gave her a rather driven look.

"While I do strongly recommend we continue to monitor, it is my opinion that the Mycoborer is less a hazard than several other biological nightmares you Barrayarans have lived with for years, not excepting this planet's own native ecosystem. Prudence yes, panic no. Add it to the list and go on, I'd say."

Tej, listening intently, blinked. "Hey," she whispered to Ivan. "That fellow's a Jacksonian. Or he was."

"I know," Ivan whispered back. "So does Gregor. Don't tell anyone else."

Gregor eyed Weddell. "Would you, personally, today, drink water taken from the river downstream of Vorbarr Sultana?" In his present mood Gregor was not above personally testing that very question, Ivan suspected. On Weddell, that was. Did he have a liter bottle tucked away behind the podium?

"Yes," said Weddell, steadily, "if it was first boiled to destroy all the eighteen other potentially lethal pathogens usually present. Normal local water treatment should protect your subjects." And anyone stupid enough to drink untreated water on this planet deserved their removal from the gene pool? Weddell, in Ivan's prior experience of the man, was perfectly capable of thinking just that, but also smart enough not to say so. Here, at any rate.

Gregor turned his head. "Dr. Allegre, has that assertion about the water treatment been tested?"

She sat up and responded, "It . . . could easily be done. It sounds plausible."

"In other words, no. Please have your people conduct appropriate tests immediately, and report back as soon as possible."

"Yes, sire." She bent her head to her wristcom.

"Very well, Dr. Weddell. Continue to monitor closely, yes." Gregor waved him back to his seat by the administrator; some heads-together conversation seemed to go, *Good, you didn't screw up*, and *So how about our funding?* Otto looked as if he didn't believe a word of it; Dr. Allegre would presumably pacify the equally dubious General Allegre, later.

Gregor stared at the rows of Arquas; the Arquas stared back. Shiv did *impassive* very well indeed. Udine threaded her fingers through her short hair. Lady ghem Estif looked willing to match her one-hundred-and-thirty years against anything Barrayar could throw at her.

"Now—in my third hat—"

But not talking through it, no, not Gregor . . .

"—we come to larger Imperial concerns."

Shiv's dark eyes narrowed in a sudden intensity to nearly match Gregor's.

"As you should realize, Barrayar has no practical interest in aggressive ventures in Jacksonian local space. But as you should be even more keenly aware, all bets are off if the Cetagandan Empire makes such a move, directly or through puppets, to gain control of your wormhole exits. My analysts posit that House Prestene is currently such a puppet, contemplating an attempt on a wormhole monopoly."

Shiv rumbled, "Other House alliances, however temporary, have traditionally resisted such attempts. Repeatedly."

Gregor returned, levelly, "Two down, three to go."

Shiv shrugged. "Fell is a tough nut to crack."

"Baron Fell is still very aged. At last report."

Udine murmured, "True."

Gregor didn't blink. "As it happens, Barrayar could use an ally in the Whole. One ally would in fact be better than five, due to, ah, reciprocal destabilization issues viz Cetaganda. For which a *covert* ally would be even more use."

"For that ten-percent finder's fee," mused Shiv, "you might find more than one House for sale."

"Yes, but no amount of money can make one stay bought. Who does not freely choose to."

"Hm."

Gregor held up a finger. "Ten percent—less expenses."

Shiv's brows rose in inquiry.

"By some miracle," Gregor continued, "there was no loss of life in last weekend's disasters."

"Are you saying you wouldn't trade in lives?"

Gregor gave him a cool look. "On the contrary. I trade in lives every day. They are the coin in which Barrayar has paid for my mistakes since I was twenty years old. But it does mean that the first item on the deductions list will not be generous survivors' pensions."

"I see," said Shiv, and "Do go on," said Udine.

"So instead, I would begin with all the operational expenses of the last week, and onwards, that this emergency has entailed."

Shiv was drawn into a *seems fair* kind of nod; a frugal wifely hand on his arm restrained further premature expression, and he settled back.

"We also, it would seem, require a new ImpSec building."

Shiv's teeth set slightly; Simon, by his widening eyes, looked as if he were stifling a cry of vicarious joy. Guy Allegre, who had shifted to the edge of his seat at the new, wider turn in the conversation, sat back in his own *Do go on* mode.

"The old building is ... extremely hard to value, in its current location. Some would consider it a priceless historical relic."

"Betan dollar?" came a low, imploring mutter from the other end of the row.

Gregor managed to ignore the interjection. "In any case, it certainly seems wise to escrow some amount of funding for its eventual cleanup or disposal."

"Mm," said Shiv.

"Much more critical is the need to escrow an appropriate amount for any cleanup of Mycoborer contamination that may yet be found. That will *not* be underfunded."

Both I.S.I. people perked up.

This won a pained grunt from Shiv. But—apparently he'd learned something about Barrayar, in this visit—no argument. Because of all the choices of points to dig in his heels about, that would have been the most disastrous. Even more offensive than quibbling over the survivors' pensions.

A very small smile curled Gregor's lips. "It will not be all take and no give, from my, er, Imperial hands, however. To help speed your and your family's return to the Whole, I propose to throw in, gratis, your own jumpship. Unarmed, but, I am assured, speedy." Gregor gave a general wave of his index finger orbit-ward.

This surprised a choke from Byerly. "Vormercier's yacht? You'd foist that—" he cut himself off.

"The décor, I am given to understand, is questionable; but the mechanics are sound. My inspecting engineers have guaranteed it. Vorrutyer here has traveled in it, and can so testify."

"Yeah, it...goes."

So long as it goes away, the quirk of Gregor's eyebrows indicated. "I expect you can get some entertainment out of its resale, later."

Shiv tapped his thick fingers together, looking amused for almost the first time this morning. "I'll look forward to that."

"The other gift I mean to give to take with you is—my personal liaison. An experienced ImpSec surveillance agent, and, as I understand it, very nearly a son-in-law. Since, I believe, you have some preferences for keeping important transactions in the family." Gregor opened his hand to Byerly, sitting in the second row next to Rish. She twisted to look at him in surprise.

This obviously wasn't the first time By had heard this proposal from Gregor—when the hell had they had time to meet?—but it was plain that he was still digesting it. "It'll be all...new," he said weakly.

Rish, recovering her composure, remarked, "I could probably help you out with that, By. Reciprocity, after all." Shiv, turning around, eyed her in tolerant speculation.

Allegre put in, as a kind of backhanded encouragement, "Your Domestic Affairs handler has been afraid you were getting stale, Vorrutyer. He thought you needed a new challenge."

No, I don't! Byerly mouthed to his lap, shoulders hunching slightly. But he didn't dare look around at Allegre while he did.

Allegre went on, "I'll leave you and the Arquas to evolve your own plausible cover story, but at a glance, you seem spoiled for choice." He managed a thin smile for Rish.

Shiv and Udine looked at each other. Udine glanced up. "May the two of us be excused to confer in private for a moment?"

"Of course," said Gregor.

They retreated to the hallway; not exactly private, there were guards out there as well, but out of earshot of the room. They were gone a long time, during which there was a lot of shifting and stretching and a run on the coffee and remaining pastries, and on the adjoining lav. Allegre and Simon teamed up to have Colonel Otto rerun his colorful visual aid a few times, at various speeds. It was really hard to read Simon's emotions, but he didn't seem to get tired of the show.

At length, Shiv and Udine returned, to take up a united stance before Gregor.

"Gregor Vorbarra," said Shiv, "I do believe you are a worthy grandson of your famous grandfather Ezar." He stuck out his hand. "You have your deal."

Meticulously, Gregor shook each of their hands in turn. "Baron. Baronne." He couldn't quite seem to bring himself to say *thank you*, under the circumstances. But he did manage, "Good luck in your future endeavors."

Shiv, about to turn away, turned back. "Emperor Gregor. I do have one purely private favor to ask."

A not-quite-nod invited him to go on.

"May I have the pleasure of informing the man known as Vigo Imola of the estimated valuation of the contents of the bunker—in person?"

A slight hesitation, as whatever lurid visions of eleventh-hour collusion crossed Gregor's well-honed imagination. Happily, his imagination didn't stop there. A faint smile turned his lips. "Fifteen percent, was it not? I believe I see your point." He motioned to Byerly. "Vorrutyer may escort you."

Armsman in front and secretary trailing, Gregor paused on his way out to deal with whatever next crisis might be crowding his queue. Because a three-planet empire delivered upset snakes by the basket-load to this man's office, every damned morning. Yeah—for all the talk of men coveting the emperor's throne, Ivan had never yet heard anyone speak of coveting his *desk*.

"Ivan." Gregor's mouth twisted. "Captain and Lady Vorpatril. I want to see you tomorrow. My secretary will call with your appointment."

Chapter Twenty-Five

When orders were dropped from that high up, they packed a lot of momentum when they hit ground level, in Ivan's experience. So he wasn't surprised when things, which had seemed to be hovering in a holding pattern for the past four days, moved fast.

Deportation was to be the cover story, it turned out, which had the added advantage of being perfectly true. Just not perfectly complete. Since the members of House Cordonah were, for their own reasons, as anxious to depart as Barrayar was to be rid of them, they swallowed the appearance of defeat and disgrace without choking, much. And also the excellent farewell luncheon smoothly supplied by Dowager Lady Vorpatril.

After, everyone was escorted by the ImpSec guards downstairs to pack except Lady ghem Estif, captured by Duv Galeni and carried off to Simon's office, along with a keenly interested Simon. The two hours they were closeted, Duv indicated to Ivan when they all emerged, were not nearly enough for a century's worth of debriefing.

"I'm going to send an analyst along on their jumpship as far as Komarr, or maybe Pol Station," he told Ivan, simultaneously calling up contact codes on his wristcom. "And one of Helen

Vorthys's postdocs or grad students, if she can scramble one in time. That'll give five to ten more days. *Damn* I wish I could go myself." He made his hurried call to the surprised but interested professora. Chasing down one of his own people took a little longer, scattered all over town as they were at the moment, but at that point, all he had to do was snap commands, and some poor ImpSec schmuck's Winterfair plans were sudden smoke. Ivan hoped there would be compensations.

"There'll be a couple of dozen theses on the declassified papers alone," Duv predicted confidently. "*With* honors."

Well, that was probably someone's idea of a reward, yeah. Because there was no accounting for taste. "You're classifying this stuff? After a hundred years? Isn't that paranoid even for ImpSec?"

"We'll be declassifying most of it as fast as we can get through it. But there are some things about the old ghem-junta...never mind." His lips compressed. And opened again to release a, "But you know that history book I gave Lady Tej?"

"Yes...?"

"I think there may have to be a new edition."

Ivan walked him out to the hallway; by the time they reached the lift tubes in the penthouse foyer, Duv was jogging, and fielding more calls from his wristcom. *Eight billion marks*, Ivan couldn't help thinking, *and he worries more about the* papers...

Or the truth, perhaps. What price that?

Gregor was providing a courtesy military jump pilot and crew for Vormercier's yacht for the run to the borders of the empire at Pol Station. This, Ivan gathered, was to make sure they arrived 1) there and 2) nowhere else. The ten days of travel time would be plenty to tightbeam ahead and arrange whatever commercial crew the Arquas wanted to hire on for the next leg. Vetted, Ivan trusted, for ingenious bounty hunters. Jet would be rejoining the Jewels, but Amiri was to travel with his family only as far as Komarr, then transfer to a government courier vessel for a free ride to Escobar, and a safe delivery back to the Durona Clinic. Any stray bounty hunter who made it that far would be Lily Durona and Mark Vorkosigan's problem; or rather, vice versa. Definitely vice versa, Ivan reflected.

His life was simplifying nicely. But not, Ivan trusted, *too* much. A little uneasy, he took the lift tube down from his mother's flat to find Tej.

∽⟡∾   ∽⟡∾   ∽⟡∾

Tej, when she'd had about as much as she could stand of listening to Amiri burble about how happy he was to be going back to Escobar, wandered into her parents' temporary bedroom. The flat had been hastily furnished with rental beds and a few sofas and chairs, the night they'd all been dumped in here by the Barrayaran authorities; a lot of the meals had been taken upstairs at Lady Alys's place. No one had urged anything more permanent.

The Baronne and Lady Alys, or rather, Lady Alys's competent dresser under their joint supervision, was just finishing packing. The Baronne was remarking, "...not my plan at all, but it will certainly do. Flexibility, as Shiv says."

She broke off and both mothers looked across at Tej as she entered, Lady Alys rather bemusedly, the Baronne...her lips tightened, but not in anger.

Lady Alys, tactful as always, murmured, "I should just see to a few things upstairs, Udine. I hope to speak with you later, Tej, dear." Motioning her dresser to close the case and follow, she withdrew. Tej wasn't sure if she was grateful or not. Spacious as the flat was, the Arquas had more than filled it; that, and all the disruptions of the past few days, had allowed Tej to dodge intimate tête-à-têtes pretty much since the rescue.

The Baronne plucked at her bangs, her new nervous gesture. Tej hoped her hair would grow out quickly.

"Have you packed?" the Baronne asked abruptly.

Tej swallowed. Straightened. "No. Nor am I going to."

The Baronne eyed the set of her chin. "You know, when your father and I told you to go with your Barrayaran husband the other day, it was merely because we hoped you could thus avoid arrest, or whatever other retribution the Barrayarans had in mind."

"Yes, I got that."

"We certainly didn't mean..."

"Mean it?" Tej suggested.

The Baronne cleared her throat. "It was a *ploy*, Tej. It was not possible, at that moment, to predict that events were going to turn out so favorably. We wanted to protect you. If not ourselves, then *someone*..."

Someone needed to baby-sit me? If Rish was going to be out of the job. "Yes. But when I said I would stay with Ivan Xav, *I* meant it."

The Baronne made an abortive gesture. "The cars are coming

to take us all to the shuttleport in another hour. Surely too short a time to make such a permanent life-bargain in."

I made it in a minute, the first time... Well, provisionally.

"How long did it take you to decide you wanted Dada?" Tej asked, suddenly curious.

"That is neither here nor there," said the Baronne. "Circumstances were very different."

"I see," said Tej, biting her lip to hide a smile.

"Also, *wanting* and *arranging* are two different things. The latter requires planning... action... sometimes, sometimes..."

"Flexibility?"

"Yes." The Baronne, realizing she was being diverted, tracked back. "Anyway, if you won't—your Dada and I were thinking—perhaps you could ride along with us. At least as far as Pol Station. It would give us more time together."

Tej controlled a shudder at the vision. She and her entire family, packed into what Byerly had implied was a not-very-large spaceship, with less escape possible than from an underground bunker. *We just had twenty-five years together, Baronne. Don't you think it's time for a* break? "I thought I'd say my good-byes right here. The military shuttleport isn't that much of a treat— I've seen it—and they'll be whisking you all through, I expect."

"I expect," echoed the Baronne, only not-disagreeing because she couldn't, at least about the shuttleport. "This all seems so rushed."

"We've had the past four days. You must have guessed something like this was coming."

"Or some Barrayaran incarceration. Which would have required an entirely novel plan. We've not been saying good-bye for the past four days!"

I was. No one noticed. Although they'd all had a lot else on their minds, to be fair. "Also, I get jump-sick, and that would be ten jumps. Five each way."

"You... might decide not to go back. You could choose freely, once you reached Pol Station."

Yes, I thought that might be your secret plan. "There would be *more* jumps, going on. And"—Tej took a deep breath, only partly for control—"I can choose freely right here. Right now. And I have." *Do I have to, like,* yell?

Thankfully not; because the Baronne, after a silence, responded,

"I suppose you will be safer here. At least for the immediate future."

Her family, Tej was reminded, wasn't exactly going directly home. Although Fell Station, as long as the old Baron was in charge, was going to make a reasonably secure initial base. "You'll have Byerly," she offered, then paused in doubt, in tandem with the Baronne. "And a war chest of, what was it, four hundred million Barrayaran marks?"

"That's only one hundred million, in Betan dollars," the Baronne was swift to point out. "A few serious bribes, some competent mercenaries, and it will dwindle in a hurry. Five percent, that tricky dealer Gregor got us down to!" This was not, Tej understood, a point *against* Gregor, personally.

"I'm sure you and Dada will be able to make ends meet somehow," Tej soothed her. "You're both very clever."

"It will be a challenge," the Baronne . . . didn't quite grumble. "But when I get my hands on those Prestenes, the retribution will be *famous*."

"Yes, make them pay," Tej agreed cordially, glad to give her mother's thoughts this more positive direction. By her standards.

"What do you *see* in that Barrayaran boy, anyway?" the Baronne asked querulously, dodging back despite Tej's best efforts. "He just doesn't seem very *ambitious*."

"Mm," said Tej. *One woman's defect is another woman's delight?* "I suppose . . . it's all the things he sees in me." *That you don't.*

The Baronne peered at her in doubt. "Which are what, Tej-love? Besides your figure, clearly." She waved away this as a given, at least with respect—or lack of respect—to Ivan Xav.

Everything, Baronne. On the other hand . . . was it really necessary to bloody her forehead trying to solve a problem already going away on its own? Within the hour, at that. That seemed a very Ivan Xav approach. So *restful*. The great charm of her and the Baronne living on two different planets, Tej decided, was that they could *both* stop trying to fix each other. She grinned crookedly, leaned up, and gave her mother a peck on the cheek, instead. "An appreciation of *his* figure."

"Really, Tej!" But the Baronne's hand stole to the kissed spot nonetheless.

Dada and Byerly arrived back then, the Baron with a heartening bustle, and Ivan Xav strolled in on their heels, ending this little mother-daughter ordeal. Moment. Again. Until the next time. Tej wondered if it would be redundant to think, *Don't ever change, Baronne.*

Tej, Rish, Byerly, and Ivan Xav rendezvoused briefly in the living room, as the luggage was staged around them.

"So how did it go with Ser Imola?" Tej asked By.

"Succinctly." By tilted a hand. "I was sent in part to impede long conversations, but it wasn't necessary. You could just *see* the man fold into himself." He added after a contemplative moment, "And prison-smock orange is *so* not Imola's color. It was all quite, quite satisfying."

"And you?" Ivan Xav asked.

Byerly grimaced, though a speculative glance under his unfairly long lashes at the listening Rish undercut his put-upon air. "Running around like a mad thing, of course. I'm going to have to leave a moving company to clear my apartment and put it all in storage. I packed last night—it was like trying to decide what to grab from a burning building. The story is I'm shipping out just ahead of imminent arrest for collusion with *your in-laws* for grand-theft-history. I am to be a Barrayaran renegade." He struck a pose. "Rake's regress, or something."

"I'm sure you'll do well," Tej tried to console him.

"It's bloody *Jackson's Whole*. Where enemies are killed and *eaten.*"

"We do not!" said Rish indignantly.

Byerly waved this away. "I speak, of course, metaphorically." Though he looked as if he weren't entirely sure.

"Well, if you get in over your head, just try channeling your great-great-grandfather Bloody Pierre," advised Ivan Xav. He added after a moment, "Or your great-great-grandmother. For you, either one."

By cast a sneer at him.

Ivan Xav grinned, undaunted. He explained aside to Tej and Rish, "It was said that the only two people Le Sanguinaire feared were his wife, and Dorca Vorbarra. And no one's too sure about Dorca."

"Really?" said Tej, the golden glasses they'd all been drinking tunnel water from the other night becoming more interesting in retrospect.

"Vorrutyer family history," By told her, "is the very essence of *unreliable news source*. Don't listen to Vorpatril." He sighed. "Though it is evident that you will. Congratulations, Ivan, if I failed to say that earlier."

"Thank you," Ivan Xav returned, bland.

And then it was time to all pitch in and help carry things down to the garage, where three luxurious governmental groundcars were pulled up waiting. Going out in style? Tej detected Lady Alys's diplomatic hand at work; the Arquas might as easily have been carted away in one big prison van.

A pair of men in black-and-silver livery arrived in a separate, quite unremarkable groundcar, and transferred to the boot of one of the other vehicles a pair of familiar, heavy boxes, with old Ninth Satrapy seals on the tops. The senior of them approached the Baron and Baronne, and saluted.

"My Imperial master's compliments, sir, and he commends to you this souvenir of your visit. May it help to speed you on your way."

Dada's brows shot up. Tej tried to calculate the value, in either Barrayaran marks or Betan dollars, of forty-four kilos of old Cetagandan gold coins, but ran afoul of her lack of experience with the antiquities market.

"Precisely two boxes out of forty," murmured Dada. "Five percent. How scrupulous of him." He raised his voice to the Vorbarra armsman. "Tell your Imperial master that Baron and Baronne Cordonah are as pleased to accept his memento as he is to bestow it."

A little edged, don't you think, Dada? But the armsman took it in expressionlessly, and marched off with his fellow to, Tej was fairly sure, deliver the words verbatim. The bulk of the payout would arrive later, by some boring tightbeam transfer. With a meticulous deduction for this payment-in-kind but, she was sure, otherwise in full.

Lady Alys and Simon arrived from upstairs, lending a touch of formality to the final farewell. Dada came over to Ivan Xav and Tej, standing together.

"They tell me," he said, "that in some Barrayaran weddings, the father is expected to *give away* the bride. That struck me as valuing her much too low."

"Just a figure of speech, sir," Ivan Xav assured him, looking amused. "In actual high Vor marriages, the behind-the-scenes dealings over the details of the marriage contract can go on for months."

"Well, that's a little better," the Baron allowed. "Your Gregor has to have obtained his skills from somewhere."

Ivan Xav added, as if by way of consolation, "And, after all, you're getting Byerly in trade."

The Baron smiled thinly. "Yes, I know..." He turned to his daughter. "Your mother tells me, Tej, that she did convey our invitation for you to ride along to Pol Station, yes?"

"Yes, Dada," said Tej. "But I'm staying right here." She gripped Ivan Xav's arm firmly; he covered her hand with his own.

"You know me—there's no such thing as a last chance this side of death," said Dada. "If ever you want to come home..."

"Thank you, Dada," said Tej, wondering how many karma points she was totting up for not pointing out that actually, he hadn't secured a home for her to come to, yet. It had better be a *lot*. On impulse, she pulled him aside, placed her hands on his shoulders, and looked him in the eye. It was a shock to her to discover they were the same height.

"Look at it this way, Dada. You're coming away from Barrayar with everyone's freedom, a ride, and a war chest. Not to mention the covert alliance with The Gregor. I can't imagine any House heir alive who could match that bride-price, right now. It's *princely*, more literally than anyone here quite lets on." *Barrayarans!* "And do you think that you'd have had *any* of it if I hadn't married Ivan Xav?"

"Mm..."

"You've got a *great* deal here. Don't screw it up!"

"But I *didn't* deal, not for him," he returned, in some very Dada-ish frustration. "And I always meant to, for you!"

"I understand." The corners of her mouth tugged up. "But Ivan Xav is a *gift*."

She leaned, not up, but over, and kissed him on the cheek. It worked to divert him, too, from his argument—he patted her in distraction. She led him back, and linked arms with her Barrayaran husband once more.

"So...take good care of her, then, Captain Vorpatril." Formally, Dada shook Ivan Xav's free hand. His eyes narrowed right down, suddenly cold and hard; his grip did not loosen. "And you'd better believe that I *can* find some way to touch you, if you don't."

"No doubt at all, sir!" Ivan Xav assured him. He flinched under the pressure of that stare, and paw, but, she was proud to see, didn't step back.

"That's *not necessary*, Dada," said Tej through her teeth.

"Yes, yes, Tej, love..."

And it was all swallowed up in last embraces, waves, cries, the clicking of silvered canopies, the hiss of groundcar engines, and...silence. More golden than Cetagandan coins.

Rubbing his hand on his trouser seam, Ivan Xav said plaintively. "Is asking *Who can I kill for you?* usually how people say *I love you* in Jacksonian?"

"No, just Dada," Tej sighed. "Though the Baronne is more dangerous—she might not *ask*."

"Ee," said Ivan Xav.

"I've been reading your histories," said Tej, giving him a hug. "Don't try to tell me some of *your* ancestors didn't think the same way. Starting with your Aunt Cordelia's famous Winterfair gift to your Uncle Aral, and she wasn't even Barrayaran! Severed heads, *really*?"

"Only the one," he protested. "And I," he added, drawing himself up with dignity, "am a *much* more modern Barrayaran."

Tej pressed a smile out straight. "I'm sure you are, Lord Vorpatril."

Their meeting the next morning with The Gregor was very short.

"Ylla?" said Ivan Xav in a confounded voice. "Where the hell is Ylla?"

Epilogue

～⌒⌒～

Senior military attaché at the Barrayaran consulate on the planet Ylla might have been a more exciting assignment had there been any junior military attachés. Or, indeed, any other employees aside from one dispirited, homesick, and slightly alcoholic consul eking out the dregs of his diplomatic career. Ivan and Tej had arrived at what passed for the planetary industrial capital—the city was about half the size of New Evias—in what was midwinter for its hemisphere: rainy, cold, smoggy, and dull. Since Tej was still in a quivering heap from far too many wormhole jumps in too-close succession, she had greeted it, and their dingy provided apartment, with no more protest than a moan.

Well, *that* wouldn't do. Hitting the consulate with what he would have considered average effort for a slow day at Imperial Headquarters, Ivan began ruthlessly applying Ops-style efficiencies to his duties, and when he ran out of those, to the consul's. It didn't take long to figure out that ninety-five percent of the consulate's business came in over the perfectly adequate planetary comconsole net, and that the consulate, therefore, could be sited anywhere with a shuttleport. Shopping for a more salubrious climate didn't take much longer. He had the whole place—lock,

stock, comconsoles and consul—moved to a large, delightful
island near the equator by the end of his third week, with money
left over in the new budget to hire a clerk. Tej responded to the
tropical light like a flower. By the end of his first month, Ivan
had his duties pared down to a neat three mornings a week with
the occasional odd hour, or pop-up trip to the orbital stations,
and after that, it was all clear sailing.

Not that people did much sailing on Ylla's extensive oceans,
nor swimming either—Yllan seawater tended to give humans
strange rashes, and while humans were highly toxic morsels in
the diet of the native sea monsters, the monsters were extremely
stupid and kept not figuring this out. But the view, out over the
swimming pool from their house's veranda, was luminous and
beautiful—he waved at Tej, over there in the big hammock—and
the sea wasn't bad to look at, either. A person of simple tastes
could live really well, really cheaply on Ylla, with the application of a little application. And with a more generous budget,
even better.

"Mail call!" he told Tej. She looked up with a wide smile
and set aside her earbug. Tightbeam messages from home were
erratic at best, what with all the jumps through which they had
to be carried; they could arrive out of order, spread out, or all
in a wodge. Today's delivery had been a wodge. He handed her
a data disc to plug into her own reader, set on the table along
with a promising pitcher and a couple of glasses, one half-full,
the other upside down and waiting just for him. "Is that iced
tea, or fruity girly drinks?"

"Fruity girly drinks. Want some?"

"Actually, yes." He kicked off his sandals, climbed into the other
end of the hammock, arranged the big cushions behind his back,
took up his own reader, and laced his bare legs with hers. She
was acquiring an almost Shiv-colored tan, which looked *worlds*
better on her than on her Dada, making her sherry-colored eyes
shine out like the gold coins on her favorite ankle bracelet—which,
along with a skimpy swimsuit, she was currently wearing. The
Ninth-Satrapy-coin anklet, and a few more stunning baubles, had
been a birthday present sent by her fond Dada a few months
back. Ivan had plans for that suit, later in the afternoon; the
chiming anklet could stay.

"Busy morning?" she inquired, as the hammock settled.

"Eh, not really. I spent most of it editing my first annual performance review."

Her brows rose in surprise. "I shouldn't think you'd need to—the consul loves your work."

"Oh, sure. I was just toning down the ecstasy a bit, before letting it loose in the tightbeam to home. Wouldn't want to give people ideas. Like, for transfers. To anywhere but back home, that is."

"When do you suppose they'll let us come back to Barrayar?"

"Gregor guessed two years, a year ago; haven't heard anything to change that, yet." What Gregor had actually said was, *Dammit, Ivan, you do realize it's likely going to take two bloody* years *for this mess to blow over! At least! What were you* thinking? Which Ivan had thought a trifle unfair, but that hadn't seemed the moment to say so. And then Ivan, too, had been permitted to discover how much packing for galactic exile on 26.7 hours' notice was like grabbing your life from a burning building.

A little silence fell, as they both began reading.

"So what did you get?" Tej inquired, when his first *Huh!* invited interruption.

"Birthday greeting from Admiral Desplains." Ivan's thirty-sixth birthday had passed very pleasantly, two weeks ago. They'd stayed home. "He tells me that my replacement is a very efficient young man, but lacks my political *nous.* And is less entertaining, thank-you-I-think, Admiral." Ivan read on. "I gather that he misses me. But that he doesn't encourage me to think of coming back to Ops, because by that time I should be moving up and on, if I'm interpreting this correctly."

"You probably are," said Tej, with touching faith in his ability to decipher elliptical hints from senior officers. Likely justified, in this case.

"You had something from the Whole...?"

"Letter from Rish." She tapped her reader. "So frustrating. She hates writing, so she never puts in enough detail, but she's too cheap to send a recording." Written messages were, indeed, the least expensive tightbeam communication to send by the long and winding wormhole routes, which was why almost everything that made it as far as Ylla was in this form. "Repairs on Cordonah Station are almost complete, she says. The reunited Jewels have danced their first public performance again, now that Topaz's replacement legs have taken. I hope the Baronne tracked down whatever nasty Prestene head-meat came up with *that* idea." She scowled. "*In* person."

Ivan had never met Topaz, but he hoped so, too. Far more cruel than shaved hair, that amputation had sounded; it had allegedly been ordered in revenge for Topaz helping the Baron and Baronne to escape their Prestene captivity, all those months ago. A loyalty now redeemed; good. The revenge cycle...he declined to touch.

"And your brother Erik? Did they finally decide if he was cryo-revivable?"

"Mm, yes, but...huh." Her brows rose. "They're still keeping him on ice for a while. You know that Prestene capturing the station was in-part an inside job? Appears Erik was the in-part part. Tired of waiting for his inheritance? And so he received the reward from Prestene that anyone with a clue might have guessed was coming...unless he saw which way things were going and turned to fight them at the end. Give him credit, Rish says, he does seem to have been thinking of forcible retirement for Dada, not patricide, but apparently someone figured out how to cut those costs. Dada and the Baronne must have *known* this, but back on Barrayar they didn't give me the least hint...Oh, my, that boy is *so* grounded! I expect my parents'll keep him as a threat in reserve for a while, in case Star and Pidge aren't able to work out their little differences as to who should be heiress. That's one way to keep them yoked together..."

Ivan tried not to picture Erik Arqua's cryochamber being used as a coffee table, but who knew? "So...will they ever revive him?"

"In a few years, I expect. When Star and Pidge are firmly in place. And then he'll get to be *their* little brother." Ivan wasn't sure he wanted to know what family memories fueled her evil chuckle. "In other words, House Cordonah's internal politics are nearly back to normal. *So* glad I'm here and not there..." Her ankle-coins chimed, as her foot rubbed Ivan's calf.

"I am, too," he declared, without reservation. "Does she write anything about Byerly?"

She scrolled on a short way. "No, not really. But if anything dire had happened to him she would have said—I think—so I suppose all is well."

"I have one from him. What's the date on yours...?" A quick cross-check assured Ivan that By's letter had followed almost a week after Rish's, so that was all right. So far. "At least I can't accuse Byerly of writing, or talking, too little. Though finding the message in the missive is a bit like looking for the meat in those meatballs they sell off the carts in the Great Square... Holy crap." Ivan's lurch nearly tipped the hammock.

Tej's bright eyes widened in inquiry.

"You know that brooch-thing that your Grandmama picked up off the floor in the bunker...?"

"Yes?"

"By finally found out what the hell it was."

"I was thinking haut-lady bio-weapons, myself, but I didn't like to say anything at the time. I didn't think we needed *more* complications to getting everyone on their way home without being jailed, and if she wanted to use them on Prestene, that was between her and the Baron and Baronne. Nothing to do with Barrayar, right?"

"Weirder than that. Even." Ivan blinked. "And a whole lot to do with Barrayar. Seems the beads on the brooch contained something like a hundred thousand sporulated genetic samples from Barrayarans born in the Vorbarra District before the end of the Time of Isolation. It was the bloody gene-survey library!"

"Oh. My." Tej hesitated. "Will the Barrayarans be mad?"

"I'm... not sure. I mean, we never *knew*."

"I suppose you do now. Byerly will have reported, right?"

"Yeah." Ivan read on. "You could—well, not you, but someone crazy could—*clone* all our ancestors from those samples, you realize? I wonder if there was anyone famous in there?"

Tej tilted her head, considering this. "That might actually be made lucrative."

"Buy your own clone of Prince Xav? Or worse, Mad Emperor Yuri ...? Ye gods. No...!" His speeding eyes widened. "Lady ghem Estif offered to sell them back to the Star Crèche!"

"That's terrible!" said Tej, but went on in earnest critique, "She should have set up a bidding war between the Star Crèche and Barrayar, at the very least! The Baronne could have advised her. What's the point of having an auction with only one bidder?"

Ivan swallowed this practical Jacksonian view without gulping, much. Or at least without comment.

Tej added, with keen interest, "What did they offer her? I can't believe By didn't find out *that*."

"He did. Ten million Betan dollars. Here's where it all goes sideways. She set up a hand-off in a neutral location—House Dyne?"

Tej nodded. "That makes sense."

"While Byerly was knocking himself out trying to steal the thing—ah, there you go, evidently he did offer to buy it, first—but he couldn't get past her. Rish... apparently refused to take sides. So anyway, they dragged this Star Crèche envoy, an actual haut lady, in her bubble and everything, though I'm not sure how you could tell—I wonder if it was Pel?—all the way out from Eta Ceta to the Whole, together with a suitcase full of bearer-credit—well not a suitcase, probably, doubtless an elegant little card, but anyway—and a platoon of really scary bodyguards. And the Dyne guy had the bond in hand, all cleared and ready to hand over. And Lady ghem Estif set the brooch down in a little force-bubble with, evidently, a hidden plasma charge, stood back, and set it off—blinding light, but no concussion—and turned it all to elemental gases. Right in front of them. By says he thought he was having a heart attack. And then he wished he'd had."

"Wow!" said Tej.

"But *why*? Why would anyone, in effect, set fire to ten million Betan dollars?"

"Well, Grandmama..." Tej pursed her lips, then took a sip of fruity drink as she apparently thought this through. "Grandmama was really incensed at being culled from the haut, back when."

"That was a hundred years ago! She's held this grudge for over a century?"

Tej gave a nod. "It's... it's a girl thing," she offered. "Ghem Estif-Arqua style."

"Ye gods." *Should I keep this in mind?*

Tej smiled a sharp little smile, and for a moment, he could see Shiv in her face. "What did my parents think about it all?"

Ivan read on. By could stand to have one of those *accuracy-brevity-clarity* tutorials, but maybe Allegre favored a different style. And he did still seem to have been quite upset when he'd composed this. *Hysterical* was probably not too strong a term. "The Baronne seems to have thought it wasteful. The Baron just laughed."

"Despite all the mother-in-law jokes everyone tells," Tej said meditatively, "Grandmama always did get along very well with Dada. I think it was because she spent the whole of her life up until the Barrayaran annexation of Komarr following all the rules, no matter how stupid they were, and being screwed over for it, and Dada finally taught her how to break them. And break away from them."

"By wants to know, did either of us—meaning, probably, you—know? About the brooch, I think he's asking, though it's hard to tell."

"Nope," said Tej. "Tell him, sorry."

"I guess."

Ivan finally started on his own frosty fruity drink—nice kick— as Tej scrolled down. "Here's one to *me* from your mother," she said. "She and Simon are back safely from their big galactic trip, during which nobody tried to kill, kidnap, or otherwise vex anybody after all. Though she says she was a little afraid for some Tau Cetan customs inspectors at one point, but she got Simon calmed down..."

Simon and Lady Alys's exile had not been nearly so summarily ordered as Ivan and Tej's, a mere suggestion conveyed through Empress Laisa to her social secretary that she was overdue for a nice, long holiday. Though Ivan doubted that any Imperial nuances had been lost en route. Ivan remembered *that* part of his last conversation with Gregor, too.

Gregor had been pacing, exasperated, when he'd wheeled and burst out: "And Simon—what the *hell?*"

Ivan hesitated, while his hope that this might be a rhetorical question died a lonely death, then ventured, "I think he was bored, Gregor."

"Bored!" Gregor jerked to a halt, taken aback. "I thought he was exhausted."

"Right after the chip breakdown, sure." *Profoundly so.* "For a while, everyone—even Mamere and Simon himself—assumed he was some fragile convalescent. But...quietly—he does everything quietly—he's grown better."

"I thank your mother for that, yes."

Yeah, really. Ivan shied from trying to imagine the biography of a post-chip-Simon minus Alys, but it might have been a much shorter tale. "He's fine when she's with him. But she's been going off to the Residence a lot, lately, leaving him to his own devices. And then Shiv came along and pushed all his old buttons, and, well, here we all are."

Gregor contemplated the *hereness* of everyone, grimly. "I see."

"I think he needs something to do. Not a full-time job. Occasional. Varied. Not too much like his old job."

"That... will take some careful thought."

Ivan hoped their long trip had given Gregor time for that thinking. He couldn't help noticing, in retrospect, that despite the reported outbreak of Imperial sarcasm, it *had* been the Illyan Plan for the Arquas that Gregor had finally adopted, more or less. And that it seemed to be working, so far.

Tej, still reading—Mamere could be chatty—went on: "Oh, good, the new ImpSec building has been dedicated. *Not* built opposite the old one. They found another site. With fewer holes under it."

"There's a kindness," Ivan put in. "Miles used to say that the one advantage of working in ImpSec HQ was that you couldn't *see* ImpSec HQ."

"They got Simon to cut the ribbon, ah, that's sweet. She says they wanted to name it after him, but he declined the honor very firmly, so it's going to go nameless for now."

"I suppose they can circle back after he's dead..." Ivan plowed on to his next letter. "Huh. Aunt Cordelia writes to me?"

"I really enjoyed meeting her and your Uncle Aral, when we stopped at Sergyar," said Tej.

"She says she liked you, too. And to be sure to allow time to stop again on our way back. She seems to assume we'll be let to come back—that's heartening. Simon and Mamere dropped in on their way home, too, evidently. Probably what triggered this. *Simon and Aral enjoyed their trip out to see the new settlement... so glad for a chance to catch up with Alys... heard all about their nice visit to Beta Colony,* yes, Mamere wrote me all about that, too... *what?*"

"What what?" said Tej agreeably.

Mamere hadn't written her only son *everything* about her trip to Beta Colony, evidently. "*She* took *Simon* to the *Orb*? Or was it the other way around...? No, I guess not. Female collusion, I bet." He read on, his face screwing up, then demanded of the auntless, and therefore blameless, air, "Why do you think you have to *tell* me these things, Aunt Cordelia?"

Tej's lips twitched. "So what does she tell you?"

"They signed up for some sort of one-week deluxe instructional course. That doesn't sound too... Role-playing? Because Mamere thought it might be easy for Simon to get into, on account of having done covert ops in his youth. And the first day was pretty rocky, but once she persuaded Simon to stop treating the mandatory psychological interest survey as a hostile inter-rogation, things smoothed out...and... Thank God, now Aunt Cordelia switches to telling me all about Commodore Jole's new sailboat—the Sergyaran seas don't dissolve human skin the way Ylla's do, happily. He took them all out for a sail, good. And no one drowned. Much better."

"Better than what?" Tej was still laughing at him, he feared.

"Just—better." Ivan took refuge in what dignity a man wearing nothing but shorts and sipping fruity girly drinks could muster. And also in the drink.

"We should go to the Orb, on the way back," mused Tej. "I mean, it's famous for its erotic arts instruction, which I've already had, but I've always wanted to see it."

Ivan was torn. "Yeah, so have I, but...what the hell is the *mandatory psychological interest survey*? Nobody ever mentioned that before." Not even Miles.

Tej brightened. "My Betan tutors told me all about that. It's not like a multiple-choice test—it's more like a brain scan, while they run all kinds of images and stimuli past you, and then put the response-data through their analysis program. They pitch it to the customers as a way of helping people with limited time sort through the menu of offerings to find what will please them most—and it does do that. But it also screens for problem customers."

"Are they turned away?"

"No, no. They just get a different level of supervision. They mean a lot of varied things by *problem*, you see. Some people are very distressed by insights that the survey reveals about them, things that they didn't want to know, and then they have to be sort of gently talked down."

Ivan considered this, warily. "I think Simon already knows everything about himself that he doesn't want to know. He never seemed much given to self-deception. All those years of nonad-justable memory."

"I can believe that."

But a new reason for *some people* not to talk much about their visits to the famous Orb glimmered in Ivan's mind. The *next* time he caught up with Miles...

Speaking of that devil. "Ah, here's one from my cousin, Lord-Auditor-and-don't-you-forget-it."

"Oh, those are always very interesting." Tej perked up.

Ivan read for a minute or so, his lips parting. "Oh, my God. The investing angel who bought the old ImpSec site from the Imperial government? Turns out to have been my clone-cousin Mark Vorkosigan."

"For a Betan dollar?"

"No, not that much nepotism. But he bargained them way down by accepting all legal liabilities. Apparently, his engineers found a way to raise the building back to ground level again! *And* stabilize the subsoil. It took several months, but they got it up pretty much whole."

"That must have been almost as bizarre a sight as sinking it was. But..." Her brows drew down. "What in the world is the man going to do with an ugly old government building? It was pretty much gutted, wasn't it?"

"Stripped more than gutted, I gather. Surprisingly intact. Mark Vorkosigan Enterprises' new headquarters? He needs one. No..." Ivan scrolled on. His lips drew back in an uncontrollable grin. "Ooh, snarky, Miles! I just *bet* you're upset..."

"Come on," urged Tej, grinning as if he were the best show in town.

"Mark's turning it into a theme hotel, restaurant, and nightclub. With an espionage museum, very educational. He plans to sell 'the whole ImpSec experience' to the tourists, both backcountry and galactic, apparently."

"Will people *pay* to sleep in old ImpSec cells and offices and things? I mean—it seems more like a place people would have paid to get *out* of."

"That was then, this is now...oh, my. Oh, you'll have to read this. Miles is *so* pissed, but he can't say so directly, because, Mark. The grand opening is in a couple of weeks. And it's already booked solid for the first two months." Ivan couldn't help adding, after a moment of somewhat skewed beatific vision, "I wonder if there'll be an *Adults Only* section...? Because, Mark..."

He wanted to go back and start over right then, just to savor the letter on all its levels, but there was more, taking another direction. "Oh, no, Miles and Ekaterin have decanted another one. Going into production, coz? I suppose you are. Still trying to outrun... everything. And pictures. Why? Babies all look alike, I swear..."

"Ooh. Send over." Tej held out a demanding hand; he extended her his reader, now displaying flat scans of what, he was assured, was a baby girl, one Lady Elizabeth Vorkosigan. His newest niece. *Uncle Ivan*, good God, the urchins would probably be up to *calling* him that by the time they got home to Vorbarr Sultana. And *Aunt Tej*, as well, now. *How is it I can have my identity changed by something I didn't even do...?*

He cautiously considered the sobriquet *Da*. That one, at least, might be his own doing...

Tej was not, thankfully, *goopy* the way some women got when presented with baby pictures. But the look in her eye was curious, and, when she raised her face to his again, speculative.

"One wouldn't," she said neutrally, "want to start an infant in a replicator here, and then have to drag it, decanted or otherwise, back through all those stressful wormhole jumps to Barrayar. More sensible to wait a bit."

"A bit," Ivan agreed. The memory of so comfortably *ignoring* his thirty-sixth birthday drifted across his mind. But some deadlines demanded attention. "You know... I'm going to be a twenty-years man in just four more years. That used to seem *forever* away, and now it's... not."

"What does that mean? In Barrayaran. Or Vor, as the case may be."

"MilSpeak. Yet another dialect for you. It's the time a mid-grade officer like me either takes early retirement—not all that early, really—or retakes his oaths and gets serious about tracking for high command. They used to encourage men to stay in, but they don't so much, these days. They'd rather have new young fellows with new young training."

"So... what do you want to do? Or do instead?"

"Opting out would be a sure-fire way to avoid unwanted promotion." He tried to remember his early military idealism, before the glitter had worn off. In retrospect, he wasn't sure it had been idealism so much as a burning hunger for a status to overawe his fellow obnoxious eighteen-year-olds. Which... seemed much less important, now.

"Is that your answer, then?"

"Might be. It also depends on the alternatives on offer. The consul thinks I should consider the diplomatic corps. That's—really not an unusual second-career path, for a twenty-years man like me."

Tej's lips curved up. "There's no one like you, Ivan Xav."

Ivan decided not to argue with this flattering viewpoint.

Tej tried it out in her mouth. "Ambassador Vorpatril?"

"Ambassador and Lady Vorpatril—they like you to come as a set. And they'd fall all over themselves for your language kink. But there's an apprenticeship first, even if I were fast-tracked. Unless we were sent to the backside of nowhere." He looked around, and added conscientiously, "Again."

Tej let her gaze pass over the golden Yllan landscape, the odd but lovely deep blue-green-for-want-of-a-better-term vegetation— much the color of a very chilled Rish—the wide, shining, corrosive sea. "Well, *someone* has to be," she allowed, judiciously.

"It could involve a lot of wormhole jumps."

"Mm, but only once every few years. I could . . . steel myself. And it would keep us far away from *both* our families."

"I can see the appeal . . ."

In all, in truth, it was a problem for another day, Ivan decided. When life and chance handed you an afternoon as idyllic as this one promised to be, it seemed profoundly ungrateful not to *pay attention.*

Ivan ran a toe up Tej's shin, and began attending.

~ *FIN* ~

Miles Vorkosigan/Naismith:
His Universe and Times

~~~

CHRONOLOGY	EVENTS	CHRONICLE
Approx. 200 years before Miles's birth	Quaddies are created by genetic engineering.	*Falling Free*
During Beta-Barrayaran War	Cordelia Naismith meets Lord Aral Vorkosigan while on opposite sides of a war. Despite difficulties, they fall in love and are married.	*Shards of Honor*
The Vordarian Pretendership	While Cordelia is pregnant, an attempt to assassinate Aral by poison gas fails, but Cordelia is affected; Miles Vorkosigan is born with bones that will always be brittle and other medical problems. His growth will be stunted.	*Barrayar*
Miles is 17	Miles fails to pass a physical test to get into the Service Academy. On a trip, necessities force him to improvise the Free Dendarii Mercenaries into existence; he has unintended but unavoidable adventures for four months. Leaves the Dendarii in	*The Warrior's Apprentice*

CHRONOLOGY	EVENTS	CHRONICLE
	Ky Tung's competent hands and takes Elli Quinn to Beta for rebuilding of her damaged face; returns to Barrayar to thwart plot against his father. Emperor pulls strings to get Miles into the Academy.	
Miles is 20	Ensign Miles graduates and immediately has to take on one of the duties of the Barrayaran nobility and act as detective and judge in a murder case. Shortly afterward, his first military assignment ends with his arrest. Miles has to rejoin the Dendarii to rescue the young Barrayaran emperor. Emperor accepts Dendarii as his personal secret service force.	"The Mountains of Mourning" in *Borders of Infinity* *The Vor Game*
Miles is 22	Miles and his cousin Ivan attend a Cetagandan state funeral and are caught up in Cetagandan internal politics.	*Cetaganda*
	Miles sends Commander Elli Quinn, who's been given a new face on Beta, on a solo mission to Kline Station.	*Ethan of Athos*
Miles is 23	Now a Barrayaran Lieutenant, Miles goes with the Dendarii to smuggle a scientist out of Jackson's Whole. Miles's fragile leg bones have been replaced by synthetics.	"Labyrinth" in *Borders of Infinity*

CHRONOLOGY	EVENTS	CHRONICLE
Miles is 24	Miles plots from within a Cetagandan prison camp on Dagoola IV to free the prisoners. The Dendarii fleet is pursued by the Cetagandans and finally reaches Earth for repairs. Miles has to juggle both his identities at once, raise money for repairs, and defeat a plot to replace him with a double. Ky Tung stays on Earth. Commander Elli Quinn is now Miles's right-hand officer. Miles and the Dendarii depart for Sector IV on a rescue mission.	"The Borders of Infinity" in *Borders of Infinity* *Brothers in Arms*
Miles is 25	Hospitalized after previous mission, Miles's broken arms are replaced by synthetic bones. With Simon Illyan, Miles undoes yet another plot against his father while flat on his back.	*Borders of Infinity* interstitial material
Miles is 28	Miles meets his clone brother Mark again, this time on Jackson's Whole.	*Mirror Dance*
Miles is 29	Miles hits thirty; thirty hits back.	*Memory*
Miles is 30	Emperor Gregor dispatches Miles to Komarr to investigate a space accident, where he finds old politics and new technology make a deadly mix.	*Komarr*

CHRONOLOGY	EVENTS	CHRONICLE
	The Emperor's wedding sparks romance and intrigue on Barrayar, and Miles plunges up to his neck in both.	*A Civil Campaign*
Miles is 31	Armsman Roic and Sergeant Taura defeat a plot to unhinge Miles and Ekaterin's midwinter wedding.	"Winterfair Gifts" in *Irresistible Forces*
Miles is 32	Miles and Ekaterin's honeymoon journey is interrupted by an Auditorial mission to Quaddiespace, where they encounter old friends, new enemies, and a double handful of intrigue.	*Diplomatic Immunity*
Ivan turns 35	ImpSec Headquarters suffers a problem with moles.	*Captain Vorpatril's Alliance*
Miles is 39	Miles and Roic go to Kibou-daini to investigate cryo-corporation chicanery.	*Cryoburn*